THE HUMAN BLEND

THE

HuMAN

BLeND

VOLUME I OF THE TIPPING POINT TRILOGY

ALAN DEAN FOSTER

BALLANTINE BOOKS TRADE PAPERBACK NEW YORK

2011 Del Rey Books Trade Paperback Edition

Published in the United States by Del Rey, an imprint of The Random House Publishing Group, a division of Random House, Inc., New York.

DEL REY is a registered trademark and the Del Rey colophon is a trademark of Random House, Inc.

Originally published in hardcover in the United States by Del Rey Books, an imprint of The Random House Publishing Group, a division of Random House, Inc., in 2010.

This book contains an excerpt from the forthcoming book *Body, Inc.* by Alan Dean Foster. This excerpt has been set for this edition only and may not reflect the final content of the forthcoming edition.

Library of Congress Cataloging-in-Publication Data
Foster, Alan Dean.
The human blend / Alan Dean Foster.
p. cm.—(The tipping point trilogy; v. 1)
ISBN 978-0-345-51198-0
eBook ISBN 978-0-345-52305-1
1. Regeneration (Biology)—Fiction. 2. Thieves—Fiction. I. Title.
PS3556.O756H86 2010
813'.54—dc22
2010015541

Printed in the United States of America on acid-free paper

www.delreybooks.com

2 4 6 8 9 7 5 3 1

Book design by Liz Cosgrove

For Allen Grodsky and Bill Skrzyniarz,
who prove that Shakespeare was wrong

THE HUMAN BLEND

1

"Let's riffle the dead man." Jiminy scowled at the newly won corpse and hopped to it.

Viewed up close, the freshly demised Meld wasn't much of a prize— but then, Jiminy Cricket wasn't much of a thief. Neither was his occasional mudbud Whispr. As Jiminy slipped the still-warm barker back inside his shirt, the two men bent over the motionless middle-aged Meld who'd had the unluck to be singled out as prey. Whispr was relieved the man had finally stopped gasping. In the deceptive calm of the Savannah alley where they had dragged the lumpy body, the dead man's penultimate air suckling had grown progressively more disconcerting. Now it, and he, were stilled.

Jiminy had not been certain the barker would work as intended. With a slapjob barker you never did know. It was supposed to identify anyone, Meld or Natural, who was burdened with a fib, pump, adjunct, pacemaker, flexstent, or just about any other variety of artificial heart or heart accessory—and at the push of a button, stop it. A barker meted out murder most subtle. More important to the wielder, it imposed death quietly. Once the barker's short-range scanner had picked the pedestrian out of a late-evening crowd, Whispr and Jiminy had trailed him until the opportunity to stop his heart from a distance and riffle the resulting corpse had presented itself.

Victim and murderers alike were Melds. Jiminy's legs had been lengthened, modified, and enhanced with nanocarbonic prosthetics that allowed him to cover distances equivalent to obsolete Olympic long jump records in a single bound. Immensely useful for fleeing from pursuers. Awkward if you wanted to buy off-the-rack trousers. Each of his bone-grafted, elongated thighbones was twice the length of those belonging to a Natural of the same height. The high-strength fast-twitch muscle fibers with their bonded protein inserts that wrapped around his leg bones were three times normal thickness while the accompanying tendons had been fashioned from synthetic spider silk.

These melded legs had struck Jiminy with the casually bestowed nickname he had gone ahead and adopted as his own. Ostensibly he was a legitimate messenger, able to leap easily from platform to platform and street to catwalk across the multitude of canals and waterways that now crisscrossed Old Savannah. In actuality, they allowed him to elude all but the most persistent hunter. Evening to early morning was when he practiced his real profession. Was when he made his money resolute. Diurnal messenger boy was his mask, moonlight the chisel that chipped it away.

Unlike his friend who had acceded to a naming by acclimation, Whispr had chosen his own Meld name. His validated moniker was Archibald Kowalski. Everyone in his family had been big—in his family "big" serving as polite synonym for "obese." Growing up an obese kid was bad. Growing up poor and obese was bad squared. So when the appointed legal hour of adolescence arrived when Archie could choose to stay natural or undergo his first legal meld, he chose to become—slim. Not naturally slim which he could perhaps have accomplished with diet or even unpretentious traditional surgery, but unnaturally slim. Meld-slim.

Set beside the grand majority of complex meld surgeries, his was comparatively simple. They removed half his stomach and the majority of his intestines. In their place were inserted a fuel cell-powered post-digestive NEM (nutrient extractor and maximizer) that drew its energy from the fortified liquids he drank. It was complemented by a compact prefood processor. Nothing custom was required—all were straight off-the-line components. They had to be. Even with the first-meld loan he took out to pay for them he couldn't afford anything fancier.

Since then, with the money he and Jiminy had aggrandized through their after-hours activities, Archie had been able to add more personalized bioganic components to the humeld that was himself. A carbo squeezer, muscle assists, and most significantly a full course of bone aeration treatments. The result was that while he stood nearly six feet tall and weighed less than a hundred pounds, he was according to all tests and measures perfectly healthy, from his heart rate to his skin color. A bonus accruing from his chosen meld was that his cholesterol and triglyceride levels were lower than a mudpuppy's pooper. He and his whip-thin silhouette were nothing exceptional. Not when compared to the average Meld—far less when set beside one who was exceedingly customized.

He could slip through spaces between buildings where the police could not follow and enter openings too tight or narrow for more intelligent but less willowy thieves. Due to his everlastingly abridged weight he walked in a permanent hush. This practice of making airfalls instead of footfalls had led to him choosing the Meld name Whispr. But unlike Jiminy he had not had it wholly transliterated to his national ident. The census still knew him as Archibald Kowalski. Only friends and fences were acquainted with him as Whispr.

He and Jiminy had not singled out the unaccompanied pedestrian for the man's heartparts. Heart components were as common as—well, as melds. Perversely, what had drawn their attention was the man's left hand. With the face of its deceased owner smudging the alley's old brick paving, Whispr was able to admire the hand more fully as his partner extracted a compact set of decoupling tools from inside his copious shirt and began the process of ampuscation. Beyond the scene of the crim out on the one-way street an occasional electric vehicle, little noisier than Whispr himself, hummed along on its predetermined path as its passengers toured the city's historical district.

In a time of rising sea levels the blocks of old buildings, warehouses, and stately homes had turned out to be easier to preserve than the natural vegetation among which they had risen. Unlike much of the native flora that dominated the low-lying east coast of the old United States, standing cypress had no problem coping with the rising water that had inundated much of the old city. But most of the other trees and bushes needed a good deal of tender loving care to ensure their continuing survival. In the historical district entire blocks had been razed repeatedly and entirely. As

with similar localities deemed worthy of preservation in Charleston, Port
Royal, and all the way down to Jacksonville, they had eventually been
placed on hydraulic platforms. So Old Savannah still looked remarkably as
it had in the nineteenth and twentieth centuries, except that the warm
Atlantic shallows now flowed sleepily beneath the power stilts that kept the
historical city high and dry.

The old town was always full of tourists. Tourists being always full of
credit cards and other instruments of financial transfer as well as marketable swag and viable body parts, it was where Whispr and Jiminy preferred to hang out after leaving their day jobs—and scan for quarry.

Working swift and efficient with the gear from the tidy tool kit,
Whispr's mudbud already had the hand half detached. Though his fingers
were natural and unmelded, Jiminy was good with them. While his friend
toiled, Whispr occupied himself keeping an eye on the distant street traffic
and riffling the dead man's pockets, taking time to look for any hidden
antitheft compartments that might have been sewn or welded into the fab-
ric. To his surprise he located the man's wallet lying loose and unsecured
in a front pocket. Such casual indifference to personal safekeeping pointed
to a criminal neglect of personal protective measures. Or worse, the possibility that the wallet held nothing filchworthy. On the other hand there
was the hand, whose construction suggested that its owner was a man of
means, or at least had access to substantial resources.

Peering close he could see that the meld component his partner was
carefully removing was an exquisite piece of work. Navahopi craftsman-
ship, perhaps. Or if it was an import, maybe Russian or Israelistinian.
When one revelation after another came to light their excitement and expectations increased proportionately. As Jiminy's work progressed, however, Whispr found his early enthusiasm giving way in his half stomach to
a slow curdling of his dinner. It was becoming increasingly clear that what
the Cricket was ampuscating was no ordinary meld accessory. This fertil-
ized the rising suspicion that the evening's prey might be no ordinary
tourist.

Maybe sufficiently unordinary that others might come looking for him.

When the manifold processes of triple-R (Repair, Replace, and Regeneration) had first become cheap and widely available, people had opted for
the best exterior matches to their truborn selves. It was only later, when
flaunting one's Meldness had become not only socially acceptable but

trendy, that such additional cosmetic expense had proven itself unnecessary. The prevailing sentiment became the same as that espoused by purchasers of costly private vehicles or fine jewelry. If you could afford an expensive bodily accessory, why not show it off? What was the difference between a tattoo and a blue you? So the titanium weave and carbonic fibers of the dead man's prosthetic hand glimmered in the dim light that infused the alley unencumbered by the ancestral wistfulness of human skin.

It was work as fine and precise as Whispr had ever seen. The bonding of metal and carbon fiber to wrist bone, tendons, and muscles was seamless. It was impossible to tell where organics ceased and modifications commenced. In addition to permitting basic grasping, each finger had been further customized to perform a different task, from airscribing to communications. The hand of the dead man had been turned into a veritable five-digited portable office.

Jiminy was all but cackling to himself as he strove to finish detaching the piece from its owner. "Swart-breath, this is terrific stuff! Must've cost tens of thousands to compile and append. Swallower will give us six months subsist for it." He leaned into his work. A surgically equipped Meld or even a Natural would have been finished by now, but the necessary additional installs would have conflicted with Jiminy's chosen meld-self. Anyway, he didn't have the inborn brainjuice to be a medmeld. He was better at running. And killing. As was Whispr.

The difference between them was that Whispr knew it. He'd always been aware of his mental limitations. Maybe that was why he had chosen a meld that rendered him even more inconspicuous than most. Jiminy was an audacious, even impudent hunter. Whispr was shy.

And wary. As Cricket labored to finish the job, his slender companion glanced more and more frequently at the street. No cops showed themselves, no guides or handlers sought their waylaid subject. For an improv hunt it had gone very well.

The sweat that coursed down Whispr's rapier-thin body did not arise from unease. The Carolina coast was sufficient inspiration for the perspiration. Anymore, it was hot and tropical all the time, no different climatologically from the east coast of central Brazil. In the old days, it was said, fall and winter had been cool, occasionally even chilly. Such weather was gone with the Change. Savannah was as tropical as Salvador.

Maybe, Whispr mused, he would have his sweat glands removed one day. He knew those who'd had it done. But the resultant requisite panting that was required to compensate for the meld was unattractive, and inspired too many inescapable jokes of the canine persuasion.

"I wonder what he did, this guy," he found himself muttering aloud.

Jiminy replied without looking up from his work. "Some kind of scribe, maybe. Or accountant. He sure didn't get by on his physical attributes." He grunted slightly as he struggled to dissolve remaining connective tissue without damaging the linkages to the prosthetic. "Visiting from New York, or London. Hope he had the chance to enjoy some good Southern cooking before we made his acquaintance. There!"

The hand came off cleanly in Jiminy's fingers. There was only a little blood. The Cricket was no surgeon, but he took pride in his work. Whispr made an effort to suppress his natural melancholy. He tried to envision the gleam that would come into Swallower's eyes when he set all four of them—two natural and two melds—on the dismembered body part. For Whispr and the Cricket, he told himself with the slightest of grins, money was at hand.

It was as his companion was stowing their five-fingered prize in his scruffy backpack that Whispr noticed the thread.

It caught his eye only because the indirect light in the alley made it stand out slightly from those surrounding it and because he had been kneeling over the body of the dead man long enough for the cadaverish topography to become familiar. Had he passed the man in the street, had he stopped to converse with him, it never would have drawn Whispr's notice. Time, light, and circumstance conspired to reveal it.

Leaning close over the body's motionless chest, he drew a mag from one of his pockets. Slipped over his right eye, it automatically adjusted to his vision. Gently squeezing or releasing the muscles around the ocular orbit increased or reduced the magnification.

His interest had not been misplaced. Beneath the lens he could just make out the minuscule hinges that held the top and bottom of the thread in place inside the dead man's breast pocket.

"Let me have your tweezers." Without taking his eye off the pocket, he extended a hand toward his partner.

Jiminy gazed edgily toward the busy street as he fumbled for the requested tool. When he was sitting down, the kneecaps of his elongated legs rose higher than his head, making him look more like his arthropodal namesake than ever.

"Here—what'd you find? Concealed credit stick?"

"Naw—I don't know what it is. Sewn inside the pocket. Maybe it's a storage device." As the perfectly miniaturized hinges yielded to the pointed tips of the tweezers the top end of the thread came free. "Leastwise, one end's got a connector. Tiny, but I can see it."

Leaning toward Whispr as far as his monstrous lower limbs would allow, Jiminy sounded dubious. "Just looks like a piece of thread to me. Don't ident what it's made of, but that doesn't mean anything. Looks like metal, but might be something else. Pretty slick piece of work, whatever it is."

Whispr nodded as he carefully slid the excised thread into an empty storage packet. Lifting his right leg he drew a finger across the side of his shoe. Reading his vitals it unlocked and slid aside to reveal a small waterproof compartment. Carefully inserting the packet into the opening, he then snapped the sole back in place.

"I don't recognize the material either, but small as it is the connector looks standard. All we need is a reader."

Knees aimed forward, Jiminy lurched to his feet. "Probably full of family pictures, maybe an address book: nothing out of the ordinary. No subsist, that's sure."

"Yo so?" Normally Whispr would defer to his more intellectually gifted associate in such matters, but not this time. "If that's all that's on it, then why go to so much trouble and expense to hide it? Why not just keep it in the wallet?"

Jiminy hesitated, then nodded approvingly. "Good point. I'm with you on sticking it in a reader." He glanced down one more time at the dead man. The ampuscated hand was not bleeding. "We're done here." He slung his pack over his back. "Let's go play money tag with the Swallower."

No one looked in their direction, much less confronted them, as they hissed out of the public parking structure on Jiminy's two-wheeled scoot. Electrically powered like every other private vehicle on the city streets, the front end had been customized to accommodate its owner's triple-length melded legs. Turning south out of the tourist area, Jiminy eased the scoot into a lane reserved for two-wheeled vehicles, set the automateds, and let his fingers relax on the U-shaped guide wheel as the road integrals took control of their direction and speed.

Relaxing in the padded passenger seat behind him, Whispr let his gaze drift away from the backpack containing the decoupled hand and to the city lights flashing past. As always at such moments, he enjoyed squeezing his eyes nearly shut to morph the glow into swathes of black-framed rainbow. Most of metropolitan Savannah's development had been inland, to the west. Walking stilts, float lots, and other advanced hydrologic technology had allowed some expansion north and south along the coast, but the costs were prohibitive compared to moving inland to higher, dryer ground.

Steady acceleration soon had them out past the suburbs. They had entered the realm of floating towns, mobile villages, and the tropical vastness that had reclaimed the shallow land from what was left of inhabited Florida all the way up to the Chesapeake Bay. Isolated larger settlements utilizing the same climate-sensitive, flexible dike systems that protected Old D.C. formed oases of below-sea-level dry land that was scattered among the reeds, jungle, and powerfully resurgent mangrove forests. Eastward of permanent urban cores, massive hurricane barriers lay flat against the water, ready to be raised at the first sign of alarm from the weather service.

Whispr knew that the season was predicted to be comparatively mild, with no more than two dozen major storms expected to strike the mainland. Though not a 3M (modified Meld marsher), he rather looked forward to hurricanes. This because despite alerted residents taking the usual traditional precautions there was always destruction, which meant salable goods and material would be available for salvage.

Stopping for a celebratory early supper at a popular seafood restaurant, he and Jiminy encountered a busload of visiting Martians. Despite thickened black skin designed to absorb the sun's feeble rays, specially melded corneas that protected their bulging eyes from Mars's harsh UV light, greatly expanded chests required to accommodate four instead of two lungs, the respiratory reducing masks they wore (a Martian would drown in Earth's far denser atmosphere), and the other biogen mods necessary to allow a human to survive on the surface of the Red Planet, their appearance was no more outlandish than that of half a hundred terrestrial Melds.

Had they been visiting Titanites, now, Jiminy and Whispr might have stared. Titan's melded natives were a rare sight on Earth because of the cost of traveling from their distant moon. But Martians—the two men paid them hardly any attention.

Besides, they were watching for cops.

Their waitress was on the upside of thirty, half blond and half redhead (straight down the middle), and four-armed. Looking at her, it was impossible to tell which were her born arms and which the subsequent biogens. Multiple limbs were a common meld useful in numerous fields besides waitressing, though all multiarms tended to be regarded by the populace at large as potential pickpockets and often treated accordingly. Sue-Ann (so said her nametag) was only interested in handling plates of fried catfish, fried shrimp, fried clams, and fried chicken, with fried okra on the side. If a customer was so inclined and sufficiently hungry they could also order their food served on a suitably flavored edible plate. Fried, of course.

Though they had not yet made the sale the two thieves felt confident in treating themselves. Whispr slipped onto a natural chair while his companion plonked himself down on a floor cushion. Though their table had been fashioned to resemble one made from an old ship's hatch cover, it was capable of the usual multiplicity of adjustments necessary to accommodate the needs of dozens of different Melds. Jiminy was able to lower the half facing him down to chest level. The food itself was excellent and cheap, and no one in the country restaurant so much as glanced in their direction.

Equipped with four arms like the waitress, the Meld mixologist held court behind a bar that had been built up of slabs of welded metal cut from ancient hydrocarbon-powered vehicles. A real antique, Whispr thought as he studied it. Something that belonged in a museum—or in the back of Swallower's shop, where advertised via the ugweb it would bring substantial subsist.

A brace of local oystermen hauled in. They didn't flaunt their melds. According to the law, harvesting of oysters in the sloughs and bays could only be done the old-fashioned way, by hand and from small boats. One burly local had the three small fingers of his left hand transformed into a shell opener. A modest meld to be sure, but not one Whispr would want to have to confront in a fight.

The garrulous oystermen were interested in drink, not fighting. Chatting among themselves they sauntered past the Martians and spread out in front of the bar, a sunburned tide of braggadocio, boots, and body odor.

"Getting crowded." Wiping his lips, Jiminy tossed the napkin onto his (inedible) plate, jacked himself up on his elongated legs, turned, and in two hops was at the door. He waited on Whispr. But then, he was always waiting on someone.

Thunder rumbled out to sea as they sped down the coast. Looking to his left from the rear seat of the covered scoot, Whispr could see flashes of lightning dancing beneath the moon. He hadn't had time to check the latest weather report (he and Jiminy had been busy killing someone) and couldn't tell if the storm was coming inland or crawling along a low pressure path northward. He desired the former. He liked the rain even more than he did hurricanes, though its arrival invariably triggered the usual jokes from bystanders about being so thin that he could stand between the raindrops.

Decelerating down an offramp Jiminy reassumed manual control of all the scoot's functions as the highway's integrals relinquished control. Here out in the labyrinth of canals, natural drainage channels, sloughs, patches of dense forest, and surviving high ground, traffic shrank to near nothing. Raised above the swamp and water on pylons of honeycomb foam, the side slip was barely wide enough for the scoot and far too narrow to accommodate a car. Its slenderness was not a problem for the isolated commuters and fisherfolk who lived in this delta since most commuted to the city via hydroskim. Greater Savannah's waterways were always more forgiving than the fixed coast roads, and never closed for repair. Off in the distance and illuminated by the moon a big six-masted container ship was slowly advancing landward, on course for Savannah port.

Sprawled above reeds and sawgrass on four separate walkway-connected platforms, Swallower's Pawn and Supply looked as if it had been hit by a bomb. In actuality it had been, and on more than one occasion. Following each incident the resilient proprietor rebuilt his business; bigger, better, and sloppier than ever. Hunks of scavenged machinery were piled high and haphazardly on two of the platforms. They showed little rust. Nobody used equipment in the American South anymore that was susceptible to rust. Not when modern materials and coatings were widely and cheaply available that could ward off or prevent it.

Such resources could not, however, prevent swamp growths from epiphytes to mosses from taking root in odd corners of Swallower's inventory. Sometimes he would spray retardant. More often he just let the growths flourish. As long as his customers could get a general idea of what lay underneath the thriving vegetation, he would declare, that was good enough.

Slowing, Jiminy coasted to a stop in the small parking area reserved for scoots. Sturdy posts kept it well above the high-tide line and adjacent to the dock. There a pair of battered, scored, heavily used skims lay next to one another, floating like giant narrow leaves on the dark water.

Swallower's shop and office were part of the circular main building—circular in shape the better to withstand frequent hurricane winds and tidal surges. Its supporting platform anchored deep in the muck that passed for ground, it rose two stories high. The few windows on the lower floor were seriously security screened. It was assumed by visitors that the second floor was where Swallower dwelled in sybaritic and debased comfort. "Assumed," because no one had ever been invited to see the owner's living quarters. Those familiar with Swallower did not press for an invitation. There are some things mankind was not meant to know.

A pair of great white herons lifted off a pylon as the two men advanced via a raised walkway that led, like the leg of some giant dismembered crustacean, from the scoot parking area toward the main structure. Silvery metal glistened inside a wrecked and salvaged industrial-grade water purification block. Within the old machine's guts something dark and hirsute wandered slow and deliberate: a bird-eating spider that had claimed it for a home. A splash sounded from the high reeds where a family of capybara, taking no chances, made haste to remove themselves from the presence of man. Long-established residents of the southeastern coast, they were good eating and knew it.

Having been alerted to the scoot's approach by the shop's automated outlying security, Swallower awaited them within the establishment's central showroom. The large, high-ceilinged, circular space was crammed to the rafters with merchandise of every imaginable shape, size, and function: everything from antiques salvaged from Old Savannah to drums holding packets of the latest liquid jewelry in suspension. Access to the doughnut-shaped central counter and the single-person elevator at its nexus fluctuated according to the constantly shifting heaps of goods stacked on the floor. Having utilized the shop's services on previous occasions, Whispr and Jiminy were able to approach the proprietor without the aid of a map.

Swallower was not the only occupant of the congested floor display. At least a dozen cats prowled the piles and patrolled the spun-carbon struts that supported the second floor. Natural and melded felines coexisted as freely and easily as did their human counterparts. All were rescued animals. A man of many contradictions, it was known that the shop owner would blow off the legs of a prospective scam artist without a second thought and then force him to try to swim back to Savannah, but would spend thousands to save the life of an injured animal. Whispr shrugged at the thought. There was no accounting for personal predilections. As for himself, he was as indifferent to the affection of animals as he was to that of people.

Swallower belched softly as he turned from studying a heads-up display to confront them. He did not ask if they were armed. If they were, shop security would never have let them past the parking area, much less across the raised walkway that led to the front door. Shadowy of skin, though not as black as a Martian, the wildly bearded mass of man was bigger than Whispr and Jiminy put together. When asked why he didn't have his obese form melded, or at least suctioned, he declared with satisfaction that not only did he take pride in his appearance, he took pride in being *naturally* fat.

"When I eat a good meal," he had once explained without hesitation, "I want the results to *show*."

The world, Whispr knew, was replete with inexplicable perversities not all of which stemmed from the endless inventiveness of melding.

The proprietor's unwillingness to fine-tune his body did not extend to his profession. Above the natural eyes with which he had been born, two specialized ocular melds coldly examined the world around them. Their installation and grafton had necessitated a slight raising of his forehead. One eye was a magnifier of considerable range while the other saw into and registered sights far into the ultraviolet. Together they enabled their owner to ascertain the veracity of numerous items that were offered to him for sale, from fine meld componentry to estate jewelry that had been unwillingly liberated from various estates. More for show than need, Swallower had commissioned a pair of customized old-fashioned spectacles—with four lenses, two set above two. When worn, they helped to soften his otherworldly appearance. This was useful in business dealings, since there was nothing soft about the man himself.

Thick fingers wrapped around and enveloped Jiminy's much smaller hand. "I know thee, Cricket." Releasing their careful grasp, they flicked in the direction of the other visitor. "As be your companion, how is the sad-eyed soda straw these days?"

Jiminy's head inclined toward the silent, staring Whispr. "Jolly as always. We just had ourselves a most fine dinner at the Bug Shack."

The proprietor's doubled brow rose. "Eating out? Do not tell me you boys hath been working?"

Jiminy winked and swung his backpack around in front of him. "Nothing special. Just another fluky salvage pickup off the street."

"Knowing thee and thy predispositions, I should rather say savage pickup." A quartet of eyes peered downward. "What hath thee brought for me this night?"

As soon as he heard their host murmur his approval of the ampuscated hand, Whispr lost interest in the negotiations. Wandering toward the rear of the shop, he lost himself in idle contemplation of the assortment of merchandise. Some of it he recognized, some he wished he could afford, some meant nothing to him. One of Swallower's many cats ambled by, paused, and whistled a merry tune. In the course of the surgery necessary to save its life it had been given a throat meld. Now it could sing like a canary, or a mockingbird. Poetic justice, Whispr thought. Bending down, he let his hand stroke it from head to hips. Its tail came up and purring commenced to alternate with birdsong.

Hundreds of containers, individual bits of machinery, partial scavenged melds, and other merchandise hung from the ceiling. Swallower's shop was a bargain-hunter's as well as a cat's paradise. Whispr figured that Swallower could have done twice the trade if he had located inland on dry ground in the commercial district of uptown Savannah. But had he chosen to do so, his business would have been subject to more than twice the official scrutiny it presently received. Like a number of other kindred independent businessfolk whose establishments operated under ambiguous circumstances, Swallower preferred the anonymity conferred by the swampy suburbs.

"Eight." Jiminy was hopping in small circles, wary of banging his head against suspended product or the exposed fiber rafters. "Whispr and me, we took on a lot of karma to get this hand. We gotta have at least eight."

"I shall be fortunate to get eight on resale." Swallower was less exercised than his visitor and no less resolute. "I can offer thee no more than three."

"Three!" Oversized leg muscles contracting, Jiminy literally hit the ceiling, albeit it was only a glancing blow. "For three I'd just go ahead and turn myself in to collect the citizen's tip! Save all this time and trouble."

Unfurling a viewer from a pocket, Swallower nudged it to life and proceeded to consult the lambent screen. "I should sayeth three and a half, but I will go four in memory of the business we have done prior to this and the business that I expect will come after."

"Four. Four is a four-lettered word." Jiminy was not mollified.

"No it is not—four is a number."

The Cricket eyed the fat man unhappily. "You're playing games, Swallower." Holding out the dismembered meld hand he waved it in the proprietor's direction. Secured in place, the fingers did not jiggle. "You want it or not? You're not the only dealer on the coast, you know."

It was then that Whispr remembered the thread he had plucked from the dead man's clothing. Should he mention it now? Swallower would likely have equipment capable of reading the contents of the unobtrusive sliver of storage media. Information was always worth subsist. But without any idea of what was on the thread, he and Jiminy had no way of pricing it. Relying on a prospective purchaser to tell you what your article was worth was a poor way to begin negotiations. Maybe they could hire someone just to read the thread. With this idea in mind he started toward the two arguers. He badly wanted Jiminy's thoughts on how they should proceed. Besides, judging from the volume of perspiration rolling down their faces, both men could probably use a rest from the ongoing bargaining.

The necessary break was supplied by a source other than the advancing Whispr when all hell broke loose. . . .

2

Like Swallower himself, the alarms whose shrieking suddenly filled the shop were anything but restrained. They howled, they clamored, they screamed for attention. And they got it.

Wrangling forgotten, owner and visitor instantly ceased their haggling. Unsettled by the cacophony, panicked cats scattered among the rafters and merchandise in a flurry of tailed shadows and militant hissing.

"What be the freak?" Exhibiting speed and agility that belied his bulk, the startled Swallower turned from Jiminy and lunged in the direction of the control counter behind him. By the time he and his visitors reached it, holos relayed by several remote pickups were already dancing in the air above the projectors. A couple of the more confident cats paused to watch, their attention caught by the internally illuminated hovering images.

Whispr's gaze went immediately to one particular oval holo. Uptaken from a unit hidden in a power tower or maybe a tree, it showed a line of high-power scoots traveling silently and at a high rate of speed down a narrow roadway. Even the dim light did not prevent Whispr from recognizing it immediately. It was the same elevated roadway he and Jiminy had recently used to access Swallower's enterprise. He stared silently. There were an awful lot of scoots, and they were transporting an awful lot of police.

They were coming this way.

Face flushed, four eyes all but alight, a furious Swallower turned rising rage on Jiminy.

"Treachery! Perfidious betrayal! Thou hath sold me out!"

Crouched down behind his upraised knees, a manifestly perplexed Cricket struggled to make sense of what the concealed security monitors were showing.

"I—I don't understand. We were careful! No one saw us—no one!" He stared down at the amputated hand. "This doesn't make any sense. It's not even a whole *limb*." His bewildered gaze shifted to another of the hovering holos. As the flotilla of police scoots materialized to fill it, the preceding image winked out.

"Mayhap thy slaying unknowingly and foolishly involved an important personage." As he spoke Swallower waddled behind the circular counter, having to pass through the police-heavy holo to reach his destination.

"He didn't look important." Jiminy was mumbling *and* sweating now. "There wasn't anything in his wallet to suggest consequence. Just the usual subsist. No spec defensive glam—nothing."

"On one thing we doth agree." A small open-sided elevator was descending slowly from the second floor. The lift was industrial grade, Whispr noted. It would have to be, to handle their host's impressive bulk. "This indeed maketh no sense."

Didn't look important, Whispr thought slowly. *Just the usual subsist.* Except for one thing. Except for the thread. Noting the fury in Swallower's expression he decided now might not be the best time to bring up the matter of the tiny, artfully camouflaged storage device.

"We didn't sell you out!" Jiminy was insisting.

Face flushed, quartet of eyes glittering, their bearded host stepped into the open lift. "Not intentionally, perhaps. I do not grant you that much acumen. But for one such as myself whose business be fencing without fences, stupidity be a synonym for blindness, and the blind sometimes cannot avoid stepping in shit." Emitting a grinding noise that was less than reassuring, the lift started to rise toward the circular opening in the ceiling from which it had descended.

"Where are you going?" Whispr asked their host.

From the depths of the ebony Assyrian beard flashed a hint of a wry smile, like a crack in dried asphalt. "*I* am going to bed. If the police wish to speak with me, I shall appear before them cloaked in coverlet and yawns, affecting an air of bemusement at being rudely roused from my beauty sleep."

Taking a long step forward, an increasingly distraught Jiminy continued to follow their host's ascent. "But what about us?"

"Get thee hence from my sight and my shop. Flee these surrounds, lest thee shortly be identified to the looming authorities as intruders whom I was compelled to welcome only under duress, and with whom I would surely *never* do business." Swallower's hand slipped to the instrumentation on his belt.

As Jiminy was readying further protest, long, attenuated shapes began to emerge from the mountains of merchandise. In slinks and links the modified serpents came squirming toward the two visitors. Neither man being herpetologically challenged, they immediately recognized the venomous bushmasters and fer-de-lance who were advancing toward them under Swallower's control. He liked his snakes as well as his cats, did their no longer congenial host, and there were far too many of the fat man's pets to shoot.

When a seven-meter-long python dropped from the ceiling to land right in front of Whispr and start toward him, the slender thief whirled and bolted for the exit. Coming to the same conclusion that trying to argue with Swallower was no longer a viable course of action, Jiminy soared over his retreating associate with a single bound. Behind them the pursuing serpents, more effective than any human security guards, halted at the doorway.

Once more outside, both men could see glimmers of light reflected from the eyes of Swallower's beloved rescued and personalized felines. Be they calico or tabby, manx or maniac, they prowled the raised walkways flashing scythelike claws on their front feet. Patterned after the killing talons of the long-extinct Deinonychus, they were as adept at cutting a man's throat as they were at disemboweling intruding rodents.

Hissing, fur standing on end, claws upraised, one overzealous stiletto cat barred their way. Jiminy cleared it effortlessly, leaping high to land well on the other side of the potentially lethal feline. Whispr, however, was forced to pause and search frantically for a way around it. Driven by instructions broadcast by Swallower directly into its brain and those of its stealthy, watchful companions, the killer kitty continued to block Whispr's flight.

It wasn't going to matter. Having safely reached the scoot waiting in a far corner of the small parking area, Jiminy slipped inside, threw one melded leg over the seat, and powered it up. Dashing toward his partner would send the security cat scrambling on all four paws to get out of the way. With the pack containing the still unfenced hand slung across his back, the Cricket accelerated. Emitting a softly rising whine the scoot headed toward Whispr.

Then veered away, heading for the raised access road that led south and away from the shop.

Surrounded by lethal felines a dumbfounded Whispr looked on as the two-person vehicle continued to pick up speed. He did not call out. He was too stunned, and there was no point. It was not as if Jiminy had forgotten about him. It was not as if Whispr had been overlooked.

There is something about the act of wanton abandonment by a friend that beggars comment. The orphaned can go to wrack and ruin in an orgy of loud recrimination, or respond with silent acceptance. It was not in Whispr's nature to do the first, and he did not have the intelligence to offer more than the latter.

Instead, he continued to stand there, gaping dumbly at the swiftly receding silhouette of the speeding scoot. Jiminy would hit an intersection and strike off safely away from the incoming police, leaving Whispr alone and isolated to answer their questions. Swallower had already as much as declared that if pressed by the arriving authorities he would not hesitate to categorize his recent visitors as nothing more than potential thieves, and that as a consequence he was relieved to welcome the police onto his premises.

Was it possible, Whispr wondered, that the approach of authority in such numbers had nothing to do with his and Jiminy's presence? Might the city or state be mounting a raid on Swallower's establishment for reasons that had nothing to do with his latest visitors? It would be easy enough to find out. All he had to do was stand right where he was and await their arrival.

For someone who had been raised in indigent surroundings and who upon maturity had drifted into a lifestyle charitably described as unsociable, this was not an option. Espying one corner of the parking area that was not infested with Swallower's damnable killer cats, Whispr bolted in its direction, put both hands on the molded plastic railing, and without hesitation leaped over the side.

Too bad about Whispr, Jiminy thought as he urged the scoot onward. Behind and beneath him the finely tuned engine whined softly as it carried him south. The willow man had been a good companion, always helpful on jobs, never extending himself beyond the limits of what he knew he could do. That was the trouble with so many contacts in Jiminy's business. Intoxicated from absorbing one too many popent plays, they all too often made the mistake of confusing entertainment with real life. Or worse, conflating the two. Be they Natural or Meld, successful lawbreakers were the ones whose names and faces you never saw splashed across the media because they never got caught. Jiminy was perfectly content to languish in prosperous anonymity. To maintain that enviable status one sometimes had to make sacrifices. Friends, family—in this instance, Whispr. Cricket knew he could find a new partner more easily than he could handle incarceration.

He smiled to himself as the scoot angled sharply to the left as it automatically leaned into a turn. Whispr's internment wouldn't cost the state much. They could lock him up in a closet. Or a golf bag.

He saw the police search unit before he heard it. Swift and nearly noiseless, it went right past him, the bright light from its belly illuminating the water and stultified swamp that flanked the narrow roadway on either side. Then it swung around in a wide arc to come up behind him. Moments later his vehicle was undergoing a scan from a wide, diffuse laser as bright as day. He hunched down as low as he could in the driver's seat and muttered a curse. There was no way he could outrun the robot searcher. If they would just ignore him long enough for him to get into Georgetown proper he could ditch the scoot and lose himself in the pedestrian crowds: one more Meld among thousands.

Alerted by the first, a second searcher drone arrived and began to track him in parallel with its brethren. Still no cops. He was only minutes from the first major Georgetown intersection. There would be traffic, offramps, shopping—not downtown, but he would have a chance. Knowing this, he did not slow or pull over even when a floater appeared overhead and in front of him. Pretending not to hear, he ignored the commands to stop.

They put a disabler on him. As it drained the battery pack that powered the scoot he felt his transport slowing. Well, he had made his best effort at flight, though he doubted the authorities would give him credit for it. Letting the depowered scoot coast to a halt on the roadway he prepared his response. Since he had no idea what was going on or what they might want him for, it was necessarily generalized. His spirits rose slightly. Maybe they just wanted to ask him some questions about Swallower's operation. It might have nothing to do with the killing at all.

As he stepped out of the scoot he walked quickly to the roadway railing. Bending over the side, he pantomimed throwing up. The movement caused his backpack to slide around in front of him. Continuing to feign upchucking, he allowed the hand to slip out of the pack. It made nary a splash as it landed in the water between support pilings and sank out of sight into the dark muck. Having thus neatly disposed of the only incriminating evidence and wiping nonexistent drool from his mouth, he felt much better about his imminent prospects as he turned to face the roadway.

Touching down in silence the floater completely blocked the scoot lane leading southward. Holding his arms above his head Jiminy blinked as handheld lights were turned on him. He was startled to see half a dozen lod cops coming his way. Expecting regular police, the presence of the lods was a surprise. Two ordinary cops would have been more than adequate to take the unresisting Cricket into custody.

All lods were Melds, of course. Four of them were characteristically enormous. Pumped full of modified HGH, their pituitaries gengineered, their bones infused with organic titanium powder, extra heart muscle layered on, the smallest of them stood two and a half meters tall and weighed a shade under two hundred kilos. For all that mass and muscle they were not slow. Meld injections had supplemented their natural bulk with many grams of high-twitch muscle fiber. It was a brave (or highly specialized Meld) lawbreaker who would directly challenge a lod.

Hands held high above his head Cricket had no intention of doing so, of course. As they drew nearer his concern gave way to a touch of ego shine. Whatever they wanted him for he could not help but be flattered by the amount of manpower and hardware that had been deployed to catch him. The lods were heavily armed and armored. Eyeing their approach, he knew he did not have enough strength to even lift one of their guns, much less aim and fire it.

"Evening, gentlewhen." The lights illuminating his face were harsh.

Unlike some of his friends he had never had his eyes melded to allow for better night vision. Or like Swallower had additional orbs added to compensate.

The nearest lod was a sergeant. A rhino in blue, he loomed over the melded flight risk and leaned forward. For a lod his voice was unnaturally, almost comically high-pitched.

"Where is it?"

Cricket responded with a bemused smile. "I guess that all depends on how you choose to define 'it.'"

The lod was not amused. Reaching out and grabbing the prisoner with one huge hand, he lifted the other Meld off the pavement. Cricket's elongated and strengthened legs could deliver a potent kick, one powerful enough to stun even a lod. He didn't dare, of course. If he used his legs against this squad they would respond by breaking them, and if he struck first he would have no legal defense at all. He took comfort in the knowledge that as with all interactions involving the police and public, every moment of the confrontation was being recorded. He would not give them the satisfaction of allowing himself to be provoked no matter how much they manhandled him.

"It's too late in the day for funny, bug-boy." The lod wasn't smiling. "Hand it over." The thick fingers gripping the detainee's shirtfront tightened ungently. "*Now.*"

Jiminy lost the smile. "Go on, keep abusing me." He nodded in the direction of the parked floater. "The result won't look good in court."

"In court. Of course." Setting him down, the lod turned to his massive colleagues, then looked back at the much smaller Meld. "You're right, bug-boy. Shaking you around would look bad to an adjudicator. So would this."

Stepping out and forward, the sergeant brought one elephantine foot down on the smaller Meld's right foreleg. The bone snapped loudly, not unlike a branch of dead pine, and Jiminy screamed like a girl. Clutching at the shattered limb he collapsed to the pavement. Widening eyes filled with unrestrained tears as he held himself, moaning. Unmoved, the police sergeant extended a huge hand downward.

"Give it over. Last chance."

"Can't be the last chance." Another of the lods was gazing emotionlessly at the writhing, whimpering Cricket. "Can't kill him 'til we have it."

"Shut up, Noril." Kneeling down beside the sobbing prisoner, the sergeant reached out and placed one hand over the other man's face. Fingers the size of small clubs began to squeeze. "Talk to me, bug-boy. Tell me where it is. Don't bet your life on the corporal's faux pas. Bet it on us recovering what you took." He relaxed his grip.

Trembling with fear and from the screaming pain in his smashed leg, Cricket struggled to raise an arm and point to his left. "There—over there. I dumped it over the side. In the water."

Releasing the detainee's face the lod sergeant stood and gave an impatient jerk of his head in the indicated direction. Immediately two of the squad moved toward it.

"Better be well packaged and not damaged. Better be easy to find," the irritated cop growled.

The water was dark, but with the advanced search gear at their disposal a badly shaken Jiminy knew these police should have little difficulty finding and retrieving the ampuscated meld hand. In any case, it was over. After recovering what they had come for they would haul him to jail to await an adjudication. That would give him time to prepare a plea.

He could blame it all on Whispr. The stick-man was not good with words and would likely put up a poor defense. As he considered his options Jiminy felt a little better. With luck he might get off being charged only as an accomplice to the tourist's killing instead of being marked as the instigator. His hesitation had cost him a broken leg, but before he could appear at trial that would have to be repaired at state expense. He might even be able to file a successful claim charging the Savannah Authority with police brutality and use of excessive force. Though things hadn't worked out as planned, he would get through this all right. He always had.

Raising a hand, he tried to block out the stark illuminators that were still shining on his face. "Could you guys maybe do something about the light? It's hurting my eyes."

"Oh. Sure." Looking over a shoulder, the sergeant spoke to one of his subordinate Melds. "The lights are hurting his eyes. Fix it."

The bigger cop nodded and the lights winked out. Jiminy had just enough time to experience a moment of gratitude when the Meld shot a necap. Landing squarely on the prisoner's head the highly charged diaphanous material adhered securely and flared once, instantly short-circuiting every cerebral neural connection. Jiminy's head slumped forward as his brain went out. The sergeant eyed the dead detainee a moment longer before turning expectantly toward the roadway railing.

"Find it yet?"

A voice called back from somewhere in the shallow water below. "Still looking, sarge!"

Muttering to himself the police noncom checked his chrono. "Hurry it up! Word from Downtown is they want it back Outown as of yesterday!" Raising his gaze he let it drift south and east, deeper into the wildlife sanctuary. Bug-boy might have been lying all along, the sergeant thought worriedly. His broken leg notwithstanding, what they had been ordered to recover might not even be where the insolent Meld had indicated.

Which made it all the more imperative that they find the dead man's missing partner as soon as possible.

WHEN THE GREATER MOON SLIPPED behind the clouds that had tiptoed north from Cuba, the owl's eyes appeared as two smaller substitute satellites. Killing claws locked it firmly in place on the mangrove branch overhanging the water as it hooted softly. Below, a brace of two-meter-long white caiman lay motionless as scabrous logs, waiting for something edible and unaware to come drifting by. The air was still, heavy, and saturated. A steady chorus of nocturnal insects voiced their approval.

Whispr was likewise wringing wet, but he was most definitely not still. Though lanky beyond imagining, he was neither weak nor feeble. His muscles were thin but strong strings and he powered his way through the water and reeds with a determination and knowledge born of frequent flights from the law.

He had tried to tell Jiminy that the dead man's hand was bad news. The quality of it, the superb workmanship, all hinted that its owner was no ordinary citizen, just as the prosthetic was no ordinary meld. Whispr did not doubt for a minute that the sudden and unexpected arrival of so many police was connected with the hand they had tried to sell. Dwelling as it did on the cusp of legitimacy as well as the edge of town, Swallower's business was hardly unknown to the authorities. Were they so inclined they could have shut it down anytime they wished. On technicalities if not on straightforward charges. The presence of custom-tailored poisonous snakes and scythe-clawed cats notwithstanding, it would not require multiple police floaters to close him up.

Had he not been on the lookout for ancillary police apparatus like the searcher drone, Whispr probably would not have seen it coming his way. Gliding silently through the air a few meters above the treetops, only its small subdued red ident lights indicated its presence. Fortunately, he had noticed its approach while he was still just out of range. Its fan-shaped detectors had not yet reached his location. He could not outrun the drone, of course. With his powerful melded legs Jiminy might be able to do so. Whispr's alters were of a different nature.

But not necessarily less effective.

A range of hardy, salt-tolerant trees rose from the swamp. Choosing the densest grove, Whispr forced himself into its center. The nearly dry land from which they sprang beckoned to traditional North American water moccasins, copperheads, and coral snakes, not to mention dangerous intertidal immigrants from much farther south like the occasional anaconda. At the moment, serpents were the least of his worries.

Finding a suitable groove in the trunk of a stately old oak, he half closed his eyes and set in motion a pair of melds that were wholly internalized. Half physical adjustment, half mental, when activated in combination they allowed him to dramatically moderate his heart rate. So much so that within moments his blood flow had been considerably slowed. Responding, his body restricted and concentrated the flow to the most important organs. One result was that unless it flew right over the top of him a police scanner would be hard-pressed to identify his greatly reduced heat signature as that of a human being.

Sure enough, the searcher drone passed well off to the left without pausing to focus in his direction. A running man, or even one standing and breathing hard, would immediately have drawn the attention of the drone's sensors. Concealed within the protective fold of his oak, Whispr did not.

Nevertheless, he remained where and as he was until the scanner had vanished in the direction of the western horizon. Reviving himself and restoring the full flow of blood to his body, he noticed a faint glow in the scanner's wake. Having nothing to do with the police search that was obviously in full swing, the faint light heralded the approaching dawn.

Breaking from the cover of the trees he resumed his muddy slog cityward. While his slender shape would allow him to hide behind pylons as well as trees, daylight would make locating him easier. Only by losing himself in a crowd could he be confident of throwing off the search.

How badly did they want him? If it was deemed serious, if the authorities were really determined, they could get a court order requisitioning copies of Swallower's in-house security recordings. These would show his visitors clearly and from every angle. Once his face and form were flashed into every police file, Whispr knew he wouldn't be able to go anywhere without being scanned and identified by one of the hundreds of ubiquitous security pickups speckled throughout the state.

To protect his continued obscurity what he really needed was a new face—or at the very least, a serious adjustment. Ideally, suitable anonymity called for a full-scale remeld. That much work would require money beyond subsist, of which he had little. As fond as he had become of his slim, flexible body, if it would keep him out of a Reducation Center he would gladly pay to pack on a few dozen melded kilos. He was far more attached to his freedom than to his shape.

Along with having no money, he had nothing to sell. Leastwise, nothing that would pay for even the comparatively simple meld he needed. What he did have was a solid if unremarkable reputation in certain illicit quarters of the Savannah area, and excellent credit therein. Unlike Jiminy and other acquaintances, Whispr rarely bought anything he could not afford. His wants being simple, he had never been in debt.

Now was the time to call those credits and cash in on that reputation. Added weight, a few basic facial manips, maybe a custom add-on or two would change his appearance more than enough to baffle the police. Of course, they were used to lawbreakers on the run changing their appearances. The eternal striving of the pursued to disguise themselves from their pursuers had stimulated comparable advances in criminology and police forensics. But if he could just acquire a few simple manips, Whispr was confident he could evade the notice of the authorities.

After all, he told himself as he plugged onward through the swamp, it wasn't as if he and Jiminy had stolen the hand of a president or a popular entertainer. Their prey might have been an important businessman, or at most a visiting dignitary taking in the tourist sights of Old Town. Surely nothing more.

He was more interested than ever to see what was on that storage thread, though.

But first he had to elude the police pursuit, then arrange for a quick manip and meld. Any mysteries contained on the thread would have to wait.

As he splashed and fought his way through the reed beds and increasingly frequent patches of damp forest he wondered if there were any amphibs tracking him. A full amphibian meld, involving the addition of gills but the retention of lungs, was much more expensive and difficult to install than a simple lung-gill replacement. Usually, hydrophilic citizens opted for the latter and a round-the-clock underwater lifestyle. More complex amphib melds were reserved for the rich, or for full-time supervisors of the huge fish and shellfish farms permanently emplaced along the entire east coast.

Because of their location amid the slowly but steadily rising waters of the Atlantic, low-lying cities like Savannah often had an amphib or two on retainer, if not a full staff like New York or Boston. There used to be whole squads of them working farther south in old Miami. But old Miami was no more, a badly sited conurbation lost to history and the rising waters that had inundated much of the Florida peninsula.

He couldn't recall reading or hearing anything about an amphib cop being part of Savannah's police department, and the water in which he found himself was too shallow to permit a gill Meld to move about comfortably. Most likely, the police would rely on their scanners to track him down. Having already avoided one, there was a good chance no others were in his immediate vicinity. He had an opening now, certainly.

As he slogged onward he wondered how Jiminy was doing. When next they met, an angry Whispr would have a few choice words for his leggy friend. Abandoning him like that. Why, it would serve him right if the cops picked him up and took him in for interrogation.

Something stung his right leg. He flinched but kept moving. Farther inland and higher up in the warm waters of the Savannah or the Ogeechee Rivers there was always the chance of encountering piranha. In their vicinity he would still be okay so long as he refrained from splashing around too much. The bite he had just incurred might have come from one of the nastier river bugs that had migrated north along with their larger tropical cousins the snakes and birds. What he really feared was the candiru, though cases involving that horrific little parasitic fish were still largely confined to the more seriously flooded Deep South.

He was feeling pretty good about his prospects until he saw the jaguar.

3

Just the nose.

Fixing it wouldn't require a meld. Not even a formal manip. Half the professionals in her tower were qualified to do the work. Rajeev would probably do it for free. Any man who could do a full limb graft (bone, cfiber, organotitanium—your choice of materials and colors, easy financing, no interest for six months) could certainly shorten a nose. For more than a year now his interest in her had encompassed all regions below the nose with an eye toward performing a procedure less complex but just as personal as a meld. They had gone out several times. He was good company, as were several of the other doctors and surgeons who had offices in the same tower. Ingrid preferred him to many of her colleagues because he was less inclined to talk business on a date. If only he could somehow resist the urge to talk cricket. Compared to the favored game of his ancestral homeland, the nuances of infectious diagnosis were a simple matter to explain.

She knew she was natural-prettier than the average physician. What had been a burden in residency had carried over into private practice. There were prospective patients who hesitated to place themselves and their illnesses in the hands of a doctor who was more attractive than the majority of the population. Especially one who was a Natural. Some male patients tended to be either too reluctant or too eager to submit to examination. Age would take care of both problems, she knew. But for now it remained an ongoing concern. Patient unease, however, tended to diminish as her reputation grew.

Despite the opinion of friends that she leave her nose alone, she was still tempted. She was aware of the importance of imperfection. Nowadays, when anyone could be perfect, perfection was impossible to define. And perfection was the least of it. Pay the appropriate license fee and you could undergo a full cosmetic meld that would leave you looking like anyone you wished. After an initial flood of Marilyn Monroes, Sophia Lorens, Clark Gables, Belmondos, Rais, Washingtons, and others, the popular trend in purely cosmetic melding (for those who could afford it) had shifted to historical figures. That fad too had soon waned. It was all very well and good to look like the Berlin bust of Nefertiti—until four of them showed up at the same melding-out party.

As the skills of gengineers and surgeons had improved exponentially, cosmetic manips had given way to practical ones. One of the first casualties of the new, more advanced procedures had been traditional sports. To be a three-hundred-kilo lineman was fine on the football field, but rendered the majority of one's daily life uncomfortable as well as difficult. What was the point in undergoing a meld to be two meters tall when the next meld raised the average height of basketball centers to three meters? You could dunk, but you couldn't enter most buildings. Or buy clothes, or ride the bulk of public transport. As for tolerating any flight on an aircraft that lasted longer than ten minutes . . .

Gradually, inevitably, composite melds became more job specific. Slender elongated fingers for everyone from assemblers to pianists. Night vision for those whose occupations were nocturnal. A decorous layer of sculpted blubber for the Antarctic colonists. Ear enhancements for musicians and voicebox manips for singers. For professional drivers it became possible to actually give them eyes in the backs of their heads, though laying out the schematics of the requisite neural processors was much more time-consuming and expensive than installing the additional orbs themselves. For the first time, workers in the worldwide sex industry were able to—enough to say that the variety and kinds of melds were limited only by the imagination of those requesting such modifications and the skills of the surgeons installing them.

Then there were the truly extreme melds. Those that were required to turn *Homo terrestrialis* into beings capable of surviving on Mars. Or even more remarkably, on Titan. Radically manipulated humans, but human still.

Leaning slightly forward, Ingrid Seastrom once more contemplated her thirty-ish visage in the bathroom mirror. Though it continued to bother her she decided that for a while longer, at least, she would leave her nose alone.

As she prepared to leave for work she spared a last quick glance out the picture window of her eighty-fifth-floor codo. The view encompassed the tourist district of Old Town and in the distance the waters that rolled in off the Atlantic's continental slope. She preferred it to the panoramas on the other side of the building, no matter how romantic Rajeev insisted the sunsets were when viewed from his domicile.

The elevator took her down past the consultation medical suites that occupied floors fourteen through ten. The six ground floors of the tower were occupied by two domain hospitals, one specializing in cardio and the other in neuromuscular. Between them and far below the building's private residences was a single commercial floor (grocery, electronics, and more) and occupying the last two levels, the Great South Savannah Meld Center. Rajeev worked there while Ingrid's shared facilities were on the eleventh floor. Their paths crossed more often in one of the building's restaurants or its grocery store than they did in any of the manifold medical facilities.

As she stepped out of the elevator and headed down the familiar hallway she passed colleagues and patients in equal number. Both groupings comprised Naturals and Melds. One might operate on the other, and vice versa. As in any successful medical practice Ingrid's patients included both. What made her stand out from the vast majority of her colleagues and what had brought her practice a certain notoriety was a unique characteristic that had nothing to do with belonging to either social group.

Dr. Ingrid Seastrom made house calls.

Disregarding the remarkable advances medical science and gengineering had made over the past centuries, one executive patient had described this inimitable aspect of Dr. Seastrom's practice as "true science fiction."

Never having actually encountered or heard of the ancient medical custom in person, she had first come across it when reading several novels set in an earlier, simpler time. Intrigued, she had proceeded to research the concept, only to discover that it still survived as a therapeutic relic in a few scattered locations around the planet. Resurrecting it for a couple of afternoons out of her workweek had done wonders for her practice.

Thursday afternoon was one of the two she had set aside for engaging in the ancient medicinal enterprise. Some of the visits she made were pro bono; her way of fulfilling her share of the mandatory national medical service. Leaving her corner of the shared offices, she took the lift down to the first subterranean garage level. Like everything else in Greater Savannah it was tightly sealed against the eventual inevitable intrusion of the ever-rising Atlantic.

Able to afford more than a scoot, her personal vehicle had four wheels. The built-to-order back end contained a complete portable medical facility, touted by its manufacturer as the "hospital in a trunk." It was not quite that, but Ingrid could do in the field what most twentieth-century medical facilities required the contents of entire buildings to accomplish.

Powered by a single battery slab her car could not achieve a high rate of speed, but it was more than adequate for traveling around the metropolitan area and taking her as far as the outlying suburbs. A good deal of the Carolinas and Georgia was still rural, especially those districts that impinged on national or international nature preserves, and many of their denizens could not afford to come into Savannah or Jacksonville for advanced medical care. It was while working among the poorest of her clients that she felt the greatest satisfaction. The government covered basic medical needs, but beyond that patients were on their own.

Among the worst cases she saw were those involving botched melds.

As a Natural, she was not expected to be sympathetic. All melds were elective, and many Naturals felt that those who chose to undergo such procedures could hardly expect understanding from their fellow citizens should adverse consequences result. That she was at all times empathetic always impressed her clients, be they highly paid businessmen or low income specialty farmers and fisherfolk.

The afternoon was unexceptional, featuring a ten-minute pause to let one of the almost-daily equatorial downpours burn itself out over the city. She had read that there was a time in the past when such heavy tropical rains had been far less frequent in the southeastern states. But there had also been a time when Old Savannah, like Old Nawlins, had actually sat on dry ground instead of having to be raised up on stilts. Having grown up in such surroundings she felt perfectly comfortable among them, of course. Ancient history was full of surprising revelations.

As the characteristically sultry afternoon wore on and she dispensed the usual much appreciated advice, recommendations, medications, injections, and minor meld repairs, her curiosity was stirred only twice. Once by an ill Natural sixteen-year-old boy who the instrumentation in the rear of her car diagnosed as suffering from dengue-h fever. She treated him and advised his concerned parents to bring him into the city for a checkup and possible isolation treatment. The second case involved a would-be professional model living in an expensive floating coastal codo whose melded left leg was showing signs of degradation of gengineered calcium sponge. An injection temporarily relieved the young woman's discomfort and Ingrid advised her to seek a consultation with the original surgeon, with an eye toward a possible remeld. This advice was not received enthusiastically.

The sun was on its way down and she was already contemplating dinner options when she parked in front of the house in the woods.

It fronted a private forestry concern. Behind the house hectares of rocket pine thrust bright green needles toward the recently rain-swept sky. Gengineered to provide two harvestable crops a year on poor soil, rocket pine had replaced peanuts and tobacco as a ready cash crop throughout many of the southern states. While the advent of electronic readers had replaced the need for newsprint throughout the world, no one had yet come up with an electronic substitute for paper towels or toilet paper. Additionally, private forests supplied incidental habitat for a far greater diversity of fauna than other farms while simultaneously serving as excellent buffers for nature and wildlife preserves.

Runoff from the recent sticky downpour was still trickling into holding ponds and tanks as Ingrid got out of the car. With her medogic tucked under one arm she strode toward the front entrance, tiptoeing around the occasional puddle. Dinner was very much on her mind.

The worried woman who met her obviously had other concerns.

"I can't believe anyone does this," she murmured gratefully as she invited the doctor inside. Her comment was typical of the reaction Ingrid received on no less than ninety-nine percent of her house calls. "Thank you for coming on such short notice." Turning, she led the doctor deeper into the spotless residence.

"You're welcome." Ingrid never said "It's my job." If she did, the flow of gratitude tended never to cease and interfered with her work.

A slidestair carried them to a second floor. The view out a flex window shifted continuously from one end of the property to the other. A few steps down an interior hallway and the mother halted briefly, waiting on a door to open.

"It's our daughter, Cara," she whispered nervously. "She didn't want us to call you. She doesn't want to see a doctor. I think she's embarrassed."

According to the stats Ingrid's office had downloaded and that had been transferred to her medogic, Cara Jean Gibson was a fifteen-year-old girl. Simply *being* a fifteen-year-old girl was embarrassing. Entering the room, Ingrid was mentally primed to confront the expected. Acne, gawkiness insufficiently improved by low-grade over-the-counter manips, badly gengineered hair, failed skin toning resulting in possible fever.

She was not prepared for what she actually encountered.

Cara Gibson was lying on a traditional bed. The underneath was fibernet, but from the looks of it the antique feather mattress on top had been lovingly restored and maintained. In contrast, the girl's head rested on a thoroughly modern aeromuse pillow that had doubtless been programmed to play her favorite music depending on how she shifted the weight of her head against it. For all Ingrid knew it was hammering away right now, transmitting the latest goolmech to the girl via direct acoustic transduction. If it was, the tune she was listening to was not a happy one.

Eyes widening at the sight of the newcomer, Cara responded to the intrusion in no uncertain terms. "Moma! I *told* you—no doctors!"

Ingrid put on her most sympathetic girl-girl smile. "How do you know I'm a doctor?"

The teen grunted, as if the visitor's identity was the most obvious thing in the world. "Musth! You barely glanced at my face before your eyes went to my head."

Ingrid spoke gently as she advanced toward the bed. "May I see your head?"

Cara Gibson turned over sharply to face the wall instead of her mother and the stranger. "Why not? It seems like everybody *else* wants to."

At least with her patient facing the other direction Ingrid did not have to worry about maintaining an empathetic smile. The girl's turn had revealed what should have been a fairly simple cosmetic meld gone wrong. It was a full quill implant, standard scarlet macaw. Bright yellow, dark blue, and intense red feathers flared in the currently favored Mohawk crest from the top front of the girl's otherwise shaven skull down to the middle of her back. The meld ensured that the feathers would continue to grow exactly as they might from the body of the bird that had provided the template DNA. Unless the meld was deleted, of course.

Ingrid unfolded her medogic. "I have to scan you to see what's gone wrong, Cara. I need your permission."

"Like my mother didn't already give you permission. Oh, go ahead." The girl didn't turn to watch. "I don't care. I'm a mess anyway."

"Maybe we can fix that." When the patient didn't reply Ingrid proceeded to activate the medogic. "And thank you for giving me *your* permission."

The readings were about what she expected based on her preliminary visual observation. Whoever had performed the meld had either used an insufficiency of bonding protein or the wrong one. More than half the quill line had refused to integrate with the underlying bone. As a result, feathers were falling out right and left. People who had undergone feather melds, often more than one, were willing to worry about appearance, but not molting.

She placed the open medogic on a nearby end table. "I think it can be fixed, Cara."

That brought the girl's face and attention back around. Her attitude underwent an immediate shift. "Really? You're not just scraping me? Joelle Richards said that once the quills start to come out you have to delete the whole meld and then there's internal bone scarring that has to be smoothed out and . . ."

Reaching over, Ingrid gave the girl a reassuring pat on her upper arm. "Depends on the severity of the breakdown. I'm pretty sure yours is salvageable." She glanced at the mother standing nearby. "First we need to treat the infection. I know it looks bad, but it's not ampstaph or anything like that. A shot of polyotic should clear it right up." She turned her attention back to the now alert teen. "I'll give you a couple of names and addresses. I'm not in a building that specializes in these kinds of melds, and you definitely want a specialist to perform the repairs, but the references I'm going to leave with your mom are for melders I know personally. Either of them should be able to restore your crest." She spared a second glance for the obviously relieved parent.

"It won't be cheap, but this time it will be done right, and the work will be guaranteed."

The grateful mother lurched forward. "Thank you, Dr. Seastrom, thank you! Cara . . ."

Mother and daughter embraced. Both were crying. Gathering up the medogic, Ingrid folded it carefully and let herself out into the hallway. To her ongoing dismay, dealing with botched melds constituted a fair share of her work. It was an unending source of amazement to her that despite the almost daily reports of deaths and disfigurements caused by unlicensed practitioners, people continued to seek out and make use of backstreet melders. Such decisions all boiled down to money, though she could not for the life of her imagine that any such savings were worth the potential risks.

Take Cara Gibson, for example. Probably engaged someone to do the feather work who had been "recommended" by a friend. A cheap unauthorized melder operating out of the back of a truck. The loss of feathers was nothing. Far more significant was the infection that had resulted from the incompetent work. Left untreated, it could have developed into something far more serious. One touch of ampstaph in the girl's upper spine could have left her paralyzed for life. Or at the very least in need of an emergency extensive back meld.

Not wishing to interrupt the emotional mother-daughter bonding, she occupied herself reviewing the medogic's readings. Infection type and rate there, recommended polyotic dosage so-and-so, muscular trauma rating, neural welds so many, growth points so many . . .

How now—what was that?

She scrolled back and enlarged one portion of the readout. There were forty-six points of quillgrow attachment along the girl's skull, neck, and spine. Forty-five of them were fashioned from the expected patented custom blend of gengineered carbon and melded proteins. The forty-sixth . . .

Most obviously, it had been installed deeper in the back of Cara Gibson's skull than was necessary. Not dangerously so, but just enough for the abnormality to register on Ingrid's sensitive medogic. The insert did not call attention to itself and could easily be overlooked. In fact, had Ingrid not been wiling away the time in the hall the information would have been automatically compressed, filed, and forgotten the instant she shut down the device. She had caught the anomaly only thanks to boredom.

Like the other attachment points it was composed of familiar organic staples, none of them expensive. That, and something else. There was an—impurity. This in itself was not what drew Ingrid's attention. It was the nature of the adulteration. In her experience, impurities tended to be irregular in form and composition. This one was anything but.

For one thing, it glistened.

After checking the readout for a third time to ensure that the anomaly was real and not a program aberration, she reentered the room. Sitting at the foot of the bed, the mother looked up in surprise. "Dr. Seastrom: I thought you'd let yourself out."

Ingrid smiled. "I have to give you those referral names and addresses, remember? And as long as I'm still here, I'd like to draw a protein sample. For future reference and for record-keeping purposes."

Mother looked down at daughter. The girl responded with a wan smile.

"Okay—I guess." Having come to trust her visitor implicitly, Cara turned over onto her stomach.

Thinner than a human hair and programmed by Seastrom via the medogic, the intelligent probe snaked its way painlessly into the back of the girl's head. Finding what it sought, it excised the abnormality that had intrigued the doctor and retracted without damaging any of the surrounding tissue. The periosteum through which the anomaly had been removed would continue to hold its feather.

Ingrid did not bother to examine the extraction and packed it away. While she could have executed an assessment on the spot she did not want to do anything that might upset the reunited and relieved mother and daughter. First she needed to satisfy her patient. Satisfaction of her own curiosity could wait until she was back in her building. Tomorrow was Saturday. Her office would be closed, and she could slip down from her codo at her leisure to scrutinize the curious finding in depth. She gave a mental shrug. Odd as its composition appeared to be on the medogic readout, the identity of the anomaly would probably yield to a simple, straightforward analysis. Most likely she was obsessing over nothing.

As she escorted the doctor out of the house, the comforted mother wanted to add a bonus to Ingrid's fee. The doctor would not hear of it.

"The look of relief on Cara's face was more than enough for me."

At the mother's insistence, however, Ingrid did depart with something called "homemade" bread. To the dubious Seastrom it *looked* as edible as the vacuum-sealed, slickly packaged product one ordered through the usual grocery channels, but confirmation would have to await tasting.

Friday night was for relaxation. She and Rajeev went to a neighborhood wordwar competition and managed to finish third in Couples while suffering only minor (and speedily repaired) emotional wounding. The exhilarating and mentally energizing bout was followed by dinner at a restaurant specializing in Titanian cuisine (methane overtones thankfully excised) and then sex, which was even more rewarding than wordwar and considerably easier on their respective cognitive faculties.

She felt exceptionally fine sleeping in the following morning. Sated as she was by the indulgences of the previous night, even the anomalous fragment she had recovered from the head of Cara Gibson did not intrude on her rest. She was so relaxed that she almost decided that analyzing it would be a waste of weekend time. More out of a need to check on several other things around the office than a desire to perform the assay, she finally got dressed and took the elevator down to her office level. It was late afternoon.

While the inlab ran penetration and accumulated stats, she busied herself with the few other minor items that required her attention. Sitting at her desk, she idly called for the lab results while gazing out the broad sweep of glass at the city beyond. As soon as the lab began to explicate results in its familiar dry voice, however, she stopped what she was doing and spun around in her seat.

The three-dimensional visual accompaniment to the formal declamation was even more off-putting than the words describing it. Gengineered carbon was present in the tiny insert, of course, and customized protein, of course, and—something else. Though it did not improve her perception, she instinctively found herself leaning toward the projection, as if the forward inclination of her body would somehow foment understanding.

According to the inlab analysis the insert contained more than the predictable carbon and proteins. Much more. Initially dismissive of what the assay might find, Ingrid now found herself staring intently. High magnification had yielded something entirely unexpected. Gengineered adhesives were present, yes. Combinant primate-avian DNA weaving, yes. Patented floridity, naturally. All anticipated, all predictable. Only one thing was present that was out of the ordinary.

The machine. It was beyond tiny, past minuscule. In structure and shape it was unlike anything Seastrom had ever seen. Under magnification it shone like the tiniest imaginable drop of molten silver. Functioning at the molecular level, its purpose was as enigmatic as its incredibly complex design. It should not have been there. It should not have been *anywhere*. And it had been removed from near the brain of Cara Jean Gibson, to all outward appearances a perfectly ordinary and classically self-conscious fifteen-year-old girl of modest circumstances and no known exceptional interests.

All of this registered on Dr. Ingrid Seastrom's mind almost simultaneously. Which turned out to be unexpectedly important, because as she was staring at it, the object vanished.

"Bring it back." She hardly recognized her voice as she verbalized the command. "The object just assayed. I want to see it again."

"The object does not exist," the no-nonsense synthesized male lab voice informed her.

Doubly bemused, she settled slowly back in her chair. "What do you mean, it does not exist? I just saw it."

The lab obediently restored the image, together with an explanation. "What you have been seeing all along and are looking at now is a replay of the primary assay. Only preliminary results are available, because the instant the object was subjected to focused analysis it vanished."

Ingrid strove to comprehend. "Real objects don't 'vanish.' It looked like it was made of some kind of alloy. Are you saying that when subjected to study it self-destructed?"

"No. It vanished."

"Explain yourself," she snapped.

"I cannot. I can only offer hypotheses. From the reaction of the object to initial probing, I believe it represents an example of delayed quantum entanglement."

"I understand the last part," she responded. "You're suggesting that the object itself was a perfect duplicate of an original located somewhere else, and that the act of viewing it in itself caused this one to disappear in favor of the other. But if that thesis is valid, then it should have vanished when I removed it from the skull of the girl where it was located. What I did with my medogic similarly constitutes probing and observation."

"I said that it was 'delayed,'" the lab replied without rancor.

"There is no such thing as '*delayed* quantum entanglement.' If the act of being viewed causes one copy or the other to cease to exist, then the nano-level device you just showed me should have ceased existing long ago."

"I agree. I told you I could not explain it. I can only report what was observed."

Seastrom sat quietly for a long moment; contemplating, digesting, trying to make sense of what the lab's AI was telling her. As much as the physical contradictions she was mystified as to what such a finely crafted impossibility was doing in the head of an ordinary teenager. An impossibility that had, to all outward appearances, done the girl no harm. And if someone wanted such a device implanted in fifteen-year-old Cara Gibson, why had they chosen to have the work done by an apparently incompetent backstreet technician specializing in cheap cosmetic melds? None of it made any sense. Of course, if she had some idea of what the incredibly sophisticated nanoscale device was designed to *do* . . .

As if that wasn't sufficient rational overload, the lab had one more for her.

"Subsequent investigation suggests that at least part of the device was composed of metastable metallic hydrogen."

Ingrid nodded slowly to herself. "Sure it was. And the pressure required to maintain it in that state was the nominal several million atmospheres that happen to exist at the center of the Earth—something not generally found within the cerebral epidermis of a fifteen-year-old girl."

The inlab did not react to sarcasm. "Atomic-level analysis revealed a crystalline lattice composed solely of protons exhibiting spacing less than a Bohr radius. This is consistent with the detection and presence of MSMH. A quantum state existing within a quantum entanglement. Observation of concurrent superconductivity also suggests that . . ."

"All right, all right—enough." What the lab was elucidating was more than mildly insane. Though well grounded in modern science, Ingrid was a physician, not a physicist, and the lab's explanation was rapidly extending into realms well beyond her level of comprehension. While she was unsure of what she was being told, she *was* sure of something less arcane but equally confounding.

An incredibly advanced nanoscale biomechanical device at least partially fashioned of a material that ought not to exist at normal temperature and pressure had been found where it ought not to have existed. Now it wasn't there anymore, which precluded further evaluation of it. If she wished to pursue the matter any further it appeared that she could rely only on the inlab's hastily made recordings of the no-longer extant anomaly. That would make it rather difficult to secure confirmation. Of anything.

She had a lot to do next week. She had patients. She had a life. Did she really want to get further involved with something that defied rational explanation?

Of course she did, she told herself. She was a doctor, all doctors are scientists, and what all scientists want to know more than anything else is what they don't know.

But how to find out?

If not overtly illegal, the presence of the device in Cara Gibson's head suggested something problematic. The fact that it had apparently caused the girl no harm was not reason enough to ignore its existence — especially given the lab's compositional breakdown. As a doctor, Ingrid was as interested in the *why* of it as the *how*. If nothing else, an interesting paper might be derived from further research into the abnormality. Whether anyone would believe certain conclusions enough to authorize publication in a respected scientific journal was another matter entirely.

From a scientific standpoint, expounding upon what she had just seen and heard from the inlab was tantamount to a commercial pilot describing a recent encounter with a flying saucer. As to the actual lab recording, lab recordings could be falsified. A report as elaborate and detailed as this one hardly seemed worth the effort to fake, but if she went public with it that would not prevent detractors from claiming it as the source of not one but several preposterous claims.

She wondered if she should share it with Rajeev, or perhaps with other professional but less intimate associates. She could imagine the reaction.

"Hi Steve, hi LeAndra. I recently removed this delayed quantum entangled piece of nanomachinery partly built out of metastable metallic hydrogen from the skull of a local fifteen-year-old girl, and I'd like to know what you think of it. Except since it was quantum entangled it doesn't exist here anymore, though it did when I first studied it. But don't let that stop you."

Oh sure.

It was plain that before she told anyone else about it she was going to have to further research the discovery (or the hallucination) quietly, by herself. Only when she was absolutely certain of the findings and had something more concrete to back them up would she risk sharing them with others. Only when she was certain, for example, that she was not being made the subject of some elaborate, albeit scientifically impressive, practical joke on the part of unknown colleagues.

Finding herself operating in the kingdom of the incongruous, she would begin with the obvious—by inquiring of her ostensibly unaware patient as to the name, nature, and whereabouts of whoever had performed on her the deceptively straightforward cosmetic feather meld. What that might lead to she had no idea.

Possibly even to a manufacturer of infinitesimally small machines that had no rational basis in known physical reality.

4

"Hey, old man!"

Turning slowly as he leaned on his cane, Napun Molé squinted in the direction of the challenging voice. He was short, his white hair fraying and thinning, a squat little fireplug of a mestizo in his late fifties who looked much older.

"Sorry—what?" Raising the hand that was not gripping the head of the cane, he pointed to the right side of his head. "My ears . . ."

Rolling his eyes, the security guard came closer. "I started to say that this is a restricted area, old man." He indicated the medium-size cargo ship, its sails autofurled, that lay alongside the dark dock. "What are you doing out here anyway, in the middle of the night?"

"Middle of the night?" Lapsing into introspection, Molé put shaky fingers to his lips. "Is it that late? I thought—I thought . . ." He looked around and blinked. "I must have wandered away from the group. We came down the funicular and . . ."

"You *are* lost, old man." The oft-restored nineteenth-century funicular that still conveyed tourists and citizens alike from the top of Valparaiso's cliffs down to the harbor lay several kilometers to the south. The guard's tone softened. "I bet your guide or tour attendants are going loco looking for you. Do you have any identification? An emergency number I could call so someone can come and pick you up?"

"An emergency—yes, yes." Reaching into a pocket, Molé brought out a cheap, battered wallet, started to fumble at the contents with uncertain fingers, and dropped it. Sighing, the guard shook his head.

"I'll get it." Muttering under his breath, he reached down to pick it up. He therefore did not notice when the hinged tip of the old man's left index finger flipped open. The programmed-protein spidersilk-derived aramid fiber that shot out automatically looped itself around the guard's neck and tightened convulsively. Eyes bugged wide, the startled guard tried to shout, but the swiftly contracting strand had already interdicted the air supply to his lungs. Reaching up with both hands, he tried to grasp the tightening filament, but it was too thin and too deeply embedded in the flesh of his throat for him to slip thick fingers between strand and skin. Blood began to trickle, then to spurt from beneath the thread, which by now had buried itself invisibly deep into his neck.

Molé watched the guard's demise evolve, until within minutes the man lay dead on the dock. His head had been half severed from his neck. A quick flick of the old man's left hand halted the ongoing contraction and rewound the lethal loop. The strand's gengineered hydrophobic properties kept the dead guard's blood from adhering to it as it was reeled back into the hollow finger.

A rapid survey showed that the killing had not been observed. Reaching down, Molé picked up his wallet. Using both hands he dragged the body of the guard to the edge of the dock and eased it over the side. Landing between the hull of the freighter and the dock's polycrete pillars, it made only the slightest of splashes.

From another, deeper pocket Molé extracted the folded dispersion suit and slipped effortlessly into the one-piece garment. Racing up the now un-guarded rampway, he found himself on the open deck of the cargo craft. Many stories overhead a few lights shone from within the bridge. If some-one was standing nightwatch they were not visible. Finding a gangway that led inward Molé hurriedly made his way deeper and deeper into the bow-els of the ship. Except for the minimum personnel necessary to sustain a watch, most of the crew would be asleep, relaxing in their cabins, or most likely sampling the delights of downtown. While some of the old city and particularly the commercial port area had been lost to rising sea levels, Valparaiso had been luckier than most since a good portion of the modern urban area was situated on the steep cliffs that bordered the harbor.

In the course of his fleet descent he passed several security cameras. By bending light around him the dispersion suit rendered him invisible to ordinary video pickups. It did not, however, prevent a wandering crewmember from nearly running into him. Despite the enhanced hearing afforded by his melded right ear, in the enclosed corridor Molé had not heard the man coming.

"Hey, what . . . ?"

Not exactly memorable last words. Molé brought the blade of supersharp extensible bone that now extended from the edge of his left hand around in a sharp arc to cut the man's throat. As the stunned crewmember staggered backward, clutching at himself with both hands in a futile attempt to stem the fountain of blood that was gushing from his neck, the relentless Molé followed up the initial incapacitating strike with a wholly traditional unmelded blow from his cane. Gagging and choking, the man went down in a heap. Unlike the security guard, Molé did not bother to try to hide the crewman. If the body was discovered before he finished his job here, it would mean that he was working too slowly.

When he was certain he was well below the waterline he selected a gently curving inner segment of hull and aimed the cane. Flipping back the rounded head revealed a dense tangle of controls. These he proceeded to adjust carefully. Sending a steady stream of liquid explosive spewing from the tip of the cane he used the solution to apply a large glistening oval to the seamless material of the inner hull. The last of it he employed to write his name in the center of the oval.

Becoming time-sensitive on contact with the air, the various chemical components of the sticky and highly volatile substance would reach critical blend in a short time. Even if it was discovered and recognized there was nothing that could be done to prevent the final denouement. Firmly adhering to the carbon-fiber hull it could not be removed, pulled apart, or scraped off. In order to accomplish that, a special neutralizing agent was required which the crew of the cargo vessel was unlikely to count among its customary stores.

He encountered no one in the course of his speedy departure. Back on the dock he slipped out of the dispersion suit, crumpled it, touched an embedded switch, and dropped it in the water. In three minutes it would have completely disintegrated and begun to disperse through the harbor. He was halfway to the lights of downtown when the pedestrians among whom he was now walking looked up and back in astonishment as a small portion of the great port was infused by a sudden burst of light as bright as the sun. Seconds later everyone's ears were assailed by the deep rolling rumble of a violent explosion.

Napun Molé did not think of himself as a commercial assassin or an industrial saboteur. He was only a simple tutor delivering education to those badly in need of it. While the ship was doubtless insured, the fiscally substantial portion of its cargo that was illegitimate was not. The owners of the vessel who had refused to pay a long-standing debt to Molé's current employers had just received an expensive lesson. If they were half smart it should not have to be repeated.

With the exception of the occasional (and always disappointed) streetwalker, neither Natural nor Meld paid the least attention to the old man with the cane as he made his way deeper into the heart of Valparaiso's nautical entertainment district. Interlocked young lovers out for the night looked only into each other's eyes. Visiting couples from Santiago strolled quietly between show venues and restaurants. Tourists in pairs and in organized groups marveled at old buildings that had been preserved, raised, and moved to higher, safely dry locations. Rapa Nuians holding dual Sudamerican and Commonwealth of Oceania citizenship eagerly scrutinized the contents of souvenir shops.

"Evening, senior señor." It was impossible to tell from looking at her whether the young woman was a natural blonde or not. Certainly the golden mane that extended from her head all the way down her spine and ended in a half-meter-long tufted tail was pure meld. Snorting enticingly through her maniped, widened nostrils she let out a little whinny. "Interested in a little horseplay?"

Looking down he saw that what at first could have been taken for four-inch black heels were in fact feet that had been maniped. In addition to hair and nostrils, she had undergone a full foot meld that had eliminated human heels and toes in favor of highly polished hooves. A small diamond flashed in the depths of the left one.

"Not my cup of tea," he replied in a polite quaver.

As he tried to go around her she stepped in front of him, blocking his path. Her practiced smile continued to invite. "It's been my experience that even old men are all equestrians at heart—when they are presented with the right mount."

The casually inadvertent "old man" designation did not trouble Molé. His actual age had never been a source of embarrassment to him. Quite the contrary. He took it as a point of pride that someone in his profession had survived for so long. Still, he was averse to the insistent invitation.

"I don't have the kind of meld that might make for a memorable evening for you, girl."

She laughed horsely. "You've got it backward, old man. It's *my* job to make *your* evening memorable."

"Then I suppose I can only accede to your persistence." He extended an arm. She immediately wrapped hers around the proffered limb.

"A gentleman, too." She squeezed his arm gently and her eyes widened in surprise. "Oh my—you're in a lot better shape than you look! I promise you a night you won't forget, senior. Or if times are difficult, an hour."

"I will do my best to reciprocate." She did not notice that the old man quaver in his voice had disappeared.

By the following morning she had, too.

The call that reached Napun Molé a month later differed from many similar calls that had preceded it only in detail. It found him lying on a water-whisking lounge on the beach at Pimento, in northern Peru. Speaking aloud the acceptance code string that activated the receiver-pickup resting in his right ear he answered the secure circuit greeting while alternating his gaze between the wealthy swimsuited women up from Lima and the fishermen demonstrating the use of their traditional reed boats. Most fishermen now were Melds, having had their bodies maniped to feature everything from gills to gengineered swim bladders.

No one paid any attention to one old man among many as Molé sat up on the lounge and swung his feet over the side. Nor did they remark on his incongruously youthful body, not realizing that the muscles it featured were wholly natural and the consequence of a lifetime of consistent serious exercise instead of a quick meld. The unusually thick soles of the feet he idly dug into the sand beneath the lounge were not manips to support creaking bones but cushions that allowed him to walk and run in near silence.

The voice on the other end of the call was atypically stressed. An

important person had met an untimely demise and the usual suspects ex-
onerated. On his person this individual had been transporting something
of immense importance. If it was not recovered certain people including
the speaker were likely to suffer. If it was to fall into the wrong hands—the
worldwide media, for example—the consequences could prove calami-
tous to the interested parties. Prattling on, the caller used the word apocalyptic. In a lifetime of practicing his vocation Molé had encountered many
synonyms for deep concern, but until now apocalyptic had not been
among them.

Despite knowing Molé as well as it was possible for someone to know
him (which was to say not very well at all) and being fully aware of his reputation, the caller still felt compelled to ask certain questions. Molé was
not offended. The more significant the job, the more that was at stake, and
the more money that was on offer, the more queries a prospective employer was entitled to ask. He replied patiently and without rancor to every
one, accepting each condition one at a time and indicating his full understanding of every relevant detail.

In response to one of the questions, as he was already mentally readying himself to start making the necessary preparations, he had to admit
that, no, he had never been to the central far east coast of Namerica.

WHISPR SPENT THE FOLLOWING DAY hiding in the center
of a dense grove of ceibu trees. There was a time not long ago when such
growths could not be found north of Central America, but with warming
temperatures and rising sea levels they, like so many other plant and animal species, had eagerly migrated northward. Once he thought he heard
the voices of visitors to the nature preserve, but he knew he could have
been mistaken. As tired and hungry as he was it was entirely possible he
had imagined the presence of other people. In any case, he never saw
them.

It was not yet quite dark again when he felt safe in leaving the temporary refuge, but he was anxious to be on the move. The sooner he was out
of the surrounding slough and swamp preserves the sooner he would be
back in the developed, civilized surrounds of the city where he could get
something to eat and find out what had happened to that bastard Jiminy.
Peering cautiously out from among the trees and undergrowth he could
see no sign of police or mobile scanners. All would be well if he could

continue to evade their notice until he could make his way back to town. A quick manip, just enough to fool the omnipresent pickups emplaced on numerous corners and shops, and he would be free to walk the streets again. The manip was vital. Once your features appeared in the continental Wanted database they were immediately accessible to every cop from Moose Jaw to Managua.

But the database could be fooled. In a time when anyone could opt for a complete and even radical body meld, a simple facial could be performed in thousands of qwiclinics, or even one of the hundreds of mobile surges that plied every continent's byways, highways, and flyways.

He was about to step out into the shallows when he heard the growl.

In early times the only dangerous large animals one had to keep an eye out for on the southeast coast of the old U.S. of A. was the occasional alligator and poisonous snake. Migrating north along with hundreds of other alien plants and animals were far more venomous New World serpents like the fer-de-lance and bushmaster, big crocodilians like the caiman and the Orinoco, dendrobates poison arrow frogs (kids were especially—and sometimes fatally—attracted to their bright, clownish colors) and a posse of exotic felines: ocelot, jacarundi, margay, and most conspicuously the one an unknowing Whispr had just roused from its morning meal.

As he stood frozen in place and staring he was able to view at close range the jaws and teeth that gave the jaguar the most powerful bite in proportion to its body size of any of the big cats. As hefty as an African lioness at a hundred and fifty kilos, the mature male lay alongside its recent kill panting like a steam engine. Stocky and incredibly powerful, the cat had dragged the young bull from the farm or feedlot where it had been slain to this island of rainforest in the midst of the coastal preserve. Though it was quite capable of utilizing the throat-bite and suffocation killing technique of its cousins the lions and tigers, unique among them the jaguar preferred to bite down into the skull directly between the ears, piercing the brain of its prey and terminating it more quickly.

As he slowly backed out of the last of the tall trees and toward the water, a wide-eyed Whispr knew that the big predator would scarcely have to exert itself to perform a similar operation on him. Maybe it would ignore him, he thought fearfully. After all, it had a whole young steer to consume.

The piercing yellow eyes never left his as it growled a second time and started to get up.

Whispr couldn't help himself. He was no action hero and this was no vid documentary. Screaming, he turned and threw himself into the shallows, flailing at the water as he tried to get away, managing in a single moment to do three absolutely wrong things simultaneously. He screamed louder when he felt a sharp, searing pain tear across his upper back. Eyes bulging, he looked in terror over his left shoulder only to find himself almost eye to eye with the big cat. But for the water that surrounded him, he would have fainted. Instead he did something entirely predictable and entirely involuntary. His bowels let loose and he soiled himself. Taken aback by the spasmodic intestinal eruption, the jaguar backed off.

Continuing to swim and kick at the muddy bottom, Whispr forced himself forward into the dense, high reeds. Behind him the predator hesitated as it tracked his panicky flight. Then it turned and splashed lazily back to the island. Whispr knew that ultimately it was not his discomfiting bodily reaction that had saved his life but the fact that the massive feline had decided the pitiful, thrashing human was no threat to an already slaughtered steak dinner.

In place of the anticipated lethal bite to the skull, Whispr had suffered only an annoyed swipe across his upper back. In the absence of a mirror he could not tell the extent of the damage. The flexibility afforded by his slender frame did allow him, however, to reach all the way around back and feel the area. The contact pained him and his fingers came away bloody— but not too bloody. Trying his best to ignore the burning he alternately stumbled and swam northwestward. The sensation was akin to someone taking a sheaf of new nine-kilo bond and dragging the edges across his deltoids: a hundred paper cuts all concentrated in the same place. He was hurting, but he would not die.

Not from the single glancing paw swipe, but just possibly from hunger. He struggled onward. Many decades of federal protection resulting in the restoration of filtering reed beds, mangroves, and sawgrass had rendered the waters of the reserve in which he found himself at least nominally fit to drink, but he was still growing weaker by the hour. It had been too long since he had last had anything to eat and his slenderized melded frame contained no reserves of fat. He needed food.

About right, he mused. He had eluded the police, avoided the dangers of the swamp, and escaped death by jaguar only to look forward to perishing for lack of access to something as banal as a vending machine.

It was midafternoon and crushingly humid when he stumbled into the isolated fishing outpost.

Dirty white, mussel-encrusted pylons supporting multiple nets speckled with electronic ministunners identified the dwelling as the home of a fisherman. Though licenses to work the broad stretches of the coastal preserves were heavily regulated, individuals or families lucky enough to have obtained one could make a good living fishing within their designated boundaries since large commercial operations were banned inshore. The majority of catches ended up in the restaurants and markets of Greater Savannah. Any excess was vacuumed up by the insatiable market of the Atlanta Conurbation.

Utilizing whatever posts, pilings, trees, and brush presented itself, a cautious Whispr slowly worked his way closer to the buildings. The cuts on his upper back throbbed. He could only hope some of the more exotic parasites to be found in the preserve had not already wormed their insidious way into the open wounds.

Outward appearances suggested that the unpretentious venture was doing well, though not making its owner rich. Fronting the water behind the wall of drying nets was a boathouse fashioned of premolded permeable foam sections painted green and brown to blend in with the preserve surroundings. A lack of sharp corners combined with deep-earth anchors kept it from being blown into the next state by the repetitious hurricanes that now afflicted this part of the Atlantic coast. The boathouse was connected by raised catwalks to a processing shed and, farther on, to a residence. Sprawling over several uplifted platforms the house looked as if rooms had been added on one at a time, one year at a time. More profits, more rooms, Whispr knew.

A pair of electric jetboats were visible bobbing inside the boathouse. Two adjacent slips were empty, suggesting that the owner/operators might be, unsurprisingly, out fishing. Whispr licked his lips. If he could get one of the idle craft started it would save him days of stumbling through the remainder of the preserve. It would also allow him to avoid the risk of trying to hitch a ride into town. Once your image was out and about, hitching became a risky proposition. Prior to picking up someone standing on the side of the road with their thumb out, a driver could run a hitchhiker's image through his car or scoot's information system as easily and efficiently as any police vehicle. "Borrowing" a private watercraft would be much safer.

Carefully working his way through the water with only his head above the surface he edged closer and closer to the boathouse. Once he thought he might have heard voices coming from the vicinity of the residence and he hurriedly ducked down behind a clump of enormous *Victoria regina* water lilies. No one appeared, however, and after a couple of minutes with only his eyes and top of his head visible he resumed his stealthy approach.

As he had surmised from his first glimpse the boathouse was deserted. Here in the middle of the nature reserve tidal current was almost imperceptible. The two docked craft sat almost motionless in the water. Trying to make as little noise as possible he used one of the dangling fishing nets to pull himself out of the water. Though it weighed next to nothing, even a melded strong man could not have torn the nephilia net. It held Whispr's weight easily.

It felt good to be out of the water. Both of the jetboats should have standard ignitions. Out here in the middle of the reserve he doubted, he hoped, that there would be any reason to secure them with a code or password. With luck they would be fully charged and ready to go out fishing on short notice—or deliver him to dockside Savannah. Seeing nothing to differentiate between the two craft he stepped gingerly down into the nearest. While scrutinizing the embedded instrument panel his tired eyes happened to fall on a choice slice of Heaven.

An integral part of the hull's shot-molded foam interior, the food compartment contained a couple of apples, several nutrition bars, tropical chocolate, and bottles of water and fruit drink. Since the compartment's heat/cool circuit was off the latter were not chilled. A famished Whispr would not have cared had they been visibly polluted. Ripping off seals he drained first one fruit drink and then another. A bar of chocolate was followed at a more leisurely rate of consumption by a mixed berry nutrition bar. Moistening on contact with air, it was the equal of the finest meal Whispr had ever enjoyed.

"You! Whatch'u think you doin' there?"

Crumbs of bar fell from his fingers as Whispr stumbled forward and jabbed frantically at the ignition switch. It buzzed once and the water behind the boat frothed as the noise of the engine rose to a soft hum. As he grabbed the wheel he looked back to see a middle-aged woman with three breasts and double-length melded fingers rushing toward him. She might have had the additional gland added for cosmetic purposes, or perhaps to help raise a brood, since she was being accompanied by a quartet of youngsters who ranged in age from ten into their teens.

"Git out of that boat!" As she gave vent to her outrage one of the older teens raised a tubular device and pointed it in Whispr's direction. At the same moment, he gunned the engine.

Snapping free of the several catches that had kept it attached to the enclosed dock the compact, wide-beamed craft shot out of the boathouse just as the teenage girl let fire with the instrument she had been aiming. Ejected under high pressure, droplets of liquid fish stunner covered him, the boat, and the surrounding slough. Fortunately he only received a diluted dose. Had he taken the full brunt of the discharge it would have short-circuited every nerve in his body. As it was the charged fluid caused him to slump over the wheel. Calibrated primarily for bass and perch, the stunner that missed him and landed in the water immediately brought a hundred or so paralyzed fish floating to the surface. Had the goo penetrated any of the boat's instrumentation it might have temporarily shorted it out as well. Fortunately the most sensitive electronics were either inherently waterproof or appropriately sealed.

Adulterated as it was, the electric liquid left him barely able to function. In Whispr's case, barely was good enough. All he had to do was keep the boat on course until the incapacitating tingling left his body. It felt as if every extremity from his toes to his hair had "gone to sleep." He fought hard against the lingering effects because he fully expected the angry fisherwoman and her litter to come after their stolen craft. As soon as sufficient feeling returned to his arms and hands he found some tools and took a moment to smash the boat's automated emergency locator beacon.

For once, however, he had caught a break. No chase materialized. Perhaps the family was unsure about the nature and capabilities of their boat thief. Maybe they believed that as a thief brazen enough to work in broad daylight he was armed. Or maybe their other craft was unseaworthy, or its power pack was discharged. Whatever the reason, by the time he found himself in the city's outer, stilt-mounted suburbs, there was still no sign of pursuit. He did not heave a sigh of relief—it would have flexed the aching skin on his ragged back—but he was considerably eased in mind.

The sooner he could ditch the craft the better. Surely by now the family would have provided the police with a description of the thief and the stolen boat. Would it be accurate enough to allow the authorities to match the description with the images taken by Swallower's security apparatus or any personal details Jiminy might give them?

He had no way of knowing that while the gentle ministrations of the Savannah police might indeed inspire Swallower to heights of ready compliance, his erstwhile partner and companion Cricket had long since passed beyond the conversational plane.

In olden times a thief might have waited until nightfall to abandon stolen transport. With the installation of automated metropolitan security monitors that could see as well in the dark as during the day, nighttime had ceased to be as much of a criminal's friend. Whispr knew he would have a better chance of avoiding attention by losing himself among a typical workday crowd full of Naturals and other Melds than if he waited until after sunset when considerably fewer people were on the streets. He was not concerned about being singled out because of his particular meld. He was far from being the only representative of the artificially slenderized walking the streets of Greater Savannah.

After cleaning himself up as best he could with the gear that was available on the boat he pulled into one of numerous public riverfront piers and docked in a public parking slip. He took care to make it look as if the boat was properly clamped in place. Then he set the timer so that the catches on the hull would disengage in twenty minutes. If his good fortune held, the boat would slip free to drift downriver with the slight current, hopefully to be run over by a big cargo vessel or float out to sea. He could not chance just pushing it away from the dock because some good Samaritan might see it drift clear and intervene to alert its oblivious "owner."

No one followed him from the pier and it was only a block to the nearest of the city's silent, automated public transport lines. As he stepped on board, one or two fellow passengers glanced briefly in his direction, then looked away. While far from being coiffed and attired to shoot a cover spread for a fashion zine, he was less grubby than any number of the hundreds of bumelds who haunted every large conurbation. Without drawing attention to himself he did his best to hide his face as well as his body from the transport's internal security pickups.

As protective measures both he and Jiminy had always utilized false addresses on all their official (and unofficial) idents. Aware of the delinquent nature of the individual they were looking for, the police would know or suspect as much. But it should still take them some time to locate his actual residence. Just to make sure and to exercise commonsense precaution, Whispr spent half the night working his way closer to his apartment. At no time did he encounter any evidence of either straightforward or surreptitious police presence in his neighborhood.

After confirming his ident the automated concierge let him in. The entrance to his apartment was nearly as constricted as the hallway. The four rooms he called home, however, were surprisingly large. More than adequate, actually. Their spaciousness reflected the success of his and Jiminy's diversely disreputable nocturnal excursions. The apartment was well furnished, familiar, and comfortable. He was going to miss it.

He could not stay, of course. The police could arrive at any moment. Nonetheless, having gambled on their sluggishness this long he decided he could wait until morning to abandon his residence. After hours and hours of slogging his way through the wildlife preserves south of the city he desperately needed some cooked food and sound sleep. He would, he could, leave tomorrow.

As was typical among those who shared his vocation there was virtually nothing in the restful apartment complex that was not rented or purchased secondhand. Nothing, in other words, that he could not leave behind without a second thought. Setting the stove to cook as much food as it would hold, he settled down to wait the ten minutes until dinner would be ready. For the next couple of months he would live on the streets with occasional forays to safe, cheap apartments. As soon as the ruckus surrounding the tourist they had killed calmed down he would begin to look for another semipermanent place to live.

But as he found out the following day, as far as his immediate future was concerned, things were anything but calming down.

5

When he left the apartment for good the following morning, the backpack he was wearing was wider than he was. Autostabilization kept the spine spanner from flopping loosely against his back. Before bidding the apartment a last reluctant farewell he had taken care to eat a full meal and to shower and depilate thoroughly. The excessive attention to personal hygiene carried practical as well as aesthetic implications. With the police looking for him the last thing he needed was to attract the attention of his fellow city-dwellers through unusual body odor or distasteful appearance.

A glance skyward hinted that it might not rain at all today, though given what had happened to the climate over the past couple of hundred years any weather prediction made more than twenty-four hours in advance had to be taken with a grain of salt water.

The kind of qwikmeld he needed could be had at any of several dozen facilities scattered throughout the urban area. Clean, efficient, and reasonably priced by dint of intense competition, any one of them would be glad to fulfill his humble requests. Unfortunately they would also as a matter of course and due to legal requirements note his presence and the procedures performed. They would also record a potentially incriminating dollop of additional information, none of which he had either the desire or intention to release. Forced to opt between cleanliness, efficiency, and fair pricing on the one hand or maintaining his anonymity on the other, he needed barely a minute to make his choice.

He went to see Barracuda.

Though burdened with an unfortunate name for a melder, Barracuda Chaukutri had not let his moniker stand in the way of devoting himself to the motto by which he ran his business, which was "Any Meld, Anytime, Anywhere." He was operating out of his third mobile surgery, the previous two having been separately confiscated by the authorities following incidents in which his semilegal melds had turned out less copacetic than some of their recipients had intended. This was most especially true of one who under Chaukutri's fuddled ministrations had expired messily and somewhat noisily. Having somehow escaped sanction, much less incarceration, for that bungled bit of organ collapse, 'Cuda Chaukutri was for the third time once again back in business.

Suitably subtle inquiries led Whispr to a bus-size mobile food operation that was currently parked to the south of a major construction project. One of several mobile kitchens that slaved to sate the appetites of the site's workers, it specialized in Indian-American food. It also provided excellent cover for Chaukutri's true vocation. The small kitchen took up far less of the vehicle's interior than appearances suggested. In addition to performing surreptitious melds Chaukutri also served up some mean pakoras. While his wife made naan up front her husband remade people in back.

The melder's reaction upon greeting his sinuous visitor was less than what Whispr had hoped.

"You—go, go on, get away!" Peering nervously out the rear service door of the industrial vehicle, the jumpy Chaukutri looked in all directions.

Whispr slipped forward past the shorter man. "Look, 'Cuda, I know I'm a little hot right now but . . ."

"Hot? *Hot!*" The outer door hummed as it slammed shut behind the skinny visitor. It was reinforced and armored against forcible intrusion. Not the sort of vehicular entryway one would expect to find in a mobile kitchen. "You are not hot, my friend. You are incendiary! You are combustible!" He grabbed Whispr by one arm. "Get out of my place before proximity to you burns up all of us!"

Whispr looked down at the excitable little man. As a marginally competent if unlicensed melder Chaukutri could have had himself melded to stand taller. He did not do so because in a surgeon slightness of stature, especially in the hands and fingers, was a positive benefit. That did not mean he had shunned productive manip entirely. Greatly enhancing the melder's already exceptional natural dexterity, each of his fingers possessed an extra pair of joints as well as terminating in a specialized and artfully concealed surgical tool.

As a comparatively unremarkable bit of melding they did not even draw Whispr's attention. The fact that Chaukutri had fourteen fingers instead of sixteen, or eighteen, or twenty slimmer, smaller digits spoke to a desire not to stray unnecessarily far from the natural. Those who did notice the enhancements and commented on them were told that the extra equipment was intended to assist their owner in his work as a chef. This was accepted because the instruments employed by a surgeon and a cook were not all that different.

Swinging his backpack around in front of him Whispr dug into its depths and fumbled with the contents. The card he flashed at his fretful host glistened as its unique, embedded, irreproducible identification matrix caught the vehicle's interior light.

As Whispr expected, Chaukutri's anxiety gave way to a rapidly escalating surge of greed. "That's a Hain Ltd. card. Stolen?"

"No." As always, Whispr's sarcasm was gently put. "I acquired it with my hedge fund profits. What do you care about—its load, or its origin?"

Reaching out, the melder took the card and examined it closely, turning it over and over between his fingers as he did so. "Can I—scan it?"

His visitor had to laugh. "If you don't, then you're not the 'Cuda Chaukutri I know. You're an imitation, and a bad one at that."

"Wait here."

Whispr watched as his reenergized host headed toward the front of the vehicle. He was uneasy letting Chaukutri and the card out of his sight, but the meld-maker had a reputation of sorts to maintain. He was an artist, not a thief.

On the other hand, it was evident from the semihysterical manner of his greeting that he knew his visitor was wanted seriously by the authorities and that there was probably a substantial reward attached to the slender fugitive.

Whispr tried not to let the extent of his relief show when a smiling

Chaukutri returned and handed the card back to his guest. "I suppose in the end money always triumphs caution."

"If it didn't," Whispr replied, "you wouldn't still be standing here and I wouldn't be talking to you. Both of us would be solid, upstanding citizens."

When the mutual laughter this image invoked finally subsided, the biosurge wiped at his eyes. "All right, all right. You know, my wife keeps saying we should forgo all this and move back to Nagpur."

"Why don't you?" Whispr's query was not in the least inhibited by the fact that he had no idea where Nagpur was.

"Because I'd have to live in Nagpur. With my wife." Chaukutri looked at his watch. "This is all very jolly, but my feeling is that we are both of us in a hurry. What is it you want done?"

"What are my options today?"

Chaukutri turned and beckoned. "Come. Let us go shopping."

The makeshift surgery's scanner took the measure of every part of Whispr's naked body inside as well as out. An analysis was performed. Options were put forward that took into account his height, weight, age, bone and muscle density, visual acuity, hearing, sexual competency, follicular health, status of vital organs, and everything else from a physiological standpoint that might in one way or another either permit or compromise any one of thousands of available melds. As the scanner generated a final tally, melder and customer passed the time discussing aesthetics.

"If you are trying to disguise yourself I suppose the first thing you want is to add some beef. Or perhaps chicken, or fish?"

Whispr shuddered as he relived his recent agonizing slog through the swampland south of the city. "No fish. I'm not particular about the protein base, so long as it's mammalian. I'll settle for something unobtrusive that doesn't smell. Even plain whey derivative."

Chaukutri nodded. He took no notes nor did he need to. Everything they were saying was being recorded.

His customer continued. "How about semi-orientalizing my eyes along with a color change? Thin out the hair and make it black instead of blond. Give the muscles a tune-up and while you're at it, add a couple of extra leg tendons." Having always been jealous of Jiminy's leaping ability, as long as he was going under the carver he might as well put a little extra spring in his step. Literally.

When they had concluded the discussion Chaukutri printed out a hard copy and studied the ramifications. "This is simple stuff, Whispr. Are you sure it is all that you need?"

His visitor nodded. "I want to look like myself, but just different enough to fool the monitors. More . . ."

". . . Natural?" the biosurge finished for him.

Whispr sighed. "Yes, I suppose so."

"It is your money." Chaukutri let out a short, contented laugh. "Well, actually I am quite certain it is somebody else's money, but that does not matter because soon it will be my money." Leaning forward, he winked. "For a small additional cost I can embed a special pheromone synth that will make you irresistible to the ladies. It comes with a verbal activation system so you only turn it on when you want to—you know. A reputable supplier offered me six of them a few months ago. Knowing a good thing when it is presented to me, I bought them all. And what do you know—I only have one left. It is a meld you cannot fail with."

"Thanks but no thanks." Whispr was firm. "Personally I think all that stuff is overrated. I don't want to draw attention to myself, 'Cuda—not for any reason and not in any way."

Spreading both hands wide the melder shrugged. "As you wish. I suppose therefore I cannot talk you into letting me make you better-looking either?"

Whispr had to grin. Ever since the advent of cheap melding anyone could look like anyone else. When a thousand men looked exactly like Admiral Nelson and a thousand women like Lady Hamilton such visages ceased to be distinctive. Not to mention the innumerable and fatal faux pas that occurred at social gatherings when two exact equals accidentally confronted one another. Far more intriguing to members of the opposite sex to flaunt an idiosyncratic rather than classic visage.

This development led to a burst of originality among facial sculptors. For a time it was not unusual to see everything from Frankenstein monsters to frogmen to sharp-tailed succubae wandering the streets of the world's more cosmopolitan capitals. It was yet another meld fad that soon faded as people quickly learned that paying for a Frankenstein or a succuba meld only gave one the appearance of such beings. As yet, no one had figured out how to meld personality.

There was nothing worse than paying for a meld that was at obvious odds with who one really was.

Someone wishing to avoid the attention of the authorities would opt to look as ordinary as possible. And all the melded-on muscle or body-integrated weaponry in the world was not sufficient to allow a criminal to break out of a modern meld-proofed prison. Years on the street had taught Whispr that the best option for avoiding incarceration was not to get caught.

Not only was Chaukutri good—he was fast.

Having been maniped before, Whispr required no instruction on how to prep. One advantage to his current meld was that his body could fit in nearly any size surgery. The bustling Chaukutri left his customer to get ready as he prepared himself to operate.

While a portion of the vehicle was given over to the preparation of Indian fast food, the bulk of the interior housed a completely portable melding theater. Disinfecting as well as illuminating, a pale lavender glow highlighted Whispr as he stripped to his skin. He had no compunction about leaving his clothes and backpack outside the sanitation tube. Chaukutri would be too busy to riffle through them. Even if he chose to do so he was unlikely to find the artfully concealed storage thread that was still the principal object of Whispr's curiosity. At present the thread's container lay concealed in a hidden pocket of his shoe. This was the safest place since the forthcoming meld might require him to purchase some new clothing. While the surgery healed, Chaukutri or his wife or a hired runner could fulfill that more mundane need. The additional forthcoming expense caused Whispr no distress.

An occasional need for a new wardrobe came with the job.

Nor did Chaukutri's unconcealed desire to get the work over and done with and get rid of him worry Whispr. After all, it wasn't as if the melder was actually going to touch him. Whispr knew there had been a time long ago when surgeons actually made *personal physical contact* with their patients. A time when incredibly delicate corporal manipulations, excisions, and embellishments had in fact been performed by shaky human fingers. The very thought of it made him shudder as he stepped into the cylinder. The transparent curved door slid tightly shut behind him.

Tilting back his head he allowed a thin tube to slide between his parted lips. It halted partway down his throat. A second tube entered his body via his anal canal and a third through his urethra. In each case there was no pain, no discomfort. Like the anticoagulant in a vampire bat's saliva, the intruding probes released salving emissions of their own. He felt soothed, not violated.

In less than five minutes his entire body had been properly sterilized, cleaned, and prepared, without harm to any of the useful bacteria in his gut. Responding to a musical tone that rose above the sanitizing tube's soft, steady beeping, he stepped out of the prep cylinder through a portal on the other side and entered the equally meticulously hygienic operating chamber. Off to his left Chaukutri waved at him from the other side of the transparent barrier. Lights on the console in front of the biosurge were alive with readiness.

Giving a nod to indicate that he was doing fine, Whispr turned, lay down on the bare, internally heated, sterilized platform, and closed his eyes against the subdued illumination. It was almost dark within the chamber. A gentle rising hum was accompanied by a tingling sensation as the maglift took hold of the iron in his body and raised him two meters off the platform. By controlling the magnetic field Chaukutri or the instruments in the chamber could rotate the patient's suspended body into any position.

The melder's voice reached Whispr through a speaker. "What kind of sleep would you like, my friend? I can offer you quite a selection."

"Something Ceylonese," the already half-anesthetized patient replied contentedly. "Surprise me."

Chaukutri nodded and proceeded to program the remainder of the sedative. As soon as the Ayurvedic anesthetic took hold he set to work programming the chamber.

Behind the transparent barrier a multitude of extraordinary instrumentation went to work on Whispr's levitated corpus. They performed their labors independent of any real-time surgical instruction. Having programmed in the melds requested by his customer, Chaukutri had only to sit back, watch, and monitor their progress. Machines did all the actual work. The presence of a human melder was necessary only for backup.

Synthesized facial bone was grafted and sculpted. Over it, delicate fine-tuning was applied to Whispr's brows and eyelids. There had been a time in Asia when rounder eyes had been considered a sign of beauty. When anyone could have whatever size, shape, or number of eyes they wished, such peripheral beauty concerns became nonexistent. Permanent ionic depilation thinned Whispr's hair while minuscule injections turned the remaining follicles permanently black from root to tip.

Chaukutri paid no heed when Whispr's entire body began to jump and twitch. It was merely a sign that chemicals and electronic stimulants which would have been the envy of ancient bodybuilders were giving his muscles an instant tune-up without damaging or overworking the fibers. Cutters opened his legs and peeled back skin and flesh. There was no bleeding at all. Each incision was accompanied by the introduction and adhesion of a mesh of hypoallergenic shunts. Instead of being allowed to leak out of his body, every drop of his blood was allowed to continue circulating normally through tubing that perfectly matched and mimicked his own arteries and veins.

Removing Whispr's choice from a container of synthetic tendons (he had opted for a set of affordable midrange models grown in Africa), emplacers set them against bone, stretched them to their proper length, and sealed them enduringly in place alongside the patient's already somewhat worn natural integuments. Informed by sensors that both of the customer's knees were exhibiting the first signs of bursitis but were otherwise in good condition, Chaukutri had made the decision on his own to have them cleaned and upgraded. He felt that while Whispr would not accede to the cost of full replacement, he would grudgingly pay for a necessary refurbishment.

As soon as the legwork had been completed and closed up and after a routine check of the patient's vitals, the machines moved on to the last of the programmed melds.

While Whispr's body cavity was cracked, flexible transparent sheeting was installed to protect his exposed organs. As he floated in the hover field everything from his serpentine intestines to his dark liver and beating heart were exposed. Bone was added to the existing skeleton to support the additional tissue to come. Adding just the right blend of muscle and fat, a pair of protein chuggers layered bulk onto the body. New cells immediately began to draw nourishment alongside the old. Obligatory additional nerves were inserted simultaneously with the extra flesh, giving the result the look of dark red silk shot through with strands of tarnished silver.

Supplementary synthskin filled in the gaps and bound together the separated halves of Whispr's split epidermis. After taking a shade and tone reading a final cosmetic touch was supplied by a sprayer that permanently matched the color of the new skin to the old.

Half an hour later Whispr was sitting up and strong enough to argue over the bill. Like the majority of basic, straightforward melds, the manipulations he had just undergone did not require hospitalization. They did, however, itch. From experience he knew not to scratch at the skin seams. Cupping a handful of Ms. Chaukutri's freshly baked garlic naan he scooped at the beans and lamb the biosurge had laid out for him in the vehicle's compact commercial kitchen. As it was now late, the serving area was closed. No one could see in through the one-way window.

Chaukutri joined him in dining. Not to scrutinize his progress but because the effort of monitoring the melding had left him as hungry as his patient.

"Since you ask for my advice . . . ," he began.

Whispr spoke between mouthfuls. "I haven't."

"Since you ask for my advice," Chaukutri repeated more forcefully, "I am telling you now. As a friend who would not sell you out to the authorities for anything less than a couple hundred thousand—get out of town. Leave Savannah. In fact, leave Namerica. Go as far away as you can manage." His tone turned wistful. "Try Mumbai, it's not a lie. Or Dar-es. Djakarta, Guangzhou, Sagramanda—anyplace big where you can lose yourself."

His patient replied sorrowfully. "I don't know any of those places, 'Cuda. I'm not a man of the world like you. I was born here. This part of Namerica is my home. If I were to do as you say, then I really would lose myself."

The melder sighed and sipped at his yogurt. "I am telling you, the word is out for you. Strong word."

Whispr set his empty plate aside and smiled. Chaukutri did good work and the expression did not hurt his customer's maniped face. "Thanks to your efforts they'll have a tough time trying to ident me now."

Chaukutri looked away and shrugged, but Whispr could see that he was pleased. "A little nip here, a tuck there, some new add-ons. Basic bone ladling, most of it. You should have gone more radical, Whispr. I could have put fifty kilos on you from top to bottom. *That* would have done it. Made you simultaneously bigger and more invisible."

His guest's smile widened. "If you had done that then I would have had to change my Meld name, too. No, 'Cuda. I needed a different look, but I still need to feel like me."

Picking up the dishes Chaukutri rose from the folding chair on which he had been sitting. "That feeling will get you much sympathy with the police when they pick you up. I have done what I can. The last I can do is wish you good luck."

Whispr also rose. "Thanks, 'Cuda. You're a real friend."

"Don't turn those mournful eyes on me—especially since I just worked on them. You are a repeat customer, that is all. I am nice to you and concerned about your fate only because it is good business." He nodded in the direction of his guest's plate. "Would you like me to wrap up some food for you to take with you?"

Whispr shook his head. "Thanks, no. One of the benefits of my fullself meld is that I don't need much food. I can't outrun a lot of my, uh, colleagues—but over a long slog I can outlast them. Speaking of which, you happen to have heard anything about my associate Jiminy? I need to have words with him."

"I have heard nothing about the gentleman you name." Chaukutri's shoulders rose and fell. "I am sure once you are back in circulation you will soon enough find out all you need to know."

Whispr did, but not in the way he imagined.

MARULA'S REPAIR SHOP WAS BURSTING with parts and components for scoots, trucks, and a vast variety of personal transports. It was where people brought vehicles to be repaired that had gone out of warranty. It was where they brought vehicles to be extensively customized. It was also where the occasional stolen machine could be sold, bought, or traded in for one Marula had made legal.

The proprietor flashed quite a few extensive modifications himself. So many that first-time visitors committed the occasional oversight of mistaking the shop's owner for one of his machines. Not only was N'da Marula not offended by such errors of identification; he was flattered by them. They only confirmed the effectiveness of the manips he had chosen to undergo.

Dark-skinned as the rest of him, his right hand was perfectly normal except for the variant sensor pads that had replaced his fingertips. The other hand was oversized, double-boned, and terminated in a clamp that had been created by fusing the bones of his fingers together and adding a second fused hand facing opposite. Mated to his enhanced bone structure it enabled him to lift and examine an entire scoot without mechanical aid. Outwardly he looked like a cross between a robot and a troll, but the shop owner didn't mind such comparisons. In the realm of extreme melds his were far from the most outrageous. For one thing, he still looked human.

His right eye had been replaced with an analytical probe whose multiple lenses were capable of extending several centimeters from the socket. Ears and nostrils were original, there being no reason to meld them. The kind of repair work his shop specialized in relied little on hearing or smell.

Seated opposite the square-shaped Marula, Whispr was virtually invisible to anyone who might chance to look into the workplace. The shop owner weighed four, maybe five times as much as his guest. A number of other melded employees toiled in the vicinity with sealers and cutters, handheld analyzers, and other gear on an assortment of vehicles ranging from single-person scoots to an elaborate limo that when finished would be the perfect likeness of an oversized horse-drawn carriage, complete with robotic horses.

"I'm taking a chance just talking to you." The lenses of Marula's melded eye kept extending and retracting nervously. "Hellslip, I'm taking a chance just letting you into my place."

Whispr shifted a little to his right in order to place himself more fully in the stream of cold air blowing silently from one of the air-conditioning vents. It was midafternoon and Savannah-hot and sticky, even inside the shop.

"If bluebreath is that huggy on us then I bet that prick Jiminy has gone to ground, too."

The brows over the shop owner's natural and melded eyes rose in concert. "Jiminy C? That's a name you don't have to concern yourself with. The Cricket has been squashed. He's dead and boned, his file filleted."

Whispr's jaw dropped as he registered shock. "What? How?"

"Word on the flyway is 'resisting arrest.'" The shop owner's sardonic grunt rose like a whale belch from the depths of his huge frame. "That's always the explana when someone picked up for questioning dies in police custody, ain't it?"

A disbelieving Whispr nodded slowly. "'Resisting arrest' is a nonstarter. That's not Jiminy's modus. Even if he had a reason to fight being taken into custody he wouldn't do it. He's not that brave. He's not that stupid."

"He's also apparently not that alive." Marula sipped from a self-chilling tankard of liquid high-potency calcium. Essential to keeping his massively melded skeleton healthy and functional, a thermos of the fruit-flavored supplement was always close at hand.

Concluding repairs on the left side of an electric two-seater, a sealer hissed loudly on their right. Whispr waited for it to shut down before continuing.

"This makes no sense, N'da. Why would the police kill Jiminy? He wasn't important."

In the absence of knowledge the shop owner was perfectly willing to speculate. "Maybe he didn't tell them what they wanted to know. Maybe they didn't want him telling someone else something he *did* know." One artificial and one natural lens focused on Whispr. "Do *you* know anything?"

"Nothing worth dying for," Whispr replied without hesitation. "We riffled a meld hand off a dead guy, that's all."

"Nothing else?" Marula was watching him closely.

"Nothing else," Whispr lied with a faculty born of much practice.

The shop owner considered. "Must have been a prodigious valuable hand. Or a mighty valuable man."

"He didn't look exceptional. A mild Meld. Ordinary tourist. Or so we thought. We didn't intend to kill him." A wan smile crossed Whispr's newly melded face. "You know how it is. Sometimes things don't work out as planned."

"Bet Jiminy C would second that. Where's this hand meld?"

"Jiminy had it."

The shop owner looked disappointed. He could always black market a hand. "If that's what someone wanted back, now that they've recovered it maybe it won't be as bad for you as word has it. Maybe after a quick scorch around town the authorities will back off."

Whispr blinked as he nodded. He was still getting used to his newly maniped eyes. "That's what I'm hoping. I'd really like to stay in the area. I'm not a traveler. This is my home."

Unable because of his mass to peer over his shoulder, Marula had to turn his whole body in order to look behind him. "Well, it's a hot home today. For all of us." Legs like mechanical lifts straightened and he extended the hand that still featured fingers. The visit was at an end.

Jiminy's dead. Wandering the halls of the specialty mall that occupied the bluff overlooking the south side of the river allowed a contemplative Whispr to wander in comparative safety among busily shopping crowds of locals and tourists. On one occasion he passed close to a couple of burly security guards, but despite the fact that there must be a sizable reward on his head they didn't even glance in his direction. He smiled to himself with satisfaction. Chaukutri was worth what he charged.

He thought back to his conversation with Marula. Had the shop owner been on the right track? Was it the ampuscated hand? Was that what the authorities wanted back so badly? But if they had recovered it from Jiminy, why kill the poor goof? Unless—unless the Cricket had managed to hide it somewhere before he had been taken into custody. If that was the case and it *was* the meld prosthesis the police were after it might explain why there was so much uncharacteristic pressure to find the Cricket's partner.

Unless it was *not* the hand they were after. Unless they were desperate to recover something else.

He did not need to remove the packet containing the thread from its hiding place in his right shoe to imagine what that something else might be.

What was recorded on that slender bit of flexible storage material? Something worth killing for? The only reason he could think of for someone to want Jiminy homicided would be to keep him from talking about what he had done. Which was to slay a visitor and take two things from him. If the street was true and the authorities were still hot after Whispr, and the reason for the hunt did not center on the ampuscated hand, then it somehow had to involve the thread. If that tiny bit of cyberforage was valuable enough to justify a custody kill by the police then it might, then it must, be worth money. A lot of money.

Before he could do anything else, before he could plan anything else, he needed to know what was on that thread.

6

It was just at closing time when the three women showed up. His wife had left to do some shopping, leaving Chaukutri to close down the cookers and bank the mobile adverts. One by one the floating ads winked out as the energy that maintained them was turned off. He was in the process of locking the counter when the Natural approached. In the absence of the usual manips she was still quite attractive, in a severe sort of way. It didn't take much imagination for him to envision her clad in polarized synthetics, wielding a . . .

"Is it too late to get some papadams?" Her voice was sweet but stilted, like chocolate that had been left too long in the sun.

He replied reluctantly. "I fear so, miss. Our cookers are just now shut down and I do not even have the wherewithal to heat up any leftovers." He glanced to his left. "I have some cold sticky buns with sesame, if that will satisfy."

"I guess they'll have to. Three, please, if you have that many."

"Most assuredly."

Slipping the trio of hand-sized loaves into an aerogel bag he prepared to hand them over. Contact with the enzymes in human saliva would set off a reaction that would dissolve the container, leaving only a trace amount of coagulated organic packaging that would pass harmlessly through the human gut. He handed over the sack in exchange for a credit stick.

That was the last thing he remembered until he regained consciousness.

Through a high horizontal window he could see that it was night outside. He was in his own surgery, seated with his arms bound behind him and his ankles secured so tightly that the flow of blood to his feet was in jeopardy. The woman who had approached him in search of something to eat was chatting amiably with two companions. Unlike her neither of them was a Natural.

They had been melded beyond oversize. It was not that they were unattractive. Their proportions were perfectly normal except for their height, weight, and enhanced muscularity. From what he could tell as he recovered consciousness both were fairly standard Amazon melds. Neither looked like an athlete. They were just large.

Seeing that he was awake the two bigs came forward to take up stances flanking his chair. The Natural confronted him.

"Your sticky buns are very good."

He swallowed and fought to maintain his composure. "We bake most everything ourselves, right here."

"Commendable." Looking past him, she nodded. "You also do other kinds of cooking."

He managed to force a smile. "Man cannot live by papadams and sticky buns alone."

"Neither can woman. Our information is that you had a recent visitor named Whispr, né Archibald Kowalski. Information about him is as thin on the ground as he is reputed to be." She leaned forward. "I'm going to take a stab in the dark and guess that he didn't come here for your wonderful food. What did you do to him? A partial meld? Full makeover?" She straightened and popped something into her mouth. Chaukutri couldn't see what it was, but her pupils dilated sharply. He tried to swallow again but his throat had gone dry.

"You are mistaken. We are old friends and he comes often to eat here."

The Natural nodded. For a second time, she looked past him. "You know, when I was young I gave some thought to becoming a melder. Circumstances led me into another line of work, but I never completely lost the desire." She gestured.

Picking him up chair and all, the two Amazons hauled him backward. Into the surgery. Chaukutri's eyes widened without the aid of chemical stimulation.

"Wait! What are you doing? There are sensitive instruments in here. Be careful, you could damage something."

"We wouldn't want to do that." The Natural's voice had fallen. "We don't want to damage anything." She waved at the nearby bank of instruments. "If you're a careful little people-baker you won't have kept any records. No records means no trails for the authorities to explore. No trails for the authorities to explore means that if your little hobby is discovered, in the absence of any examples or evidence to produce in court, they can't haul you in on charges of performing dangerous melds. Which means that the only records are likely to be in your head." As the two bigs stepped out of the surgery, the Natural scowled at him.

"It's time to perform some information recovery. What did you do to, or for, this Whispr? It is vital that we talk with him. He and a friend stole something many others are looking to recover. There is much at stake, I am informed, besides money. My sisters and I hold no unreasonable expectations: we will be quite content to settle for the money." As the door to the surgery slid shut she strolled over to the bank of darkened instrumentation. "It's last chance time, little baker." She giggled unpleasantly.

Even as he struggled against his bonds Chaukutri was watching her intently. "You know I cannot tell you anything about meldwork that has been performed in confidence. I am sure that if you continue to ask questions of relevant parties you will make Mr. Whispr's acquaintance soon enough."

"We don't want to make it 'soon enough.' We want to make it yesterday." A hand reached down, elegantly ringed fingers dancing over buttons and switches without quite making full contact. "I think I remember what this one does, but I'm not sure—"

"Don't touch that! It . . . !"

When his wife returned from shopping and found him slumped over inside the surgery, she started screaming very loudly. Chaukutri was not dead. The meldwork that had been performed on him reflected an expertise that belied the operator's inexperience. His arms had been modified into wings, his eyes enlarged beyond practicality, his mouth replaced

with a beak. Coarse feathers erupted from his skin while his now permanently bent legs terminated in feet that were broad and webbed. His
mouth-beak had been widened into a permanent smile the writer Hugo
would have recognized instantly.

Taken in toto the extensive meld was not unappealing—at least to children. Chaukutri now resembled a well-known and widely popular children's cartoon character. Such animated melds were not unprecedented.
A few were eagerly sought-after and costly. There was only one drawback
to the far-reaching work that had been carried out on the man slumped
unconscious in the chair.

Every bit of it had been carried out without the benefit of anesthetic.

IN AN AGE OF RADICAL cosmetology when the unusual had
become the norm and the outrageous common it took a particularly exceptional meld to attract attention. For many that was reason enough to
undergo melds that could be classified as extreme. "Look at me!" was the
cry; sometimes strident, sometimes subdued, sometimes desperate, that
had accompanied the first radical melds. Nowadays such once drastic
manips were sufficiently widespread so as to rarely draw interest.

In the same way that three-meter-tall guards and three-hundred-kilo
linemen had spelled the end of professional basketball and gridiron football (along with most other organized sports), so too had outlandish cos-
metics performed purely for the sake of reckless narcissism fallen rapidly by
the wayside. They had given way to melding carried out for more practical
reasons. Better long-range vision for enthusiastic bird-spotters, larger hands
for chefs, enhanced lungs for singers and specialized lips for all manner of
brass and woodwind players, curved thighbones for enthusiastic bicycle
riders, and greater sensitivity to changes in pressure for airline pilots.

Hobbyists were able to indulge in melds that allowed them to immerse
themselves more completely in their favorite activities. With the advent of
off-loadable organic storage banks capable of holding millions of old memories, brain melds proved not only impracticable but unnecessary. Then
there were the melds that could be applied to pets as effectively as to their
owners.

And as with all progressive leaps in technology, sex was forever in the
forefront of new developments. Thanks to continuing advances in melding
nearly anything that could be imagined became attainable.

Notwithstanding all of this, the complete face and body melding that had over a period of more than a decade completely remade Luther Heeley Calloway of Boudreux Island still marked him as something special among the melded masses. For one thing, no one had called him Luther or Calloway for a long time.

He was simply the Alligator Man.

"Why?" was inevitably the first question asked as to why he had chosen to undergo such an elemental transformation. The Alligator Man's reply was as uncomplicated as it was sufficient.

"I like gators. Always have. Admired 'em, respected 'em, used 'em, and et 'em. Always thought it would be great to look like 'em. Found out I could. Did."

Whispr knew about the Alligator Man. As did anyone who prowled even occasionally among the underworld of Greater Savannah. But he had never met him. Making his way downriver under cover of darkness, changing at the last minute from one commuter ferry to the next to throw off any possible police tail whether automated or human, he finally reached the low-lying complex of islets known collectively as Boudreux Island just after seven in the evening.

The Alligator Man did not greet him. The five-meter-long reptile that did raise its head behind the transparent autodoor caused Whispr to involuntarily jump backward half a meter. His newly enhanced and not yet entirely healed leg tendons protested at the sudden exertion required of them.

The loglike crocodilian yawned, displaying a toothy gape that was a perfectly primeval threat. "State your selfness." The demand issued not from the depths of the enormous maw but from a speechbox that had been melded to the monster's back just aft of the weighty skull.

"My name is—I'm called Whispr. I can show ident. Prior to today I resided at . . ."

The synth voice cut him off. "You are recognized, Whispr. Our files are extensive." Lumbering aside on four clawed legs, the security pet made room for the visitor to enter as the portcullis door whirred upward. "Please come in. And don't mind Lucius. He's well trained, completely under control, and less inclined to gnaw on the legs of visitors than your average starving fried-chicken aficionado."

Despite this dubious reassurance Whispr knew he had not traveled all this winding way to be dissuaded by a melded reptile no matter how big or carnivorous. Although he effected his entry with more velocity than was normal, his stride expressed confidence.

"Come around to the back." Wired to the reptile's brain the permanently affixed voicebox crackled encouragingly. "I've just finished up for the day, but I always have time for another customer. You are another customer, aren't you, Whispr-man? Otherwise you're wasting both our time."

"I hope I am." Foolishly Whispr realized he had addressed his reply to the uncomprehending reptile. Meeting the gaze of the quadrupedal guard he found the latter's eyes cold and empty.

Everyone knew why the Alligator Man was so called, but it was one thing to hear a secondhand description of the melds that had been performed and quite another to encounter them in the flesh.

Whispr's host smiled. It was both impressive and off-putting.

"Call me Gator."

For thousands of years it had been a customary coming-of-age rite for young men in the middle and upper Sepik River region of Papua New Guinea to scar their bodies as an homage to the sacred crocodile in the belief that doing so would allow them to partake of its strength. This was done by using a sharp knife to make multiple one- or two-centimeter-long slits in the skin and flesh of a young man's back. Ash from a recent fire was then rubbed into the bloody open wounds. As the slits healed over the ash they formed raised bumps that strikingly resembled the ridged scutes of a crocodile.

Contemporary melding technology allowed such modifications to be taken to extremes undreamed of by Sepik villagers.

Whispr could not help but stare. No doubt his host was used to the attention, expected it, probably even welcomed it. Whispr found himself speculating on Gator's social life—and more. Short of encountering an alligator woman via a box portal his appearance was not likely to draw the interest of any member of the opposite sex—or of any sex, for that matter. Still, Gator was doubtless satisfied with the transformation he had paid to undergo or he would not have done it. The man's succinct explanation notwithstanding, Whispr could not keep from continuing to wonder why.

In an age of melds, there was no accounting for individual decisions. As for himself Whispr quite liked alligator. Preferably the tail, fried and dipped in dressing and then slapped between the two halves of a fresh baguette.

The melds made his host look bigger. Most prominently in the face, though the rest of the body was in proportion. Unable to avoid staring at the results, Whispr could not imagine what it had all cost. It was clear that whichever surgeon or consortium had performed the work had been especially skilled.

Gator's jawbones had been extended and strengthened. Human teeth had been removed and a full complement of crocodilian orthodontics installed in their place. When the man closed his mouth, selected white canines jutted outside his closed jaws just as they did in his reptilian namesake. Black slit, gold-flecked pupils replaced round blue ones. The external ears had been removed. At least, Whispr noted as he shook hands with his host, the man kept the prominent claws on his hands trimmed.

Given Gator's customized appearance it was hardly surprising that of all the melds the man had undergone, some of them self-evidently painful, the most extensive work had been done on his skin. Even the tail that had been appended to his lower vertebrae and now extended behind him for a distance of more than a meter did not draw as much scrutiny as his modified epidermis. Tails of all kinds were a common meld especially favored by women. Crocodilian skin was not.

The nodules and scutes looked as if they had covered Gator from birth. Ranging in hue from dark green to black they shone in the room's light like fine leather. Which they were. A side benefit of the aesthetics was that their owner was encased in the same natural armor that protected everything from caimans to garails. Eyeing his host, Whispr could not tell how fast the man was capable of moving, but between teeth, tail, and tough hide he would be a formidable opponent in hand-to-hand combat.

He had not come here to fight, however, nor to admire his host's extraordinary meld. He had come because among those who practiced professions suspect and illicit, Gator's technical knowledge was famed throughout the southeast coast. Whispr needed to engage the man's brain, not his teeth. His host's physical appearance was immaterial. Among melds eccentric and extreme, Whispr had encountered his share.

And there were forever rumors of the far more . . . outlandish.

Shaking hands was not a problem. Staring into those reptilian eyes was not a problem. The proximity to so many threatening canines was not a problem. The only problem Whispr had with the engineer concerned not his physicality but his price. Upon hearing it, he shook his head regretfully.

"I can't pay you what I don't have."

"And I can't work without being paid." Rising on leathery, claw-tipped feet shod in industrial-strength sandals Gator nodded in the direction of the front door that had admitted the visitor. In response to its owner's movement the white caiman that had parked itself there reluctantly ambled off to one side.

Whispr was desperate. He was also caught in a conundrum. He couldn't sell the enigmatic thread until he knew what was on it. Without knowing what information it contained he could not set an asking price. He had already taken a risk in coming here because once Gator knew what mysteries were contained on the thread he might well try to buy it for himself at a greatly reduced price.

Of course the thread might contain nothing of value whatsoever, or even be blank. But if that was the case, why were the police so interested in him? The murder of a tourist or any out-of-towner always provoked a heightened response from the authorities, but nothing as excessive as what he had recently experienced. It suggested that the thread must be worth something. He had to find out. Given such desperation, among contacts both real and rumored, the Alligator Man would be the first choice of anyone to try to unravel the thread's contents. But he was not the only choice. Unable to meet his host's required fee Whispr turned to leave. Before he reached the workshop door he heard a word both desired and fraught with uncertainty.

"Wait."

Whispr turned back. At a distance his host looked more inhuman than ever.

"All you want is the information on a single storage thread decrypted and read?"

"Or parsed." Whispr tried not to show any emotion. "I'd settle for parsed."

"I don't do half-assed work." Gator grinned, and it was a truly remarkable thing to see. "I'll read it whole entire or naught. I'm past parsing. I have more professional pride than that." Still chuckling he extended a leathery green-black palm in his visitor's direction. "Let's see this thread you say your life is hanging from."

Whispr proceeded to remove the packet from the hidden compartment in the sole of his right shoe. He worked carefully, though the thread had shown typical resistance to damage. Based on what he knew of it thus far it was more likely to be misplaced, overlooked, or lost than broken. He handed it over.

Taking the transparent packet deftly between two claw tips, Gator brought it close to his face. The silvery filament seemed to absorb rather than reflect the light in the heavily adapted living room.

"Mighty small piece of something to have caused you so much grief. The death of your partner at the hands of the authorities, you say? May their genitals undergo explosive melding!"

"I don't know for sure that he was murdered because of this. It might have been over something else we took, or because of the person we had to kill. Or something else. But I feel sure that it must be valuable, somehow."

Reptile eyes met his. "And how pray tell do you know that, Whispr-man?"

His visitor did not look away. "Because there was only one of these on the dead man. When there is only one of something and a lot of trouble is taken to conceal it, value is usually an attribute."

"Hmm. We'll see." Holding the packet firmly, Gator beckoned. "Come with me."

Part laboratory, part machine shop, part techrap, the workroom where Gator performed his unlicensed magic took up most of the back part of the house. Windows offered a view of one of the slithering Savannah River's glistening moonlit tributaries. Something whose ancestors had migrated north from the Orinoco to settle happily among the cypress screamed softly from the trees. Whispr had no time to appreciate the real estate. He had to keep an eye on Gator. Despite the identification provided by the thread's distinctive visual qualities Whispr had no intention of becoming a victim of an amiable switch on the part of his far more knowledgeable host. If at all possible he was not going to let the thread out of his sight.

A long workbench ran beneath the windows that overlooked the river. Here the lugubrious tributary of the Savannah flowed slow as black Jell-O. Hundreds of years ago the space between bench and windows might have been filled with hammers and saws, drills and awls, boxes of nails and spools of wire. In contrast, the skills of contemporary advanced technology demanded more mettle than metal.

Holding the thread steady in a portal beam Gator examined it closely while the projector ran a preludial analysis. "There's a connector on one end. Reckon you noticed that already." Whispr nodded. "Nonstandard contact, but my gear can adjust for that. The thread itself is interesting. Not a carbon derivative. Definitely metal. Lightweight even for something that's just a bit of thread. That said, the actual composite could be any one of a thousand functional storage alloys. I don't suppose you have a clue as to its chemical configuration?"

Whispr shook his head. His redone hair itched and his eyes still felt a little tight in their recently maniped orbits. "Uh, something-oxide?"

"Nothing like a little specificity to help a man out." Gator sighed. "I suppose what it's made of isn't nearly as important as what's on it. You need to know and I'm curious."

Leaving the projector's analyzer to finish its work Gator moved to another station farther down the workbench. As Whispr looked on, his host carefully slipped the thread into a tension capsule. Once it had been drawn taut with the connector end left free, Gator then gently inserted the capsule into one of several receptacles on the top of a gray box. On the instrument's front panel a trio of green telltales immediately winked to life. Almost as rapidly they began to turn red, one at a time. In spite of his radically melded face Gator still managed a frown.

"That's odd."

"What's odd?" Looking from host to box and back again while seeking enlightenment, Whispr found none in either location.

Without replying Gator removed the capsule from the gray box. Continuing down the long workbench he flipped open the transparent cover of a much smaller device and placed the capsule on the pad within. Once the cover was softly snapped shut he adjusted the controls that speckled a protruding panel on the instrument's front. A pale blue glow filled the chamber and enveloped the capsule. Moments later a multidimensional, much enlarged image of the small cylindrical container and its inscrutable contents were projected into the room.

"Resolve subject matter." Unlike his body there was nothing reptilian about Gator's voice. It was full and mellow and occasionally bordered on the operatic. He glanced at his visitor. "This is how you read storage media while bypassing the connector. You go straight in and pull the information straight out. No messy intervening physical security to deal with."

The capsule image vanished, leaving behind only the enlarged likeness of Whispr's prized thread hovering before the two men. Drawn taut, it pulsed beneath the probing azure aura of the analytical beam that had been focused on it.

"Content resolution unsuccessful," a synthesized voice declared.

For a second time Gator frowned. "Repeat procedure." The same number of moments passed as previously, and generated the same disheartening response. "Explain failure," he demanded curtly of the machine.

"Content is encrypted."

The techrap looked relieved. "Is that all?" Moving to the workbench, he fingered additional controls. Two more pieces of equipment came to life; one to the right of the capsule-holder, the other that was built into the shelf beneath it. After a delay of a minute or so one, or perhaps both of them, beeped softly.

"Decryption failed."

Was that a hint of confusion in the gray box's synthesized voice? a perplexed Whispr wondered.

Leaning his back against the workbench and sliding his tail onto a vacant shelf Gator crossed leathery arms as he stared at the floating image of the uncooperative thread. "Military level?" he inquired aloud.

"No." Gray box's response was unexpected. "Beyond military. Beyond anything in my files or that I can access via the box. I can distinguish patterns within. But as soon as they are pursued, holes are encountered."

"Utilize the patterns to construct temporary bridges." Gator was now utterly involved in the probe, Whispr saw. Had the engineer possessed a brow, it would have been deeply furrowed.

"That has been tried. Thus far no bridging effort has proven successful."

Gator nodded with satisfaction at this first sign of encouragement, however inconclusive. "'Thus far.' Keep at it unless and until you hit a wall." Remembering that he was not alone, he looked over at the blank-faced Whispr and explained patiently.

"For every hole in an encryption pattern it is possible to construct a bridge based on the underlying nature of the encryption pattern itself. It might fall into place on the tenth attempt, or on the trillionth. But the number of possibilities is finite. While we're waiting for the box to find one we might as well eat something. You like Italian?"

Never one to turn down a free meal, Whispr avowed as how he did.

Almost as distinctive and engrossing as Gator's appearance was the sight of him using a special utensil to shovel penne pasta into his crocodilian jaws. They ate in the workshop. It would not have surprised Whispr to learn that Gator slept there as well, comfortably ensconced among his instruments and tools, his pet caimans and garails.

The gray box and its wireless attendants were still humming away trying to unlock the secrets of the thread's contents when farther up the workbench the portal beam analyzer chimed for attention. Carrying his now almost empty plate of self-heating pasta Gator rose from where he was sitting and ambled over to study the readout. Having long since downed the last of his own meal Whispr watched as his intent host stared fixedly at the wisp of screen.

"Well, what's it say?"

Though not words of magic, Whispr's query broke the spell that seemed to have overtaken his host. Gator blinked and turned to him. "At the outset we encountered an oddity. Now I find that compounded by an impossibility." Whispr's response to this avowal consisting of blank incomprehension, his host hastened to explain. "It is the thread's composition. It's chemically absurd. It's physically preposterous.

"Under normal pressure and temperature metallic hydrogen shouldn't even exist."

HOURS PASSED, NIGHT DEEPENED, AND the Alligator Man seemed to grow more and not less energized as one tantalizing clue about the mystifying thread after another was disclosed by his interlinked complex of instruments. Minuscule as they were, periodic revelations emerged only after long periods of analysis by multiple devices. As midnight snuck up on the two Melds and then fled, Whispr found himself having to struggle to keep from nodding off. Fortunately, a refrigerator in one corner of the workshop proved to be an inexhaustible font of chilled stimulants. So he was able to stay awake but grew increasingly edgy doing so.

Not Gator. The more he learned about the thread's composition, if not its still impenetrable contents, the more determined he became to winkle them out.

"Look at this." Holding a hard copy in front of the sleepy Whispr he shook the reusable paper violently. "According to the laws of physics and

metallurgy not only is the thread's atomic structure unparalleled, it's unreasonable. It shouldn't exist." Crocodilian canines ground against heavily
maniped jaws. "Even if this thread contains no information of value, my
friend, even if it turns out to be completely blank, the remarkable substance of which it is composed is worth a great deal. Any manufacturing
concern in the world that deals in exotic metals would . . ." His voice
trailed off, the need to articulate his thoughts overcome by the visions they
had begun to inspire.

"Then," Whispr ventured hesitantly, "you can see someone paying for
it even if it can't be opened or decrypted?"

Gator turned back to his hopeful guest. "I can see more than that." He
gestured at the workbench where the gray box and its companion devices
were still struggling furiously to try to decipher the thread's contents. "For
one thing I can see that the time has come for us to work out an arrangement." As he continued speaking every word echoed as if freighted with its
own punctuation. "I have excellent commercial contacts. This is potentially big, my slender friend. Very big." His gaze drifted ceilingward and
elsewhere. "It is," he paused for emphasis, "unsurpassingly *large*."

It was at that point and on the cusp of incipient mutual celebration that
the alarms went off.

Articulating an expletive that was more consciously reptilian than anything he had uttered thus far, Gator rushed to a battery of small projectors
installed at the far end of the techrap. The images they displayed of hus-
tling, disembarking armored squads were intimidating. As they were
meant to be. The arriving cops were not trying to mask their presence.
Spreading out from multiple transports they were approaching the complex rapidly and on foot. A pair of heavily armed police watercraft idled at
a distance from the building in order to cut off any retreat via the river.
Auto minihunters had perched themselves in the surrounding trees. All of
this disheartening visual information arrived in the techrap courtesy of automated security pickups hidden among the dense vegetation and
mounted on the backs of Gator's modified free-roaming pets. They were
well and truly trapped, a despondent Whispr decided.

Except they were not.

"Follow me." Hissing a single code word his host shut down the security
pickups and turned away. Devoid of options or ideas, Whispr complied. If
Gator thought that in the panic and confusion his guest might forget a cer-

tain small sliver of specious metal, he was mistaken. Whispr followed, but not before flipping up the transparent cover of the analyzer and recovering possession of the study capsule that now contained the thread. Hurrying to keep up with his host he alternately ran and hopped as he placed the capsule back in the secret security compartment in the sole of his right shoe.

If nothing else the arrival in numbers of the authorities at Gator's establishment confirmed that the thread *had* to be the object of their attention. Such extensive forces would never be deployed by the city or the state just to pick up a single questionable homicide suspect. Multiple squads of heavily armed police would not have been sent out to arrest someone like himself on suspicion of participating in an ordinary murder. Their appearance only lent reinforcement to Gator's preliminary assessment of the thread's value.

If only, Whispr told himself as he followed his host down through a flawlessly camouflaged trapdoor in the workroom floor, he had some idea of what was *on* the damned strand of metal. As far as its ostensibly unique composition was concerned that was of less interest to him than it evidently was to his host. Whispr really could not have cared if the thread had been fashioned from arc-welded fairy wings.

Had his admittedly limited scientific knowledge extended farther into the realms of physics and metallurgy he might have realized that fairy wings were more likely constituents than the reality.

Since Gator's house and techrap complex were built on pylons out over the water Whispr was not surprised to encounter a slice of river in the compound's basement. In light kept deliberately dim that barely illuminated the patch of dark water, long streamlined shapes gradually resolved themselves into living creatures. Lying largely submerged, they were the contours of nightmare. Though the prospect in the basement resembled a clichéd scene from a bad horror vit he was not afraid. In an age when animals as well as humans had been subjected to every imaginable kind of advanced melding one truly could no longer judge a book by its cover or the reactions of a creature from its appearance.

Slightly awash, a sturdy platform extended outward from the bottom of the last step. A flick of a concealed switch accordioned the stairway upward until it lay flush with the underside of the residence. At Gator's command two of the largest floating shapes, driven by lazy sweeps of enormously powerful tails, approached the platform. Unlike those of other crocodilians their ebony scutes stood up like those of a dragon. The black caimans in Gator's basement, however, were not creatures of imagination. They were very real. A squinting Whispr could just make out the control box that had been melded to each of their spines just aft of the skull. He had expected to see something of the kind. What he had not anticipated was the other equipment that was fastened to the broad, armored backs.

Gator was already in the water. "Hurry up! My decoys are already out in the river. They should draw the boats and airborne hunters away and hold their attention long enough."

"Long enough for what?" Hesitating only briefly, Whispr eased himself into the black water. Kept perpetually in shade by the house above, it was unexpectedly cool.

If he had known he was going to be spending this much time running from the police through water, he mused, he might have asked Chaukutri for a fin meld.

"Long enough for us to get away," Gator told him.

Further verbal instruction proved unnecessary. Whispr simply emulated his host's actions as the Alligator Man removed and donned gear from the long narrow container secured to one caiman's back. Mask for the eyes, compact oxygen extractor and minirespirator for the lungs. Puzzlingly there was no sign of foot fins, webbed gloves, or an underwater scoot. As he soon found out, these appurtenances would not be needed.

The rubberized grip ring that had been melded to the caiman's back just above its shoulders was sturdy and wide. Because of the caiman's sluggish metabolism the ring's presence did not harm it. Slipping the oxygen extractor's respirator into his mouth, Whispr fumbled with the mask. He barely had time to clear it before Gator gestured to him (or maybe at him) and plunged downward atop his own scaly mount.

Lying down and forward Whispr let his body stretch out along the caiman's spine as his saurian steed took him beneath the surface. Guided by signals from Gator the pair of powerful six-meter-long crocodilians and their human riders passed beneath the plastic overhang that formed the lower exterior rim of the compound and shot out into the open river. The pressure of water pushing against his mask prevented Whispr from guessing whether they were traveling upstream or down.

Something bubbled off to his right. At first he thought it was a big fish that had been startled by the passage of the two predators. Only when the noise and disruption was repeated several times in rapid succession did he realize the cause.

Projectiles, moving fast through the water. Whether auto-hunter or actual police, someone was shooting at them.

Following Gator's directions the caimans went deeper and initiated evasive action. Quick as they were, they were organics and not mechanical submersibles. They were not even as agile as otters.

He knew it immediately when Gator got hit. The Alligator Man nearly lost his grip on his mount. Even in the murky water the trail of darker liquid that started to swirl from his left hip was identifiable. Whispr had seen too many men bleed not to recognize the source.

His host gestured one last time. Perhaps he also conveyed further instructions to the caiman's headbox. Regardless of the cause Whispr found his mount turning away. Was Gator initiating separation to make it more difficult for the police to track them? Or was he sacrificing his guest, delivering him to the authorities in order to facilitate his own escape now that he had been wounded? Whispr had two choices. He could let go of the ring and let himself float to the surface. Or he could take a chance on his host's integrity and hang on. He chose the latter. If nothing else, it was less tiring.

Something tore into his right side.

He couldn't tell what he had been hit with. The persistent burning sensation hinted at something other than a simple slug. But since he had been struck while he was beneath the surface and since his experience of fighting underwater was limited, he could not be certain of anything. Looking back and down, fighting to hang on to the control ring, he saw long strands of his shirt trailing in the water like bleached seaweed caught in a current. There was also blood, but not as much as he feared and considerably less than he expected. Had the shot internalized and was even now sapping his life force or had he only been struck a glancing blow? Warm water and adrenaline combined to mute the effects.

There was no muting the persistent throbbing, however. He hung grimly to the grip ring as the caiman maintained its powerful push toward a programmed and unknown destination. Time enough, Whispr told himself through the pain, to learn how badly and by what he had been hit when eventually he emerged from the water. No more shots struck him. A glance downward showed that he was not losing much blood. After awhile it dawned on him that his mount must have either eluded or outswam any police pursuit. He was going to be all right. He was going to make it.

All he had to do, he told himself as the underwater vista surrounding him grew more and more blurry, was not black out. . . .

"COME OUT NOW, with your hands up and empty! We know you're in here, Kowalski!"

The cordon of cops advancing steadily deeper into the techrap complex knew nothing of the sort, of course, but based on the frantic research performed by the Center over the past couple of days there was a decent probability that the fugitive who was the subject of so many recent bulletins might indeed be found seeking out the just barely legal services of one the Alligator Man, né Luther Calloway.

The corporal who was on point and who led the way in had neither the manner nor the meld for subtlety. Working with hands the size of hams he simply leaned his considerable weight on the front door and pushed. To the officer's surprise, the barrier was surprisingly flimsy. Having been warned to expect everything from reinforced portals to automated weaponry and having thus far encountered neither, he and his colleagues relaxed slightly in spite of themselves. Relaxed, but did not let down their guard.

The sergeant was not allowed to do so. As the woman in charge, relaxation was a luxury of which she could not partake. "Relaxing" while an assault was in progress would look bad on her record, and since the movements and actions of every city cop were transmitted continuously for the purpose of permanently recording such movements not only by their own individual sealed personnel monitors but by those of their fellow patrolling officers, she could not apply for nor hope for any personal privacy time until the raid had been concluded. The compact devices allowed monitors at the Center to keep track of the actions of everyone on the municipal force. Backup could be deployed without having to be requested, help sent to an injured officer unable to respond, situations analyzed in real time by experts in specialized fields.

The continuous recordings also did an excellent job of cutting down on incidents of police brutality, with consequent benefits not only to the officers who had to function under constant surveillance but to the taxpayers as well.

Within minutes the armed men and women who had spread throughout the building began to trickle back toward the entrance to report. Gathering around the sergeant they comprised a wide spectrum of Naturals and police-specific Melds. The commtech had remained with her throughout the dispersal and search, ready to make use of the instrumentation that had been melded into his body and in a few instances linked to his own nervous system. Even among Melds, Officer Raymer was unique in that he stuck his two specially melded fingers into open electrical sockets not by accident or because of some perverse fetish but because the gesture was designed to recharge the batteries that were emplaced in his buttocks.

"Nobody here, sergeant. The place is empty." The young officer reporting was not out of breath. It was just that while impressive for a private, one-man operation, the techrap and integrated living quarters did not occupy a great deal of floor space. Checking the interior had required only a short time.

"Not unexpected." The sergeant was disappointed but not surprised. Similar simultaneous raids were taking place all over Greater Savannah. Still, given its level of importance this was one collar every commanding sergeant wanted to make. Word had seeped out of the Center that whoever brought in the Meld called Whispr could look forward to not just a commendation but possible immediate promotion. Why the low-class Meld was such a catch she could not imagine, unless he had somehow managed to seriously offend someone important.

Not her job to wonder, she reminded herself. Only to apprehend. Despite the succession of negative reports from the members of her squad she was loath to quit the riverside techrap so quickly.

Opening his eyes, the commtech spoke up. "Auto-hunter reports are all negative, sarge. Same from our people on the river."

"The river." It was a short mantra, but one worth investigating. She turned to her squad. "Check the lower floor."

"This place is a one-story, sergeant." The officer who spoke up sounded apologetic.

"Then check the understory," she snapped. "Check the friggin' mud. You find anything bigger than a crawfish, I want to talk to it."

They fanned out anew. It wasn't long before they found the camouflaged trapdoor.

"Think they're down here?" The patrolwoman spoke as she knelt and began tracing the fringes of the locked opening with her scanner.

Holding his riotuss casually, her companion shrugged. "Could be. Good place to hide from infrared pickup." He nodded at the almost imperceptible lines that marked the edges of the portal. "If so, they sure are being quiet."

Something on the underside of the barrier clicked and the lightweight but strong panel popped upward a centimeter or so.

"That's got it," she murmured. Rising, she drew her sidearm, aimed it at the portal, and glanced at her partner. "Ready?" Raising the muzzle of his riotuss, he nodded. The ammo gauge on the crowd-control weapon read full.

With the toe of her right boot she flipped the door up and open. It fell backward on the floor with a soft bang. The riotuss's search beam illuminated a slick surface below: water black as onyx.

"Kowalski, Calloway—come on out! Game's over."

There was no response from below. No sound, no movement. Looking to her left, the officer who had opened the doorway fastened her gaze on a dog-sized storage cylinder. Pushing it with her left foot she shoved it toward the opening until it tumbled in. There was nothing sham about the splash that resulted. The river below was real and not a projection. She edged toward the silent gap.

"I'm gonna have a look."

"Slow," her companion advised her unnecessarily.

With a nod she dropped silently to her knees, then to her stomach. Lying prone, she stuck the muzzle of her weapon and then her head into the opening. The light built into the end of the barrel swept the underside of the techrap.

"Nothing," she reported just before the Orinoco crocodile shot like a missile from the depths of the dark water, clamped its jaws shut around her head, and dragged her screaming into the water below.

At this point the erstwhile occupants of the complex who had been the subject of the raid were summarily forgotten in the ensuing confusion, panic, and unregulated hysteria that resounded piercingly not only throughout the heretofore silent techrap but via a multitude of active links through the no longer phlegmatic souls at police Central.

7

"Really, I must speak with the fellow. He is my late wife's cousin's youngest son."

The ramshackle residence hotel located in one of Savannah's poorer districts being too low on the scale to afford a customized Meld (or even better, an automaton), its front desk clerk was a Natural. As a Natural he needed less coddling than a Meld and less maintenance than an automaton. He was also adaptable. Fully cognizant of his exalted position as decision-maker in matters of admittance, he took his time studying the supplicant before deigning to respond.

The poor old guy certainly looked harmless enough.

"Everyone calls your skinny whip-guile relative Whispr. Tell me his real name."

The elderly visitor did not hesitate. "Archibald Kowalski. The family is from a little town up north—Pittsburgh."

None of which meant anything to the clerk. He had solicited an answer simply to see if the visitor would have one. Whether it was accurate or not was immaterial. What mattered was that the old man had replied promptly and without hesitation. The clerk sighed.

"A duplicate keystress'll cost you twenty, if you want to sit in the room instead of the hallway."

The oldster dutifully slid a charge tic across the desk. Both of them knew that the clerk could have let the hotel's visitor into the room in question for free, just as both of them knew he would not do so. A ritual as old as the first time one Cro-Magnon provided space in his cave to another, the exchange was soon concluded.

"None of my business," the clerk murmured as the visitor deftly palmed the keystress, "but is this a family visit?"

The shuffling senior smiled slightly. It was impossible to tell just by looking at him if he was Natural or Meld. He was a short, sorrowful-faced little fireplug of a man, stocky but not fat beneath his cheap garb. On the street no one would look at him twice. Presumably it was an incurable (or too expensive to fix) spinal disease that caused him to bend forward slightly at the waist. His eyes were brown and his nose appeared at one time long ago to have been broken in several places and poorly reset: in an era of melds and other medical miracles such sloppy work was a sure sign of frail finances. There was a healthy glow to his full cheeks that stood in contrast to his otherwise genteel shabbiness, indicating that even if he didn't dress well, he ate well. The fringe of unkempt white hair that haloed his otherwise bald head was thick and several centimeters long.

Yeah, he's a Natural, the clerk decided as he appraised the pitiful coiffure. Even a poor Meld would go either all skin or all hair, both cosmetic choices that were equally easy to obtain. He realized that the old man was still speaking to him.

"I don't mind telling you. My late wife's cousin recently passed on. I am here to convey the news and to inform Archibald that he has been left a small inheritance. I come in person instead of sending the information via the box because I have papers with me that he must sign in person in order to claim the sum."

Grunting acknowledgment of this explanation, in which he had no interest whatsoever, the clerk turned back to the soft porn projection in which he had been immersed. Half-meter-high dancing nymphs swirled around him, cooing and caressing. He smiled like someone in the throes of a pleasant drug-induced daze. In boxland did the entertainment moguls a pleasure dome decree.

"Got us a rich lodger, eh? That's a first!"

"Oh no, not rich. Not at all. But it is only fair that Archibald receive that to which he is entitled from those who wish it upon him." As he stepped into the open lift and turned back to face Reception the elderly visitor bowed slightly. Even lost within the lascivious projection the clerk was visibly startled. In his entire life he could not recall anyone ever having bowed to him.

Lucky bastard, this Koo-kowski. None of his relatives had ever left the clerk anything except misery.

In the hallway on the sixth floor the old man pressed the keystress to the center of Room 684's handleless door. A synth voice warbled "Recognized" and the barrier obediently slid aside. The internal room lights came on as he entered. There were not many of them and they were weak. This the visitor expected.

"Hello?" he called tremulously. "Whispr? Archie Kowalski?"

In the absence of a reply he began a slow search of the living area. It was not spacious enough to qualify as modest. Tiny, perhaps. There was one living room and a bathroom. A cooking unit sat on a table next to an old food preserver that hummed too loudly. Nothing in the cubicle was elaborate enough to qualify as décor. Painted with receptors, the blank wall opposite the narrow, pushed-apart twin beds served as the sole viewing monitor. Inspecting the room's electronics the old man could not find evidence of a proper projector. Primitive accommodation indeed, whose sole virtue was its cheapness.

He checked the single built-in closet. It held a change of clothing, some personal items remarkable only for their insignificance, and little else. As he peered into the depths of the food preserver the visitor's nose wrinkled. The fare was all of a piece with everything else in the cubicle.

It was unfortunate that the Meld called Whispr was not there, but the oldster was a patient man. Settling himself on one of the beds and stretching out his legs he activated the cheap house monitor and leaned back to watch a nature documentary. The natural world was a particular love of his, be the subject matter unmelded or otherwise.

Long after night had fallen he still had not eaten. That did not trouble him. He was used to going long periods without eating. Around eleven p.m. the door announced an arrival and the old man rose from the bed. He would surprise the renter. Moving off to one side he stood against the wall and waited. As he did so, his spine unbent. A professional acrobat's trick, it would have astonished the sleepy-eyed desk clerk.

A figure entered, carrybag in hand. Moving slowly and clearly tired from the day's exertions, he set the carrybag down on the table beside the cooker and turned. As he did so his eyes widened slightly.

"*U'af,* who are y . . . ?"

Melded muscle-twitch fibers contracted throughout the old man's body as he cleared the space between them in a single bound. When the startled resident reached for something in his left pocket the quartet of tentacles that extended from the four fingers of the oldster's left hand snapped whiplike around the man's left arm and wrenched it violently sideways. Crying out as the intruder closed on him the resident used his other hand to pull a knife from a scabbard under his shirt and thrust wildly forward. It skittered off his attacker's chest, the fine point unable to penetrate the flesh-toned organic Kevlar meld.

"*Harami!*" the resident screamed. "*Itassal bil bulees!*"

Even as he worked to bind the younger man's hands the suddenly uncertain intruder wondered why he should be calling for the police in Arabic. Was the use of that language some sort of code he shared with someone elsewhere in the building? Or was it being employed to trigger a defense mechanism or activate a concealed communicator? While his earlier search of the tiny apartment had turned up neither potentially problematic installation it was always possible something had been overlooked.

Slapping sealant over the man's mouth the oldster threw him down on one of the beds. When he tried to struggle back to a sitting position his assailant wrapped two finger-tentacles around his neck and drew a thumb-sized cylinder from a shirt pocket.

"This is only a simple neuralizer. You can buy one in many stores or via the consumer box. You know what it does. Delivers an incapacitating electric shock." He leaned toward the man thrashing around on the bed. "However, if I were to press it against your left eye and fully discharge it . . ."

No one needed to project any images. The man on the bed immediately stopped fighting.

"Before we go any farther, let me assure you I mean you no harm." The oldster smiled reassuringly. His appearance was that of a favorite uncle or doting grandfather. "Odd as it may sound at the moment and under the present circumstances, I don't want to hurt you. I only want something you have. Do you understand?"

Still wide of eye but beginning to calm down, the man on the bed nodded slowly.

"Good. My name is Napun Molé." He sighed as he saw the man's brows furrow in confusion. "It is pronounced 'moe-lay,' not 'mol.' The word comes from the Aztec and refers to a sauce made with cacao or chocolate and spices—not to the little burrowing mammal of which you are doubtless thinking. Nor, for that matter, does it have anything to do with the unit of measurement that represents Avogadro's number and is used for weighing atoms, molecules, and elementary particles." His expression tightened. "I am Mol-é, not 'Mole.' Please do not forget that when you address me. If it is easier for you to do so you may use my first name, which proffers no such confusion." As he spoke he continued to play with the neuralizer, passing it from the fingers of his right hand to the bizarre tentacles of his left. These continued to extend and retract as he talked.

"As I am sure you are already well aware the police have also been looking for you and for the item of interest in your possession. Please don't insult me by telling me you don't have it. If you had not taken it and it was not in your possession or at least under your control, you would not have been striving so strenuously these past several days to avoid the attention of the authorities. Those who want it back—my employers—have no interest in you, your future relationship with local law enforcement, or anything else. For all they care you can go blithely about your business and on your way or find yourself helmeted beneath a truther. It is of no consequence to them, or to me." His eyes gleamed and suddenly he did not look as old as he was.

"But I will have it, or you will suffer. I am very adept at what I do and I can spend many hours making you believe you are dying. Except that you will not. You will wish that you were, but you will not." He paused. "Do we understand one another, Mr. Kowalski? Or Whispr, if you would rather be addressed by your Meld name."

Behind the sealant, the figure on the bed was making violent muffled sounds. Molé nodded perceptively. "I will remove the sealant now. If you scream or yell for help, I will be forced to silence you. It will be unpleasant for you. It will be more unpleasant the next time you regain consciousness." Reaching forward and down he used the tips of his melded tentacle-fingers to peel back the sealant that covered the man's mouth.

There was some coughing and sputtering before the figure said, "I don't know what you talking about and I don't know who you talking about! My name is Ali al-Thuum! I am a part-time cook at the Ghadames Restaurant on Mirabile Street. Please, I have a family in Sahara States who rely on the little money I can send them. What is it you want from me?"

The old man considered. Reaching down, he unzipped the shirt beneath the cheap coat he wore. As he passed the palm of his right hand over his belly the accessible chipped library that had been installed in his stomach came to life. While the bound man on the bed looked on with a mixture of curiosity and apprehension, his elderly captor proceeded to verbally access his own stomach. The flesh that framed the storage insert was aged, but all muscle.

The conclusions Molé drew from querying his internalized database were irrefutable. He had the correct address and apartment, all right—but the wrong man. Shutting down the library he zipped up his shirt and regarded the immigrant cook.

"I regret this episode of mistaken identity, Mr. . . . ?"

"Al-Thuum." Visibly relieved, the younger man's heart rate began to slow, his blood pressure to drop, his excessively dilated pupils to contract. Molé knew all this because the sensors that were components of his left eye meld told him so. The individual who had been mistaken for Molé's quarry tried to smile. "I can feel sorry too for what you said earlier because my name sometimes also causes me embarrassment. But it is my family name and I will not disown it."

"I'm not interested in your name or anything else about you." Molé's response was as indifferent as it was calm. "What I'm interested in right now, the only thing I am interested in right now, is the location of a man named Archibald Kowalski, also known as Whispr, who is the tenant of record for this apartment."

"I shouldn't tell you that," al-Thuum mumbled as he looked down at himself.

"Of course you should." Molé shook his head slowly. Sometimes he could never decide if people were stubborn or just stupid. "Otherwise you will die a slow and painful death. I'll find him eventually anyway. You know that I will. Listen to my voice and you will know it. Look into my eyes and you will find this confirmed. To me your demise will be only an inconvenience. Your inconvenience will be far greater, and permanent."

"I don't know where he is."

The elderly grim-faced captor edged the neuralizer toward al-Thuum's face and the younger man flinched. "Honestly, honestly! I do not. He sublet these rooms to me only yesterday." Bound hands flailed sideways as they struggled for purchase on the mattress. "See? There are two beds. His only condition of the subletting was that he be allowed to sleep here from time to time."

A number of the remarkably tiny, astonishingly sensitive, and profoundly expensive sensors that comprised Molé's left eye played over the man on the bed. At the same time Molé inhaled deliberately of the bound young man's body odor in hopes of isolating and identifying certain potentially revealing pheromones. Insofar as this exceedingly sophisticated combination of sight and sound was able to ascertain, al-Thuum was telling the truth. There was also no indication that he might be involved in a physical relationship with Molé's target.

It meant another delay. Another inconvenience. But then, the truth was often inconvenient.

"When might he be back?"

The man on the bed shook his head. "I don't know that, either. I don't know anything about him, really, except that he needed money. That's why he moved into this place and almost immediately agreed to sublet it to me. At least, that's what he said."

For someone on the run it made perfect sense, Molé knew. Rent living quarters so you would have an address and a place to eat, sleep, and clean yourself, but utilize it only when there was no alternative. Meanwhile sublet to keep it occupied and have the look of being lived-in, but not by you. What information he had been able to glean on this Whispr person suggested he was not particularly bright. In the light of present circumstances that assessment might have to be revised. Even in Molé's chosen profession general intelligence evaluations had a difficult time gauging street smarts.

A pity this wretched émigré was not fat, or female, or otherwise melded. Any of those characteristics would have been sufficient to physically distinguish him from the loose description Molé had obtained of his quarry and the whole awkward confrontation could have been avoided.

"I can wait," he declared softly.

"You might have a long wait." Al-Thuum coughed again. His expression wrinkling slightly in disgust, Molé decided he would not want this gentleman cooking his food. "The last time I saw him he said he might be away for a while, and just to keep his bed clean and made up in case he should return unexpectedly."

The hunter nodded. "Yes, you're right. I could linger here for days, or weeks even, wasting time while he and the important article he carries with him journey ever farther from Savannah. Now that you mention it, renting this residence and then subletting it to another might be nothing more than an astute ploy to induce someone like myself to squat here and wait for him to fall into my lap." He straightened. "I thank you for reminding me of something I should have thought of for myself."

Smiling weakly but hopefully the immigrant cook extended his trussed hands. "So you'll be leaving, then."

"Yes, I'll be leaving. Immediately."

Al-Thuum shook his bound wrists. "Could you release me?"

The old man stared down at him. "You might attack me."

"I have no reason to do that."

"You might call the police."

"I wouldn't do that, either." The younger man's smile was fading fast.

"You might contact the police and tell them what occurred here."

The smile now gave way to a reprise of earlier fear. "*Laa*, I promise I won't do that. Why should I? I barely met this Whispr, I don't know him, I don't care anything for or about him. Or for you, for that matter. I only want this whole last hour to go away. I just want to go to sleep, wake up, and go to my job tomorrow. That's all. I will not present a danger to you, sir."

"No, you won't." Molé was in agreement as he drew the gun.

The clerk barely glanced in the old man's direction as the elderly visitor walked silently through the small lobby and out the single entrance onto the street beyond. Once outside and several blocks distant from the miserable residence hotel Molé allowed himself the freedom to curse aloud.

Nothing made him madder than having to work with bad or misleading information. Had the suppliers of that information been present he would have had a harsh word or two for them. And likely something more physical as well. There was nothing to be gained from cranking about it now, he sighed to himself.

His quarry still might return to the apartment he had sublet. Having employed certain liquids and methods to dispose of the corpse he had left therein, Molé had also left behind a handful of tiny devices that would alert him to the arrival of whoever might visit next.

In the meantime, there was ample mean time. Molé had other leads to follow, other ways of locating his target. Greater Savannah was a good-sized metropolis, but the hunter was used to working places like Chengdu and London, Kairo and Sagramanda. Someone hiding out in Savannah was unlikely to be able to continue to escape his notice for very long. The Mole's reach, as his uncaring and unsubtle employers were fond of observing, was wide-ranging. No one could escape it for long.

All this money and effort, he mused to himself, to recover a single storage thread. He wondered what information it contained that made it so precious to those who had engaged his services. Valuable enough to enlist a hunter like himself as well as spending to corrupt a diverse menagerie of municipal authorities. Someone was pouring out money like water.

Ah well. Whatever was on the thread did not matter as long as an equitable portion of that money fell on him.

Only a few citizens out for a late night stroll bothered to glance in the direction of the hunched-over old man. Those who did, did so out of concern for his safety and presence in what was a less than salubrious corner of the city.

They need not have worried.

Traktacs.

Whispr didn't have to see them. The angry linear marks where they had penetrated his skin were evidence enough. That was what had hit him on his underwater flight from the Alligator Man's dwelling. They were also an indication that the authorities wanted him alive. Not out of any concern for his health or fear of public indignation should his head happen to get blown off, but probably because he could not be allowed to die until he revealed the whereabouts of the stolen thread. If the police had been certain it was on his person they would have used more deadly force and he would likely already be dead. A supposition was therefore easily inferred: keeping its location a secret was vital to keeping him alive.

Not that any of that would matter once the traktacs began to activate.

Each of the dozen or so tiny pellets contained its own transmitter and power source encased in a biodegradable husk. When these finally dissolved inside his body the pellets would begin broadcasting. The husks served a double purpose: to act like the casing of a bullet and protect the transmitter inside, and to give a target shot with them an opportunity to turn him or herself in before the organic outer shell fully dissolved. Once it did, a compelling combination of homing signals and internal irritants would be released. The former would allow the police to track down the source of the broadcasts while the latter would render the subject thus afflicted increasingly uncomfortable within his own skin. For one who had been hit with traktacs there was only one remedy: the removal of every last one of them before they could begin broadcasting their location.

To anyone familiar with such an intrusion the size, color, and shape of the entry wounds shouted the distinctive signature of traktacs. Only the police and the military had the authorization to utilize and the inclination to use such specialized stalking ammunition. It would therefore be presumed by anyone asked to treat such an injury that the patient was wanted by one official institution or another, else such devices would not have been inflicted on the patient. Whether they chose to treat the wounds or not, any legitimate physician was required to report such a request. It therefore behooved the increasingly uncomfortable Whispr to seek immediate relief from one who was not legitimate. This led him to seek out a mobilemed he knew well.

When he wasn't playing the blues through the straight-line sax that had been melded from an additional radius, an operation that had left him with three instead of two major bones in his left forearm, Cyrene Pope (everyone who knew him called him Righteous) performed the work of a wandering physician. He did this only with what he could carry on, or as a part of, his profoundly melded person. Whereas in earlier times as eclectic a personality as Righteous Pope might have collected tattoos or metallic body modifications, such iconoclasts now accumulated a highly personalized diversity of melds. The musician-medic boasted so many he barely looked human.

Beneath his chin, a radical throat meld had produced an organic speaker. Linking to his melded forearm, it allowed him to amplify his music without the aid of mechanical supplements. While the fingers of his sax-arm remained perfectly functional, those of his other hand featured medic melds that allowed him to perform all manner of on-the-spot minor surgeries and bodily repairs. Attached to his lower ribs, his bloated flanks featured compartments holding medical supplies that could be accessed by rolling back flaps of self-adhering skin. In addition to the various skills he had mastered, Righteous was a walking dispensary. Very useful for treating someone injured on the spot, or who wished to avoid certified medical treatment. Licensed treatment was better, safer, and guaranteed by the government, but it was also intrusive. A fair segment of Righteous's clientele preferred his makeshift surgeries to having to report cause and location.

Whispr found him on the riverfront plying both his music and his medicine beneath the old bluff warehouses. While some of the blocky structures could trace their noble commercial ancestries all the way back to the eighteenth century, they were all antique shops and restaurants now. Thoroughly gentrified, as were their patrons. That didn't keep people from stopping to listen to Righteous's music, or seeking treatment from him for scrapes and bruises, or furtively purchasing from his internal body stock the occasional semilegal recreational pharmaceutical.

Whispr waited beneath a sprawling shade tree on the faux stone riverwalk until Righteous concluded his business with a well-dressed young couple. As soon as the Naturals continued on their way, hand and drugs in hand, he hurried forward.

"Don I know you, mon-man?" Unlike many who chose to maintain at least one natural eye, both of Pope's were full melds. One to aid in his medical work, the other simply to gleam large and bright while shining forth a gold-tinged beam of its own. To a devotee of cosmetic melds, appearance was every bit as important as practicality.

Not wanting to draw attention to himself, the slender supplicant slowed as he drew near. "They call me Whispr."

"Whispr—right! Speak up, mon-man. Make yourself known." Amused at his own sally, Righteous let out a prodigious laugh. Whispr waited until the jovial human who was still just barely identifiable as a member of the species calmed down.

"Got a problem," he murmured.

Righteous grinned broadly. "Lady got you down? Cat got your tongue?" The flesh beneath his left arm bulged, parted, and before folding back in on itself revealed a small tongue. The musical Meldman roared again, but less stentorian this time. "Serious now, mon-man, what can old Righteous do for you?"

After one more scan of the immediate riverfront surroundings to make certain as best he could that no one was watching, Whispr turned sideways, lifted the hem of his shirt, and exposed his right side to the musician-medic's melded eyes. Golden light illuminated the bright red spots on Whispr's skin while the other eye scrutinized and took readings. When he had finished the examination to his satisfaction, Righteous straightened. His smile had vanished and he was now dead serious.

"Looks like you been attacked by a covey o' drunken hummingbirds, my sibilant friend." He lowered his voice conspiratorially. "Either that or you done caught yourself a consignment o' traktacs. Course, it might be nothin' but the first stages of a bad case o' shingles. That I can treat. And I doubt any hummers gonna mistake you for a flower." He shook his head sympathetically. "But traktacs, now—those little screamers are bad news. Baaad news."

Dropping his shirt hem, Whispr growled under his breath. "Tell me something I don't know, bone-music. Why the hell d'you think I came to you?" Like marbles on marble, his eyes were in constant motion, continuously searching their surroundings for signs of approaching police.

"To avoid the official hell, I've no doubt." It was a solemn Righteous who now met the anxious Whispr's gaze. "Traktacs—damn difficult little buggers. I can hex a stall on 'em, but I can't do an extraction. If I try without knowing the individual codes, never mind the group signature, all the procedure'll do is set them off. Every one of them." Tilting back his head slightly, he squinted skyward. "The Savannah strikers'll be down on you like hail in December. They'll pound you flat and spatula you off. I don't want to be next to you when that happens."

"I don't *want* it to happen." Whispr chewed his lower lip. Around the two men, who appeared to be engaging in a perfectly commonplace afternoon conversation, tourists milled contentedly while locals sauntered in and out of the upscale restaurants and shops that lined the edge of the bluff.

"If you just do the stall, what happens next? I've only heard about traktacs. I've never had to deal with them." The slender thief's expression was one of despair, his voice thickly beseeching. "When your stall wears off I'll be just as vulnerable to trace as before."

Righteous nodded agreement. "One way or another, my friend, you've got to get them out of your body without setting the nastily loquacious little nobbers off."

"You said that can't be done." Whispr's tone was simultaneously hopeful and accusing.

The musician-medic shook his head. "Huh-um—I said that *I* couldn't do it. Don't have access to the right tools. Expensive, sophisticated." He performed an unexpected and surprisingly nimble pirouette. "Do I look like either?"

Whispr was crestfallen. "Then what can I do?"

"I got couple o' names. Docs who are repute-revered for giving treatment without asking too many questions. Not because they're off-wire like me and mine but because they actually believe the oaths they've taken: to render ministration without mulling. To treat without judging. Course, confronted with an officially inflicted infiltration like the one you got they might as easily turn you right in as prescribe you a pill." He studied the other man somberly. "That said, one of them's still your best chance. After I install the stall I'll give you names and addresses. You decide to supplicate on them, that's up to you."

Whispr's shoulders sagged. "I don't have a choice."

Later, as Righteous was arranging his fantastic array of physical melds preparatory to temporarily freezing the ability of the traktacs embedded in the other man's body to communicate with their law enforcement host and broadcast their location, Whispr thought of something else.

"One more thing. I don't have the money to pay you right now. But I expect to shortly."

Righteous grinned. "That's okay, my friend. The stall's a cheap insert. I'll stick it between two ribs, right in the center of where you were infected. It'll give you seventy-two hours of anonymity. Best I can do. After that, the traktacs' signal will override the install. You'll have three days to get rid of the little hugger-muggers before they start bawling to the hop-cops. Me, I reckon if you ain't evicted them by then you're a pretty high priority candidate for pickup anyway. As for payment, I'm not worried. I know as soon as you can that you'll compen and sate."

They moved toward a secluded, tree-shaded area behind a shuttered cotton-ice stand where Righteous could perform the stall install in privacy.

"How do you know I will?" Whispr was genuinely curious.

"Because if you don't, my friend, then I'll find you and kill you. Or hire one of our mutual friends to do the deading deed." Before commencing the on-site riverside outpatient surgery the musician-medic blew a brief underlying tune on his orthopedic radial sax, scoring as well as underscoring the threat he had just made with an appropriate snippet of man-music blown through his own bone.

. . .

As HE EXITED THE PUBLIC transport the following morning Whispr proceeded on the belief that Righteous's work was as good as his name. It was an assumption he had to make. It wouldn't do any good to doubt it. If the traktacs embedded in his right side were now active and functioning and had not been temporarily stalled by the work of the musician-medic, the police were likely to land on him at any minute. The surest proof he had that the street doc had done his job properly was the undeniable fact that so far Savannah's ugliest handpicked blues had failed to do so.

That did not guarantee everything Righteous had told him was truthful. Seventy-two hours stall-time, the mumed had promised him. Three days in which to liberate himself from the traktacs before they reconstituted their programming and he lost the protection provided by the provisional electronic scramble.

Assuming Righteous had been straightforward, Whispr could have taken a day to relax. *Sure he could,* he told himself. Just like when they used to give the condemned rolled tobacco to burn between the lips prior to execution by firing squad. Death anticipating death. Having always been a firm believer in no time like before the present, as he strode down the pedestrian path he studied the first of the two names and addresses Righteous had slipped him. Preferring to walk, he disdained the use of the parallel moving walkway off to his right. Not because he was a resolute believer in daily exercise but because the walkway's protective transparent sides made it too easy for someone to be trapped within. Better to rely on one's own two feet (or more, in the case of those Melds sporting multiple manips).

Even allowing for his naturally slender limbs, he was able to move faster than ever now thanks to Chaukutri's excellent tendon melds. As long as he kept to open, old-fashioned, paved static paths he could take flight in any direction he wished at any moment he chose. He retained, as he and his friends were fond of referring to it, fleedom of movement.

It was for other reasons entirely that he found himself more than a little uncomfortable in his present surroundings.

Here in the northwest district, well above Old Savannah and its flatland flood-prone suburbs, rose the residence-office towers of successful and important commercial enterprises. The university tower was here too, along with its attendant stadium and other athletic facilities. There were banks and businesses, gleaming white and silver spires dedicated solely to habitation, soc schools for teaching children how to survive in contemporary society, manicured parks and rambling upscale entertainment venues. What there was not were any individual residences. Even for the wealthy, land in central Savannah had become too pricey. Those who wished to live in mansions had been banished to the country.

Around him people of all sizes, shapes, colors, and melds wandered at leisure or with purpose in mind. Melded construction workers with huge muscles and oversized hands were repairing a length of rubberized boulevard. An impossibly long-limbed street vendor was hawking fast food from a cart whose clever design resembled a miniature nineteenth-century paddle-wheel riverboat. The solar-driven paddle wheel powered the cart's cooker, refrigeration, and insistently flashing lights.

Many of the residents here were Naturals, but they did not comprise the majority of strollers. Not at this time of morning. Most of the casual walkers were teens. Able to attend soc in either the morning or the afternoon and do their academics at home, they were free to enjoy the rest of the sunny, humid day on their off time. In contrast to the workers they were made up of an equal number of Naturals and Melds.

It had struck Whispr on more than one occasion that each year the population seemed to consist of fewer Naturals and more Melds. That was the impression he held, anyway, however unscientific his own personal sampling might be. Certainly it looked that way when one encountered groups of perambulating preadults. All hung together, of course, Naturals and Melds mixing as freely among their age groups as did adults. In the first years of readily accessible and affordable melding there had been some unspoken segregation, but that kind of social shun had long since been relegated to the past. Nowadays boys and girls, androgynies and Melds, socialized without giving the interaction a second thought.

He found himself musing on beauty. "Natural" was in itself a kind of beauty to be admired. Adept and diverse as it was, melding could only advance beauty so far. Restricted to modification of the purely physical, it could do nothing to beautify an individual's inner self. There was as yet no meld for personality, for a sense of humor, for wit or for compassion. Or for love, he told himself.

Invent that one and become the richest person on Earth.

Home to two hospitals, a fully accredited meld center, and medical offices as well as shops and dwellings, the main entrance to the tower he now found himself standing before boasted three levels of security. Not as extensive as one would encounter at a government building, but daunting nonetheless. He tried to put a hint of jauntiness in his step, to act as if he belonged. Very soon now he was going to learn the efficacy of Chaukutri's melds and see if they were sufficient to fool general public security. Given the exceptional speed and ferocious nature of the official pursuit that he and the late Jiminy had attracted, he had no doubt that the likeness of his premeld self now occupied a prominent place in every security and alert file in southeastern Namerica.

Singly or in couples or in small groups, residents, workers, and visitors were passing through building Security in both directions. Whispr tried not to make eye contact, did his best to avoid drawing any casual glances in his direction, and struggled to blend in with the crowd. This was made easier because his melds were not radical, especially when compared to some that were being discharged from the tower's hospital facilities. One way or another, in a hurry or taking their time, every one of the building's occupants or visitors had a destination in mind that likely did not cause them to all but quiver in a rictus of anxiety. That unsettled state of mind was reserved, Whispr was certain, solely for him. The deeper into the structure he progressed, the more he was certain he could not go through with this. Or if he did, that it could not end any way but badly.

True, Righteous had assured him that both the physicians whose names the street surge and musician had provided came highly recommended through the regional box. But a recommendation was not a guarantee, and yesterday's ally could easily turn into tomorrow's turncoat. Whispr shook his head mournfully. What certified doctor with a legitimate public practice would risk treating a multiple wound that had patently been inflicted by a branch of officialdom? Suddenly next in line to enter the first stage of Security, he took a deep breath and stepped forward, to find himself enveloped in a softly purring green halo.

He was about to find out.

THE MONSTER THAT WAS chasing her wasn't there.

That was because it was entangled, of course. And now it had entangled her. It was silvery and shapeless, tiny and enormous, heavy as a sun and light as a feather. In and out of reality it burst, one moment threatening to crush her to a pulp, the next to envelop her in an alien embrace that was hot, was cold, was freezing, was burning up. Ingrid Seastrom screamed but made no sound. It did not matter because there were none around to hear.

The forest was filled with splinters. Underfoot as she ran was a surface composed of sequoias three centimeters high while around her blades of sharp glass hundreds of meters tall thrust skyward. Everything was the reverse of what it should be, oppositionally ornery, mary mary quite contrary how does your cosmos grow? As she fled in terror from the horror that was implacably closing in on her, from a dreadfulness she could not resolve, she felt little pieces of her mind sloughing off; memories rendered as dandruff. Felt her self remorselessly disintegrating, each fragment floating free on the sweltering humid air only to be swallowed up and digested by the indistinct ogre she was unable to elude.

Hot clammy fingers adhesive with moisture reached for her. She could not escape them because she was entangled with them. Once she had been absorbed by her shadowy pursuer she would cease to exist. Or would it be the monster that would cease to exist? With quantum entanglement one could never be sure which would be destroyed and which would survive, which was the original and which the copy.

It was upon her now; sultry, steaming, smothering. When she opened her mouth to scream again, it slithered down her throat and began to choke her. Perspiration stung her eyes like a hundred minuscule bees. She couldn't breathe.

With a gasp she sat up in bed, her heart pounding, sweat cascading down her body in salty runnels, and knew instantly the cause.

Hormones.

Damn it, she told herself. *This has got to stop.* Sliding unclothed out of the bed, her progress lubricated by the same perspiration that had contributed to her awakening, she stumbled into the bathroom and cursed at the shower. As soon as she entered, water of a preprogrammed temperature materialized all around to strike her body from every direction. Inhaling deeply of the warm, soothing wetness, she let out a long exhausted breath and began to relax. The shower was the personal luxury of which she was the most fond. It was also the most expensive. As a respected and successful physician, she could afford it. She owned little in the way of jewelry save for one flashy sphene bracelet, did not take expensive vacations, and the typical social expenses of an attractive woman her age were generally picked up by the men who asked her out. She felt no guilt over the sophisticated shower.

Especially right now.

As the water was whisked away to be recycled by the building, she stood with her arms held away from her sides while the facility gently dried and scented her. One step beyond the utility's one-way glass wall, the ground fell eighty-five floors straight away to the ground. She could see out and no one could see in, but it was no shower for an acrophobe.

More than anything, she was angry at herself for continuing to suffer from such nightmares and not doing anything about them. She was a *doctor*, for goodness sake! This early morning's unenchanted death dream made twenty or so she had suffered this month. While the particulars of each nightmare differed, the underlying paradigm was the same. Something was chasing her, some unknown horror, and it always involved entanglement of a sort. Sunday night her imaginary tormentor had been a monstrous water-dweller. Before that, a gruesome flying creature.

Physician, heal thyself. Or at least call a colleague. There were plenty of readily available medications that would mitigate the effects of the hormonal changes her body was undergoing. She had put off taking them: a fine example for a medical practitioner. *This evening*, she told herself. Before lunch she would file a request to fill the pertinent prescription and it would be ready for pickup when she finished work. As if the discomfort and personal embarrassment the nightmares were causing her were not enough, there was the matter of continually having to change the bed.

At least she could look forward to the fact that it was Friday. Saturday lay uncommitted before her, open and inviting. Maybe she would call Suzanne and Leora and the three of them would go down to Dubaia Park for the weekend, letting themselves luxuriate and unwind among the welcoming spas and sensoria of the south coast's strand of artificial islands.

The mere thought was enough to reenergize her. So much so that this morning she decided to spurn the usual severe white unisex medical garb in favor of a lightweight business suit of robin's-egg blue, one short of sleeve and tremulous of hem. It would brighten her colleagues' day as well as her own. She smiled mischievously to herself as she imagined Rajeev's reaction to it. Though he didn't see them often, he was of the considered opinion that she did indeed have legs.

Before she left her apartment and took the elevator down to work she thought to check on the lab report that had nagged at her ever since she had first listened to it. The notion of tiny vanishing devices fashioned of impossible substances was sufficiently thought-engaging to push the last remnant memories of her most recent nightmare clean out of her mind. While ongoing speculation as to the source and function of what she had extracted from the back of Cara Gibson's head produced only greater confusion and bemusement, these were at least a welcome relief from continuing anxiety and frustration over the inescapable hormonal changes that were taking place within her own body.

Work itself was also a great help. Even for a general practitioner such as herself, far more concentration and effort was demanded than had been for her long-ago predecessors. Like her, they had prescribed aspirin and bed rest, had set broken bones and administered vaccines, had been required to observe symptoms and call for specific tests to isolate certain diseases.

None of them, however, had been asked to identify the cause of infection in a third eye. None had been expected to diagnose whether the progressively collapsing bone structure of a complete facial remeld should be attributed to failed surgery, inadequate maintenance on the part of the patient, or the insidious effects of a recently banned self-administered tanning additive.

Though she dealt with no one under the age of thirteen, there were still children present in the office antechamber. Accompanying adults seeking treatment and advice, the kids kept the atmosphere lighter than that generally found in specialists' offices. Maybe it was the presence of the candy robot Ingrid had acquired several years back. The mechanoid entertained, and dispensed sweets, and joked around, and generally made life easier for her adult patients by diverting their progeny. Ingrid had never thought of the robot as a tool for bringing in business. In truth, she had more clients than she could comfortably handle and was regularly forced to turn prospective patients away. She hated to do it, but the alternative was to exhaust herself, to the detriment not only of her own health but of her work.

It wasn't her unarguably capable skills but rather her concern that marked her as an exceptional doctor.

Even allowing for the fact that she had a competent office staff whose work was supplemented by up-to-date automatics, the morning passed with exceptional efficiency. Chosen on whim, her outfit had the desired effect not only on Rajeev but on everyone who saw it. Women complimented it, men ogled it, a few men complimented it and a few women ogled it. She drew equal attention from both Naturals and Melds. Even in modern society it was still recognized that certain aspects of physical attractiveness transcended time, space, and elective body modification.

After an excellent lunch at Laziiz, a restaurant with a view that blistered from the east wall of the tower, she returned to her office suite rejuvenated by all the attention that had been paid to her, even by strangers. And also by the knowledge that once she had seen to the afternoon's pro bono patients she would be free for the weekend. In her mind, the artificial beaches of Dubaia were looking more and more attractive.

It had been a long time since the passage of the law that required every citizen to donate a certain number of hours per week to community service. For all its unpopularity when introduced, as a way of reducing the cost of government it had proven to be an undeniable success. What those forced to participate in the program got out of it, Ingrid had reflected on more than one occasion, was entirely up to them. Whether janitor or jailer, lawyer or landscaper, butcher, baker, or candlestick maker, the PSP (public service program) could either leave one feeling better for having helped out one's fellow human, or that they had simply been taken advantage of by the government. The viewpoint one took was usually a matter of personality as well as perspective.

Personally, Ingrid enjoyed her pro bono time. There wasn't much that made her feel better than resetting a twisted muscle, layering fresh bone over a fracture, or administering a successful epidural to someone suffering from a bad meld. Since the government paid for all medications, she felt no hesitation in handing them out freely but wisely. There were impoverished old folks whose youthful melds had begun to break down, poor but sturdy men and women in the throes of Mali cough, furtive and ignorant twenty-somethings whose medical difficulties were indicative of having engaged in the right sex in the wrong place, or the wrong sex in the right place.

Occasionally her office saw to immigrants whose illnesses required full body scans and subsequent library searches. She treated each and every one of them with the same concern and compassion she lavished on her paying patients. Though her PSP efforts brought in no money, she had grown wealthy in grateful tears and thank-yous.

Last visitor of all today was this slender fellow, recently enhanced of thigh and calf, oddly ill at ease in her antechamber, who according to her receptionist had insisted on *being* the last patient of the day. An odd request, Ingrid mused as she examined him. The usual wish of her patients both pro bono and paying was to see her as soon as possible.

He didn't look sick. Scrutinizing him as his own attention wandered from her to her professionally decorated surroundings to the spotless floor and back again, she found herself doubting that he had ever looked completely healthy. But according to the preliminary checks and initial readings she took there was no overt indication of illness. The man didn't have so much as a head cold. She sighed resignedly. Another hypochondriac. He wouldn't be her first. And contrary to popular thinking, hypochondria was not an affliction confined exclusively to the well-off.

Still, she told herself, he was the last patient of the day. She might as well complete the exam by running the usual full-scale body scan. The poor skinny fellow probably hadn't had one in years, if ever.

"Stand over there please." She held no clipboard, no compact recording device. Half a dozen linked recorders, some highly specialized, were built into the walls and ceiling of the gleaming, pale blue examination room. He nodded, complied, and retreated a couple of steps until he was standing within the main medical scanner. She did not ask him to remove his clothing. It was not necessary. "Hold still. This scan will complete your exam. You may breathe, if you wish."

He didn't bat an eye and his expression did not change. If she *had* been carrying an old-fashioned antique clipboard she might have written down, *"Note patient's prior surgery: sense of humor removed."*

Sitting back in the self-powered wheeled chair that motored around the office in response to slight shifts of her weight, she studied the readouts as information became available and was transmitted from the body scanner. Blood pressure: slightly elevated. Heart rate: faster than it ought to be but within tolerable parameters given the visitor's claimed age. Presence of detectable melds: leg tendons upper and lower, hair follicles, ocular orbits . . . it was neither a long list nor a distinctive one. Very minor biosurge work compared to what she saw and dealt with every day.

Body fat, sectional proportions, muscle density, presence of required trace elements in the blood, kidney-liver-spleen-heart-testicular function, neural activity, cognitive functions, digestive system—one by one the scanner broke down, analyzed, and reported back on the general condition of the subject. As she perused the flow of information and used it to build up a picture of the visitor's health, Ingrid's mind was already turning to thoughts of lying on a warm beach in as little as possible while doing as little as possible and imbibing as much as possible. She managed to lose herself in coastal reverie while absorbing, digesting, and contemplating the visitor's condition.

Right until the alarm went off.

9

Ingrid's daydream vanished consciousness like at a concert. The same in-office experience that allowed her to diagnose and deal with patients while paying only half her attention to them abruptly jolted her back into full awareness of where she was and what she was doing. Muting the audible alarm with a verbal command, she now turned all her powers of observation onto her visitor. In sharp contrast to her response, he had been neither surprised nor startled by the alarm. His nonreaction spoke volumes. If anything, his attitude verged on the apologetic. She grew tense.

"You knew that was going to happen."

Whispr nodded without meeting her accusatory stare. "I had a pretty good idea something might. I mean, I knew they had to show up sometime during the exam. I just wasn't sure how soon or under what circumstances."

She blinked uncertainly. "'They'?"

Taking a deep breath, he turned sideways to her and pulled the hem of his shirt out of his pants. Raising it toward his armpit exposed a smattering of tiny red bruises on his back. Her inspection was fleeting.

"Not chicken pox and not fleas. But I suspect you're already aware of that." She was more upset by the unanticipated revelation than she cared to admit. Adopting a professional approach in the presence of the unexpected allowed her to remain calm. "Why do I have this uneasy feeling that you know full well what set off my system?"

He let the shirt hem fall from his fingers. Neither was particularly clean. "I've been shot."

"So I infer." Inclining her head slightly, she nodded toward her instruments. "From the looks of your skin and the readouts I'm seeing, my guess would be police traktacs. But if so then they should be broadcasting. They're not. At least, not on any frequencies detectable by my equipment."

"I was able to arrange a three-day stall. The instant it expires I'll start blasting out signals all over the southeast." Unexpectedly limpid eyes locked on hers. "There's no way to stop the transmissions. You know that. All I can tell you is that I have plenty good reason to believe my life's at stake. It would sure help me out if when these little pieces of electronic shit resume broadcasting, they do it from someplace other than my ribs." He risked a smile. "Like from the bottom of a toilet, maybe."

She studied him without instruments, doing her best to try to generate a picture of her quietly desperate visitor. He did not look, sound like, or otherwise strike her as a violent person. There was a disarming innate shyness about him. Working in his favor was the fact that he had come to her office as a supplicant, making no demands and issuing no threats. Of course, that could easily change if she refused to help him. On the other hand, it was unlikely that whatever branch of law enforcement had invested him with the traktacs had done so out of boredom or a lack of other subjects for target practice. She knew it had to be something serious. Casual muggers, sneak thieves, and bar brawlers did not generally attract the attention of traktacs. The Greater Savannah Authority wanted this man badly or he would not have been shot with the minuscule locators.

Her continuing silence was making Whispr edgy. "Can you get them out?"

"Of course I can get them out." Should she call for help? Or just run from the examination room? "The question is, should I?"

"You're a doctor," he challenged her. "I'm someone who's been hurt. I need your help. I swear to you on my best friend's life that I haven't hurt anyone or damaged any property."

She wasn't buying it. "Then why do the authorities want you badly enough to inflict you with traktacs?"

That, at least, was a question to which he could reply honestly. "I swear to God I don't know. I mean, I have an idea, but it's only an idea. I'm not really sure. I think it has to do with money, but not with any money I stole."

He was being evasive, which was hardly surprising. The beckoning languor of Dubaia Island was fading from her thoughts. There was no reason why it should. All she had to do was tell him to wait and that she would be right back. Once clear of the examination room she could activate a floor-wide alarm as well as instructing the office receptionist to call the police. Claiming the need to take additional readings and prepare the necessary instruments for extraction would allow her to stall him until they arrived. Washing her hands of him would be easy. She had almost decided how to proceed when he did something that caused her to hesitate.

In obvious pain, he winced and grabbed at his side. He could have used the brief burst of suffering to play on her sympathy, to plead, to try to make her feel guilty. He did none of them.

Traktacs were small, but they were still an alien intrusion in the body. Quite likely some were impinging on nerves. She could remove them, eliminate the pain they were producing, and *then* notify the police. That way she could fulfill the Hippocratic obligations according to which she had lived ever since she had received her medical degree and still turn her patient over to the authorities without feeling more than the slightest twinge of guilt.

"All right. I'll take them out. But you'll have to dispose of them yourself."

He looked shocked, as if he did not really believe that she was going to help him. The disbelief began to dissipate as she approached him holding a small device from which protruded what looked like a large opaque magnifying glass.

"Lift up your shirt again and hold still." He complied and she passed the lens over his side. The scan didn't take long. He was the skinniest nonstarving person she had ever seen, but he did not register on her instruments as unhealthy. Stepping back, she inserted the narrow end of the device into a slot in a nearby console. Telltales came to life as she waited for the readout.

Within moments she was examining a dimensional projection of the affected area. Whispr gawked at the glowing image as it hovered in the air between them. The projection was a perfect representation of the right half of his torso. Utilizing voice commands Seastrom caused the projection to focus in on specific areas. Imaged blood flowed through the network of arteries and veins while a detailed visualization of his right lung expanded and contracted in perfect parallel to his actual respiration. Zooming in on an area in the vicinity of the fourth rib brought a flurry of minuscule round objects into view.

Traktacs.

Marveling at the pulsating, lambent representation of a living part of himself that was as much an advance over the old MRI as the X-ray was over imperfect pencil sketches drawn from life, he swallowed. A couple of the tiny transmission devices had penetrated deeply into his body. "How— how are you going to get them out?"

"I have a flock of trained ravens that will peck them out of your flesh." Confronted with a stare of incomprehension, she rolled her eyes and explained. "Just take off your shirt, go over to the exam table, and lie down on your left side. Raise your right arm and put it across or behind your head, whichever is more comfortable."

Whispr did as he was told, wondering not for the first time if coming here had been such a good idea. He was placing himself at the mercy of this woman. Suppose there was now a reward out for him? Suppose she knew, or suspected, that such was the case? She could inject him with anything, knock him out, and have him all nicely sedated and packaged for the police while she waited for them to arrive and pick him up.

He had little choice. The traktacs had to go. He had to trust *somebody*. Her back was to him as she busied herself placing selected equipment in a sterilizer cabinet.

"You're not going to have to cut me, are you?"

She glanced back over her shoulder at him. "Where do you think you are—some back alley in Katanga?" Turning, she approached the table holding gleaming instrumentation in both hands. He saw that she was now wearing gloves.

"Taking them out won't null the stall, will it? It won't do me any good if the procedure nulls the stall."

She made a face at him. "I have no idea, Mr. . . . Whispr. This isn't the

sort of infection I usually find myself dealing with. I'll get them out. After
that you'll just have to take your chances." Her eyes met his. "Unless you
want to climb off that table, pull down your shirt, and leave."

"No. No," he mumbled disconsolately. "I have to lose them. You're my
best hope."

"Lucky me." Her voice dropped to a murmur as she bent toward him.
"You're going to experience a chilling sensation. It's the usual combinant
disinfectant-anesthetic spray. I think we can get by with a local."

He was relieved to hear it. At least she wasn't going to knock him out.
His wits had been all that had saved him numerous times in the past, and
he wanted them about him now. As far as he was concerned, so long as she
removed the traktacs he was ready for her to proceed without the aid of *any*
kind of anesthetic.

Something hissed like a student whispering in class and his side went
numb from underarm to waist. The application stung a little, as if he had
inadvertently pressed wet skin against an open freezer. Inquisitive as
always, he strained to follow the procedure as she began to work.

As she flipped the surgical lenses down over her eyes and began probing with the extractor, Ingrid noted his interest. *Scrawny but tough*, she decided. The typical patient undergoing this kind of multiple extraction
would by now have turned their head away from the site or at least closed
their eyes. Not this Whispr fellow. When she made the first insertion he
continued to track the probe with almost as much intensity as the doctor.

Sliding into his flesh, the slender probe's integrated ultrasonic rejuve-
nator induced temporary metabolic stasis in the muscles and nerves it
pierced. Using her lenses to peer far inside the patient's body, Ingrid aimed
the tip of the probe toward the traktac that had penetrated the deepest.
The choice was standard for invasive outpatient surgery. When extracting
foreign objects, be they splinters, screws, or bullets, always remove those
presenting the greatest danger first in order to minimize trauma and the risk
of complications.

Whispr said nothing, did not so much as flinch as he watched the
probe slowly squeeze into his body, linger for a moment, and then slide
back out. As the procedure was repeated, one traktac after another *pinged*
percussively as it was transferred to a waiting glass dish. With his flank efficiently anesthetized, he felt nothing. The only pain was psychosomatic.
He was at once engrossed in and divorced from the process, as if he were

viewing a projection of someone else's body. He found the entire procedure very impressive, not least of all because the woman performing the surgery was as easy to look at as she was skilled in her work.

Tic-tic-tic—seven, eight, nine little gray spheres accumulated in the dish. Other than the pings they made as they were dropped onto the glass and the steady breathing of doctor and patient, it was dead quiet in the room. Not many more to go. There was no bleeding. The tiny holes and shafts made by the multiple insertions healed behind the probe as it was withdrawn.

"Last one." A moment later she was holding the business end of the probe over the collecting dish. Oozing from the instrument's tip, the last of the itching, intrusive traktacs dropped onto the glass. Taking a long breath she sat back, pushed the lenses up onto her forehead, and rubbed her eyes. "You can sit up now if you like. Somebody doesn't like you."

He straightened on the table, letting his shirt fall down to cover the site. From armpit to waist he looked as if he had spent an hour under a heat lamp. His side ached in the places where she had been working, but not to the extent that he could call it pain.

"Somebody like you, for instance?" he opined.

She looked surprised. "I never said I didn't like you. I'm neutral on the subject. Considering your probable social status, I'd say that's probably giving you the benefit of the doubt."

"Righteous was right about you." Still sitting on the examination table, legs dangling, he worked to close his shirt. "You're a real throwback: a doctor first and foremost. A doctor before anything else."

"So I've been told, on occasion. It beats being handed a service plaque at a medical convention." She frowned slightly. "'Righteous'?"

He turned cautious again. "My professional reference. Did you get them all? The traktacs?"

Her expression twisted. "Are you questioning my professional competency?"

"No, no," he replied hastily. "I just—it would only take for one to be left behind to make everything you just did a waste of time."

"They're *all* out." Her tone was stern. "As it is time for you to be." She nodded in the direction of the door. "You're my last patient of the day—of the week—and I have plans." Thus far those plans existed only in her head, but the reality of the anticipation was sufficiently strong that she did not feel like she was lying. And why should she care anyway if she bent the truth a little for this melancholy and socially dubious charity case?

As he slid off the examination table he eyed her uncertainly. "You're not going to call the police as soon as I'm out of your building, are you?"

Turning away from him she busied herself with shutting down equipment for the weekend. "I was able to treat your traktac infiltration but I'm afraid I can't do anything for your paranoia. I took care of your most obvious problem and now any remaining problems are entirely your problems." Dumping the traktacs into a small glassine envelope, she handed them to him. "Of course, the longer you stay here the more opportunity I have to change my mind."

He nodded understandingly. Lean as he was, he reminded her more than anything else of the occasional stray dog she encountered from time to time in the city parks. Sodden and shaggy mutts drawn to the city's green spaces for access to their automatic watering systems—and any edible leftovers abandoned by uncaring picnickers. These clever stray canines were smart enough to avoid the park electronics that were designed to discourage their presence. Just as this Whispr individual and his advisor had been smart enough to identify her as one of the few regional physicians bound tightly enough by their Hippocratic oath to help him in his moment of need without turning him in.

Had he been telling her the truth? Had he been harried with traktacs because of a dispute over money, as he claimed, and not because he had murdered some innocent in their sleep? She still didn't think he looked much like a killer, and not just because of his skeletal appearance.

She chided herself. Her knowledge of the facades of convicted murderers had been acquired from casual perusal of the news and popular entertainment. Bodily dysfunctions she could diagnose with little effort. Mental ones lay outside her realm of expertise.

To her surprise she heard herself saying, "I don't know what you've done, but why don't you turn yourself in? Do the right thing, assume any debt you owe to society. Turn your life around. You don't strike me as addled. You're slim but based on what I see not physically impaired. Good health is a windfall for which even the most elaborate melds can't compensate, and you seem blessed with it."

How much of what she was saying came from the heart, she wondered even as the words left her lips, and how much from a desire to assuage any lingering guilt over the service she had just provided to someone wanted by the authorities?

Whispr knew he ought to have felt insulted by her rebuke, no matter how well intentioned the sentiments. Had any of his street acquaintances ventured such unsubtle advice he would have told them promptly and in no uncertain terms where they could file it. But coming from her, after what she had just done for him, the suggestions left him feeling not angry but—uncomfortable. He chose to test their veracity by seeing just how far he could push her.

"There's one more thing you could do for me, doctor. Ms. Seastrom."

"'Doctor' will do nicely," she replied tartly. "And for some reason you're still here."

He held up the little bag of traktacs. "I can lose these before the stall gives out. Dump them in an estuary, down a public toilet. Mail them out of the country. But no matter where they fetch up, sooner or later and most likely sooner the authorities in the area will catch the signals and they'll be traced back to their point of origin. To Savannah. I know traktacs." He spoke with confidence. "Try to destroy them and they'll rightquick broadcast their location, even if they have to punch the signal through a stall." He was eyeing her intently.

"The one thing that would really help me out now, now that you got them out of my body, would be if they could be deactivated." He indicated the examination room. "You got all kinds of advanced gear here. I guess some of it would let you turn medical implants on or off remotely. You probably do it all the time as part of your work." He jiggled the contents of the envelope.

"I bet you can turn these off." He eyed her somberly. "That would *really* set me free. If I sent these to Istanbul, Interpol would pick up their signal and notify the police back here. Then they'd be able to trace them to the point of mailing and they'd know I'm still around. But if the little bastards never *start* broadcasting—nobody would know where to begin looking for me again. I'd have my life back. Or at least some freedom of movement."

He was pleading with his eyes as well as his voice. By now she was having serious second thoughts about what she had already done. "I think you'd better leave, Mr. Whispr." The words emerged hard and unyielding from between her lips as she edged toward a particular console. "I'm starting to think maybe I might have made a mistake, Hippocratic oath or no oath. Consider yourself fortunate that I've helped you as much as I have. What happens to you now is none of my business and none of my concern—except that you're still here in my office. Get out, Mr. Whispr." One hand hovered over the contact plate that would summon an emergency surgical crew. They weren't the police, but their presence should be sufficient to forestall any trouble.

"Just 'Whispr.'" His whole body gave a despondent heave. Was he going to cry?

"Whatever. Leave, while you still can. If you can't accept that I can't and won't do anything more for you, appreciate that compared to most of the street folk who come in here you've already received more than your fair share of pro bono time and effort."

So that's it. His thought was mistaken, but the notion took hold and he clung to it desperately. *She wants to be paid.* His misperception was understandable. The lives of nearly everyone he had ever had dealings with in the course of his adult life invariably revolved one way or another around money. Specifically, the lack of it and how to rectify the deficiency.

Not that it mattered. He knew that the pittance he could access would not buy two minutes of this esteemed physician's time.

Except maybe . . .

Setting aside the clear envelope that held the threatening traktacs, he lifted one leg and began fumbling with his right shoe. "I can't pay you," he began timidly, "but maybe we can work a trade. I have something that I think—no, that I *know* must be worth a lot of money!"

Watching his trembling fingers fumble with the shoe as he struggled to maintain his balance, Ingrid truly felt sorry for him. But not sorry enough to lavish any more time on his problems. The more he scrabbled and groped at himself, trying to locate something inside the scruffy footwear, the more she felt he was relatively harmless. A glance at the time projection that drifted decoratively around the walls of the examination room just below the ceiling revealed that afternoon was marching ever remorselessly toward evening. Her homeward commute was vertical and short-lived, but still constituted precious off-time that he was wasting.

"I'm afraid I don't operate on a barter system, Mr. . . . . Whispr. It doesn't matter anyway. I'm a doctor, a general practitioner. Not a police tech. With the instruments I have here I *might* be able to deactivate the little locators

I extracted from your side, but circumstances and moral constraints dictate that I . . ."

She stopped in midsentence to gaze at what he had removed from a compartment concealed in the sole of the shoe. Her initial sight of it made her want to break out in sad, disparaging laughter. Reflexive closer examination of the capsule hinted at it—hinted at . . .

Within the transparent capsule lay a small bit of thread. To all outward appearances the thread was metallic in composition. One end terminated in a tiny but recognizable universal connector. The alloy of which the thread had been fashioned had a peculiar, distinctive cast. The way it caught the soft but bright light that suffused the examination room suggested something at once briefly glimpsed and familiar. As she stared at it the silvery mottling seemed to change and flow before her eyes. That was preposterous, of course.

More than anything else the thread's general appearance reminded her of the singular sheen on the advanced molecular-level biomechanical insert that she had removed from the follicularly melded pate of young Cara Gibson. With one significant difference. Unlike that supposedly quantum entangled nanoscale device, this one showed no sign of disappearing.

Could it be touched? Could it be handled and manipulated? Could it (most likely of all) be entirely unrelated to the mini mechanical mystery she had encountered earlier? Was she ascribing unknown potential to it out of yearning instead of common sense? And if it did possess anything other than the most superficial similarity to that baffling set of inlab conclusions that had been drawn from the Cara Gibson incident—how had it come to be in the possession of this downcast street person?

"May I—can I—see that?"

Whispr was instantly on guard. "You know what it is?"

"No. No, I don't. I don't have a clue. But I may—I may have once encountered something similar." Sensing his unease, she hastened to reassure him. "If you want to try and trade something so insignificant for my services, particularly for services not commonly rendered, I have to know whether what you're offering is worth anything, don't I? Surely you don't expect me to take your word for it that it's valuable?"

"N-n-no, I guess not." Reluctantly, he handed over the capsule. His willowy, sun-browned fingers covered her pale palm like a predatory crab dropping gently down atop an oyster. As she stared closely at the thread inside the capsule he watched her intently. "Did you mean to say that you've seen another thread *like* this one?"

"Not a thread, no. Something that might possibly be made of the same material, but smaller." She looked up at him. "Much, much smaller. It had kind of the same color and shine. I took it out of the back of a young girl's head. It was part of a bad meld."

Whispr frowned. "A bad meld? That's all?"

It made no sense. Why would the Greater Savannah authorities be so anxious and commit so much in the way of resources to recover something that had to do with a social function as common as melding? Unless maybe the thread contained the record of some really important individual's particular meld. Despite the vast range of modifications that were freely available to all, there were still such things as illegal melds. Maniping an arm into a gun, for example, was more than just frowned upon. You needed a special permit. Then there were melds that were socially frowned upon, many of them often of a bizarre sexual nature. And if the person who had undergone the illegal or perversion meld was famous . . .

Yes, it was starting to make a little sense. He still had no proof of anything, no facts, but at least now he had a theory. Gradually, his suspicion of the doctor's motives was becoming subsumed by his desperate desire to have some answers.

So excited was Ingrid at the discovery that the tiny item her strange visitor was offering to swap for her services might peripherally resemble the nanodevice she had removed from the teenage girl that it did not occur to her that due to the increasing lateness of the hour she was now alone with him not only in her office but in a large part of the medical complex as well. This Whispr person was not only her last pro bono patient of the day, he was her last patient of the week. Her receptionist had departed and the offices and medical suites with which she shared the tower floor were also rapidly emptying out. Of course building security, live as well as automated, was always available and on-call twenty-four hours a day. But still, if her visitor intended her harm it would take time to produce a response.

None of this intruded on her musings. Her thoughts were entirely on the metallic thread and any secrets it might hold—provided that it didn't vanish under her gaze. Understandably, her visitor was equally enthralled. Had she known more about his background, she might have worried.

They spoke little as she carefully removed the thread from its protective capsule, inserted it into an appropriate office inlab receptacle, and waited for the sophisticated medical analyzer to do its job. Eventually the lab's synthesized male voice announced the arrival of preliminary results. Ingrid did not hold her breath, but she was focused. Left to himself, Whispr let his gaze rove over the multiple readouts that had begun to appear on a monitor while simultaneously trying to make some sense of a series of scrolling projections floating between the doctor and a wall. Their meaning being as alien to him as Malagasy he was grateful for the accompanying synth voice even if he could only make sense of a little of what it was saying.

"MSMH." The inlab's AI spoke confidently. "Insofar as I am able to determine, this storage medium is composed largely of the same material that was found in the smaller and more complex sample that you earlier submitted for analysis. However, there are also significant differences."

Whispr's brow furrowed. "What's it talking about, an 'earlier' sample? Like that piece of a bad meld you mentioned?"

Ingrid ignored him, intent on the readouts and projections. "Specify the differences."

"One end of the thread appears to terminate in a simple connector common to a wide variety of commercially available storage devices. I believe it may fit one or more flex plugs located elsewhere in this office." Ingrid felt a little thrill of anticipation race through her at this revelation. *Patience*, she told herself. The inlab AI continued.

"Also, and most significantly, I can find no indication or evidence that this device is entangled. Though if such entanglement is among its inherent properties, it could conceivably vanish at any moment. Insofar as I can determine, however, it appears to be stable. If it is entanglement-reactive to simple observation, mine has not triggered such a feature."

Remarkable, Ingrid found herself thinking. Given its astonishing composition, the mere fact of the thread's enduring stable existence hinted at a knowledge of metallurgy beyond anything with which she was familiar. Not that it was a specialty of hers, but the use of a diversity of medical instruments carried with it a certain minimal knowledge of their makeup. The creation of stable MSMH might of itself make the thread incredibly valuable.

As to what it might have stored on it . . .

Interrupted by a querulous voice, she was startled to see that the patient had come up right behind her. She saw him before she heard him—a quality that might go some way, she realized, toward explaining her visitor's Meld name.

"I don't understand a lot of what your machine is saying." His tone was timid, his attitude challenging.

Trying not to show that his proximity was making her nervous, she edged away from the slender, looming presence. "Chiefly, it's saying that this thread is made from an unusual metal."

Whispr perked up. "A valuable one? I told you it was valuable."

"I didn't say it was valuable," she half lied. "I don't know much about metals." A delicate hand gestured toward the slot that held the thread. She was glad she didn't wear good jewelry to work. "I do know that if the lab analysis is right, this is an unusual material. Now we need to try and find out what's stored on it, if anything. Maybe if the container isn't valuable, the contents are."

"I already had friends try to find out," he told her. "They couldn't get at any contents."

She had to smile. "I don't know what kind of instrumentation your friends used, but the equipment in my office is pretty up-to-date. Some of it might be more advanced than anything your friends were using."

His eyes met hers before she could avoid them. "I hope so."

As she carefully extracted the thread from the study slot it struck her that this afternoon's ongoing activities had nothing to do with the practice of medicine and a great deal to do with activities she was aware of only from watching the news and casual entertainment. But curiosity continued to overcome apprehension. They had already established the extraordinary nature of the thread's composition. Suppose that was compounded by the discovery that it also held information of value or importance? What then? Among her friends and professional acquaintances she could count a considerable number of specialists, but "fence" was not one of them. Stealing another surreptitious glance at the man who had brought her the thread, she had no doubt that he would know exactly where to locate such a person.

What was she thinking? And what was she getting herself into? She had already taken one risk by treating him.

She ought to send him packing. Right now, this minute, before things grew any more complicated. She insisted to herself that she held back from doing so only out of scientific interest. She wanted to know what, if anything, was on the thread. More crucially, she *needed* to know in what way if any it might be related to the vanished nanodevice she had removed from Cara Gibson's head.

Conveying the thread to another part of the inlab, she started to insert the end featuring the connector into the nearest self-adapting flex receptacle—only to have it snatched from her fingers. Startled, she turned on her visitor. He was not just thin—his reflexes were lightning-fast.

"Wh—why'd you do that?"

His expression was impossible to read. "You want to know what's on this, don't you? To see if it's valuable?"

"So do you," she shot back accusingly.

"Utterso. But there's something even more important to me." Digging into a pocket with his other hand, he pulled out the envelope containing the extracted traktacs. "Do what we talked about first. Deactivate these. Then I'll let you try to access the thread." He taunted her with the transparent container full of seed-sized transmitters. "That was the deal."

She wasn't sitting at home on her couch munching popcorn and watching an entertainment vit, she told herself. She was participating in one. Like the rest of real life there was no fast forward and no rewind. She could continue, hit ERASE or . . .

"Give those to me." She extended a hand and tried to ignore his knowing smile.

Deactivation proved less difficult than she feared. The band the traktacs broadcast on was straightforward and easy to find. While she had never had occasion to perform such work herself, the requisite mechanical means were at hand—as they would be in the office of any recognized and bonded physician. It was just never used because such interference with official police instrumentation was . . .

She concentrated on the work.

Her AI handled the necessary programming. Once that was completed it was a matter of subjecting each tiny pellet to the appropriate modulation by the inlab's instrumentation. As each small but critical adjustment was completed she would pass the now harmless position locator back to the man from whose torso it had been removed.

When she handed over the last one he held up the glassine bag, carefully and slowly counted its contents, then pocketed it and looked back at her. For a brief moment he did not look either melancholy or forlorn. He looked dangerous. Maybe murderous dangerous. But the sensation passed quickly.

There are all kinds of entanglement, she thought. Including emotive ones. As a physician she had to cope with them every day—though they usually involved a patient's reactions and not her own.

"How do I know you did anything except put these under a bright light?" he asked her.

She slipped into her best doctor-knows-all mode. "You don't. You have only my word for it that, as a physician, I fulfilled my end of the bargain."

She could see him debating with himself. Then he smiled—tightly, showing no teeth as usual, and passed back the thread. Taking it, she exhaled softly. Until that moment she had not realized how afraid she was that he was going to take it and run. Or worse. She suspected he did not because he wanted, he *needed*, to know as much as she did what, if anything, lay stored within the hair-thin strand of outrageous silvery metal.

Returning again to the instrumentation best equipped to answer that question she started to push the end featuring the miniconnector into the self-adapting flex receptacle—and found herself hesitating. Whispr was watching her closely.

"What is it? What's wrong?" He indicated the waiting console. "Why aren't you trying to see if it will plug in?"

"I have reason to wonder whether or not the contents might be something illegal." She met his gaze without flinching. "Especially if it *does* turn out to be valuable."

Her visitor might occasionally be slow of speech but there was nothing sluggish about his mental faculties. They suggested someone who rather than being stupid took time and care to think before he spoke.

"What about the similar thing you said you took out of a girl's head? The thing that was part of a bad meld? Was it illegal?"

Now there was a notion deserving of contemplation. "I—I didn't actually give it much thought. It was just something peculiar that didn't belong. It was the strangeness of it that interested me. I never really considered whether it might be illicit or not. I just thought it was an atypical component of a bad job."

He nodded toward the thread she was holding. "Maybe that's all this is.

Strange and atypical doesn't mean illegal. It's enough for you to know that I got it from somebody who didn't need it anymore."

Clearly that was all the explanation she was going to get out of him. It would have to suffice—for now. "Another possibility, and one that's even more likely, is that it is of military origin."

That would explain a lot, Whispr realized. Not only the strange metal of which it was made but the exceptional effort the authorities had been expending to track him down. With a start he realized that the unusual amount of resources which had been deployed in that effort might have nothing to do with the fact that he had been involved in a robbery gone wrong but instead were directed solely toward recovery of the storage thread. The police, the government, might not be interested in him at all. In which case by returning the thread—anonymously, of course—the heavy pursuit might be called off. Return the thread now and he might be able to strike a deal.

She was still holding it between two fingers. He could easily snatch it away from her and bolt from the office. But no matter who was looking for it and no matter how important it might be, he remained tantalized by the potential it represented. He knew he wouldn't be able to decide which way to jump until he found out what was on it.

As usual, greed overpowered common sense.

"Why are you looking at me like that?" Taking a guarded step backward, she noted uncomfortably that he was standing between her and the exit from the inlab.

"Sorry. I get lost in my own thoughts a lot." He made himself smile. "Sometimes I have a hard time finding my way back. A friend once told me it's a side effect from taking too many cheap meld drugs."

The regret with which he spoke left her staring blankly for a moment. Then she reacted, with a smile of her own. It faded quickly as she returned her attention to the thread.

"You understand that if this *is* military and my equipment here does succeed in accessing the thread's contents, the act of doing so might well set off an alarm ten times stronger than any traktac and send out a locator broadcast of its own?"

He had already come to the same conclusion. As well as another. If he snatched back the thread and fled, he would have to start all over again trying to find someone with access to instrumentation capable of penetrating its secrets. Mentally, he flipped a coin.

"Plug it in," he said with conviction. "Let's see what happens."

Expressing satisfaction she turned away from him. With the dexterity of an accomplished physician she slid the thread connector first into the open flex receptacle. Immediately above it and as soon as contact was made, a telltale on the console flared to life.

10

Regrettably, the light was red. Frowning as she leaned toward the console, Ingrid murmured a succession of commands. Intermittently, the telltale would go out. On the occasions when it came back on, it was always the same disheartening color.

Whispr stood it as long as he could. "What's happening?"

Intent on fine-tuning the instrumentation she barely glanced in his direction. "We have a connection, but my inlab isn't reading any contents."

"You mean the thread is vacant?" That didn't make any sense, he thought. Why would anyone go to so much trouble to conceal an empty storage device?

"It's not that," she told him. "I can't tell if it's empty or full to the last byte. What I am telling you is that my equipment can't read this medium, whatever it is."

"How can you have a connection but not even be able to tell if there's anything held in the volume?"

Stepping back from the console, a frustrated Ingrid gestured at it. "You don't believe me? *You* ask it. I turned off the coding—it'll respond to anybody's voice."

Accepting the challenge Whispr stepped forward and began mouthing commands at the console. It replied immediately, politely, and with the same blanket declamations of negativity that had greeted the doctor's more precisely phrased inquiries.

"Maybe a more advanced reader . . . ," he mumbled unhappily.

"Perhaps. But as I told you, the electronics in my office are very up-to-date. They have to be, in order to keep up with the latest medical data. Furthermore, in addition to the public box the technical specs of my inlab are tied into all the other private ones in this building, including the hospital's. We all share information and analytical capabilities. Everything except patient and associated privileged information." She looked back at the flex receptacle.

"I agree with you that if we have a valid connection the equipment should at least be able to tell us if there's anything stored on the medium. That it cannot suggests that it contains proprietary coding as advanced as the composition of the device itself."

Whispr prided himself on his ability to see the world around him realistically. Among other things that meant being able to admit when you had reached the limit of your personal knowledge. So he was able to confess ignorance without shame.

"Don't feel bad," she heard herself saying. "I'm not sure what to do next, either. There are more powerful readers and other instruments that can probably tell what's inside this thing."

"Then let's use them."

Her hesitation was conspicuous. "I think if this storage device was mine, I'd want to study it some more before I would risk that. For example, subjecting it to scrutinizing radiation could bypass the coding—but it might also destroy or damage whatever is stored on it. Before I'd go deep-probe I'd want to try and get inside using less invasive technology. I propose that—"

Her suggestions were interrupted. Not by her visitor but by a chirp from the console. Leaving Whispr to wonder what was happening, she turned quickly to the readouts.

"We've got a response," she finally informed him. Her eyes flicked over the information that had suddenly and unexpectedly appeared on the main monitor. "It's putting out a signal. Very weak, bordering on the undetectable. And it's got to be powered by the tiniest battery I've ever encountered." Looking back at him, she tried to be reassuring. "I doubt it's summoning the police, if that's what you're worrying about. Its strength is much too weak. I imagine that anything capable of picking it up would have to be exceptionally sensitive and specifically attuned to listen for it. Unless this is an example of still another technology that's new and incomprehensible and previously unencountered."

Military. More and more that was looking like the most likely explanation for the thread's impossible composition and cryptic content.

Whispr tried to wrap his mind around something else that made no sense. "How can something that small and thin be putting out *any* kind of signal? Seems to me the whole thread would have to be devoted to power generation and that wouldn't leave any room for information storage or anything else."

She shrugged helplessly. "I have no idea, Whispr. Maybe it can change physical states, from storage to transmitter power. Between this and the encounter I had with the device I removed from that girl's head I'm starting to think that someone, somewhere, is doing a little real-life rewriting of the physics textbooks."

"Is it directional? The signal, I mean."

She eyed him in surprise. "I can't figure out if you're knowledge-challenged or just knowledge-specific."

He smiled diffidently. "Actually, I'm stupid, but I do know a few things."

She turned back to the console readouts. Nothing to trace there. Her shoulders slumped.

Whispr could see that investigation-wise the doctor was at a dead end. Not one to linger in an atmosphere of unproductive circumstance, he started toward the instrumentation.

"I guess this is as much as I'm going to learn in your office. Thanks again for all your help, medicinal and otherwise. I promised you payment if you deactivated the traktacs. I keep my word, Ms. Doc. As soon as I find someone willing to buy that thing, whatever it is and regardless of whether it can be read or not, I promise that I'll pay you—something." He reached for the flex receptacle.

Her palm came down on a contact nearby. A sheet of hard transparency slid down to cover the opening to the receptacle. Grimacing,

Whispr put a fingertip on the covering and tried to push it back up. It didn't budge. She withdrew her hand from the contact and backed up as he reached toward it. No matter how hard or how many times he pressed it, the receptacle's protective cover remained in place.

Coded, he told himself. Matched to a command or to her handprint. Either way, he knew he could eventually break in and get the contact to work. He was good at breaking into things. But he was curious.

"Why'd you do that? Your equipment can't read the thread. It's no good to you."

"Or to you." As she replied, she heard a tiny voice in her head shouting. *What do you think you're doing? You're all alone here, everyone else has probably gone home, this guy isn't big but he's strong and desperate, and you're confronting him over—what? The unknown?*

Employing much harsher and less politely acceptable silent musings, Whispr was wondering much the same.

"You can't stop me getting it back. It's my property. I'll find something. I can use a chair, if I have to. I'll break it open."

It struck her abruptly and unexpectedly that a single trailing letter constituted the only difference between thread and threat. Banishing the less than noteworthy insight from her thoughts, she surprised herself by continuing to refuse to buckle to the demand of her taller, probably stronger visitor.

"I mean it when I say that I don't know if there's anything on that thread. But I feel that after everything I've done for you that I now have an equal right to know if there is. I've helped you twice now. You say you'll pay me. I have no guarantee of that." She indicated the receptacle. "You can pay me with knowledge. More fulfilling to me, cheaper for you. And there is this similarity of manufacture between the thread and the device I removed from the girl's head. It's important to me to understand and to resolve that. It's a matter of medical knowledge."

"I might trust you more if I could see that 'device' you keep talking about." Whispr held his ground. "Where is it?"

"Elsewhere." She improvised hurriedly. "It's not currently accessible. It doesn't matter. I have records of it that I can utilize for direct comparison. There's no need for you to concern yourself with its location." It was her turn to eye the receptacle. "I want to know what, if anything, is on that thread. You want to know what, if anything, it's worth. If we continue to work together we can achieve mutually beneficial and nonconflicting aims."

"'Work togeth . . .'" He gaped at her. The woman staring back at him was smart, she was a successful nonmeld physician, she was pretty—she might as well be from a different universe. He shook his head slowly but forcefully. "I just finished 'working together' with an old friend. Now he's dead. Partly because we worked together. Doesn't that scare you?"

She swallowed. "Yes. Yes, it scares me." Having taken the first step off the precipice she found herself continuing to plunge helplessly. "But I don't care. I've only ever seen one other thing like that thread, and neither of them make any sense. I don't know for sure how much yours might be worth, but a part of me won't rest until I understand one or both of them better than I do now. I'll try to explain this to you, Whispr—I don't have any choice in the matter. Now that I've seen them, I *have* to understand them." She paused and stared hard at him. "It's called 'science.'"

Whispr reflected that to someone like himself and to most of his friends, such an attitude would be called "senseless," but he kept the thought to himself. "Supposing for the moment that I might consider going along with something like this—why should I?"

She thought fast. "You don't have access to the kind of expensive, specialized scientific equipment that I can call upon in the name of 'research.' I don't have access to the kind of, uh, specialized resources that you do. We each have detailed knowledge in our respective—fields. Maybe I can figure out the secrets of this storage medium without you. Maybe you'd eventually be able to do the same without me. But there's no guarantee of either one working, and we have a much better chance of learning what we want to know if we pool our resources."

He shook his head in disbelief. "I wouldn't have figured you for someone who would take a chance on someone like me."

"Neither would I," she responded unapologetically, "until just now." She nodded toward the sealed receptacle. "The thread, it changes everything."

"That's your opinion. I still think I can solve it without you. And when I do, I'll keep my promise to pay you." He started again toward the console, looking around for something heavy with which to shatter the protective transparency that now covered the plug-in.

Her thoughts raced. She knew she couldn't deny him physically. Anyway, if she tried to do so she might end up losing more than just an opportunity.

"I can also help you to hide from the authorities."

That gave him pause. Even absent the matter of the mystifying thread, it would have given him pause.

She rushed on. "Just because you're rid of the traktacs doesn't mean they won't run you to ground tomorrow. If everything you've told me is true they'll still be hunting you because they want the thread back."

He nodded slowly. "That's—right. What exactly did you have in mind?"

I don't have anything in mind, she told herself a bit hysterically, *because I'm sure by now that I must have lost it.*

"I'll—I'll hide you. I have a big codo. There's plenty of room. While we try to solve the thread you—you can stay with me."

There, she thought. Four successive terse statements; all true, half of which marked her as self-designatedly certifiable.

"No one will even think to look for you in a private residence, much less in my place."

"You're kidding," he shot back. "You're just trying to stall me until you can think of something else. Or call the police."

"I swear it—Whispr. You can live in my place. Until we unravel the insides of that thread." Seeing that he remained doubtful she tried to think of a rationale that would appeal to him on his own terms. "Besides, your promise to pay me will mean a lot more if I can keep an eye on you and the relevant property."

"I'll be damned." A hand featuring heavily weathered, impossibly slender fingers stretched out toward her. "You've got a deal, Ms. Doc. And to show you that I mean to keep my part of the bargain I promise not to kill you in your sleep."

As she shook his hand, feeling the coiled strength in the serpentine digits, her responding smile was twisted. "I'm relieved to hear it, Whispr." She let go of his hand and the fingers slid away from her flesh like so many snakes slithering back into their den. Dividing her attention, she walked back over to the console that was now dominated by the shuttered receptacle.

While he watched her work the instrumentation, he admired the play of muscles and other things beneath her clothing. She was moderately fit, but he wouldn't have called her athletic.

"You have my label," he murmured softly. "What shall I call you? You're a Natural, so you don't have a Meld moniker. I can't keep calling you 'Ms. Doc.' What's your first name?"

Concentrating on reopening the receptacle, she barely glanced in his direction. "Why don't you just call me 'doc'?" Not wanting to irritate him this early in their new business relationship, she added, "Until we get to know each other better."

He was disappointed, but accepting. "All right—doc. Only problem with that is it makes me think of some old guy with a long beard wearing a white coat. You got the white coat but you don't look anything like an old guy with a long beard."

"I can see that you could've made your way through life on flattery alone," she replied absently. "*There.*" The protective panel slid back to reveal the silvery thread. Plucking it carefully from the flex plug receptacle, she slid it back into its protective capsule. A quick check of another instrument revealed that the device was still generating its minuscule emission. To what end and for what purpose remained as much a mystery as its composition and contents.

Feeble as the output was, perhaps the device was some kind of limited-range homing signal, she mused. If that was the case then she might have the opportunity to learn the nature of the thread's contents from its owners themselves. At which point, if such a get-together eventuated, it might be reassuring to have someone of Mr. Whispr's idiosyncratic talents present.

When he started to reach for the capsule she instinctively dropped it down the front of her camisole. The instant she did so she grasped that this might not be the most rational response to his reaching. The realization that where such an action would give someone like Rajeev pause, it might mean less than nothing to her visitor. Her breath caught in her throat for just an instant, until he smiled and shrugged.

"If you want to hang on to the collateral, that's okay with me." His voice was devoid of worry. "Now that we've come to an agreement I know you're not going to run out on me." He smiled, and it was a genuine smile this time. "I know where you live. Or I will, as soon as we get there." He looked toward the doorway. "How many k's to your place?"

"Less than one," she told him. "All of it vertical."

. . .

WHISPR WAS NOT AWED by her dwelling, but he was quietly impressed. In company with Jiminy and others he had stolen from more elaborate surroundings. Possibly it was the sheer tidiness of the place. It was as clean and orderly as his unmemorable succession of habitats had been grubby and chaotic.

Not unlike his life, he thought.

She showed him the spare bathroom, which was indeed spare but positively luxurious compared to where he had recently performed his hygienic ablutions. The compact eating area featured a self-cleaning cooker and plates made out of material more solid than cellulose derivatives. He could dine when and as he chose, Ingrid told him.

If she had known how little time he'd had during the preceding several days to pause and eat, she would not have been surprised at the ravenousness with which he proceeded to consume an imposing quantity of food.

He apologized afterward as he lay slumped on the big U-shaped couch in the common area. "I don't eat like this all the time."

"Only when you're running from the authorities?" she challenged him.

"No," he countered without rancor. "There are times when I don't have enough money to pay for food. When it's on offer I tend to eat everything in sight."

She slowly looked him up and down. "At least you'll never have to worry about going on a diet."

"Wouldn't want to." He patted his nonexistent stomach. "Inherited genetic predisposition as well as physical manip. This is what I opted to be. This is what I *wanted* to look like."

She considered. "Mind if I ask you why?"

His reply was unexpectedly terse. "Yes. I do mind."

That was the one and only time she queried him about his chosen meld.

While she dove into the global box the following day to try to learn everything she could about MSMH, he spent the hours wallowing in utter luxury. His only regret was that there were fewer of them (the hours, that is), because he did not awaken until some time after noon. It was the longest period of continuous sleep he had allowed himself in a very long time. Safe and secure in her upper-level codo, in an upscale secured building, he was able to close his eyes in peace and shut down the auto-matic reflexes that he normally engaged to wake him at the slightest sound. Such reflexes were vital to ensuring survival on the street, where anyone at any time might slit your throat for your money. Or your shoes. While discovering that you had no money might prompt regret on the part of your murderer, it was better to avoid such possible post-homicidal mis-givings by not getting yourself killed in the first place.

At his initially hesitant but increasingly confident command, the cooker in the trim and efficient kitchen area dispensed real bacon (not soy) and real eggs (not self-coagulating flavored albumin), together with real coffee, real sugar, real . . .

It had been so long since he had tasted real anything that the flavors were almost new to him. His shocked taste buds and overwhelmed diges-tive system both threatened rebellion. It was one uprising he put down ruthlessly, as the most difficult part of the meal proved to be keeping it down afterward. Unused to bona fide food, the risk of losing it via violent upchucking was all too real. He solved the problem by distracting himself with the entertainment system in the living area. When he activated the vit, the floor-to-ceiling windows darkened commensurately, threatening to send him off to dreamland all over again.

As he ate and relaxed, his host ignored him. Seated at her home station Ingrid recited a steady stream of vorec commands to speed-whip through readouts and dimensional projections faster than he would have been able to read one. Occasionally he would look up from the ambient enter-tainment and its cone of constrained sound to peer across the room at her. Above her station he caught glimpses of rapidly merging sentences underlying swiftly flowing imagery. Multisyllabic expressions, technical terms, incomprehensible lexi accompanied diagrams and schematics as alien to his experience as the construction plans for spacecraft.

Leaving the entertainment projector running, he stepped beyond the boundaries of its focused sights and sounds and wandered across the room until he was standing behind her. A glance showed that the capsule con-taining the inscrutable thread lay on the small desk near her right arm. He could easily have grabbed, whirled, and fled from the codo. He did not. In-stead, he waved at the colorful scientific projections and readouts.

"What is all this?"

She spoke without looking up. "We don't know what's on the thread, but unless my inlab's gone completely haywire we do know what it's made of. I'm trying to find out what company or government might have made a recent breakthrough in metallurgical research or the relevant high-pressure physics or both that would enable them to manufacture something like this."

He nodded to himself. What she was presently doing he could not do. Not only was he unable to comprehend the information that was being mustered, he did not have the background, the knowledge, or the where-withal to call it up in the first place.

As he stood and watched, his attention slowly shifted from the gush of incomprehensible data to the technical sorceress who was summoning it forth. She was wearing a loose-fitting one-piece lounger of some pale yellow airfleece material. Her new blond haircut was short and severe (the time and resources Naturals devoted to physically manipulating follicles never ceased to dumbfound Melds). What was visible of her body beneath the airfleece was anything but severe. He wondered why she wasn't partnered. He did not know her well enough to ask. So instead of asking, he leaned forward and kissed her lightly on the back of her neck, his lips just brushing the short hairs there.

She whirled as if she had been shot. Her expression was such a clashing jumble of surprise, terror, and uncertainty that he almost burst out laughing.

"Don't . . . ! What do you think you're doing?"

For once he did not need an interpreter for her words. "I kissed you."

"I know what you did." She had backed as far away from him as the chair at the box station allowed. "Why did you do it?"

Simultaneously smart and stupid, he told himself. Typical of her kind.

"To see how you would respond. Did you like it?"

She wiped furiously at the back of her neck, as if someone had spilled hot soup on her skin. "No, I didn't like it, Whispr. And if you do anything like it again, if you even *look* like you're going to do something like it again, our business relationship will be terminated forthwith!"

His expression excessively somber, he nodded slowly, gently mocking her without words. "Okay. Got it. I regard myself as suitably chastised. If you're so outraged, how come you didn't hit out at me?"

"I'm sitting down. I can't reach you." She started to get up. "If you'll just stay there, I'll rectify the oversight."

Raising his hands defensively, he backed away. "All right, all right. Take it easy, mind-muffin. I promise I won't touch you again." He nodded in the direction of the thread. "Where I've come up from, money trumps sex every time."

"*Sex?*" She found herself sputtering. The idea that this slow-witted vagrant, this street-scum, this stick-insect of a Meldman would even *entertain* such thoughts . . . would conjure such imagery . . .

For a moment she thought she was going to be physically ill.

"Calm down." By now he was more annoyed than offended. "Can't blame a guy for trying."

"Next time you 'try,' I'll shoot you. With whatever is at hand." She was actually shaking. Not violently, but enough to get the point across. "Can't blame woman for blowing your fool head off."

Turning with a sigh, he returned to the far side of the room to once again immerse himself in the entertainment cone. Regaining control of herself Ingrid returned to her work. It took several attempts with her unsettled voice before the vorec recognized and acknowledged her commands and resumed the research she had been pursuing. Occasionally she thought she sensed a presence and would jerk around sharply to look behind her. On each occasion she saw nothing. Insofar as she could tell, the only time her guest stepped out of the entertainment cone was to get something to drink from the refrig.

Gradually she allowed herself to relax enough to slip back into deep study mode. By early evening the cavalier imposition of earlier that afternoon had begun to diminish in memory and importance. Only rarely did it intrude on her concentration or interrupt her train of thought.

Mind-muffin . . . ?

ONE CORNER OF THE LIVING area floor inflated to form a guest bed that was only temporary, but it was worlds away from the assorted platforms on which Whispr usually slept. Long after his host and erstwhile business partner had retired for the night he lay awake on the cushiony surface, unable to fall asleep because of the unaccustomed softness and silence. The nocturnal view from the eighty-fifth floor revealed a whole new world: the glistening spires of Greater Savannah and the electric suburbs that stretched off in all directions. To the west he could make out the vast floating commercial hub of the port and even the pair of thousand-meter-long cargo ships that were moored there, their towering carbon-fiber masts aglitter with running lights.

This was truly another world, he concluded. Another planet. In the bedroom off to his left slept a woman who was not only smarter than him, more attractive, a Natural, and cleaner, but one so determined to find answers to complicated questions that she would invite someone like himself to spend the night in the same habitation as her. An admirable and potentially useful acquaintance was Dr. Ingrid Seastrom. What he had told her earlier when she had so forcefully rejected his clumsy advance was true, but to Whispr such unattainability only enhanced her allure.

As sure as blood flowed through his veins, the door to her bedroom would be locked. She might even have armed herself, though he doubted she owned a deadly weapon. Her type would be much more likely to have a nonlethal protective device. A vomitizer, perhaps, or something that would spew blinding lenscoat.

He smiled to himself. If she thought any kind of internal door lock could keep out someone with his experience, she was only fooling herself. Once in the bedroom, surprising her while she was asleep, he could easily force himself on her. He pictured the many ways she might respond to such an intrusion, knowing as he did so that the various scenarios spinning through his mind were little more than sheer fantasy. More likely, the act of simply entering her sleeping quarters unannounced would put an immediate end to their recently established business connection. It was vital to maintain that relationship—at least for now.

Relationship? Had their association advanced far enough for him to legitimately employ that terminology? Even on a solely commercial basis? It smacked of an intimacy that existed only in his addled imagination.

He wanted her.

Denying the desire that coursed through him would have demanded self-deception. He had made an advance and been harshly rebuffed. More importantly than wanting her physically, he needed her intellectually. One did not have such problems with the box, which was sexless unless programmed to be otherwise.

As he lay on the bed pondering the much too rapid and far too extreme changes that had overtaken his life in the course of the past week, city lights and inner longing conspired to keep him awake until well into morning. Only then did the exhausting events of the previous couple of days finally connive sufficiently to render him unconscious.

11

"I'm going to have to show the thread to Dr. Sverdlosk. He'll want to take his own readings in order to run his own programs and analysis."

Bestirring himself, Whispr slid his legs off the inflatable bed. Might as well get up, he told himself. His coffitte had already turned tepid and was in need of a recharge. It was amazing how quickly one could get used to the finer things of life.

"You're not going to leave it with him?"

"No." Fully dressed and ready to go out, Ingrid had stopped by the half-open front door to look back at him. "I'll be right beside him while he takes his measurements and I won't let it out of my sight. I don't think there'll be any problem."

Whispr still wasn't happy. "Sure you can trust this boffin?"

Ingrid tut-tutted. "That paranoia of yours again. I've known Rudy ever since I took up both personal and professional residence in this building. He's one of my closest friends and a dear colleague. Honest, dependable, wide-ranging in his interests, generous with advice, and something of a mentor."

"Sounds like the perfect boyfriend." Whispr couldn't quite keep the sneer out of his voice.

While the memory of his earlier unwelcome advance had begun to fade, a certain frisson of tension still scented the codo like spoiled cheese. She was grateful for the chance to make light of it.

"Rudy? He's seventy-something. A little too old for me."

Whispr brightened immediately. "As opposed to me?"

"Natural or Meld, you're too skinny," she shot back. "Also too forward, too rough around the edges, too unstable, too—"

He cut her off. "Too much. I get the picture." He raised his self-heating glass in sardonic salute. "I guess I'll have to satisfy myself with reloaded coffittes."

"Don't overdo it. Someone as naturally jumpy as you doesn't need to add caffeine." The codo's front door slid all the way aside and she started out. "I've put a hinder on one half of the drink dispenser. No alcohol or other stimulants."

He shrugged. "I don't indulge as much as you seem to think. I've seen too many friends lose their lives at the same time as their inhibitions." He offered a casual wave as she departed.

Then he spent the next hour fruitlessly trying to rescind the block she had placed on the kitchen dispenser.

SVERDLOSK HAD AGREED TO MEET her in his offices during their mutual lunch hour. Although the enigmatic thread was not far from her thoughts she still had to deal with her regular clientele as well as new patients and referrals. Her preoccupation was apparent to staff and friends alike.

"You are distracted, *dyevooshka*." Sverdlosk's eyes twinkled beneath brows bushy as rainforest caterpillars. With the crinkled skin beneath his eyes, full mane of white hair, and perfectly trimmed short white beard, he looked like a secondary character from a Chekov play. In fact, he looked much like the playwright himself would have looked had he lived to such a respectable age. There was nothing grandfatherly about his manner, however. Certain men are forever thirty—if only in their minds.

"You have no idea." As she replied she was reaching into the secured pocket over her left breast. Reading her finger, the flap unsealed and allowed her to remove the small clear capsule that had been secreted within. Without the slightest compunction she handed it to the senior physician.

Whispr's wariness may have infected her, but so far she was free of his frightful paranoia.

Sverdlosk pushed out his lower lip, eyed her questioningly, and then turned his attention to the capsule's contents, rolling the transparent cylinder back and forth between his fingers. At a touch, magnifier lenses flipped down over his eyes. A Meld in his position would have undergone and employed an artificial vision enhancement. In lieu of that and like Seastrom, the physician had to rely instead on traditional medical tools.

"So? I see a little silvery thread with what I suppose is connector on one end. Some kind of storage appliance?"

Ingrid nodded. "I think so. A standard flex plug-in accepts it, but nothing in my office or codo can read it—or even tell me if there's anything on it." She readied herself. "Then there's the matter of its composition. *That* I do know."

White brows drew together slightly. "Maybe storage medium is an electrophoretic geloid. That's a new technology not every reader can access. What about the composition?"

She stared evenly at him. "I've checked it several times. It appears to be some kind of metastable metallic hydrogen."

This time the heavy white brows threatened to merge. The senior physician gazed anew at the capsule's contents. "It cannot be 'some kind' of metastable metallic hydrogen. Is either MSMH or is not. I will surely find out." He looked up at her. "If it were anyone else save a close friend of mine telling me this, I would say that my time was being wasted with joke."

Ingrid rose from her chair. "It's no joke, Rudy. Run your own tests. I'm sure you will anyway. What I need to know is what, if anything, is stored on that thread." She paused, then hurried on. "I have reason to think it might be worth a lot of money."

"Knowledge is its own reward." The physician replied without hesitation. "But money is nice supplement. Now you have me very interested even if is nothing on thread. But if material is anything like what you hilariously claim it to be . . ." The eyes twinkled again. "For such a friend and colleague with such a fine mind behind the find and also fine behind I will do this at no charge. Give me couple of days."

She nodded. "I've got to get back to my office. Rudy—swear you won't discuss this with anyone else. Not even with other close friends, not with anyone."

"Oh? And why not?"

She chewed her lower lip. "I have reason to believe there are other people who think that whatever is on that thread is valuable. Some of them might not be—nice."

He chuckled. "So! Is big secret. Okay, Inny-grid. I tell no one." He held the capsule up to the light and squinted at the contents. "What is tucked inside you, little hair of the impossible metallic hydrogen dog? What could make you so valuable as to so worry Ms. Inny? Scientific secrets? Wonders of the universe? Politicians' affairs with maybe names and dates and favorite fetishes? Dr. Rudolf will winkle them out of you." Lowering his gaze, he grinned through his beard at the waiting Ingrid. "End of the week at latest, I will have something to tell you."

"You seem very sure of yourself, Rudy."

He sat back in his chair, an elegant portrait of false modesty. "If I were not, I might like some of my less so-sure of themselves colleagues sometimes lose a patient. I never lose a patient. I will call you when I have something."

She nodded. "Use my emergency line if you have to." As she turned and went out, the door to the Russian émigré's inner office slid silently shut behind her.

Rudolf Sverdlosk brought the capsule close to his eyes and regarded it through the magnifiers. It did not look in any way remarkable. It most certainly did not look like something that had been contrived from a material that ought not even to exist under the normal temperature and pressure present in his office. Or anywhere else on the surface of the Earth, for that matter. Was it a hoax? Among the physicians who worked in the medical tower Ingrid Seastrom was known for her expertise in several areas, but practical jokery was not one of them. The more he thought about what she had told him, the longer he contemplated the thread within the capsule, the greater grew the urge to begin submitting it to tests and challenges. He quietly hummed a nearly forgotten Urals folk song.

Patients to see first, he told himself. Fun time after.

His intent was to subject the thread to a preliminary test or two at the end of the workday, and if anything worth pursuing turned up, to resume the examination in more detail the following afternoon. But the enigmatic material would not let go of his imagination.

It was after ten when exhaustion and eyestrain finally drove him from his otherwise empty offices and out into the sultry night. He sought succor and a change of scenery in a favorite neighborhood all-night café. His head was throbbing from the strain of trying to make sense of the thread while his mind whirled with possibilities. Though it was muggy on the street outside, like any good scientist lost in contemplation he was essentially immune to the weather.

He was not, however, immune to the attentions of his fellow citizens.

The café he frequented often enough for the waitresses to know what he wanted without him having to order it lay around one more corner. He was about to turn it when the pallid wall light that illuminated the sidewalk was partially blocked by three women. Two were Melds. One, a straightforward cosmetimax Meld, had chosen to adopt the striking blond appearance of an ancient cinema actress named Monroe. In contrast, her slender companion stood over two meters tall and reflected extensive internal melds. Sverdlosk saw that the bones of her arms and legs had been replaced with one of the more popular sinuousity condrites. As a consequence, her arms and legs were stiff enough to support her weight in spite of having been rendered nearly as supple as tentacles. Her ears tapered to points that accented the bony crest of her skull. Both sides of the latter were lavishly inlaid with intense phosphorescent tattoos.

In contrast, the Natural who stepped forward to confront him was as plump and homey-looking as a middle-aged pitchwoman for homemade pies. At least, she was until she opened her mouth. Though deep and husky, her voice was calculatedly feminine. She put him in mind of a career bureaucrat who might have an interesting secret life. She also favored candor over good manners.

"Dr. Rudolf Sverdlosk? Our monitoring of certain recent scientific inquiries suggest that a piece of private property we've been trying to recover might recently have passed into your possession. If that's so, we need to know what you've learned about it. If it's not so, we need to find out why our monitoring has singled you out as someone worthy of questioning."

The Russian responded with the practiced smile that invariably reassured patients and regularly intrigued women much younger than himself.

"Yes, it is sticky out tonight, isn't it?" He gestured past the pair whose appearance was no more outré than that of numerous other melded Savannahians out for a misty nighttime stroll. "I am on my way to get something to drink and maybe a little chocolate piroshka. If you want to talk, is much nicer to talk over black tea and—"

She hit him. In the face, and much harder than he could have anticipated. As he collapsed onto the sidewalk a detached part of him dispassionately analyzed the blow and came to the conclusion that appearances notwithstanding, she was not a Natural. Unlike her companions, she only looked Natural. How otherwise to explain being struck by what felt like a fist of solid steel than to recognize that he *had* been struck by a fist fashioned of solid steel? Or by something equally dense and unyielding beneath the perfectly realistic skin?

His systematic analysis was confirmed when the woman knelt to grab the front of his jacket and yank him toward her. Sinuous Meld wrapped her unnaturally supple arms around his torso and pinned his arms at his sides. Ancient cinema actress Meld was aiming a weapon at him while chewing on something crunchy that stank of lavender. The taste of salt was strong in his mouth. His probing tongue located the socket of the tooth that had been knocked out. He coughed, spitting blood.

"So. Not tea-drinkers, then."

The plump woman's Meld was not perfect. Or perhaps it was merely worn and in need of an upgrade. When she knelt before him, still gripping the front of his shirt, her metal patellas made squeaking sounds as they rasped against hidden internal cables.

"Listen close, doctor. My friends and I are not out here wandering the streets in search of relaxation. We are on a job. We are working. You will answer my questions promptly because we do not like to waste time. Also because if you try to evade them or stall us we will have to jog your memory by every so often removing parts of your body." Her eyes gave him a quick once-over. "You are a Natural. Losing body parts would be unpleasant.

"You are maybe studying an unusual piece of metal. You have maybe learned something about it. All we want to know is what you have learned. Anything you might have found out. Something you might suspect. We believe that it may recently have been given into your care by someone else. What we do not know for a certainty is if it is still in your possession or how much time you have had to spend examining it. We believe it to be worth a great deal, but there is much we still have to confirm." Letting go of his shirt, she stepped back to gaze unblinkingly down at him. "Tell us, doctor. What do you know?"

He swallowed salty stickiness. "I know that I need drink of something stronger than tea."

The woman did not smile as she turned to her companions. "I think sometimes old men are braver than the young ones because they feel they have already lived their lives and are going to die soon anyway." She nodded at sinuous Meld. "Spread his legs."

While still restraining his arms, the tall Meld's lengthy limbs reached downward to wrench Sverdlosk's thighs apart. He tried to resist, feebly.

Pausing a moment to make certain that he was watching, the plump woman kicked off her shoes. Then she lifted her right leg high off the ground and slammed it back down. The steel heel slammed into the sidewalk, leaving a cup-shaped dent several centimeters deep. Her attention returned to him.

"Maybe a certain part of your life is over already for you. Maybe not. Maybe you are a self-confessed celibate. Talk now, or I will resolve any ambiguity regarding this matter."

Cinema star Meld suddenly looked past them all and her eyes widened slightly. "Floater!"

"*Sewap!*" The deceptively homey interrogator looked up sharply, favored the wheezing Sverdlosk with a last quick, murderous glance, then whirled and raced off around the corner the doctor had nearly succeeded in reaching. The two Melds who accompanied her had to work hard to keep up.

For all its synthesized solicitousness, the police floater that dropped down beside the still seated Sverdlosk was as welcome a sight to the injured doctor as an Orthodox archangel.

"You are hurt, sir. The perpetrators have fled. I will summon medical assistance."

Sverdlosk struggled to stand, only to fall backward and hit his head on the sidewalk. The strobing lights that straightaway speckled his vision distracted him somewhat from the throbbing pain in his mouth and jaw. "I don't need medical assistance. I'm a doctor."

They were the last words he managed to utter before he passed out.

. . .

"WAKE UP, INGRID. SOMEONE needs to talk to you. Wake up, Ingrid. Someone needs to talk to you. Wake up, Ingrid, someone . . ."

"I'm awake," she mumbled as she rolled over in the bed. Whoever was trying to contact her through her secure number, she knew it was not her shady guest. Her bedroom door was locked and had he somehow managed to circumvent the privacy code, she would have heard his voice and not that of her codo.

The mildly sexy talking portrait of a favorite dramat star retreated from where it had been hovering above the foot of her bed. As it did so it melted into a similarly sized likeness of her friend and mentor Dr. Sverdlosk. His image was not that of a dramat star. The shock of it smacked her in the face like a bucket of chipped ice and caused her to sit up fast.

"Rudy . . . my God, what *happened* to you?"

"Three nightmares happened to me." Sverdlosk's lips moved only enough to form words, relying on the communicator's amplification ware to render them audible. "All of them female. At least, I am pretty sure they were all female. They didn't boast about it."

"Where are you?" She slid her legs out of the bed and activated the caffeiner. Continuously tracking her eye movements the room's comm unit adjusted the doctor's image so that it stayed in front of her. "Are you in your office? I'm coming right down."

"No you are not, Inny." Despite his unmistakable frailty his tone was firm. "I not in my office. Thanks to recent ingestion of very pleasantly enervating cocktail of designer pharmaceuticals I am actually at present resting a number of floors farther down. Level Four, to be exact."

She felt more than a little insensate herself. "You're in the hospital."

"To be exact, yes," he acknowledged. "I am afraid I currently too anesthetized to fully appreciate irony of situation. Or the location." As his head came slightly off the aerogel pillow that was supporting it his tone grew more intense. "Listen to me, Inny. These female but decidedly unfeminine Melds who confront me last night—they know about the thread that you gave me to research. They wanted to know if I had learned anything about it."

Reaching for the ready cup of instant caffeine Ingrid nearly knocked it out of its bracket. "What did you tell them?"

"I tried joke with them. Maybe when they receive their melds they also inoculated against irony. Notice I still not laughing myself. Doctor's orders. No muscle spasms, not even to laugh.

"Smart people best at playing dumb. I tell them nothing. Not even about possible MSMH construction. *Nothing*." He tried to sit all the way up, failed, then had to wait for a scolding beep from one of the instruments near him to cease before he could resume talking.

"I can access my office from this bed, Inny. Is nice that I am in same hospital as my own home and offices. Will make for short commute when they letting me walk again. First thing after I regain consciousness and can think straight, I erase from here what not much I had recorded about your suddenly problematic little thread. I even revoke indication of its existence."

She inhaled sharply. "The thread! It's still in your—"

"No is not," he exclaimed, interrupting her. "I use office remote to order it sent out via our building's internal delivery system. System works good for groceries, medications, toys, toxic storage threads. . . ." A hint of alarm crept into his voice. "You not receive it yet?"

"I just—your call woke me up. It's Saturday, you know."

"Thank you for remind me, Inny. I not have to cancel any appointments. Maybe come Monday I am unexpectedly called home to Vladivostok for indefinite period of time. Family emergency. Is not lie." He managed a painful smile. "I am member of my family, no?"

She was trying to get dressed, chug the remainder of the cup's contents, and carry on the distressing conversation all at the same time. "I'm on my way to check my delivery receptacle right now, Rudy."

"Good. I will wait to hear confirmation." He lay all the way back down. "I in no hurry."

The floating portrait followed her out into the main living area as she ran a forefinger up the front of her jumpsuit's seal. Unnatural rumblings sounded from the vicinity of the airbed that had been inflated on the far side of the room. A wraith or her houseguest, she mused. One and the same. Believing she heard her name called, she ignored the faint query.

With relief she saw that her codo's delivery container was not empty. It held several small packages. Two were pharmaceutical samples that as soon as she picked them up began to squeakingly explain why she should start to prescribe them for her patients. Another was a greeting from an old boyfriend that began to unfold and enlarge even as she slapped it down. The last was . . .

Running her thumbprint over her name unsealed the package and exposed the interior. Inside an inner, padded box was a small transparent capsule containing a single by now all-too-familiar storage thread. One that had in the brief interval out of her possession seemingly turned toxic.

"G'morn, doc." The wraith had awakened. Sitting up and straining to see over the crest of the intervening couch, Whispr ran a hand through his disheveled hair as he tried to focus on the rapidly moving mistress of the codo. Apparently preoccupied, she was studiously ignoring him. "Sleep well? I sure as hell did. Best sleep I've had in . . ." He broke off, seeing that she was not just ignoring him but ignoring him resolutely. "Is everything . . . ?" he began.

"Get rid of this thread." Along with his battered likeness, the voice of Dr. Sverdlosk was trailing the anxious Ingrid around the codo. "Is not worth whatever is on it. Not even if it really is made of impossible metal-magic stuff like MSMH. Go on boat picnic today, have good time—and throw it in deep part of river. Or better still, out in ocean somewheres. Same cheerful femmes that thrash-trash me may come looking soon for you. Tell them you take truth drug, anything they want, and when they ask about thread you can tell them truthfully what has been done with it. This is best advice cagey old beat-up doc guy like me who loves you can give you, Inny."

"I'm coming down there." Her tone was grim. "What section and room are you in? If you don't want to tell me over the tower's comm system, I can find out for myself at the hospital. Then we can . . ."

Being a doctor, Sverdlosk was accomplished at interrupting. "So. Here is orders. You don't come to see me, pretty Inny. Much as I would enjoy company of your warm self sitting on side of my bed is not good idea right now. These people, whoever they represent, maybe others, might be watching me from first minute I admitted. Might be watching me now. Get rid of thread. I go on vacation as soon as I can arrange discharge. Never speak to me about it again, ever. I take emergency leave to visit Old Country and see grandchildren—who I would like to live to see grow up." Before she could protest or offer an objection, his image began to dissipate.

"Good-bye for nowadays, Inny. Take care of yourself. Watch where you walk at night. Throw away thread. Maybe you also take hurry-up vacation. . . ."

Sverdlosk's image vanished. When she anxiously called for reconnect, the link was refused.

"Your friend didn't sound too good. Didn't look so good, either."

She whirled. Her guest had come up right behind her. *Whispr is as Whispr does*, she told herself.

"I heard most of it." Surprisingly, he did not look frightened. Only pensive. As if he always planned his life one step ahead, whether contemplating a break-in or breakfast. "I've always been one for knowing when I was operating out of my depth. Maybe your colleague is right." A small sound made him whirl toward the front door. "Maybe we *should* get rid of the thread. I always prefer to acknowledge an ill omen before it's pulled tight around my neck."

Ingrid stood there, holding a long-since drained caffeine cup in one hand and the capsule in the other, halfway between kitchen cubby and main living area. What had she gotten herself into? Galileo only had to worry about the Inquisition.

It was plain from his words and appearance that poor Sverdlosk could easily have ended up dead last night. Were his interrogators on to her already? Did they have ways of tracing the tower's internal communications structure and know that he had just spoken to her? Or that so many people's object of attention had already been delivered to her codo? If the latter, she might expect to hear an old-fashioned knock at the door at any moment. Or given his assailants' lack of social graces, their arrival and intentions might be announced in something other than a civilized manner.

And there remained the question of what to do with and about her seedy houseguest.

"No." She muttered an immediate response. "As a woman of science, I'm in too deep. It's hard to describe, Whispr. There's a name for people like me. Every time we learn something it only drives us to learn ten things more. It's never enough. As far as this thread is concerned I'm like a fish that's taken the bait. I can't let myself off the hook until I know what's on the other end of the line." She smiled tightly at him. "I can't jump off until then."

"Or," he countered, "there's also the chance that if you stay on the line you'll end up fried and consumed, with someone spitting out your bones."

She looked away. "Okay, so maybe it wasn't the most propitious analogy. But I can't let go of this until I know what it's all about, Whispr. I just can't. No matter what Rudy or anyone else says." She turned back to confront him. "If you want to give up on it, to back out now, I'll understand.

I'll just have to proceed on my own and I won't think any the worse of you."

Startled to discover that his host thought of him as anything other than a piece of human flotsam that had washed up on the shores of her office seeking repair, he was slow to respond. When he finally did reply, all his confounded thoughts would allow him to stammer was, "Curiosity killed the cat."

"Except for the ones who manage to find the mice."

He stared down at her. "This really has nothing to do with subsist for you, does it? You could care less about whether that filament of misery floss is worth a million bucks or a million cents. You just want to know the why and where and how of it."

"That's right, Whispr." She nodded solemnly. "Knowledge for knowledge's sake."

"I wish I had a dozen credits for every supposedly smart friend who lived by that philosophy. If we happen to find out that it's worth a lot of money, you won't mind then if I get all hungry and aggrand some for myself?"

Her smile returned. "I wouldn't expect you to do otherwise. Does that mean you're going to stick with this?"

"Oh, you can bet your right-so, but not here. If whoever's trying to claim the thread is close enough to it to hop all over your friend, then they're too close to it and to us. Anyway, as far as the thread is concerned he pretty much told you to forget he exists. He's right when he indicates that when the foul folk are getting that close to you, it's time to get out of town." He looked once more toward the front door. "My gut tells me it's time we do like he do."

She was tentative but agreeable. "If you think we should base ourselves elsewhere for a while, then I guess I should follow your lead. This kind of thing is your area of expertise, not mine. Any suggestions?"

It made him feel disproportionately good to know that in one area, at least, his thought processes were working ahead of hers.

"I've heard there are some especially knowledgeable linkies in the outer Miavana area, working out of the waterlands west of the city. Your creaky guy-friend made noises about taking vacation time. How do you fancy a holiday?"

She considered. "It wouldn't be as if we were taking off for India. Miavana's not far. I could still keep in touch with my office and oversee ongoing treatment of my regular patients and . . ."

"Forget that, Ingrid." He caught himself, surprised at his unexpected presumption. "Can I call you Ingrid?"

"You just did. If we're going to try and follow up with this anonymously, you constantly calling me Dr. Seastrom might be a little counterproductive."

He nodded. "I'm sorry, but once we leave here you can't have any contact with your office, your patients, this colleague of yours who got his face squared—no one. The Nasty who are after the thread have already shown themselves persistenters. You can bet wet that as soon as they're onto you certain they'll be monitoring every communications channel in Namerica that has your ident affixed to it."

"I suppose you're right. You'll have to excuse me, Whispr. I'm kind of new to all this. Doctors are used to straightforwardness, not subterfuge."

"Subterfuge is my life, or I wouldn't have one." He did not go into details. "We'll go by rental. False names. I've got appropriate ident and I can fix you up with one fast. Money debited to new cards through double intermediaries so it can't be traced." His meld-slender form straightened. "See, there are all kinds of talent in this world, doc. Ingrid."

"And plenty of operations of the nonsurgical kind, apparently." She looked around the codo, wondering what kind of accommodations they would be able to manage surreptitiously. At least there would be no shortage of options in a tourist and vacation Mecca like the South Florida waterlands.

"When should we get started?" she asked him.

He did not smile. "We already have."

She nodded and headed toward the bedroom, where he longed to follow but knew he could not. Certainly not until this business of the thread had been resolved. Only then would he feel free enough to push other matters. Until that time they would have to function closely together yet apart. And not only because he had found himself drawn to her from the first moment she had placed a gentle healing hand on his traktac-infested body. There was more to it than that. For one thing, as much as he was attracted to her, he didn't trust her.

If she was half as intelligent as she appeared, she would treat him the same way.

12

The codo was quiet, the codo was safe, and at three in the morning the codo was very dark. Because its lower floors were occupied by a hospital and associated medical offices, the tapering spire's security was much tighter than that of the average codomercial tower. Additionally, each private residence boasted its own customized refuge arrangements. These ranged from extra locks, to simple alarms, to government-registered active deterrent systems. By law the latter could encompass and include everything from narcoleptizing misters to high-power small-caliber arms.

None of this mattered to the Natural who carefully opened the door, nor to the two Melds who crowded close behind her. Deactivating a lock required as much artfulness as disarming a weapons system. Given ample experience in all facets of entering residences and businesses uninvited, the leader of the trio of intruders had no difficulty utilizing the sophisticated instrumentation at her disposal to allow her and her cohorts to enter the darkened dwelling without making any noise.

Ahead of them a short hallway opened onto a pleasant, neatly laid-out living area. The dimly glimpsed fixtures and fittings that furnished the high-floor corner codo indicated that its owner had good taste as well as an ample income. Valuable pictures and marketable gimcracks were ignored, however. The three had come to rob, yes, but their sole interest lay in a single, tiny, easily pocketable device. Not expecting to find it lying loose on a table or in a cabinet, their intent was to save time by simply requesting it from the current owner. If all went well the one-sided transaction could be accomplished quickly and with a minimum of fuss. That it might take longer and necessitate other than verbal persuasion was a consideration the invading trio had come prepared to implement.

Stepping past the stout woman who had expertly bypassed both the tower and the codo's integrated security, the replicant of a movie star from long ago gestured silently to her right and beckoned for her companions to follow. Pushing wide a half-open door revealed a dark bedroom, the light emanating from its walls muted almost to nonexistence. Blackout glass eliminated any glow from the tower across the street. There was just enough illumination to allow the intruders to see the single large bed with its aerogel pillows, yeast-float mattress, and scented floral-decorated coverlet that smelled fragrantly of bougainvillea.

Two of the women unsheathed simple weapons: a blade and a shocker. Having to bend to avoid scraping her crested skull against the ceiling, the third reached into a purse to bring out a roll of sonitape. Used for sealing small cracks and openings in enclosed spaces where recordings were to be made, the soft, stretchable material also made an excellent gag.

Gripping the shocker, the sturdy woman in the center directed the doppelganger of the ancient actress to go left. The taller woman half walked, half slithered around to the other side of the bed. At a signal from their leader the two Melds leaned forward simultaneously. As the coverlet was wrenched aside, fingers both bony and flexible reached down and forward. They closed around nothing. There was nothing for them to close around.

The bed was empty.

For the first time since she and her associates had broken into the codo, the chubby woman spoke. The curses she uttered were no less pungent than the fragrance that rose from the tropical bouquet–programmed coverlet.

Looking askance at her boss, the movie star Meld gestured in the direction of the main living area that they had noiselessly bypassed in order to get to the bedroom.

"Maybe she fell asleep in an entertainment bubble."

"Maybe she's voiding her bowels." The plump woman whirled. Both her eyes and the blade she was wielding flashed in the subdued light. "Find her!"

They barely had time to return to the codo's largest room when the crested flex-armed Meld bent double, made a hushing sound, and pointed with one all but jointless arm. Her companions nodded understandingly. Without a word having to pass between them, all three melted back into the shadows.

Responding to an arrival the hall walls brightened with enough light to illumine the entrance to the codo. A single figure stood silhouetted in the doorway. Quietly, it closed the door behind it. No internal lights picked up the photonic slack. But then, the deceptively plump leader of the invasive trio thought, someone familiar with the codo's layout would not need to activate its internal illumination.

She did not have to gesture or speak to her companions. They knew what to do. Figures that were scarcely specters edged off in opposite directions.

Moments later struggling noises scored by unreserved confusion filled the room with sound and motion. The trio's leader frowned. The voice that now rose above those of her cohorts was not what one would expect from a youngish female physician startled by intruders in her own home. In truth, it was neither youngish nor female. Once again flicking to life the blade she held, she used its glow to locate a nonaural control switch. At her touch, gentle illumination flooded the codo.

A figure struggled in the grasp of the two Melds, but it was not the one the intruders had been expecting. It was elderly, male, and utterly lacking in promise. Another professional acquaintance of their target? the Natural wondered. But if that was the case, what was he doing in the physician's apartment at this time of the morning? Did Dr. Ingrid Seastrom have a thing for old men? Did she perhaps *like* to be surprised in the middle of the night? Was this unprepossessing soft-footed nocturnal visitor all part of some creepy fetish? She shrugged. In her time and professional life she had seen enough so that little surprised her. Oftentimes the more intelligent the individual, the more bizarre their private obsessions.

Well, she mused to herself, if this prowling white-haired oldster was in search of the codo's owner, whether it be for reasons professional or

perverse, he had been preceded in disappointment by her and her colleagues. On a more hopeful note, he might know where she was. Putting
on her best matronly smile, she stepped forward out of the shadows and
into the subdued light.

"Now what do we have here? A thief of hearts—or of the more mundane
variety?"

Eyes wide and fearful, the oldster hung slack in the grip of the two
Melds. "I don't—who are you people? What are you doing in Dr. Seastrom's
home?"

The portly leader of the invading trio felt a twinge of disappointment at
the mention of the mildly honorific "Dr. Seastrom." The elder's choice of
words seemed to rule out any sort of perverted amorous rendezvous. Further questions would therefore be restricted to the ordinary.

"I might ask you the same question." Sitting down on the arm of the
woven free-form couch, she toyed with the slender blade that now shim-
mered with its own pointed internal illumination. "Are you a friend of
Seastrom's? If your answer is yes, we have questions for you. If your answer
is no, then that raises an entirely new and unexpected suite of inquiry."
Her gaze narrowed. "How either proceeds is entirely up to you."

The old man sighed. "Yes, I can see that. Please don't hurt me. I will
respond to the fullest extent of my ability to do so. What is it that you want
to know?"

Still playing with the knife and making sure as she did so that the im-
mobilized oldster had a clear view of the lustrous blade, the woman began
organizing questions in her mind. Might as well begin with the obvious,
she told herself.

"What's your name, old man?"

His tone by turns pleading and deferential he responded softly and
without hesitation. "My name is Napun Molé," he said just before the
middle finger of his left hand lengthened explosively into a meter-long
shaft of pointed carbon-ceramic alloy that went right through the throat of
the startled tattoo-crested Meld holding on to his left arm. Retracting almost as swiftly as it had extended, it left blood fountaining in its wake.

To her credit, the dead actress Meld gripping his other arm brought her
shocker around and forward to slam into his ribs. A crackle of electricity
filled the air, followed by pale smoke and the scent of ozone as the dis-
charging weapon was shorted out by contact with the dissipation weave

that had been melded into the Molé's muscles. She ducked as he swung at her, the blade now protruding from the side of his left hand whistling through the air over her head.

Straightening as she recovered from the shock of the senior's reactions, the trio's leader took aim and threw the blade she was holding. Even as it left her fingers she was already reaching for her concealed sidearm. The sharp-edged metal tore through the back of the old man's clothing to bounce off his reinforced flesh. As it did so, he fired his left index finger. The single pellet thus discharged detonated against the Marilyn Meld's neck with enough explosive force to blow her head off. It landed near the kitchen area, ricocheted off a cabinet, and lay still, a macabre echo of a glamorous past framed by a spreading pool of blood. Spurting crimson from its open neck, the decapitated torso remained erect a moment longer before collapsing to the floor.

Uttering a fluid, energetic flow of expletives in several languages, the surviving woman leaped behind one curve of the couch and held down the trigger of her sidearm. A spray of small-caliber explosive shells tore up the workings of the other side of the living area and the kitchen. Faux upholstery, carbon-fiber framing, molded crystal, reinforced glass, and a wide assortment of other contemporary decorative materials were shredded like cardboard in a tornado.

Propelled by a pair of superior-grade military spec leg melds, the Molé kicked off the floor, bounced off the ceiling, and was grazed by shells as he slammed headfirst into the woman who had nearly emptied her weapon. The air went out of her lungs as the impact cracked her sternum. Bright red pain threatened to overwhelm her vision as she staggered backward. With her free hand she drew her other sidearm. In lieu of a multiplicity of smaller ammo, this one was defined by the size of its barrel. It only held four shells, each one of which was capable of demolishing a vehicle of considerable size. Its employment would bring building security (if they weren't already on their way) and municipal police running, but at this point she didn't care. She knew now she probably had only one chance to put her deceptive assailant down. If that meant razing the codo above or below this one along with their respective inhabitants, that was the kind of collateral damage she would gladly rationalize later.

She did not get the one chance.

Before she could fire, the Molé had picked up the nearest section of couch, spun around twice to give it added momentum, and flung it in her direction. Melds that had replaced his lower spine with powerful recharge-able organic servos gave the segment of flung furniture tremendous kinetic force. It slammed into the fleshy woman with enough impact to lift her off the floor. By the time her finger contracted reflexively on the trigger of her larger-caliber handgun, the resultant shot went harmlessly wild. Harm-lessly, because she was already outside the building, having been smashed through one of the tough but not indestructible reinforced floor-to-ceiling glass panels.

Wishing for a sudden airfoil Meld did not make it a reality. In confir-mation of one in a long line of thousands of demonstrations proving the truth of Galileo's original experiment, both she and the portion of couch hit the sidewalk eighty-five floors below at the same time.

Surrounded by the wreckage of the codo, Napun Molé took stock of his surroundings. He was not pleased. He had arrived in silence and, he had believed, in secrecy, only to be grabbed and confronted by three women about whom he had immediately been certain of one thing: they were not members of the same profession as Dr. Ingrid Seastrom. He had not needed to wait for their questions to divine their purpose in invading the good doctor's living quarters. Self-evidently not representatives of the local police, their presence and attitude could only point to an objective similar to his own. They were also after the thread.

Very disturbing, he thought as he walked into the kitchen to get himself a drink of water. He was careful to step around the spigot of blood that con-tinued to pump in steadily decreasing volume from the neck of the tall, bony-headed, already dead Meld whose throat he had pierced. For one thing, the appearance on the scene and attempted intervention of outside interests was a most unwelcome infringement on the claim to the thread that had been staked by his employers. For another, in the course of the preceding squabble his suit jacket had been torn in at least two places. It was all most disconcerting.

Word was slipping out where knowledge of the thread should be invio-late, he mused. Too many people were learning of its importance, if not what was on it or what it signified. Unlike what those lying dead on the codo floor and the now carmine-blotched street outside believed, a great deal more was at stake than the mere abstraction of wealth. A great deal more. Everything tonight had happened too fast. There had been no time for assimilation; only reaction. As a consequence he had been forced to make a mess. Those who had charged him with the recovery of the thread would not be pleased.

He was none too happy himself. Downing the last of the water he initiated a swift, methodical, and professional search of the rooms. Even a basic residence would boast at least one basic box outlet. Someone of Seastrom's persuasion was likely to have access and a projector in every room.

The main living area and the kitchen having been largely destroyed, he had to go into the bedroom before he found an intact vorec. That was all he needed. Utilizing the usual omnidirectional pickup it would enable a resident to command access from anywhere in the codo.

Removing a special and highly illegal convertor from a pocket, he started speaking softly into the tiny but sensitive diaphragm. There was no immediate response from the codo's box. That was to be expected. It would take time for the ware inside the convertor to detect and decipher the codes and tonalities that were specific to the codo's owner. Only when that had been compiled could he then proceed to the next step of having himself recognized as an accepted user by the doctor's residential programming.

He was patient and prepared to wait for as long as required—or at least until Security put in an appearance. Helpfully, the coughing of the tall Meld whose throat he had lethally perforated had finally ceased. The choking sounds had been a minor distraction.

The amplification and sensitization meld that had replaced the normal organic hearing apparatus in his right ear alerted him to the presence of numerous moving figures in the distant hall well before they arrived.

His hearing told him that they were advancing cautiously. That was only common sense, given the amount of destruction that must by now have been reported by other residents living in the vicinity of the badly damaged codo. As he rose from the bed he strained his specialized hearing meld to the utmost, but he could not tell from cursory analysis of the still distant footfalls whether those making the semistealthy approach were building security or regular city police. The former he might be able to deal with. The latter, if present in any numbers, would pose a real threat.

Anger and frustration in equal measure surged within him. He eyed the convertor. He was close, real close to breaking the codo's individual coding. He could sense it. But proximity was not resolution, and if he was hauled in to jail or shot, having come close to what he was after would be small consolation. Muttering invective that was in shocking contrast to his homely appearance, he pocketed the convertor, flung the vorec onto the bed, and abandoned the room. No one saw him leave.

Just as no one saw the diminutive but stocky figure making its way through the jagged-edged breach in the exterior wall of the codo and around the smooth, sheer side of the tower, where it proceeded to scurry down the back side of the building on two pairs of very expensive and ultra-secure gecko pads.

The methodical approach of the tactical squad that had been dispatched in response to calls from several frantic residents of the tower whose residences bordered that of the respected Dr. Seastrom allowed the single remaining live occupant of the codo to depart the devastated premises unseen and in silence. By the time the armored police entered the ruins, the only ones left to greet them were two female Melds, both very dead. Initial supposition was enough to tie them to the shattered remains of a third woman whose body had been found splattered on the pavement eighty-five floors below. Only after a quick, efficient search revealed that the codo was now devoid of any threat did the arriving police allow themselves to relax.

"Wonder what happened here?" the sergeant-in-charge muttered to himself as he flipped up his protective visor. As Forensics arrived and began their work, a corporal kicked at some of the debris that lay scattered across the living-room floor. Her gaze rose to the hole in the tempered glass wall opposite, through which the clammy night air of Greater Savannah was presently entering.

"Maybe the one on the street lost a fight with the two Melds."

The sergeant grunted and rubbed at his melded left eye. It was a high-grade Mark I-Five police issue, but from time to time it still bothered him. "From the looks of this place, they all lost. No sign of the owner yet?"

The corporal murmured into the vorec that hung by a thin wire just in front of and below her lips. An audio meld would have eliminated the need for both the support wire and the pickup, but she was a Natural.

"Not yet. Nothing from air or land Scanerch. For all we know she could be out on a date." A thin smile creased her lips. "Or an overnight. Communications is presently trying to make contact with another physician who works in this building—a Dr. Rajeev."

"I hope they're both out canoodling on a paddle boat somewhere." Walking over to the gap in the wall, the sergeant looked out and down. Having spent eighteen years on the force he had no fear of heights, or much of anything else. "According to Records she's a well-regarded and long-established physician. She'll have good insurance."

"She'd better." Raising her forearm-length riot gun, the corporal used the muzzle to indicate the surrounding devastation. "She's gonna need it."

Her superior sighed. "Might as well get out of Forensics' way. You know those guys—always telling us that no matter where we step, we're infringing on potential evidence."

"Yeah." Turning her head slightly, the corporal sipped cold Boost from the tube that projected from beneath her armor. "It's been a slow night. Maybe HQ will just let us hang out here until shift's over."

The sergeant nodded approvingly. "Nobody has to shoot, nobody gets shot. My idea of a good way to end a night shift. If we're lucky, they'll locate this doc and bring her here. Be nice to see if she can shed some illum on this mess."

The corporal readily agreed, but they were to be denied.

Despite the best efforts of Greater Savannah Central to find her, Dr. Ingrid Seastrom's location was not established by sunrise, at any time in the course of the following day, or at all.

THE OBJECT OF THE SAVANNAH police department's interested but not as yet overly anxious search had spent some very early morning hours changing her hairstyle and hue, eye color, and adding enough collagen and osseoputty to completely if temporarily alter her appearance. Trying her best to look and act like a typical tourist, she leaned back into the passenger seat of the silent electric roadster. A lightweight, wide-brimmed hat shielded her face while employing a patented heat transfer system to cool her head. There was no need for sunglasses. The color-shifting contacts she had placed over her eyes earlier in the day offered ample UV protection. They would also change tint every few hours, running the currently trendy optical gamut from dark purple to light amber.

"I feel fat," Ingrid Seastrom grumbled for somewhere between the hundredth and two hundredth time as her left hand felt gingerly of the still tender skin around her artificially expanded cheeks.

"It wouldn't matter."

She looked over at the driver. Unfolded behind the controls, Whispr looked less alien and more normal than usual. "I don't understand," she said.

"I never met a woman who didn't feel she was fat. Unless she'd bought into a meld like mine. Even then, you sometimes hear it." He turned to her, his tone carefully neutral so that she would not think he was trying anything. That lesson had been learned. "Thirty kilos or three hundred, it doesn't matter. You all think you're fat."

"*You're* the one who underwent an extreme slenderizing meld," she shot back accusingly.

He kept his attention on the road ahead even though the roadster's autopilot was locked. Steering, braking, and acceleration were controlled by the sensor strips embedded in the pavement. Here along the Atlantic coast such automated control was critical to preventing accidents from blocking the one major north-south roadway. Braced and reinforced to withstand the most powerful hurricanes, the vital transportation link was elevated high above the waters that lapped beneath. Where towns such as Gifford, Jupiter, and Lake Worth had once stood, porpoises now frolicked while swarms of protected sharks prowled among drowned homes and businesses.

"True, but in my case it had nothing to do with vanity. It was a decision based wholly on practicalities and necessity."

"Which, as you have already said, you decline to elaborate upon."

He looked over at her, taking his ease as he let the road drive the car. He only paid occasional attention to the roadway in case a police vehicle happened to put in an appearance. Now approaching the outskirts of Miavana, they had encountered only normal patrols.

"Just like I'll continue to do so, so you might as well save your breath."

Turning away from him and lowering her gaze, she caught sight of herself in the right-side mirror. *Fat*, she thought glumly. Having to endure an intentionally inflicted poor self-image while attempting to unravel the secrets of the thread was not a downside she had foreseen in making the hasty flight from home. She was half tempted to call off the whole increasingly bizarre business and return to the comforts of predictable daily routine and her cozy codo. But only half tempted. The other half would not rest until she found out what, if anything, was contained on the storage thread of extraordinary composition.

"You're sure you know people here who can help us find out what we want to know?"

Whispr nodded. "Like me, they tend not to hang around in any one place for too long. But they leave trails, hints, traces, and allusions. I'll find them. I'll find them, and you'll pay them."

"I'm starting to wonder if that's a fair division of responsibility," she replied coolly.

"Too late to wonder, doc. We're here."

Verbally, musically, and physically, the roadster signaled that it was returning control of the vehicle from pavement to driver. When the changeover occurred Whispr took command smoothly, taking the second turnoff as he guided the rented car inland away from the coast. Off to their left could be seen the slowly disintegrating towers, most of them residential, of old Miami. With their lower floors submerged beneath the rising waters they had long ago been abandoned to the unsympathetic tides of the Atlantic. Home now only to birds, hydrophilic animals, and a number of transient humans, the primitive steel and concrete of which the buildings had been constructed was crumbling bit by bit into the warm and persistent salt water.

The disintegrating debris formed an excellent foundation for spreading mangroves and new coral. Contented fishermen plied their trade among the architectural wreckage. Shuttled out from the city, boatloads of air-conditioned tourists gawked at the collapsing structures much as their Antarctic counterparts gazed upon calving glaciers. Alligators, caimans, and American and Orinoco crocodiles sunned themselves on decaying slabs of prehistoric retirement dreams.

Ingrid had never been to Miavana. Able to afford more expensive vacations, her brief periods of downtime had taken her to the more exotic and distant parts of the Caribbean. She had never traveled farther than Curacao, had not yet been to Europe. It was not that she was particularly a stay-at-home. "No time," was the simple explanation she gave to friends who inquired. Like so many other nearby tourist locations, Miavana too had been skipped over. Until now.

Except, she reminded herself, she was not on vacation.

While periodically inundated throughout its history by hurricanes and the sinkage of land brought on by the pumping of too much groundwater, parts of the old city had once rested on actual semidry ground. Or so she had read. Now "the Venice of North America" existed solely on stilts and pilings driven deep into bedrock as the city kept reinventing and raising itself to stay ahead of the rising sea level. Except for a few irreplaceable monuments like the Doge's Palace and St. Marks, the original Venice was of course long gone. It was now a destination only for enthralled scuba divers and a home only to those who had undergone full gill melds.

Throughout all the changes Miavana had retained its historical predilection for pastel hues. Leaving the rental roadster at an automated drop lot, Ingrid and Whispr joined a dozen commuters aboard a mechanized shuttle heading into the city proper. The sun was hot and the air clammy but inside the air-conditioned transport it was comfortable and cool.

"Where are we going?" she asked her companion.

His reply was not what she had been anticipating.

"We're going to see a doctor," he told her, plainly relishing her reaction.

"To get these temporaries removed?" She indicated her puffy cheeks and temporarily resculpted nose.

"That wouldn't be smart. I know about the thread, but you're one up on me, doc. I may look useless and act dumb, or act useless and look dumb, but I don't miss much. One thing I do have is a good memory. You tried to access the thread, with no luck. Same for your unfortunate co-doc. So I've been thinking that maybe we should try a different approach."

The shuttle slowed into port to unload a quartet of bored-looking commuters clad in business shorts, shirts, and protective hats. "What kind of 'different approach?'" she asked warily.

"Well, if we can't figure out what's on the thread, maybe we can learn more about its composition. I'm thinking in particular about the piece of the same stuff you said you got out of the head of that girl you worked on. You said that it disappeared soon after you started trying to research it. That it was 'entangled,' or something."

Ingrid nodded. "That's right."

Leaning close, Whispr whispered intently, "Wouldn't it be interesting if there were more of such things floating around? Other nanodevices made out of the same stuff? Find some of them and we might learn some-thing about the thread's origins, if not its purpose."

"Yes." Her heart thumped. "Yes, that would make sense, Whispr. Pro-vided the device and the thread really are related, as their similar composi-tion seems to indicate. But how can we do that safely? If I were to put out a general inquiry among the medical community, word would likely get back not only to the police but to the owners of the thread. They'd find out that somebody is looking into—into whatever it's all about."

He smiled as the shuttle pulled away from the dock. "The medical community I move among is different from the medical community you're talking about. Among the 'practitioners' I know, nobody shares info unless they get paid upfront." His swagger abruptly collapsed into embarrass-ment. "I haven't got any money to pay them."

She sighed tiredly. His confession was hardly unexpected. "We're sup-posed to complement each other, remember? You find somebody who knows something about either the thread or the implant that I extracted, and I'll compensate them for whatever they can tell us." She let her gaze roam the stilt-mounted towers and sweeping art-deco revival architecture that rose above the canals and lagoons the shuttle was traversing. "This is my vacation money down the drain anyway."

Whispr was silent for a while before venturing unexpectedly, "I guess if you're really interested in science—I mean really interested—it can get in the way of real life."

She had to smile as they disembarked at the next shuttle stop. "Whispr, for someone interested in science, it *is* a way of life."

He nodded as he led the way across the dock toward the nearest build-ing's climate-controlled access corridor. Off to their right a trio of two-meter-long white caiman were sunning themselves on the edge of the shuttle dock. Looking like a pair of undertakers preparing a corpse for embalming, a cou-ple of lugubrious jabiru storks were pecking apart the remnants of some of-fice worker's fastfood lunch. Repositioning his backpack against his thin shoulders, Whispr slowed so she could catch up to him.

"If science is a way of life, give me hard liquor," he told her decisively.

Whether quip or comment, she chose to ignore his assumption as they entered the building. The characterless corridor led into the depths of a nondescript ten-story commercial edifice. The poverty of the building's clientele was defined by the structure's lack of windows. Fewer windows meant no views of the water outside but lower aircon bills. Walking along beside her guide, Ingrid was not displeased.

"This doesn't look too bad. Is this where we're going to try and meet up with some of these contacts you've heard about?"

He chuckled. Even laughter, she reflected, was squeezed from his lips like exhaust from an old engine: breathy, muted, and sometimes difficult to clearly comprehend.

"There should be a rental office in the back where we can pick up a personal watercraft cheap and without having to present any ident except the security deposit and down payment. Keeping no records means no records that can be traced." He indicated their discreetly severe surroundings. "We'll have to do some hunting. The people we've come here to try and find won't be found at a commercial address or hanging around a major downtown shopping area.

"For them, this is paradise."

THE SMALL ELECTRIC RUNABOUT they rented could seat two only, with barely enough room behind the pair of ejectable, floatable bucket seats for their modest luggage. Though a good swimmer and comfortable in the water, Ingrid found the restricted dimensions of the rental watercraft more than a little off-putting. She was acutely conscious of the fact that decades of global warming had allowed not only crocodilians to move north from South America but also a troubling assortment of dangerous snakes, poisonous insects, and carnivorous fish. The two-person runabout looked hardly big enough to resist the attentions of a middle-aged anaconda.

Whispr seemed comfortable enough in it, however. At least with him doing all the driving she could relax a little and enjoy their surroundings.

After spending the night in a small hotel they started off bright and early the following morning. Less than an hour had passed before they began to leave the city and its flotilla of waterborne commuters behind.

They were heading inland—wending their way into the swampy, semi-protected morass of steaming muck and swamp that had once been central Florida. The mix of Everglades, rain forest, and intrusive seawater now extended all the way across what remained of the peninsula to the island citadel of Fort Myers. Anyone in search of contiguous solid ground had to travel north until they hit the heavily reinforced Orlando-Tampa seawall.

Within the lush tangle of riotous greenery lay impenetrable mangrove jungle, kudzu dead zones, pockets of dry land long since colonized by invasive plant species from farther south, stilt towns that on a far smaller scale struggled to replicate the architecture and structural engineering of the city the two visitors were leaving behind, vast stretches of protected parkland and nature reserves, the isolated glitterflash of Seminole gambling islands, and the increasingly isolated suburbs of Miavana itself. It was to one of the most distant of the latter that a confident Whispr was now steering the nearly silent watercraft they had rented.

Another hour of watching little but greenery race past moved an increasingly restless Ingrid to ask, "Are we still in the city?"

"Technically, yeah. Miavana's municipal boundaries run a third of the way to the Gulf. But the main populated part of the metropolitan area is just a strip along what used to be the coast, from where the submerged highway used to go out to the Keys all the way back up to Jacksonville."

She frowned. In her course of studies geography had always taken an academic backseat to more career-relevant subjects like biology and the other life sciences. "What are 'the Keys'?"

Whispr nodded to his left. "String of islands that used to curve out into the Gulf from the southern end of the state. Been underwater a long time now, I guess. Real popular with the sea Melds who live there. Supposed to be good diving for Naturals and the rest of us, too."

"You dive?" She eyed him in surprise.

"What, are you kidding me?" He shuddered slightly. "Swimming I like, but if I have to stick my head underwater for any length of time I get claustrophobic. The way I feel about it, if Nature wanted us to swim like fish she would have given us all gill melds."

By now they were encountering as many reed- and grass-choked channels as those that had been cleared for travel. Whispr slowed down to keep from clogging the boat's jet intake.

"You can tell we're getting into the low-rent district." He indicated one old channel that hadn't been cleared in years. "Bad road maintenance."

Ever since Whispr had opened the watercraft's canopy and reduced their speed in order to save battery power she had begun to succumb to the morning's rapidly increasing temperature.

"When do we get to—wherever it is we're going?"

Bringing the craft around to port he nodded toward a tight cluster of stilt-mounted structures. They seemed to materialize out of the cloying humidity like a mirage in the desert. A notably cheap and badly constructed mirage.

"We're here." A touch on the accelerator began to reduce their speed.

She studied the approaching heat-sink of a minor municipality. At least on initial view, "here" looked decidedly unpromising.

13

The town of Macamock Hammock (Macmock to the locals) consisted of a few hundred homes and associated commercial structures built just above the dark water and linked together by a web of scoot trails and walkways whose deteriorating condition would have sent a nonbribed transit inspector into a spasm of despair. To someone like Ingrid Seastrom who hailed from a modern metropolis like Greater Savannah it was astonishing in an age of water-resistant polymers, ceramics, and carbon-fiber construction to encounter a boogeyman from the past that had been largely banished elsewhere.

Rust.

She had to double-check with her companion to convince herself she was not seeing things. But rust it was; not dark red paint or some aging polymer binder. A number of the community's oldest standing structures actually were fashioned of ferrous derivatives. Some had collapsed to form scattered small pockets of sharp-edged red reef within the boundaries of the town itself. When they drew nearer she saw windows that were empty of glass or equivalent solid transparencies.

As Whispr guided their boat into an empty berth at a public dock she found herself growing increasingly doubtful of their prospects. Macmock hardly looked like a hotbed of cutting-edge technology, medical or otherwise.

"You really think we have a chance to find out anything useful here?"

"If I didn't, I wouldn't have brought us." Extending a slender but strong arm he helped her out of the watercraft and up onto the dock. Having acknowledged and recorded the rental's ident, the dock's automated steward was demanding advance payment for berthing privileges. Ingrid paid, using the new card she had picked up in order to maintain anonymity during the journey. Providing additional security an appropriately complex tailing algorithm would disperse the details of the transaction once it had been processed, thereby preventing anyone from tracing it back to the source. Shouldering their packs, they headed into town.

As they walked, they passed a number of working fishermen making preparations to take their special shallow-draft boats out into the vast Florida waterways. Several trappers were layering legally taken caiman and croc skins onto a preservation pallet. A small refrigerated cargo craft was loading cases of frozen, locally butchered capybara cutlets.

Passing swiftly overhead, a singular shadow caused her to glance upward. It had been cast by a patrolling raptor the size of a small pilotless drone aircraft. Noting the direction of her stare, Whispr shielded his eyes with a hand as he squinted at the sky.

"Harpy eagle. I've heard they do well in Florida since finding their way up here a couple of decades ago. Lots to eat. Must be hell on the local poodle fanciers."

Every day she spent away from Savannah and in Whispr's company was another day Ingrid realized how divorced her life had become from the comfortable world she had made for herself. "Are they dangerous?"

"To humans?" Whispr turned thoughtful. "Not that I've heard. Though if I had a kid younger than three I wouldn't let it go crawling around outside with one of those killer canaries circling overhead. Just to be on the safe side."

They turned down a main pedestrian walkway. It was flanked on either side by scoot paths. Since stepping off their rented watercraft she had seen nothing bigger than a two-person scoot. South of the Tampa-Orlando seawall there were no surface vehicles because there was virtually no surface left. For a long time now everything in South Florida from people to cargo had moved by water. It was a region where outside the artificial comfort zone provided by climate conditioning, everything moved slowly, in time to the rhythms of warm water and warmer air. What in a cooler clime would have been described as sluggish in the saturated tropics was regarded as only sensible.

Their present surroundings were all very colorful and atmospheric, she thought to herself. What they were not, was encouraging. She wiped sweat from her forehead.

"I'll say it again, Whispr: this place doesn't exactly strike me as being on the cutting edge of medtech development. Whatever metals they favor here, I don't see MSMH being among them."

He did not sound discouraged. "And as with any folk, Natural or Meld, who eke out a living on the knife edge of what's barely legal, I'm sure there are more than a few townsfolk who'd be pleased to hear you say that. Sometimes, doc, anonymity is the best fertilizer."

Making their way along the walkway's edge, she stumbled over something firm and rubbery. A glance downward revealed a small brown corpse upon which a colorful assortment of tropical flies were enthusiastically banqueting. Where another visitor might have made a face or gone queasy she did not. As a physician she was comfortable with a vast variety of blood and guts. But neither did the sight inspire a gleeful chuckle.

Whispr spared the small swollen corpse a look. "Nutria. Local vermin." He inhaled deeply of the saturated air, his chest hardly seeming to expand as he did so, and grinned. "Kind of like me."

She shook her head. "Not you. You're not local vermin. You're just visiting."

"Hey," he quipped back, "how many vermin can boast that they're traveling with their own doctor?"

"I'm not your doctor," she reminded him firmly. "I'm your partner."

He nodded in the direction they were walking. "Heads up then, partner. That's where we'll be staying."

A two-story structure loomed directly ahead of them. In design it was severe, in execution contemporary. As with every other structure they had passed, an amorphous solar veneer coated all but the north-facing wall and the photosensitive windows. At the sight she heaved an inward sigh of relief. If hardly luxurious, the place at least looked modern and clean. The dozen or so watercraft parked at the nearby dock attested to the boatel's popularity. She wanted to ask if it was the best place in town but caught herself as soon as she realized it might be the only place.

The decorative sculpture out front piqued Whispr's curiosity and for a change she was the one able to provide explanation.

"It's an old boat," she told him as they headed for the lobby.

"I can see that," he responded, "but what's that thing hanging off the back end?"

"I think it's called an outboard engine. You know—one of those motive devices that was powered by a petroleum distillate? Back when petroleum was common enough to use as a fuel?"

He was clearly fascinated by the rusty relic of a bygone era. She would have gone into more detail except that as they entered the lobby she was nearly overcome by a blast of air-conditioning.

The boatel's modern exterior did not extend to check-in. Instead of the usual automated console, there was a human receptionist. The middle-aged man boasted a couple of cheap webbing melds between his fingers. Also between his toes, the latter being visible above the double-wide sandals he wore. Whispr leaned toward him and smiled.

"One room with—"

Stepping forward, Ingrid cut him off abruptly. "Two rooms." She also smiled at the clerk. "We do so treasure our individual privacy."

Judging from his stolid reaction to their byplay, as long as their method of payment proved acceptable the receptionist could not have cared if they had voiced their intent to room together in concert with a pair of full Piscean Melds, a magician, and a couple of the howler monkeys descended from escaped zoo animals whose eerie calls crisscrossed the Everglades every sunrise and sunset.

"What now?" she asked Whispr as they walked toward their lower-floor rooms. If he was upset by her curt dismissal of his desire to stay in a single room, he gave no sign.

"Tonight I'll take a walk around town and put out the word that we're here looking to buy some special, expensive rainforest hallucinogens. The naturally harvested illegal variety—not those that are government approved and available in the familiar mass-produced packs from your local NDA drugstore. That should be enough to stimulate feelers from one or more of the local entrepreneurs that I'm told do business in this area." He eyed her somberly.

"I'm pretty careful when I do my shopping, doc, but you should know that there's a chance of running into a slumming undercover poc. It's always a risk. But if I should get picked up, you'll be in the clear, and no matter what happens afterward there'll be no clean connection between you and me or between me and the thread. I'll just be hauled off and charged with drone-drugging."

"How very reassuring," she commented dryly. "Assuming that *doesn't* happen, then what?"

He was warming to the plan. "Once I've made a local contact we can rely on, we can set aside bogus drug requests and work through him or her to try and find out more about the thread and what might be on it. If everything I've heard is still valid, this floating shingle of a town is a gateway for all kinds of sensitive information and products to enter and leave the country without going through the usual official channels. It's a covert conduit and distribution point." He looked around, forever conscious of their immediate surroundings and anyone who might have wandered within hearing range.

"In the meantime, as far as anybody is concerned we're just tourists."

"Okay." Waving her key over the receiver on the front of the door she was rewarded by a soft click as it opened. "While you're scoping out the town and dropping your inquiries I'll be touristing my in-room facilities. Get back to me when you've learned something or you're ready to eat."

He looked at her in surprise. "You desire my company for lunch?"

"Don't let it go to your head—or anyplace else," she warned him. "I just hate eating alone. I have to do too much of it."

As he turned to retrace the path to the lobby he left a thin smile in his wake. "Nice to know that at least I rank one step above 'alone.'"

IF ONLY HE COULD THINK of a way to prolong this trip for as long as possible, Whispr mused as he followed an elevated walkway deeper into the older part of Macmock. Traveling around the country with a woman who was both more intelligent and more attractive than himself, having her pay for everything, was about as pleasant a set of circumstances in which he had found himself in quite some time. Eventually, of course, she would figure out that he was stringing her along. At that point she'd probably throw a little lady-doctor hissy fit and ditch him. That likely blowup would rouse no tears from him. He had spent most of his life being abandoned; first by family, lately by friends.

Until the inevitable confrontation he would enjoy the sights, the weather, the opportunities, the comfortable paid-for lodgings, and the good food. There was only one problem with the otherwise entirely agreeable scenario. It nagged at him like a cactus thorn that had broken off beneath his skin and begun to fester.

She trusted him.

No question about it. Oh, maybe she didn't trust him enough to share a room with him, but she was essentially trusting him with her life. After all, there was nothing to prevent him from turning her over to those who would hold her for ransom, or to the government or private individuals who so ferociously sought recovery of the thread. So what if he didn't learn what was on the thread or the details of its (according to her) unusual manufacture? He could pocket whatever reward or payment was offered for its recovery and vanish back into the familiar underworld of Greater Savannah. He could take any of those options. Except for one thing.

She trusted him.

Why this should nag at him like an allergic reaction to optistash he did not know. They were not old friends. She was not even a friend of an old friend—just someone whose professional services had been recommended to him. He owed Dr. Ingrid Seastrom nothing. As she had informed him, the minor extraction she had performed for him had been carried out pro bono. Okay—deactivating the traktacs, that had been a windfall bonus. Sure, he had promised to pay her for the work, but if he didn't and just walked away from her, what was she going to do? Call the cops and explain that he owed her for illegally deactivating their tracking devices?

Trust, trust, trust—why did it plague him so? It wasn't as if his conscience was any bigger than any of the rest of him. No doubt what he needed to make sense of it all was a morality meld. Except, to the best of his knowledge there was no such thing. Which meant that he was stuck with his own inescapable ethical recriminations.

Maybe it was the fact that no one of Ingrid Seastrom's social standing had ever trusted him before.

You're an idiot, he told himself. *Why not just admit that you're in love with her, or at least in lust? You know that isn't going anywhere, and you know she'll continue to reject you, yet you keep hoping. You keep fooling yourself.* On the other hand, wasn't that what love was all about? Self-deception, blinding oneself to one's own fallacies and follies? You know that love is nothing but foolishness and self-delusion held in stasis.

Which, he reminded himself, was still better than any state of existence he had inhabited during the past ten years or so.

"You look like someone who could use a zoe, broth-brother."

The Meld who had spoken was leaning against the faltering walkway railing. What made his presence distinctive and immediately identified him as a local was the fact that he was standing not on the walkway but on the other side. The exceptional leg meld he had undergone had produced stiltlike lower limbs two meters long that terminated in widely splayed feet suitable for providing support on sand and mud as well as solid ground. Standing *in* the water *below* the walkway he was still eye level with Whispr. A convenient stance for challenging less attenuated strollers.

Slowing without immediately responding, Whispr took a moment to check out their immediate environs. A local multimeld couple was strolling arm in arm in arm. Off to his right and away from the pedestrian walkways a Natural whose skin had been burnt sienna supervised a quartet of automatics that were off-loading catfish into a chilled, self-powered transport hopper. Several of the catfish were giants—more descendants of Amazonian immigrants carried northward by changing currents and patterns of ocean life. In the distance music drifted from a local café, a rejuvenating rejiggered bubbling bouillabaisse of southern Americana, salsa, and electronics that Whispr identified as the latest technopone.

But of overt undercover agents out trolling for prey he could detect no evidence.

"Not zoe," he told the man who had undergone the swamp strider meld. "Brain stuff more expensive, less stable. Mind trope—not trip, not tripe. Food for haute thought. Barf me a river, giver."

The strider's expression narrowed. "It would help if you named a tributary. Tickle me one."

Resting his arms on the shaky railing, Whispr evinced a false interest in the murky water below. "Might have a something that's worth something cubed. Need an appraisal."

Tottering slightly atop his impossible legs, the swamp strider regarded the supplicant suspiciously. "Plenty of dealers in Miavana. Easy access from there to the rest of Namerica and all points south and east. Why come here to the hot zone?"

"Plenty of watchers dealing watch on the dealers in Miavana, too." Whispr offered a conspiratorial smile. "I prefer the words of the choir invisible."

"Yopers, you do look like the type who don't want to be seen. Turn sideways and a dance step makes you so. Brisk wind blow you away; all crow and no scare."

From the other side of the walkway railing, Whispr met his gaze evenly. "Less wind in the waterlands. And I'm still here."

The strider sighed and shuddered impertinently. "You selling and not buying. Why should I drop on you anything heavier than loose vowels?"

Whispr deliberately wiped long, bony fingers across a shirt pocket. "Maybe I *could* use a zoe."

Now the strider returned the visitor's smile. "That better. Business always better two ways from yesterday. Tell me what you trying to price. Weevil wax? Gotagod extract?"

"Hard goods." Whispr kept his voice down.

"Jewelry? Instruments? Piece of equipment? Art? Sanitaried shellfish?"

"If I knew, I wouldn't need the appraisal," Whispr replied sagely.

The strider gave a favorable nod. "Broth-brother has spent time studying spiff from scum. Cannot he tell poor Molpi *anything* about the nature of his goods?"

Whispr took another sweeping gander at their immediate surrounds. No one was so much as glancing in their direction. "Two bits both metal, but we don't know for sure they are. Don't know for sure what they do. Can't tell by looking what they signify."

"In muck there is mystery, as my Meld-father used to say. What you looking for is a muck diver. See Tomuk Ginnyy. Tell her Molpi sent you."

"Directions?" Whispr asked.

The strider laughed softly. "Trouble with directions is they work both ways. I perceive you, broth-brother, but I don't know you. And not knowing you, I don't outloud homes of my friends. Herewith . . ."

Reaching into a pocket he withdrew a sleek, classy, utterly contemporary communicator. Flicking fingertips across the control panel he extended the device toward his customer. Bringing forth his own unit, which was not nearly as stylish or costly as the strider's, Whispr touched the upper contact to its counterpart on the strider's device. As opposed to an over-the-air transmission, information exchanged thusly, via actual physical contact between devices, could not be intercepted.

"Gratitude," Whispr murmured as he turned to leave.

Words accompanied the hand that reached out to restrain him.

"Long knowledge, short memory, broth-brother. Remember that we spoke of zoe-buying, and that my information does not come free. Rest-rooms are only for customers. Now—what z-kind tempts you?" He grinned encouragingly. "What's your flavor? I got four dozen different, each of them mind-polish slick and smooth."

A reluctant Whispr turned back. He had not really expected the strider to overlook their briefly voiced arrangement, but there had been no harm in trying to slip away without buying anything. Now that he mused more on it, however. . .

"No flavor," he told the strider. "Normal duration and size will be fine, but blank."

The strider's eyes twinkled. "Oh ho so? You going to mix your own neurostick?"

"Why not?" Now that business between them was on the verge of being concluded, Whispr allowed himself to relax a little.

Molpi the strider leaned close, encouraging his customer. "Want to share the details with a broth-brother? Purely out of professional interest, of course."

"Sorry," Whispr told him. "But I can tell you that my intentions are clean and single-sourcing."

Standing back away from the railing, the strider looked disappointed. "Each to his own taste, I suppose. Myself, I prefer to stir and shake before indulging."

Whispr dropped his gaze, looked up knowingly. "You almost have to. It's your business."

"ARE YOU SURE YOU KNOW where we're going?"

From where he was sitting in the small electric flatboat's driver's seat, hands locked behind his head and legs stretched out over the port side, Whispr smiled lazily over at her. "Of course I don't—but the boat does."

Luxuriating in the breeze that was temporarily keeping her cool if not

dry, Ingrid tried to relax and enjoy the panorama of surrounding swamp
and rainforest. "What if your contact sold you a mess of pottage and we're
just zooming around aimlessly through government-protected morass?"

Whispr refused to be drawn in to an argument. Smart though she was,
Seastrom had an annoying habit of worrying every little detail until it
screamed for surcease.

"I've been around a little, doc. You're experienced at identifying diseases. I'm good at spotting pretends. Our sourcer fit legit." He closed his
eyes, letting the information he had entered into the boat's autopilot direct
their course. "Besides, if we just keep going, we'll know we've been done
wrong when we hit the Gulf."

She was only partially mollified. "We're going in circles."

"Of course we are," he readily agreed. "The path to people who like
their privacy always goes in circles. Start on the outside of a web and keep
walking the circles inward and eventually you find the spider."

It was not an analogy that made her feel particularly better, but it was
evidently the only one she was going to get.

If one traveled in a straight line, the woman the strider had identified
as Tomuk Ginnyy did not live far from Macmock. Traveling the circular
route whose coordinates had been supplied to Whispr took a couple of
hours, at the conclusion of which Ingrid's relief at arriving at an actual destination nearly overrode the uncertainty in her mind and the soreness in
her buttocks.

A handful of small houses occupied every square centimeter of the
island's buildable land. The remainder was overrun by enormous liana,
vine, and Spanish moss–draped rainforest growths. Indigenous cypress and
salt pine stood shoulder-to-shoulder with ceibu, mahogany, and dragon's
blood trees whose ancestors had migrated northward from South America.
A small family of tamarins chattered in the miniature canopy while the
long furry arms of a creature Ingrid only vaguely recognized bridged a cap
between two branches. In no great rush to complete its transit, the three-
toed sloth ignored the disembarking fellow primates below.

Like the spokes of a wheel, individual boat slips radiated outward from
the round island's circumference. Unlike in Macamock, here there were
no streets, no walkways. The islet was neither large enough to require
them nor important enough to warrant them.

Passing the first structure, which had been slapped together out of poly paneling and sealant, they encountered what appeared to be a man in a bear suit. Or a bear in a man suit. Either way, an appalled and slightly intimidated Ingrid reflected, here was an individual who would unquestionably have benefited from a meld. Not to mention a bath.

Surprising her yet again, Whispr blocked the shambler's path. "Looking for a lady understated of profession and name of Tomuk Ginnyy."

Man-bear growled at the visitor. Looking at him, it was impossible to tell where his briar patch of reddish beard ended and his flourishing chest hair began. "No fishing here, wub-bub. No sights to see." Raising a massive, hairy arm that protruded from a short dirty sleeve, he pointed eastward. "Miavana's that way. This ain't no tourist stop."

"Really? A long Meld named Molpi told me this Tomuk is a good guide to local sights."

The large local blinked. "Molpi the strider? He sent you this-a-by?"

"No," Whispr snapped by way of reply, "we picked this architectural highlight out of a waterland guidesite." He took a long, deliberate peer past the man. "Or maybe I ought to say archaeological."

Anger flashed in the local's eyes, only to be replaced almost immediately by amusement. Raising his other hand, he jerked rightward a thumb the size and color of a decomposing crawfish. "Third house over. Go circumspect, be polite. Folks hereabouts tend to snack on surprises." With that he pushed past them, lurching toward a nearby dock. To Ingrid's relief, it was not the one where they had berthed their rental craft.

From the outside the dwelling to which they had been directed was less than imposing, but in the limited time she had spent in Whispr's company Ingrid had learned not to judge anything, be it people or possessions, from appearance. Money flaunted was money waiting to be stolen. Power displayed was power inviting a knockdown. From somewhere within the habitation a querulous voice responded to Whispr's query.

"Molpi sent you?"

When Whispr nodded affirmatively, the woman who had materialized in the doorway stepped back inside. A low lintel forced them to bend as they entered. It would also, Whispr reflected appreciatively as he pushed through a second inner door, make awkward the aim of any unwelcome intruder.

Inside the double entrance Ingrid twitched in delight. The temperature within the residence was not merely cooled—it bordered on the arctic. A visitor who stayed for twenty minutes or so would start to shiver. The astonishing artificial climate bespoke not only eclectic taste but also the ability to pay for it.

The interior of the main room was a cross between an electronics lab and a Mongolian yurt. Seemingly according to whim rather than any well thought-out decorative scheme, assorted primitive devices shared space with far more modern ones. In the center of the domed, circular chamber's ceiling an ancient but dead-silent splay of jointed fan blades pushed frigid air downward. Ingrid quickly edged off to one side, where if not warm it was at least less glacial.

A short stout Meld in her midforties, their host revealed in the course of making introductions that she was an immigrant from Thule. How a Greenland Inuit had ended up in the steamy South Florida waterlands was a tale she did not seem inclined to elaborate upon. She looked perfectly Natural, Ingrid saw, except for her feet. They were enormous, rough-skinned, and clad in custom sandals. The initial meld had been for snow-shoe feet. In the course of her permanent move to the waterlands, she had decided to have the broadpod meld redone into flippers. The result was recognizable if less than perfect. What the émigré Eskimo now had were crude seal feet. Ingrid looked once, evaluated, and raised her gaze. She was far from shocked. As a physician she had seen far more unusual melds than this.

"Enough chat-chit," their stocky host chirped. "I'm a busy lady. You say Molpi sent you to me? That's good enough." Naturally chubby cheeks bunched up in a rosy maternal smile. "He knows I'll have his testicles melded if he sends me anybody suspect." She looked speculatively from Ingrid to Whispr. "What can I do for you charming folks?"

His task accomplished, Whispr moved aside verbally as well as physically and let Ingrid take over. Stepping forward, she identified herself as a physician who was researching a particular, peculiar, possibly unauthorized, and potentially dangerous medical implant. From her backpack she removed and activated her own unadorned professional comm unit. The two women lapsed into silence as they spent several moments studying the projections the device projected into the air in front of them.

"Now that's something you don't see every day." Their host squinted at one small portion of the infojection. "Might even be something you don't see any day."

"Can you help us?" As she spoke, Ingrid held her unit close to her waist. Her breath formed small cumulonimbus in the chill air in front of her lips.

The Inuit turned thoughtful. "Not without being able to directly input at least some of what you have just shown me. I could describe it in my own words and formulae, of course, but a half-assed evaluation is likely to be slimmer and much less accurate." Turning flinty, her suddenly unblinking stare locked on the taller woman's gaze. "It's up to you. Did you come here for results or just to see if your panties would freeze?"

An uncertain Ingrid looked to Whispr for advice. He shrugged bony shoulders. "I'd say the same thing."

The doctor nodded and followed their host over to a console. Shown a contact point she extended her unit toward it—and hesitated.

"The information I'm transferring concerns a nanodevice that I removed from the head of a young girl. What I"—she glanced quickly back at the watching Whispr—"what we want to know, if you can find out for us, is not only what it does but whether my initial analysis of its composition is correct, its factory or country of origination, and any additional relevant details you can uncover."

She touched her unit's contact to the open port on the console. Information was soundlessly transferred. When the exchange had been completed, their host took a seat before the console and began to verbally and manually manipulate some very elite instrumentation. As the thickset woman concentrated on her work Ingrid quietly moved back until she was once again standing beside Whispr.

"If she's just researching the same lines of inquiry that I did in my office then we've come an awful long way for nothing."

Whispr was watching the Inuit operate. "There is the global box everyone knows, and then there are the box channels that exist outside what is known. There are legitimate, accessible sites, and then there are those that have been rendered intentionally difficult to visit. There are some that when found fail to acknowledge their existence or will just vanish at the mere hint of a probe. It takes more than a tech to get inside them: it takes an artist." He nodded toward where their now silent host was bent at her labors.

"Look at her. She's not the type to waste time rescanning the obvious. That doesn't mean she's going to find anything. But I can tell that she's looking. Looking hard. Looking serious. And there's something else that recommends her."

An increasingly intrigued Ingrid looked on as multiple data projections began to appear both in front of and behind their host's station. "What else?"

"She hasn't set a price on whatever she might find. That's a sure sign of someone who's secure in their abilities. If she didn't think she could teach us a something or two she would have asked for a fat credit transfer up front."

The expanding cloud of projections that continued to fill the room were as eclectic as the dwelling itself. Pink, pale blue, dark yellow—in appearance and content they favored the pastel as much as the obscure. Cartographic renditions in three dimensions shouldered aside slowly rotating images that were snippets of planet. Arcane chemical formulae vied for place of prominence with exploded schematics. Names accompanied portraits of Naturals and Melds that were individually framed with their own curriculum vitae. Little of it made any sense to the small audience consisting of an entranced Ingrid and a befuddled Whispr.

As time passed and they continued to look on, the froth of ever-changing projections began to condense. Portraits merged with reports, chemical analyses with designs, and geography with geology as rumor was reduced to speculation in a kinetic kitchen of cautionary collation.

Surely such a grand miscellany of information brought together from such a diversity of sources, Ingrid thought as the multitude of projections continued their compaction, *must* add up to something more than nothing.

Anxious to find out, Whispr took a step toward the woman hunched over the main console. "Don't hold back on us, Ginnyy. What've you found out?"

The cheerful cartoon of a woman swiveled around to face them. "Found out? I've found out that I want nothing to do with what you two are trying to find out. You keep poking an inquisitive stick into a deep dark hole and you better be prepared for whatever comes crawling out. Maybe a gopher. Maybe a big snake. Maybe a swarm of Isula that will nibble you down to nothing from the toes up. Me—I like my feet, even if I do take a size forty-eight triple N and gots no toes." She raised her left leg and wiggled the flattened, oversized appendage in which it terminated.

Whispr fidgeted. "We're not interested in your feet, Ginnyy."

Her head snapped around to face him. "No? You should be, stick-man, because they're what happens when you pay too cheap for somebody to remeld an earlier meld. You end up with shoddy work, like me. You end up with the unexpected." A short, thick arm waved through a couple of the nearest enduring projections. They broke apart like sugared smoke and quickly recoalesced in the wake of the dissipating gesture.

"Unexpected like this, for example." Rising from the chair she walked into the midst of the colorful hovering projections and proceeded to single out one seemingly unrelated floating quirk after another.

"Here's an inconsequential fragment of news about a fifteen-year-old boy in Kiev who coughs up a bunch of junk among which the attending physician finds this strange little object that he can't identify. He puts it in a storage vial, seals it, and when he gets back to his lab to examine it further he finds it's not there no more. An inexplicable disappearance, he calls it." Taking a step backward, she entered another complaisant projection.

"More than a hop and a skip from Kiev we find something similar reported from the Shanghai Urban Ring. Subject is a sixteen-year-old gymnast. Here's another, from the Gulf of Arabia. Lots more seemingly unrelated medical nonsense from Trincomalee, another from Seattle, two from Nairobi, a comparative plague of half a dozen reported from South Lima." With a wave of a hand and a voiced command, the hazy images vanished back into the closely linked instrumentation that had given birth to them.

"Different countries, different continents. Male and female subjects. Some healthy, some not. All apparently unharmed by the actual devices, but none of the reports can state for certain because as soon as the devices' discoverers move to examine them more closely, they're not there anymore. Some of the doctors and other discoverers doubt that they ever were. Rather than report the impossible many of them account for what they've seen by explaining it as some kind of physiological mirage." She was staring intently at the silent, listening Ingrid.

"But you don't think they're mirages. Do you, Ms. Thoughtmuch?"

Shaking her head slowly, Ingrid opened a sealed pocket and brought out the capsule. When the Inuit reached for it, the doctor shook her head again and refused to hand it over. Their host was reduced to squinting at the tiny cylinder resting in her visitor's palm.

"What is it?"

"Some kind of storage thread—we think," Ingrid told her. "We haven't been able to find a reader capable of accessing the contents, and it appears to be made of the same unlikely material as the implant I removed and that you just researched for us. If they're all made of the same material, then somewhere there exists an engineering and manufacturing concern that's figured out how to do the metallurgically impossible. Not to mention having developed a method for covering up whatever it is that they're doing by employing quantum entanglement." Repocketing the capsule, she gestured at the center of the room where the rapidly clearing air had recently been occupied by diverse projections of questionable content.

"Not only do we want to know who is behind all this, we want to know how they do it, and why."

Ginnyy nodded sagely. "So would I, after having skimmed the information I just called forth. Except that I'm not going to go into it any further. Because I did manage to find at least three similarities in every recorded instance." She paused for effect. "Every one of those now-you-see-it, now-you-don't little gizmos, irrespective of locality, health, gender, ethnicity, or anything else, was removed from a Meld. Not one of them was extracted from a Natural. And all of them were young. The oldest for whom I could find a report was nineteen. The youngest was twelve."

Whispr's voice was pitched lower than usual. "You said you found three similarities. What was the other one?"

Tomuk Ginnyy's lips tightened. "Every single young person who'd had one of these mysterious disappearing objects removed from their bodies had previously undergone a botched Meld that later had to be fixed. Without exception."

Listening to the Inuit, absorbing her words, Ingrid was immediately put in mind of Cara Jane Gibson and her slipshod, bungled cosmetic meld.

"So what we've got is a clear connection between the nanodevices, bad meld work, and young adults."

Ginnyy nodded. "Unless additional research turns up something contrarian, like non-Melds who show the implant or older adults who still retain it."

"But what's it do?" a mystified Whispr wondered aloud. "What are they for, these tiny machines that disappear if anyone tries to study them?"

"I certainly don't know." The Inuit switched her attention to him. "I don't think I want to know. To me a combination of bad melds, unauthorized cerebral implants, and elaborate secrecy screams stay away, don't touch, keep off the lawn. You two want to pursue this further"—she gestured in the direction of the shirt pocket where Ingrid had deposited the thread-holding capsule—"you need to talk to someone else. I'm just a small-time scanner and I can already smell that this is beyond me. Any additional follow-up calls for someone with more skill and more guts than I have." She turned back to her console. "You need to talk to Yabby Wizwang."

The visitors exchanged a glance. It was an ident neither of them recognized. Had they encountered the name previously they were unlikely to have forgotten it. Any instinctive reaction Whispr might have had he deftly repressed. New to the underworld to which he had introduced her, a less tactful Ingrid could not keep herself from grinning.

"You're kidding," she heard herself saying.

Tomuk Ginnyy did not smile back. "If you want, I'll set it up. Yabby's work doesn't come cheap, but he's the best. Compared to him, I'm just your local small-town directory service. Yabby, he's true global. But before I initiate contact for you, I've got three requirements."

Anticipating what one of the three might be, Ingrid was already reaching for her wallet. "Name them."

"One, you pay me what you owe for my work today. Two"— she shifted her attention to Whispr—"if you find out what the hell all this is about, what's behind it, and what's going on, you share the information with me. But discreetly. I'll set up a secure two-way contact for us. I'm intrigued, but I'm an old lady and I don't want any trouble."

"And three?" Ingrid pressed their host.

Some of the boisterous self-confidence seeped out of Tomuk Ginnyy. "You run a checkup on me, Mizdoc." For a second time she held up one of her oversized feet. "I've got my own substandard slipshod meld. Maybe I'm no kid anymore, but I was once. For all I know I'm walking around right now with one of these teeny little cryptics in my own skull."

"Based on the information you pulled together and just showed to us," Ingrid reminded her gently, "you really are a bit too old to fit the indicated demographic."

"I don't give a narwhal's bunghole—I want you to check me out."

Repressing a smile Ingrid proceeded to do so, as thoroughly and effectively as she could without the appropriate medical gear. If Whispr could not assist directly, he did at least make a show of concern. And while he was showing concern, he also managed to swipe the activated, blank zoe strip he had purchased from the swamp strider across the back of the doctor's bare right leg just beneath the hem of her shorts. Scarcely sensing the fleeting, featherlight touch, Ingrid Seastrom put the ephemeral contact down to a passing bug and ignored it as she continued her examination of their host.

14

The houseboat didn't look like much. The confusion of tropical flowers and emerald-green bushes crowding the top of the single-story, flat-bottomed craft might hide sensitive antennae, or they might be nothing more than decoration. The ropes and vines falling down its sides and trailing in the tepid water might comprise part of a larger disguised pickup and broadcast array, or they might be used only to tie the boat up at isolated moorings or wharfs. Nothing about the sizable but sluggish-looking craft suggested that it was home and place of business of the individual whom Tomuk Ginnyy insisted was better qualified than anyone else in the waterlands, legit or illicit, to probe the mystery of vanishing cerebral implants from young adults. Or to try to penetrate the secrets of an incomprehensible storage thread whose composition verged on alchemy.

More than anything else, Ingrid thought as Whispr steered their rented watercraft toward the unanchored, unlovely boat's starboard side, the exterior of their slowly drifting destination hinted at an owner/occupant who was slovenly and unkempt in his personal if not his professional habits. Its appearance certainly jibed with the doubtlessly made-up surname Wizwang.

Still, Ingrid reminded herself, it was unlikely Ginnyy had taken her money only to set up an appointment with an itinerant trapper or fisherman. There being no time to confirm from other sources the purported skills of the prober they were about to meet, they would have to render any such judgment themselves. She and Whispr could only hope the residents of the waterlands were not having a little fun at the visitors' expense. She was tired, hot, sweaty, and still unable to get the last images of the badly beaten Rudolf Sverdlosk out of her mind.

As their boat's bow clamp-locked on to that of the larger craft a high-pitched voice piped up from somewhere unseen. "Are you the two travelers Tomuk Ginnyy said she was sending to me? Because if you're not, leave now before I release the bees."

Bees? a bemused Ingrid thought. Had their morning appointment in the middle of the swampy waterlands been made with a distinguished dissident prober or an amateur apiarist? Following Whispr out of their boat, she found herself standing on narrow decking bedecked with moss, mushrooms, and other fungi. She wondered if all the dense sprouting was intended as decoration or camouflage.

Maybe both, she told herself as she followed her lean companion into a nearby opening in the windowless side of the boat. Seen from a distance, whether at the surface or from a satellite, the vegetation-covered craft would more than anything else look like an island of floating vegetation.

A welcome blast of cool air greeted them as they stepped through the climate curtain. The temperature on the other side was perfect; nothing like Tomuk Ginnyy's arctic ambiance. Ingrid relaxed a little. Their host might be cautious, eccentric, and a celebrated hermit, but he was also human.

Eccentric, she soon learned, did not begin to describe Yabby Wizwang.

The shirt and shorts-clad boy who greeted them looked to be about ten. Curly of hair, amber of eye, slender of form, his suntanned skin smooth and unblemished, he rose and came toward them from where he had been sitting in a wooden chair whose butt-bowl had been scooped out of a single cypress stump. Ingrid smiled at the unexpected presence. Though never having practiced as a pediatrician, she had occasionally dealt with children and their inevitable afflictions. Putting her hands on her knees, she bent over to smile at him.

"Hello. We've come to see—I'm guessing maybe it's your father?"

"My father's been dead for sixty years, but if you don't mind the sight and smell of advanced decomposition I expect I could arrange for you to make his acquaintance." Though eye level with her chest, the boy was staring at her lower body. "Tomuk said you were a physician. For a Natural, you've got nice legs."

"Excuse me?" she stammered in confusion.

"In due time and as necessary." The boy turned and beckoned. "Come with me and we'll get started. I usually allow up to five minutes for dim-witted gaping, but there are a number of things I want to get done today besides accommodating you, so you'll just have to get in your quota of obtuse oculations while we work."

Whispr could only stare speechlessly. Yabby Wizwang was the most perfect Meld he had ever seen.

When he pointed that out to his companion, Ingrid at first refused to believe it.

"How can you tell?" she whispered as she waited for him to catch up to her. "He looks exactly like a Natural child."

"That's the beauty of it." As a lifelong Meld himself Whispr did not try to hide his admiration for the culmination of innumerable surgical intercessions that their host represented. "Maniping someone to look like a Meld is nothing. Doing a Meld that perfectly mimics a Natural requires not just money but real skill." He nodded at the childish figure that was leading them deeper into the bowels of the foliage-draped craft. "Whatever surgeon or group of biosurges did this were artists as much as doctors."

Ingrid was still reluctant to countenance her companion's conclusions. "I have to ask," she blurted in the direction of their host, regardless of how the query might be taken, "but how old are you?"

The boy looked back over his shoulder. "Seventy-four next month, Legs. And just so you should know, there's one part of me that hasn't been maniped. You've got at least an hour to guess which it is."

Definitely not ten years old, she swore then and there. But why invest what must have been an enormous amount of time, money, and suffering— for this? To look like a child permanently? In the course of her studies and her career she had encountered hundreds of Melds, but never one like this. There was no suggestion, at least not yet, that their host fancied himself Peter Pan or some other notable child character from literature or the arts. Why then go through everything that must have been required in order to achieve this particular, peculiar, intentionally stunting Meld? She had to ask that, too, and also about the origin of his outré moniker.

They descended a stairway that soon opened into a room below the waterline. It was so packed with electronics there was barely enough room for its idiosyncratic owner and a couple of visitors. Wizwang settled himself into an ambient chair whose internally cooled padding folded affectionately around his limbs. There being no other furniture in the room his guests could choose between sitting on the floor or remaining standing. Whispr opted for the latter. Conscious of their host's unsettlingly childlike eyes wandering over her from hair to toe, Ingrid also elected to remain upright.

"My name? It's a joke, of course." In keeping with his incredibly elaborate meld his voice was preadolescent high-pitched, but there was nothing childlike about his diction. Nor the gaze that he used to pin her in place.

"I wanted something appropriately absurd and incongruous to fit my chosen Meld, which self-evidently is also a joke. How more amusing to live life than to make your own physicality into a permanent gag? How better to fit in with the rest of the Cosmos, which is also a joke? Read your Melville." Boyish, hairless arms spread wide to encompass everything as he tilted back his head and looked upward. "All of this, all of existence, is a gag, a trick, a hoax that our genes devised to keep us from going crazy from thinking about it too much." Lowering his eyes and dropping his arms, he favored her with a lopsided grin.

It was then and there that she came to the conclusion that their host was at least half mad.

"God doesn't play dice with the universe," he continued, reiterating an old and usually misunderstood quote. "He plays practical jokes with it. Didn't you know? That's what the universe is: a witticism, a one-liner with a many-googooplexed set of variations, designed to amuse its inhabitants and alleviate their boredom. Anyone who makes even a casual study of the cosmic neighborhood sees that it's nothing but sham, pretense, and fraud pressed into the service of untrammeled hilarity. The cosmic con." He leaned back in the soft cooling bulk of the chair. "Given that consensus I consider Wizwang, as a name, to be positively conservative."

To Whispr their host's declamation was nothing more than incomprehensible rant, but Ingrid found herself intrigued despite herself. "If all of it, if the entire cosmos, is nothing more than a deception and a joke, then what are we?"

Wizwang was clearly pleased by her interest. "Us? Isn't it obvious? We're the punch line. Through our activities and by our actions we reassert the truth of it every day."

Interesting as the ravings of the partially mad man (mad boy?) were, she and Whispr had not come all this way and expended so much effort just to wile away the day in barmy philosophical explication.

"Did Ginnyy tell you why we need your help?"

Sequestered deep within his womblike chair, he shook his head. Boyish locks fluttered. "She said you seemed candid and sincere, that your request would interest me, and that you could pay. You have five minutes to confirm all of those things or I release the bees."

Finally, Whispr thought. Something he could relate to. "You keep talking about bees. Is beekeeping a hobby or something?"

Their host's laserlike gaze shifted to the other Meld in the room. "Yes, but it's not mine: it's theirs. The bees keep me, I don't keep them."

Whispr eyed the boy-Meld blankly. "I don't understand."

"That's because you don't understand bees. Few people do. I much prefer their company to that of my fellow delusional primates." He jerked a thumb toward the bow. "They tend to stay forward. Unlike humans, they fully understand and are in complete harmony with their place in the ongoing cosmic joke. That's why unlike us they're only a minor anecdote and not a punch line."

Flowers, Ingrid realized with a start. The drifting houseboat was covered in flowers. It was not all camouflage, then. At the risk of pushing their host farther from brilliance and deeper into madness, she voiced another query.

"Your bees, do you talk to them?"

"All the time," Wizwang assured her cheerfully.

"And—do they answer back?"

"Depends on what the day's buzz is."

She hesitated, smiled, lost the smile, ended up uncertain. "You're joking with me again."

"That would mean there are jokes within jokes, doctor. Like bacteria inside cells within bodies. The bees and mes, it's a symbiotic relationship." He grinned at her, a childish grin that was anything but. "You really want to sit there and spend the limited time I've carved out for you talking about honey production?"

More unsettled than she cared to admit, she fumbled with her shirt pocket. "I've got something to show you—and no, it's not what you're hoping to see, so you might as well stay in that chair."

"Tch. And just as I was about to elaborate on the specificities of my own meld." He sniffed. "Buzzness it is, then. Show me something, and bee quick about it."

The cosmos might not be founded on jokes, she told herself as she drew forth the capsule containing the storage thread, but this craft and its singular landlord certainly were.

He slipped the thread into a custom modified reader and began working on it even as she brought him up-to-date on everything she and Whispr had learned. Unable to tell if he was ignoring her or not, she contented herself with recitation until she had delivered the last bit of potentially pertinent information.

They spent the next half hour trying to contain their impatience while their host worked. He made no comment and raised no objection when they chose to occasionally wander outside. The waterland scenery constantly changed around the slowly drifting houseboat, its position continuously monitored and rejiggered by silent subsurface thrusters commanded by the craft's GPS. Whenever midday's oppressively hot and humid atmosphere began to weigh on them they would wander back downstairs and immerse themselves in the main cabin's perfectly maintained climate.

During one muggy jaunt around the boat's exterior Ingrid found herself entranced by the sight of a flock of snowy egrets and roseate spoonbills commuting to and from a roosting tree. Their continuous calls and cries resounded like half a ton of tinfoil alternately being crumpled and unfurled. As she was drinking in the beauty of the avian mural, a bee hummed past her face, buzzing an arc toward the boat's bow. Black and yellow, it looked like a perfectly ordinary honeybee. Given its compound eyes, it was impossible to tell in which direction it might have been looking. For no especial reason, she thought it might have been looking at her.

"Doc! Ingrid!"

Dragging her thoughts away from potentially unsettling hymenopterian possibilities, Whispr's shout drew her back toward the belly of the boat. A look of satisfaction on his too-young face, Yabby Wizwang was waiting for her.

"Tomuk Ginnyy's search was even more on the mark than she thought."

Ingrid joined Whispr in regarding their diminutive host. "What does that mean?"

Sliding out of his enfolding chair, their host underscored his points with a flurry of energetic, seemingly random jabs at and into the glut of three-dimensional projections that now filled the air of the cabin.

"She found evidence of these peculiar implants that quickly vanished as soon as they came under observation." Whirling, he indicated his main console. It was so obscured with flex-plugs and add-ons that little of the base unit could be seen. "I've been able to correlate that information to-gether with what you've given me." He paused for emphasis. "There aren't dozens of these occurrences. There are hundreds. Perhaps thousands. And who knows how many more that haven't been reported, either because those who are afflicted with one of these devices don't wish to file a report or because they're not even aware they've been so infected."

It was the first time in their frenetic acquaintance that Whispr had heard the attractive doctor whistle. "Incredible. Is there a locus for the out-break?"

The melded eccentric shook his head. "Naturally I went ahead and recorded every reported incident. From what I've been able to collate, oc-currence is worldwide and relatively evenly spaced. Whoever's behind this evidently favors a comparatively egalitarian stratagem. Though to what purpose I cannot begin to divine." Pausing in his pacing and gesticula-tions, he turned to face her. Seventy-four-year-old acumen stared out of a ten-year-old's eyes. "I don't suppose you could enlighten me further on that?"

Whispr glanced briefly at Ingrid, then back at their host. "We were kind of hoping you could do that for us."

"Unlike some, I am not one who finds mutual ignorance comforting." Lowering his gaze Wizwang fell into contemplation that was, as was the rest of him, half brilliant and half mad. "Whatever have you two stumbled onto, nosy doctor and pawn of the night? It must mean *something*. There is money behind this or it would not be a worldwide, albeit widely scat-tered, phenomenon. Where there is money there is purpose. Power, art— at this point it's all pure supposition.

"I think it would be reasonable to assume that every one of these de-vices was implanted as part of the process of 'fixing' a previous bad meld. Such treatment would provide the perfect opportunity for participants in this scheme, whoever they are and whatever it may be, to install the implant while carrying out repairs to the existing broken meld. Of course, just because that appears to be the logical modus does not mean it is the only way this has been done. There may be thousands of Melds, but apparently not Naturals, who on examination would also reveal the presence of one of these implants."

"But why?" Whispr repeated. Though intellectually well out of his depth, he was not afraid to show it.

"Why indeed, stick-insect?" Though he was replying to Whispr, Wizwang's attention remained focused on Ingrid. "To paraphrase Clausewitz, 'Medicine can just be war by other means.'"

That comparison caught both of the houseboat's visitors off guard. Was their host simply trying to shock them? "What are you talking about, Yabby?" Whispr mumbled.

"Large-scale clashes between nations and groups of nation-tribes has for some time been recognized as impractical and counterproductive. It's bad for business and destroys or uses up that which war was once fought for, namely resources. But cultural conflict remains an issue for our wretched joke of a species, a philosophical appendix. Contemplation and consideration of a possible eventual conflict between Naturals and Melds has long been a fashionable subject among overwrought academics in search of a topic that would guarantee them publication. Perhaps these implants are in some way related to preventing that possibility." His voice dropped but did not deepen. "Or preparing for it."

"Oh, come on!" The outrageousness of Wizwang's speculation took Ingrid aback. "Ever since the first full cosmetic meld was auctioned off by Singapore Surgeons, Inc., there's been nothing to suggest the existence of that kind of controversy."

"Not on a governmental level, no. But there's plenty of it among and between individuals, doctor." Off to one side, a solemn-faced Whispr was nodding knowingly.

"There are laws against Meld prejudice in every country," Ingrid continued angrily.

"Laws are sufficient to stifle many kinds of antisocial behavior, but not bigotry. Prejudice is like stomach bile: controllable to the point of invisibility, but always present and just waiting for a chance to blossom and consume its host from the inside out." Turning sharply, he strode over to the customized reader that held the enigmatic silvery storage thread and leaned forward to examine a single readout.

"Nothing. Either this precious artifact of yours is empty, or else my equipment has so far been unable to break its encryption. I can't tell because the instrumentation is still working. It hasn't given up. Or your encapsulated thread could be a maguffin."

"A what?" Whispr exclaimed.

"Something designed to throw the curious off the real track. To divert attention from this plague of—so far—harmless-seeming vanishing implants."

"I don't think it's that," the slender visitor opined softly.

Wizwang's response was more indifferent than contemptuous. "Why not?"

"Because a good friend—well, a friend, anyway—of mine died because of it. Because I've nearly been killed in the process of hanging on to it." He cast a self-conscious glance sideways at Ingrid. "Others have been hurt, too." One slim arm rose to gesture in the direction of the reader that presently held the thread. "I don't know what if anything is on that thread but in my experience people don't kill to recover something that contains nothing."

Wizwang nodded pensively, no longer indifferent. "It's possible that the owners of the thread might only be striving to protect the secret of its unique manufacture. I'm not surprised that I haven't heard about this. Media coverage of violence that involves industrial espionage is inversely proportional to the size of the companies involved. Lids are clamped and sources muffled—or extirpated. Explanations for everything may well be contained on the thread itself."

Ingrid pointed toward the reader. "But you said that your equipment can't get into it."

"Time, my succulent general practitioner, is the key that unlocks many secrets."

She made a face. "If you're trying to impress me by speaking in aphorisms, it's not working."

"Pity." Small but shrewd eyes met her own. "Perhaps I should try a spew of sexual entendres. Oh, right—you're a physician. References of any sort to the act of reproduction will not faze you. Or would they?" Before an increasingly and visibly aggravated Ingrid could respond, he concluded, "I see I have you well riled, but not off balance. This is proof you will not tip easily." Barely pausing for breath, he proceeded to switch subject matter with disconcerting ease.

"There's a bar on eastside Macamock called Fillie Gumbo. Meet me there at ten tonight. I'll either have some answers for you or I'll have given up. Either way you're buying and I'll be bringing my appetite."

"Now why would anyone want to skip an invitation like that?" Whispr commented sardonically. "Why should we leave the thread with you?"

"Because I'm your last hope of finding out what if anything is on your thread or you wouldn't be here now. Because I'm known and therefore can be trusted." He looked again at Ingrid. "Because I want to see what Legs here wears to a nightclub, even a cheap one. Tonight. Be there or bee ware," their host advised him. "Nobody stiffs Yabby Wizwang."

Whispr sniffed meaningfully. "Not with *that* body."

Their host's cheeks started to flush, and then he smiled. "You have hidden depths, stick-man. You must, or one of your social status would be dead by now." He turned back to Ingrid. "Keep an eye on this one, doctor, lest in an inopportune moment you hear him say, 'Physician, peel thyself.' I wouldn't trust him in my bathroom unmonitored."

She looked over at Whispr, who was gazing back noncommittally. "We're partners in this. It's strictly a business arrangement. At my insistence, not his."

Wizwang's wispy brows rose slightly. "Should I find anything on your prized thread more outrageous than that admission, I will be surprised indeed."

15

Built on short narrow pylons out over the water at Macmock's western edge in order to take advantage of the frequently spectacular southern sunsets, the Fillie Gumbo would not have passed Savannah's riverside building codes. A spiderweb tissue of salvaged polymers, recycled cypress and mahogany (the only woods the local tropical termites would not eat), nonferrous metals, and an assortment of colorful building materials of dubious origin and possibly toxic content, the establishment was nonetheless extremely popular with the locals who were themselves of equally polyglot composition.

Some of the Naturals Ingrid observed eating, drinking, and arguing as she and Whispr made their way beneath the arched glowing entrance and out onto the expansive, well-lit, and decomposing mist-cooled deck were less admirable representatives of the human species than the often cheaply melded counterparts with whom they shared the bar and tables. The bar itself was fashioned of what had once been a piece of structural art. Its architectural glory in the past, the once vertical supportive column in the shape of a stylized mermaid lay on its side. It had been reduced to serving as a tittering footrest for backcountry drunks; its former beauty degraded, its original raison d'être dishonored by vomit stains and the untold involuntary discharges of multiple overstressed bladders. Even Whispr shied away from it.

There was no need to squander time at the bar anyway since the individual they had come to meet was already seated at an oval table by the water's edge. The seeming incongruity of a small boy hoisting a large beer attracted no attention. Recluse though he might be, it was apparent from his half-empty mug that Yabby Wizwang was well known here.

Ingrid automatically took the chair opposite him while Whispr sat between, facing the water instead of their host. While the establishment's surprisingly advanced misting system did its best to cool the air it could not entirely bring the nighttime heat and humidity into the realm of the comfortable.

Setting down his beer, Wizwang stared across the wooden table at the doctor. "You'll pardon me if I don't say that I love you for your mind. Mind I've got." His deceptive ten-year-old eyes roved.

She proceeded to do her best to support the contention that it is possible to ignore someone and engage with them at the same time. "We're here, you're here. Have you learned anything?"

"Yes." Leaning back in his chair he turned his head to his right to drink in the dark horizon. Out in the Everglades a few specks of light marked the locations of isolated stilt homes and commuting watercraft. "I've learned that there are drawbacks to confining oneself to the body of a prepubescent."

"We'd really like to socialize," Whispr commented dryly, "but you know how it is when people are trying to kill you. Especially for what you don't know."

Their host looked over at him. "Try as I might, I can't decide which of you two is more likely to be voted the life of the party." Digging into a pocket he brought out the capsule containing the storage thread and passed it back to Ingrid. Despite the guarantees he had given she was more than a little relieved to have it once more in her possession. Whispr's expression showed that he felt exactly the same. She hurried to tuck it away.

"Maybe there's instrumentation in the bowels of the Septagon that can crack the contents of that sliver, but I don't have access to it." Wizwang had turned deeply serious. "Until you showed up with it I'd never met a piece of hairware my gear couldn't unlock. This failure is a first for me.

However," he added encouragingly, "the time I spent working with it and attempting to learn about it was not a complete failure. Serendipity is a wonderful thing, especially when one starts digging into continental police records."

Instantly on guard, Whispr started to rise. "You've been researching us."

Small boyish hands made placating gestures. "Easy, easy, scarecrow! Everything is connected, everything is linked. I am very fond of links and, I flatter myself, enormously skilled at following them. What I did manage to discover should be all to your advantage and to the benefit of your searching. If a butterfly dies on the other side of the planet, what does it mean for us here?"

Only partly mollified, Whispr continued to glare at him. "That we know there's one more dead butterfly in the world."

"Not a man who likes to take in the big picture, I see."

"Spend too much time looking at the big picture and you're liable to miss the gun aimed at your head," Whispr shot back.

Ingrid intervened hastily. "What have you found out?"

Pressing one among the many assorted images that were embedded in the tabletop, Wizwang ordered another beer. "That you're not the only ones in this part of the world interested in storage devices made of MSMH."

Ingrid's thoughts flashed immediately to the trio of Meld miscreants who had nearly killed Dr. Sverdlosk while trying to extract information from him about the mysterious thread. "By chance are any of them melded women?"

Wizwang looked uncertain. "No, no women. I just happened to come across one, and it's a man."

"You're sure?" she pressed him.

"If you doubt my ability to tell the difference, come over to my side of the table and sit on my lap."

She kept her seat. "I'll take your word for it, Yabby. You say this person knows about MSMH storage threads?"

"I don't know if he knows about them, but it seems that he's interested in them. I came across him because he's been making comparable inquiries in parallel places. Nothing about head implants in adolescents. He just seems to be interested in the successful manufacture of MSMH and its possible use as a storage medium. Since he's been as discreet about it as you and the stick-man here, I responded tentatively and in kind. Once I established to my satisfaction, which I assure you is as demanding as your own, that he seemed reasonably trustworthy, I began to exchange information with him."

"You talked to someone else about our thread?" Whispr was aghast.

Wizwang favored him with a look usually reserved for invertebrates. "I told you I took care. Having met and learned from you, I was able to exchange certain credentials with this individual. He revealed enough to indicate to me that he knows things about your thread that you do not. In contrast, you have access to information concerning it that he would badly like to sample for himself. Being as happy as any middleman to take a cut from both sides, I have arranged for you all to meet."

Ingrid looked over at her companion. "What do you think, Whispr?"

Her willowy companion did not hesitate. "I don't like it one bit. Just because this guy isn't one of the lipsticked abyssuggers who pack-jumped your colleague doesn't mean he might not work for the same outfit that sent them on an infocrawl around Savannah. He could be bait to draw us out." He glared anew at their host. "What guarantee do we have that you're not setting us up?"

Wizwang stiffened visibly. "First, my wary whipsnap, I wouldn't do any such thing because my reputation hereabouts and faraway is worth far more to me than any piddling fee I could collect from turning you over to those who wish you ill. And second, had I desired to do so, this meeting would not now be taking place. Easier to sell you out at your cheap hotel than to waste time chattering with you beforehand. And I would have kept the thread."

Ingrid was not entirely convinced, but her eagerness to learn more about the thread outweighed her concern. "Where is this meeting to take place?"

"At my home, you're welcome very much. Another layer of security for you for which I expect no recompense." He sneered at the brooding Whispr. "Or thanks. Tomorrow morning anytime after sunrise. Before you come, have some breakfast, mainline some caffeine, sip-sup some local juice. I know that I will. So, I suspect, will this interested but chary third party. Then the four of us will cojoin to celebrate a collusion of the un-knowable that hopefully will result in at least a modicum of enlightenment for all."

"Or there could be a shooting," a still dubious Whispr muttered.

"Ever the optimist," Wizwang observed mildly. "I suppose one should not expect even a meager measure of jollity from one of so spare a frame and countenance."

Conversation momentarily ceased as their host's latest brew arrived, foaming mightily. Eyeing the condensation on the sides of the chilled mug, it occurred to Ingrid that neither she nor Whispr had ordered any-thing. Her dry throat colluded with her stressed mind and she ordered a drink from the compliant tabletop.

"I guess what you're saying is that you can't help us any further but maybe this person can." Whispr threw her an agonized glance, but she ig-nored him. "We'll be there. I don't know what else to do."

"When you don't know what else to do, do what someone who does know what else to do does." Wizwang lifted his mug in salute. "Drink up, hope for the best, and let the piss dribble where it may." He downed a long swallow through lips that appeared better suited to sipping milk. The con-trast was jarring.

When their own drinks arrived Whispr tried to have the last word on the matter. "I don't care what you said on your fertilizer barge. You set up this meeting so you pay for the drinks. We're trying to minimize our exposure down here."

Wizwang looked ready to protest, then shrugged juvenile shoulders. "A sampling of local libations, one of which is for a pretty lady? I think I can be that magnanimous. I'll fold the cost of your respective lubricants into your final invoice anyway and you'll never know the difference."

A bemused Whispr looked over the top of his glass. "Of course we will. You just told us that you're going to pay."

"I did? Pay no attention to my aimless ramblings." His small body forced him to rise and lean forward in order to hold his raised glass over the center of the table. "Here's to the unraveling of secrets, the uncovering of information, the explanation of impossible metallurgy, and mutual profit." Polycarb glasses clinked.

It was about then that the fight started.

The fracas was initiated by two Naturals. It was not related to the presence of the visitors from Savannah, it carried no Machiavellian subtext, and it had been sparked by a difference of opinion as old as mankind. One man took exception to something that another man said, or was perceived to have said, or he imagined to have been said, to the woman who was sitting with the offended. An escalation of execration ensued that rapidly devolved into physical conflict.

The smaller man pushed the larger man. The larger man pushed the smaller man, who fell into his girlfriend, who despite the presence of the subtle gripping upholstery beneath her butt that had been engineered to hold wavering drunks in place promptly toppled off the stool on which she had been sitting. As it invariably does in such situations, bawling led inexorably to brawling.

Picking up a chair, the bigger man threw it at his opponent, who ducked lithely. Sailing over the bar, the decidedly unaerodynamic furniture struck the unsuspecting human bartender a blow sufficient to knock him unconscious. He had not seen the errant seat coming his way because he had been in the process of trying to alert the local authorities to the budding conflict. Recovering, the sniveling girlfriend's determined defender responded with a twirl and leg sweep redolent of the best capoeira to be seen in Salvador's backstreet rodas. Taken by surprise, the bigger man still managed to stumble clear of the attempted takedown.

Unfortunately, this sent him crashing onto a table occupied by two Meld couples. Unwillingly transformed from observers to participants, they commenced to pummel the larger Natural. As one of them boasted four arms and the other a set of powerful tentacles, he instantly found himself subjected to a serious mauling. Seeing that the matchup had now become unequal, several hitherto uninvolved bystanders who happened to be acquaintances of the bigger man promptly joined in.

By now a good portion of the bar's population was engaged in ritual battle, motivated by increasingly angry words and fueled by various distillations of grains and tubers, not to mention a soupçon of exceedingly powerful synthetics. Naturals scuffled with each other and with Melds, and vice versa. An increasingly anxious Ingrid saw no evidence of any Natural-Meld sociocultural war here. Though on ample display, the loathing and dislike being exhibited was entirely egalitarian. Naturals bashed Naturals and Melds clobbered Melds with equal enthusiasm.

"This way!" Painfully aware that a superior intellect was as useful in dealing with a conflagration of drunks as a bucket of magnesium powder was in putting out a kitchen fire, a concerned Wizwang hurried to lead his visitors clear of the escalating conflict. Hugging the railing that separated bar from swamp the three of them worked their way around the edge of the overwater platform, striving to make it to the exit before any of them could be caught up in the increasingly bloody wrangle.

Having chosen an inopportune moment to attend to a personal matter, the bar's bouncer finally appeared in the entrance whose succor Ingrid, Whispr, and their host sought. In fact, he did not merely appear in the entrance—he occupied it. The initial attraction of heavy mass-muscle melds had faded as soon as it was realized that the caloric intake and exercise needed to maintain them required more dedication than most people were willing to contribute. However, the big muscle meld was still sought after by those for whom it represented a professional as opposed to merely a cosmetic enhancement.

Advancing with a menacing scowl while trying not to step on those who had fallen or been knocked down, the Fillie Gumbo's long-haired bouncer began separating combatants by picking them up, pulling them apart, and tossing them aside. Since he stood over two meters tall and weighed somewhere in the neighborhood of a quarter ton, none of the Naturals or Melds presently engaged in physical disagreement saw fit to contest the bouncer's progressive deconstruction of the circumstances in which they found themselves. Cuts and bruises were overlooked and insults forgotten as the bar's enforcer wearily plowed his way through the swiftly disintegrating skirmish. As near as Ingrid could tell, he never hit a single participant.

While rapidly dissipating, though, the widespread clash had not quite concluded. With her fascinated attention focused on the bouncer, she failed to see one of the participants stumbling in her direction. Fortunately the traditional fisherman Meld's left hand, whose fingers had been maniped into a series of four reels, was not mounting any hooks. Melded to mute the glare off water, his maniped eyes were glazed. Adapted for waterproofing, the skin of his legs that was exposed beneath his ragged-hemmed shorts scraped roughly against her. Seeking safety from the potentially dangerous drunk a jumpy Wizwang darted behind an overturned table. Whispr did not.

"Hey, fack off, squint-face!" Despite a notable disparity in mass, her slender companion unhesitatingly inserted himself between her and the weaving, oncoming local.

Lashing out as he spun around, the latter struck at Whispr with his reel hand. The blow hit home. Seeing his opponent still standing, the drunk looked surprised until he remembered that he wasn't wearing any of his work hooks. Even so, the bare-reeled swipe was edgy enough to rip through the bottom half of Whispr's thin tropical shirt and into the flesh beneath. He staggered from the blow. Astonishing herself, an infuriated Ingrid picked up a bottle and swung at their attacker. The wild swing connected with the fisherman's nose, itself middling melded the better to allow its owner to cope with having to labor all day in high heat and humidity.

Blood flowed. She gasped. Not at the gush of blood, a sight with which she was intimately familiar, but at the realization that she had initiated it. All her adult life she had worked to stop such outpourings.

"Dear me, doctor," a voice called out. "I didn't realize that you, of all people, had also bought a ticket to this backwater travesty of primate interaction." Having edged his way around the rapidly subsiding fight, Wizwang was beckoning to her from his latest place of concealment near the Fillie Gumbo's entrance.

Regaining control of her actions if not her emotions, Ingrid resumed her jerky stop-start flight in his direction. As they retreated Whispr continued to position himself between her and the remaining brawlers. Though admirable, his incongruous chivalry proved unnecessary. The last of the fighters was either down, had given up, or like one overwhelmed Meld seeking to escape the attentions of the determined bouncer, had leaped over the railing to land with a percussive splash in the dark water below.

Safely outside the bar Wizwang hurried them past buildings that alternated between hopeful and ramshackle.

"My transport's right over here. I'll run you around the island and back to the boatel." He glanced over at a panting, wide-eyed Ingrid. "Safer than trying to walk. The town streets are well lit, but so are too many of its citizens."

"Thanks," she responded gratefully. Her attention shifted to her other companion, who continued to remain alert for any further trouble. "Thanks to you too, Whispr, for . . ." Her words trailed away as she caught sight of something plastered against his skin where his lean flank had been exposed by the flailing fisherman. Her lips parted and her eyes widened slightly as she recognized it.

"That's a zoe." Their eyes met awkwardly and he quickly looked away. His obvious discomfiture heightened her suspicion. Then she remembered something brushing up against her when, at Tomuk Ginnyy's request, she had examined the insistent Inuit for a nano implant.

"You . . ." She stammered as she stared at Whispr. "You've been *wearing* me!"

From the time the ungainly, quiet Meld had first entered her Savannah office, this was by far the most outwardly uncomfortable she had seen him look.

"I—I couldn't help myself, doc. Ingrid." The look on his face was pathetic, his tone rife with heartbreak. "You know I'm attracted to you. Have been since when you first treated me. I know I can't—I know you don't want . . ." His voice trailed away into wretchedness, his halting words like pieces of shattered glass being dumped into a big-city gutter.

Torn between outrage and pity she struggled with a response as they stepped down into the quietly chuckling Wizwang's small green-sided runabout. Their host's unconcealed amusement rendered the situation even more embarrassing.

"But a *zoe*, Whispr. . . ." She stared at him. "That's, that's just so— *rude*."

Utterly miserable, he said nothing and seated himself as far away from her as the little commuter watercraft would permit. She was unreservedly grateful that for once Wizwang elected to close his eyes and especially his mouth to the obvious, resisting what must for him have been an overpowering urge to offer mocking comment. Wordlessly he guided the small boat around the island and back to their boatel's dock.

Though she knew full well what a zoe was she had never before been subjected to one. Leastwise, not to her knowledge. While perfectly legal, the deployment of a zoe implied consent on the part of the subject. What Whispr had done was akin to a kind of theft. Acting without permission, he had lifted an assortment of intimacies from her and placed them on his person.

Originally developed for use by emergency medical response teams, on contact a zoe strip took the measure of numerous components of the individual against which it had been swiped. It was the high-tech, biologically sensitive, full-body equivalent of a tongue swab. The contaminants thus acquired could be analyzed in a lab or, if the activated zoe was then pressed against another person, used to transfer all manner of useful compounds from a healthy person to one who was ill. The degree of absorption, acquisition, and delivery depended on the strength of the zoe.

From the one that had been brushed against Ingrid, Whispr had acquired certain antibodies, pheromones, and other chemicals, including a tiny but measurable dose of estrogen and its related compounds. None were obtained in dosages strong enough to change him physically. The jolts he received from wearing the zoe were strictly emotional and mental; a kind of chemical pornography. Or so the act was viewed by those against whom it was employed without consent. As for the formerly unaware subject of the attention, Ingrid had made her feelings known.

She said nothing else. There was nothing to add. Reaching down, a disconsolate Whispr picked at one end of the adhesive strip until he had peeled enough of it off his skin for his fingers to get a grip on. Slowly, deliberately, and no doubt reluctantly, he pulled it off and tossed it over the side of the boat. In the absence of current it lingered there, floating on the surface like a discarded exclamation point emphasizing the gap that still lay between them. She was relieved when their host nudged his watercraft up against the small dock and she was finally able to disembark.

They ate apart that night. Morning brought an uncomfortable breakfast accelerated by hasty words. By the time they were back in their own rented craft and speeding through the waterlands toward Yabby Wizwang's floating residence they were speaking to one another again. But the camaraderie that had begun to develop in the course of their journey south from Savannah had receded like the tide that lapped against the surrounding islands and pockets of vegetation. They were not quite formal with one another, but anything resembling a closer friendship had been set aside.

Smartly, Whispr did not push matters. The doctor felt wronged and made no attempt to hide it. There was nothing more he could think of to do beyond the verbal and physical abasement he had already performed that would better show the depths of his confusion and contrition. He would just have to wait it out, hoping that like a bad cold her anger and resentment would fade away.

In any case there was no more time this morning for further recrimination. Wizwang's jungle-covered houseboat loomed ahead and Whispr began to moderate their approach. As soon as their craft adhered itself to the floating bit of rainforest Ingrid stepped up onto the bow without waiting for him to lend a helping hand. A few bees swarmed curiously around her before heading off on their morning rounds. Looking on, Whispr amused himself by thinking that they were checking her out.

He had never held any interest in insects except for ways to avoid them. Instead, his attention was drawn to a second, battered, nondescript waterlands runabout that was fastened to the stern alongside their host's own personal commuter transport. Did Wizwang have two such craft and they had simply missed seeing the other in the course of their earlier visit—or was the unknown individual who espoused mutual interest in such things as MSMH and enigmatic storage threads already here?

Then, as his gaze wandered over the dark water, he spotted the alligator lying motionless alongside the new craft and knew the answer. It was not the hulking crocodilian itself that offered the revelation but rather the small yet efficient vidup situated atop its head and between its eyes.

The individual with whom Wizwang had so carefully nurtured contact was already chatting with Ingrid when Whispr descended to join them in the main cabin of the houseboat. He grinned at the newcomer.

"Gator."

"Sleep me with saurishians if it isn't Whispr-man!" The reptilian figure responded to Whispr's terse greeting with the astonishing toothy smile the other Meld remembered so well. Wizwang was plainly as startled as Ingrid by the instant rapport between the two men. Her lower jaw dropped while the eyes of the faux ten-year-old widened in disbelief.

"You two *know* each other?" Wizwang made an effort to recoup his poise. "I suppose I shouldn't be so surprised. There cannot be very many people who are aware of the existence of these implants, the storage thread, or the remarkable material out of which they appear to have been fashioned."

Leaving a gaping Ingrid in his wake Gator walked over to Whispr and took the other man's hand in his scaly fingers. Whispr eyed him guardedly.

"I thought you'd be dead, or in jail. I saw you get shot."

"It was a near thing." The Alligator Man tapped leathery fingers against his shirt-covered side. "My melded skin helped. Tough stuff. I did just get away. I did my best to get you to safety but until now I had no idea how you had fared. Glad to see you made it out all right. What brings you to the waterlands?"

Whispr nodded toward their host. "You already know or you wouldn't be here. Information. Trying to find out more about the storage thread I brought to you."

"The contents of which our diminutive but knowledgeable friend here hasn't been able to crack, either. Or so he's informed me. When he told me he had been in contact with others who were familiar with the same supposedly unfeasible material I had no idea it might be you." Looking back, he gazed appreciatively at Ingrid. "You've moved up in the world since our initial meeting, Whispr-man. How long have you two been . . . ?"

Her tone frosty, Ingrid interrupted. "We have not been 'anything,' Mr. . . . Gator. I am Dr. Ingrid Seastrom. . . ."

"'Doctor.'" Where eyebrows would have been, the narrow horizontal scutes above Gator's eyes rose slightly.

" . . . to whom Whispr came for treatment of his injuries. He subsequently offered me the opportunity to try and read the thread in the hope that it might contain information he might use to obtain money with which to pay me for the services I had performed. I'd had a previous encounter with an inexplicable cerebral implant apparently manufactured of the same improbable material as the thread. Naturally, encountering another object fashioned of the same impossible material piqued my interest. From a purely scientific standpoint, of course."

"Of course," observed Gator, politely noncommittal.

"We subsequently agreed to see if we could unlock the mystery of both the thread and the material of which it had been fashioned by pooling our resources and working together." Her eyes flicked to Whispr. "We bring different skills to the inquiry."

"I'll say," murmured the admiring Gator.

Whispr hurried to change the thrust of the discussion. "How'd you loose the police?"

"The same way you did. By making use of my knowledge of the Savannah wetlands and the submarine abilities of my maniped aquatic companions. Give me a live being every time that actually lives in a difficult environment over mechanical devices supposedly built to cope with it."

He turned back to Ingrid. "Tell me what you know about the material and the thread and then I'll tell you what I've learned since your friend Whispr-man and I were compelled to part ways."

She found herself hesitating and looking over at Wizwang. "Maybe this Meld knows Whispr and maybe Whispr's had contact with him, but he's new to me. How do I know he won't suck up everything we've learned and then just hop in his boat and waft on us?"

Whispr struggled to repress a pleased smile. "You've learned a lot in a short time, Ingrid."

She flashed him a look. She was still angry at him because of the zoe, but her initial white-hot outrage was starting to dim. For one thing, try as she would she could not get the memory out of her mind of the utterly dev-astated look on his face when his ruse had been discovered.

Their host spoke up. "I told you last night that I take suitable precau-tions. I've delved into Mr. Gator's background and reputation, and I'll vouch for him."

Ingrid peered across at the wizened ten-year-old Meld. "And who vouches for you, short stick?"

Whispr whistled tellingly while Gator contributed a knowing snigger.

To his credit Wizwang showed no annoyance. "If you don't feel that you can trust me by now, then why are you even here?"

Ingrid hesitated. Aware that the resulting silence was of her own doing, she realized it was up to her to break it.

"All right, then."

After a confirming nod from Whispr, whose judgment she had after all agreed to rely on in such matters, she proceeded to detail in layman's terms everything she and her slender companion had managed to learn, separately and together, about the thread. Much of this was already known to the Alligator Man from his own hastily performed research in his own lab. The details concerning the inscrutable cerebral implants—their na-ture, the fact that they had thus far been reported only in those of a certain age who had undergone bad melds, and all the rest—were however en-tirely new to him. Noting that he was recording everything, Ingrid con-cluded uneasily but with resignation.

"You're up-to-date now on everything we know. Now tell us what *you* know. What, if anything worthwhile, you've learned since you and Whispr—parted."

"I think you'll find something to interest you, doctor." Gator's tone had changed from jovial to somber. "Not that I know anything about the contents of your storage thread—if there are any. I don't. What I *did* succeed in finding out, after casting my head upon the waters in the form of a great many exceedingly covert inquiries, is that there actually is *one* company that is rumored—and I have to emphasize rumored—to be working on a manufacturing process that would allow for the utilization of metastable metallic hydrogen."

Whispr spoke up. "For storage? Or for the kind of implants Ingrid just told you about? Did you find out anything that might explain how these implanted devices disappear when someone starts to examine them?"

"The business of entanglement? Nothing on how that might be accomplished, no. Sounds like magic to me." He eyed Ingrid meaningfully. "But then, so does the ability to make MSMH under terrestrial conditions, much less build something out of it. As I say, there are just these rumors. Nothing at all conclusive."

"We give you facts, you give us gossip," Ingrid grumbled.

The Alligator Man was impassive in the face of her displeasure. "That's more than you had before I gave it to you."

"What's the name of the company?" Whispr demanded to know. Picking at a downward protruding tooth, Gator looked over to him.

"It's Sick."

Ingrid's expression contorted. "I'm not surprised, but what about the company?"

"Allow me to elucidate." Wizwang was relaxing in his special chair. "I believe your nobby-skinned acquaintance is referring to the South African Economic Combine. Though its acronym is SAEC, it's commonly pronounced 'Sick.' Or sometimes 'SICK, Inc.' among those with an economically inclined humorous bent."

"Oh," a chastised Ingrid murmured, "*that* SICK. I know the name, of course, though I've never had any dealings with them."

"Why should you?" their host observed. "You don't buy medical technology directly from them. You use what is purchased by secondary companies and then moved along the supply chain to local dealers and related establishments. SICK makes a great many products, of course, as well as dealing in raw materials. A consortium of that size and power would be interested in dealing in a substance like MSMH in its raw state as well as in the form of finished manufactured goods." He bowed theatrically in Gator's direction.

"I congratulate you, master of a maxillofacialist's reverie. Only a rumor it may be, but one with some perceptible grounding in economic reality and likely worth pursuing." His gaze crossed back to Ingrid. "As for you, mistress of elegance and knowledge, not to mention a fine set of—"

"We'll follow up on it," she said quickly. "It's the only real lead we've come across." She eyed the self-satisfied Gator. "However nebulous the facts supporting it. Right, Whispr?"

Her companion's reaction was distinguished by a notable lack of eagerness. "Ingrid, I don't know." His gaze flicked from her to Gator to Wizwang to finally settle on his own nervously shifting feet. "If Gator's infoup is right and it's SICK, Inc. that's really behind all this, it would go a long way toward explaining a lot of things. Why the police didn't hesitate to vanish my friend Jiminy, how they latched on to Gator so fast. . . ." His voice rose along with his gaze as he met her eyes. "I'm not like you, doc. I don't care what's on that thread except how it can be translated into subsist. But there are more important things than money."

"Why, Mr. Whispr, sir," a mocking Wizwang declared from his chair, "you are in truth bulging with surprises for someone so slight in both substance and stature. I would never have expected to hear such a noble if clichéd assertion fall from what remains of your lips."

By way of reply Whispr offered up an obscenity that relied for its effectiveness more on tradition than originality.

"It's still our only lead," Ingrid pointed out plaintively.

"You don't get it." Whispr fought to make her understand. "You don't mess around with a consortium like the SAEC. There are Western rules, and Asian rules, and then the rules of companies that make them up as they go along. That holds especially true for most of the big companies that have risen up south of the equator."

A somber Gator was nodding knowingly. "When it comes to the uninvited poking around their business, these big multinationals can be—impolite, doctor. Behind the smiling suits and flash melds are ugly little men making big subsist from nasty machines. The kind of people who inhabit the darker corners of urburgs like Karachi and Macao, Saopan Paulo and Joburg. They don't play nice. Owning a professional degree wouldn't impress them. Or restrain them."

Ingrid refused to be dissuaded. "We *have* to pursue it. We've come this far. I once told Whispr I couldn't rest until I found out what was on the thread—even if it turns out to be nothing." She took a deep breath. "Despite everything that's happened and despite what you're telling me now, I still feel that way."

"Actually, you can. Rest, that is."

Holding the blunt and brutal short-barreled twin-triggered flurry out in front of him, Napun Molé descended soundlessly from the accessway's last step and into the cabin.

16

"Please keep your hands where I can see them. Please do not move any more than is necessary to breathe." Molé gestured with the flurry. The weapon was lightweight, big-mouthed, and lethal. "I would just as soon not kill anybody."

"We are in agreement." Sitting up stiffly in his enveloping chair, Wizwang stared fixedly at the newcomer. "Who are you, old man, and how did you get past my security?"

"My name is not important and often confusing to those who do not know me. Since you will not have the opportunity to know me, you will not be unnecessarily confused. As to your security—what a funny-looking little Meld you are!—I suppose it qualifies as sophisticated for this backwater blackwater segment of a submerged state. I am used to dealing with far more elaborate defensive measures. I assure you I have on my person enough equipment to defeat everything up to and including the surveillance facilities of a small military base. That which was emplaced to safeguard one houseboat did not delay me more than a few minutes." His attention shifted to the openmouthed Ingrid.

"Your activities, on the other hand, Dr. Seastrom, have been grounds for a good deal of irritation on my part." With the muzzle of the weapon he gestured at Whispr, who had been looking frantically and unsuccessfully for a hatch to bolt through ever since the heavily armed oldster had entered the cabin. "Why couldn't you simply have left this sorry individual alone, or treated him and sent him on his way? Had you done that you could now be back home in your comfortable codo in Savannah relaxing in the midst of a mindless entertainment vit while, as most women of your age, pondering whether or not you are teetering on the biological cusp of sacrificing family for career." He shook his head sadly. "Instead you are here, where I may unwillingly resolve that conundrum for you by blowing your head off."

She had thought herself inured to the imagined dangers presented by possession of the thread. Proof that she was wrong was doubly confirmed; by the shaking of her body that began in the pit of her stomach and spread to her arms, and by the trickle of warm liquid that had commenced running down her left leg. Trembling visibly, she looked to her left. Her partner, her companion, her advisor, Whispr was paying no attention to her. If she expected him to leap to her defense, either physically or verbally, she was plainly badly mistaken.

Only Gator's voice remained unshaken. "There's no need for slaughter. You yourself just said you'd rather not kill anybody. Tell us what you want and we'll give it to you. If it's money I can . . ."

The old man almost came close to smiling, though the eventual expression was far less pleasant. "Oh please, don't insult me. Would anyone, especially someone my age, go to all this trouble and come to this stinky hot place in search of mere lucre? If robbery is what was on my mind I would have set to work in Miavana, where there are actually things worth stealing."

"If not money, then what?" Whispr felt he had to ask the question even though he was sure he already knew the answer.

"I don't mind heat, but the humidity in this part of the world really is appalling." The intruder returned his unblinking gaze to the shivering Ingrid. "In concert with another revolting Meld, the stick-insect standing alongside you killed a courier and stole from him something that belongs to my employers. The courier's death is of no consequence. What was taken is very much of consequence. He brought the stolen item to you. My employers want it back." Once again he gestured with the murderous flurry. "This will conclude much more pleasantly for everyone if you simply hand it over to me."

Ingrid swallowed. Quite to her surprise she heard herself saying, "I don't know what you're talking about."

Molé rolled his eyes. This time, he did laugh. It was a subdued, soft sound, almost like a muffled cough. "Come, come, woman. When I was in my youth I played this game and enjoyed it. I used to play many games in which I no longer indulge. Not because I have lost my delight in them but because my time has become more precious than the transitory amusements they once afforded. You have the thread. This is known. You lent it to a colleague of yours and he subsequently returned it. That is also known. Therefore you have it now."

Her eyes widened. "You—your people are the ones who beat up poor Rudy!"

Molé's weary sigh reflected his boredom. "If you are referring to the assault that was perpetrated on the person of a certain Dr. Rudolf Sverdlosk, your accusation and your anger are misplaced. That involved neither myself nor those for whose satisfaction I am engaged."

A surprised Whispr spoke up. "Another outfit besides the one you're working for knows about the thread?"

"Too many know about it, my angular friend. Not what it is, not what it contains, only that it is valuable. Especially to certain concerned parties, my employers being foremost among them. Knowledge of this matter has already spread too wide and is renowned, even if only as hearsay, by far too many. All disquiet will be resolved, however, and everything returned to normal when the article in question is returned to its rightful owners. Which shall be directly."

Even though it might reveal knowledge that could potentially seal her fate she could not help herself from asking questions. This is a condition that afflicts the majority of hopeless addicts. In the case of Dr. Ingrid Seastrom, her drug of choice was science.

"What about the juvenile nanodevice implants that are also made of MSMH? How does the thread relate to those?"

"Nanodevices? Implants?" Demonstrating yet another of his artfully veiled talents, Molé managed a passable imitation of her voice. "'I don't know what you're talking about.'" For a final time he gestured with the flurry. "Please give me the thread. Since I know it's not in your boatel room. . . ."

"How do you . . . oh." She caught herself. If this strange little old man could get past Yabby Wizwang's sophisticated residential security he surely would have no trouble breaking into and searching the contents of an ordinary commercial dwelling.

"Unless," Molé continued, his unblinking eyes flicking in Whispr's direction, "your companion is currently holding it. Whoever has it please just give it to me. I don't search live bodies."

"We—we don't have it, really," she stammered. "It's back in Savannah, in a safety deposit. You don't think we'd actually bring it down here with us, do you?"

"No, I don't *think* you would. I know you would. With apologies, doctor, this is an area of expertise where you are out of your depth. Your knowledge of such dealings extends to what your pathetic companion may have told you and to what you may have seen portrayed in cheap popular entertainments. To employ that medium's time-honored if hackneyed vernacular, you are stalling. This is how I deal with stalling."

The flurry went off. Despite the deceptive gentleness of its exhalation, Whispr flinched and Ingrid, unashamedly, screamed. Once again, only Gator held his ground.

She looked down at herself. Having already released her bladder, her leg was no wetter—neither from urine nor blood. She had not been hit by the blast. Neither had Whispr, who rose slowly from the crouch into which he had instinctively dropped. Gator had barely moved. Bewildered, she looked to her right. As a physician she found the sight of so much blood alarming, but only from an academic standpoint.

The hundred or so explosive darts that had emerged from one of the flurry's twin barrels had shredded Yabby Wizwang from the waist up as thoroughly as if his body had been pressed through a giant cheese grater. The visual consequences made it look as if he had simultaneously been attacked by a dozen crazed barbers wielding straight razors. So overwhelming was the trauma to his system that he had not even been able to pump a last burst of shocked air out of his shrunken lungs and past his juvenile vocal cords. Blasted back into his chair, blood draining from his minced corpse and onto the deck of the cabin, it was impossible to tell that he had undergone extensive melding to make himself look like a ten-year-old. In death as in life he still looked like a ten-year-old. Harder to discern than true age was that the flayed form had once been human.

Belying his advanced years while demonstrating his experience, Napun Molé had reloaded the instant after he had fired, extracting one shell among several from the bandolier slung beneath his loose-fitting, garish tropical shirt. His voice had not changed in the slightest when he resumed speaking.

"Please now, Dr. Seastrom. The thread? I assure you it will not be damaged if the destructive effects just applied to your host have to be repeated on your own person. The metal is stronger than you may imagine." Holding and balancing the flurry with his right hand, its short stock jammed into the crook of his arm, he extended his other hand expectantly.

The black caiman that leaped on him from behind nearly got him.

Even as she threw herself toward Whispr, Ingrid could not decide which astonished her more: the fact that the Alligator Man had somehow managed to silently signal his maniped reptilian accomplices that he was in need of help, or the fact that a stumpy-legged crocodilian like a three-meter-long caiman could get that far off the floor.

Molé was surprised but not taken. Whirling, he unleashed both barrels of the flurry. The foreparts and front half of the leaping reptile disintegrated in an expanding sphere of blood, teeth, scales, and bone. Enough kinetic energy remained from its jump, however, to drive a portion of the organic debris into the assassin and knock him to the floor. A second caiman followed close on the armored heels of the first while yet another was smashing its way through the largest of the portside windows. Each had attached to its skull a similar tiny manip implant that allowed Gator to control and direct them.

Seizing a stunned Ingrid as well as the opening, Whispr yanked her in the direction of the cabin's other entryway. Pursued by violent curses in several languages, the muted but lethal *phut!* of the flurry being fired again, Gator's half-hysterical bellowed commands, and a succession of primeval crocodilian roars, they climbed and stumbled desperately up to the main deck.

"Wait, wait!" After half dragging her up the steps, Whispr now fought to hold her back. She soon saw why.

Along with the dark water in which it sat, the boat's deck was alive with giant reptiles. Every species currently known to reside in tropical Namerica was represented: caimans black and white, alligators, crocodiles American and Orinoco. In response to Gator's call they clambered over the sides of the houseboat, the smaller craft moored against it, and each other in their haste to force their way into the main cabin. Glancing back down the stairway Ingrid saw something massive, toothy, and glittering of eye coming her way.

"Whispr . . ." Without waiting, she pushed past him. "They're not after us anyway."

"What makes you think they can tell the difference between . . . ?" He didn't have time to finish the question because she didn't give him any.

For whatever reason—the persistence of Gator's summons, the natural attraction of the frenetic action occurring within the cabin, sheer dumb luck—none of the reptiles swarming the houseboat changed tack to lurch in their direction. One lumbering armored monster did take a snap at Whispr, who eluded the potentially bone-crunching bite with a twisting leap worthy of a celebrity ballerino. Ingrid gasped—she was beyond screaming—as something tore away a piece of her shorts.

They made it to their rented watercraft which was, for the moment at least, thankfully unoccupied. Whispr disengaged the link locking it to the larger vessel. A quick spin of the wheel and a moment later they were accelerating away from the overgrown houseboat as fast as torque could be acquired.

Luggage being deemed less important than living, by mutual consent they did not go back to their rooms at the Macamock boatel. Instead, Whispr headed the speedy little watercraft straight toward distant Miavana. New clothes could be purchased. Personal effects could be replaced. Everything that mattered was already in the boat and intact: themselves, their individual faux idents, and most important of all, the thread. Far more important than recovering anything trivial from their rooms was the need to put as much distance as possible between themselves and the houseboat—in the event a fearsome and singularly ferocious old man managed to survive the dinosaurian assault Gator had thankfully unleashed upon him.

Tense behind the manual controls, sweat pouring off his bladed countenance, Whispr peered across at her.

"You look like hell."

Her attention concentrated on the swamp and waterland ahead, she barely glanced in his direction. "That's not surprising. I usually look like I feel." She shook her head slightly, ever so slightly. "He just *killed* him. Killed Wizwang. No warning at all. He didn't even say he was going to shoot. He just killed him. To make an example for the rest of us. I was looking at his face. His expression never changed."

"Whose expression?" Whispr inquired with grim humor. "The old man's, or Wizwang's?"

"The old man's. I didn't get a chance to see Wizwang's. When I did look he—there wasn't anything left to make an expression with."

Whispr maintained a death grip on the manual steering, unwilling to relinquish control of their craft to the boat's deactivated autopilot. The last thing he wanted was to give the elderly horror that had come after them a chance to take control of the watercraft's instrumentation.

"Yeah. He just went on and on about his 'employers.' Not 'employer' . . . I'm sure he used the plural."

Ingrid nodded in confirmation. "That's how I heard it. I wonder if he was referring to SICK?"

"One thing's sure," Whispr responded. "He wasn't referencing any political authority. That's how I took it, anyway. The cops might bend far enough to kill somebody like Jiminy during a pursuit, but granting permission to shoot some innocent Meld just sitting in a chair . . ." He shook his head. "You'd have to be pretty damn twisted to approve something like that. I hold with Gator's opinion: if the SAEC is working on ways to manufacture this MSMH stuff, then they're the ones most likely to know what's on an unreadable storage thread that's made from it. Not to mention why it's worth killing for. Not that it matters."

She turned from the vista of swamp and rainforest ahead to look across at him. "What do you mean, Whispr?"

He kept shifting his attention between her and the waterway in front of them. "Haven't you had enough, doc? I mean, how many folk have to die before it's enough? How many lucky jumps do you think you get before your name shows up on the Lucifer list? If we go to the authorities with the thread and everything we know and make sure there are publicams and private pickups present when we do the handover, there'll be too much publicity for those involved or bent to do anything to us. They'll have to be satisfied with recovering the thread and leaving us alone. We can get out of this *alive*. There might even be a reward for coming forward with what we know."

What Whispr said made sense. She thought about it long and hard. For a good five minutes.

"We've already talked about this, Whispr," she finally told him. "I'm not giving it up. I can't. If you want to go home, I'll understand. I'll keep the thread as payment for helping you with the traktacs."

"Yeah," he mumbled, "you've already said that. You know, for a woman of science you sure can catclaw cling to an outmoded, illogical theory."

Her brow furrowed. "What outmoded, illogical theory?"

"The one that says that if you keep on with this fanatic's quest you'll still manage to make it to your next birthday."

While she had not gotten over her indignation over the zoe, she still had to smile. "It's nice of you to care, Whispr."

"I *don't* care!" he yelled. "I could care less if—ah crap, forget it. Forget everything. It doesn't matter anymore, I guess. We're gonna die anyway."

"That's the spirit!" Reaching over, she gave his right shoulder a gentle squeeze. "I like a man who's driven by optimism."

"Driven to madness, you mean," he muttered darkly. But his shoulder tingled where her fingers had gripped him. That wasn't logical either. He eyed her in wonderment. "People sure can change fast, and I don't mean by melding. You're not the same twitchy tight-ass doctor who treated me in Savannah."

She spent awhile digesting that while they powered on toward Miavana as fast as the compact rental craft could carry them.

"So," she finally asked him, "you sticking with this and with me, you staying here in Florida, or are you going back to Savannah?"

He guided the boat around a floating mass of emerald-green, meter-wide *Victoria regina* lily pads. Panicked frogs the size of his open palm scattered in all directions, prompting a brief surface-shattering attack by a couple of lurking pirarucú.

"I go back to Savannah without the thread for justify, I get picked up or killed by the cops. I stay here, I get killed. I go with you, I get killed. Not an easy call, doc."

Turning away from him she watched the line of exotic vegetation flow past off to starboard. "Your unremitting sarcasm demeans you, Whispr."

"Really? I thought it defined me as a realist. You're a physician, Ingrid. Not an industrial spy, not a professional probe. Keep on with this and you're gonna find yourself way out of your depth and eventual-like singing with the Choir Invisible."

She looked evenly at him. "You didn't answer my question."

He gave a violent shake of head, thoroughly annoyed with himself. "Of course I'm sticking with you. If only to get an apology before we're both shot, or decapitated, or however badly this eventual-like ends. How the hell do you expect to learn SICK's secrets when they have toxic scum like Molé working for them?"

"We don't know that he works for them," she countered. "He never identified his 'employers.'" She turned thoughtful. "But based on what Gator told us he found out, it's the logical place to start. We'll try and learn what we can from SICK, Inc. by doing the last thing a company with their reputation would expect."

"What's that—no, I don't want to guess. Tell me—Ingrid."

"We'll go there."

"Excuse me?" He looked over from the controls.

"To SICK, Inc. Wherever their main research facilities are located. I don't know that location offhand, of course, but I think I read in a business journal somewhere that their corporate headquarters are in South Africa. Their principal research setup would be the logical place to try and find out if they're working on something as improbable as a technique for manufactured MSMH."

Whispr nodded slowly. "Yeah, that makes sense. What doesn't make sense is how in the name of all that's melded you think you're going to get yourself, or me, or the both of us into the R&D facility of a major multinational concern that's legendary for not playing nice with competitors or, for that matter, governments."

"One step at a time, Whispr."

"One foot in the grave at a time. Oh well, never in my most stim-aided dreams did I ever think I'd ever get to Africa. As long as you're paying, doc, I'm with you on this suicide express." He was growing wild-eyed. "To the terminal Terminal where we'll be terminated, that's where we're heading!"

She did her best to calm and encourage him. "Don't be so negative, Whispr. Think about it. Aside from the business of the implants, if the SAEC *is* working with MSMH and is after the thread and suspects that I have it, the last place their hired hunters like this Molé person would expect me to show up is at the front gate of one of their own administrative or research centers."

"With good reason." He turned thoughtful. "I just have one condition for staying on this doomed night train."

"Name it."

His words were suddenly filled with a wholly unexpected yearning. "If we're going all the way to Southern Africa having to avoid hired assassins the whole time, before I die I want to see some wild animals. I've only seen them in vits. Never expected to see them in anything *but* vits." He turned to face her. "I want to see lions, Ingrid. I want to see elephants. I want to see gemsbok and reedbok and steenbok and every other kind of bok."

Her reply was somber. "This isn't a vacation, Whispr. You yourself have missed no opportunity to point that out."

He was unshakable. "That's the deal, doc. Ingrid. I get to see my animals or you can go get yourself killed all by your smarmy upperclass know-it-all lonesome."

She shrugged. "Animals. Okay, we'll make time."

A slow smile spread across his face. "Look at it this way: if we act like typical tourists, maybe no one will pay any attention to us."

She perked up. "You believe that?"

"Not for a minute. But optimism-wise it's the best I can do right now." He shook his head gloomily. "SICK, Inc. We'll just stroll in through their front gate and ask to speak to whoever's in charge of arcane product development and nonsensical metallurgy."

Ingrid went quiet, letting him steer the boat, pondering his last offhand comment. In subterfuge as in medicine, she concluded, there is virtue in directness. If that wasn't a contradiction in terms. And she knew a contradiction in terms when presented with one.

It perfectly fit her present situation.

THAT HIS IRRITATINGLY NIMBLE QUARRY was utilizing automatically rotating random idents did not surprise Molé. It was not something he had anticipated, but it was something he was prepared to deal with. That employment of the mildly sophisticated technique for continuously concealing one's identity arose from the street experience of the inconsequential Meld who had been his original quarry he had no doubt. That a Natural citizen of Dr. Ingrid Seastrom's social strata was traveling in the company of an individual like this Whispr and was making use of the miserable Meld's decidedly nonmedical learning was rather more surprising.

It would not matter in the end, of course. The outcome was fated. His recovery and return to his employers of the precious storage thread had suffered a temporary delay. While he disliked delays, he was quite able to accommodate them. Through their obstinacy and ignorance his quarry was only delaying the inevitable. And perhaps accumulating considerable future unpleasantness for themselves.

Though it took a little time, it had not been difficult for someone of his determination and experience to learn where the pair intended to travel next. Conveniently, the two small commuter watercraft he had seen fastened to the houseboat of the late iconoclast Yabby Wizwang had displayed vehicle identification information near their bows. The first he had traced as belonging to the interfering but undeniably interesting reptilian aficionado known as the Alligator Man. The other had been rented to a Ms. Arlene Verdoux. A little illegitimate digging through the right corners of the local box brought forth the watercraft rental company's security image of Ms. Verdoux, whose likeness was, unsurprisingly, a close match for that of Dr. Ingrid Seastrom of Greater Savannah.

Breaking into the closed security systems of transport networks required a certain higher level of skill, but it still did not take him long to match up a Ms. Judy Davis with a Mr. Elon Danovich. Names could be altered with frequency, comparative ease, and the right program, but changing appearances took time and meldwork. While he would not have been surprised to see Archibald Kowalski subject himself to an extensive facial meld at a moment's notice, it was something far less likely to be expected of a Natural like Ingrid Seastrom. As it developed, while their names were shifting like the wind, their physical appearances stayed more or less constant.

So it was that in due and not disproportionate time he learned that Ms. Davis and Mr. Danovich had departed on a JALAA flight to Tokyo. Why Tokyo? He would find out when he found them. With a sigh, he prepared to make the necessary travel arrangements. Tokyo was a big place, far larger in extent and population than Greater Savannah. But the fact that he would be looking for a pair of gaijin would reduce the necessary search time considerably. As he packed his small bag and prepared to depart from Miavana he had no doubt that the runners and the thread they carried with them would be in his hands within a week at most. They really had no idea who they were dealing with.

But then, neither did anyone else who had ever been unfortunate enough to look over their shoulder and catch a glimpse of Napun Molé.

"So," INGRID WONDERED AS she settled back in Seat D, Row Ten, of SAA's evening Miavana-to-Cape Town ramjet, "what makes you so sure this Molé creature isn't on the flight behind us?" She twisted around in her seat. "Or even in the back of this same plane?"

Whispr was as relaxed as he had been in some time, luxuriating in the kind of air travel he had never expected to be able to experience.

"Because he's not looking for our current idents, doc. He's looking for the previous ones, and right now Judy Davis and Elon Danovich are on their way to Tokyo." He smiled to himself. "I don't know if it's fair, but my experience says that each time you successfully employ a new ruse it gains you another year of life." He snuggled back in his seat.

"While we were getting ready to leave I broke into JALAA's reservations system, picked out a couple of passenger names at random, and time-subbed our prior idents for those of an actual couple going to Nippon. Instead of finding our Cape Town reservations, anyone researching our previous names or appearance will be shunted to theirs." He chuckled to himself. "With any luck, Molé-man is already on his way in the opposite direction from ours."

Ingrid considered. "He won't be happy when he learns that he's been tricked."

Whispr's amusement vanished. "What difference does that make? When he or his associates eventually find us it won't matter if they're laughing hysterically or growling in anger when they finish us off. But I think I've bought us some time." His smile returned, albeit muted. "It's funny—I don't care so much about learning the secret of the thread any-more, as long as you're satisfied to accept it as payment—but I do want to see the animals." His gaze locked on hers. "You have your obsession, I have mine."

Having delivered himself of that assessment, he set about learning how to use the plane's in-flight entertainment system, as delighted by each new offering as a kid with a new netglobe. Leaving him to his amusements, Ingrid chose to accept his assessment of their current prospects. If the assassin who had been set on them really was on his way to Tokyo, they should have at least a week or more to move about freely and make open inquiries in Cape Town—after setting aside a suitable period for wildlife viewing. Once they arrived she could renege on that agreement, of course. Doing so would also likely see her chances of learning anything about the thread without first getting herself killed reduced to near zero. In a place as foreign and dangerous as Southern Africa she would need the street smarts of her disreputable, seedy, and somewhat smelly companion more than ever.

As the plane climbed to the edge of space she found herself worrying about her friends and patients back home. What would they think when her "vacation" time ran out and she failed to return or contact anyone? She missed her comfortable codo and the modern conveniences and enhancements she had for so long taken for granted. She missed feeling safe. And she knew she couldn't contact anyone, personal or professional, lest the communication be traced back to the location from which she initiated the contact.

Her fellow passengers were starting to settle in for the duration of the flight. No one was looking in their direction. Environment lenses flipped down over his eyes, Whispr was completely lost in whatever entertainment he had plunged into.

Reaching into a pocket she withdrew the transparent capsule, unsealed it, and extracted the thread. Holding it up next to the small window caused it to glisten silver and metallic in the polarized light. How could something so small and difficult to get into fuel so much violence and death? If she was fortunate enough to learn the secret of the tiny storage device's contents, would she learn the answer to that as well?

And despite everything she had told Whispr, in her heart of hearts did she really want to?

READ ON FOR AN EXCERPT FROM

BY ALAN DEAN FOSTER

PUBLISHED BY DEL REY BOOKS

Whispr knew for certain that he was in Africa when the pair of black leopards shot past him in the airport corridor. His companion, cautious business partner, overbearing scientific advisor, and (dare he think it?) sometime personal physician, Dr. Ingrid Seastrom, let out a gasp and dropped to her knees as one of the big cats forcefully brushed her right leg in passing. Unlike their now panicky intended quarry they tore through the terminal in complete silence. An equivalent airport Immigration and Security team back home in Namerica would have used dogs, an admiring Whispr thought as he watched the two carnivores take down their target. Amid screams and shouts, other equally startled arriving passengers were quick to scatter and give the cats room.

Pinning him to the ground beneath weight, fang, and claw they did not begin to devour the man they had trapped. In its excitement the larger of the two felines urinated on the frightened captive's legs. The smell of buttered popcorn filled the terminal. As Whispr had quickly assumed, both melanistic predators had been thoroughly maniped. Snapping against their muscular chests and flanks, loose-fitting lightweight vests flashing the SAEC's bright colors identified them as members of the Helen Zillie International Airport's security team. Strips of gleaming metal set atop their skulls between their ears testified to the skills of the biosurges who had installed the controlling implants.

Like the vests, the complex neuroplants were also probably South African Economic Combine products, Whispr mused. With impossibly slender and deceptively strong arms he helped the stunned Ingrid to her feet. The secrets of one peculiar kind of advanced SAEC technology—SICK technology—was what they had come all the way from Georgia and Florida to try to unlock. Less dramatic and more subtle, their purpose unknown, the quantum entangled nanoscale implants that had first intrigued and subsequently inveigled Ingrid Seastrom were infinitely more sophisticated than straightforward animal manips.

"Startled me." Ingrid continued to mumble to herself as she straightened her pantsuit.

She wasn't worried about her temporary dishabille or the fact that she had been knocked down. Overriding any and all other concerns was the need to keep safe the tiny silvery storage thread of metastable metallic hydrogen that lay hidden in a sealed security compartment within one cup of her brassiere. She worried about the shard's security because it represented a whole series of scientific breakthroughs and unknown social possibilities, some of them sinister. Whispr worried about it because if it were to be damaged or destroyed it surely wouldn't bring as high a price as it would if they could keep it intact.

Knowing her to be a consummate worrier, he wondered if Seastrom ever worried about *him*. Ever since he had obsessively but foolishly planted that scent-sucking zoe on her in Florida she had held herself even more distant than ever. Despite this her continuing disinterest in him in no way lessened his feverish desire for her. But he had vowed to act the gentleman, much as that remained an abstract concept to a street survivor like himself. Not because he didn't feel the urge every day, every hour, to pull her close to him and press his mouth against hers, but because at this point in their relationship it would be a bad move from a business standpoint.

He looked at her, drank in the sight of her, with great pleasure every chance he got. Even in her current disguise mode with her blond hair blackened, her cheeks puffed with temp collagen, the additional weight she had put on, and the contacts that changed her eye color every couple of hours, he still found her irresistibly enticing. He loved the way she looked, the way she walked, even the slightly stilted professorial way she talked. His attraction had nothing to do with the fact that he was a Meld and she was a Natural. Knowing full well that she would find any such expressions of admiration on his part unutterably annoying, he kept them to himself. Besides, they had work to do and surveillance to avoid.

Unlike the terrified young man who had been taken down by the leopards and was now being rescued and arrested by the big cats' handlers, they had made it quietly through Immigration and Customs without any difficulty. Traveling with only hand baggage, they headed for the nearest Transportation kiosk. Some of the other disembarking passengers had stopped to watch as a trio of cops placed the unfortunate lawbreaker in securestrips. None of them were citizens of the SAEC, for whom such sights were old news.

"I wonder what they're holding him for?" As Ingrid looked back at the scene she saw that the young man still wore a look of utter terror. She didn't blame him. Not with two full-grown maniped male black leopards hoping to make hors d'oeuvres of his toes and barely restrained by their handlers.

Whispr was more interested in finding immediate transportation into the city proper. He had been witness to far too many arrests to find this one worthy of his time, the exoticism of the circumstances notwithstanding.

"Probably trying to sneak into the country illegally," he opined. In the old days, he knew, the frenetic apprehension and subsequent arrest would likely have involved drugs. Imagine locking someone up for possessing recreational pharmaceuticals! What little he knew of history never failed to amuse him.

"As I understand it there's three Africas: North, Central, and South. North is philosophically and spiritually confused, Central is like downtown Old Atlanta at two in the morning—only with a quarter billion people, and the South is where everyone in the Central and much of the North wants to be. Mostly because the SAEC and the South is where the subsist is." Turning, he nodded back in the direction of the now stripped and secured illegal visitor.

"Gotta give the crazy Natural credit. Instead of sneaking across the border through a tunnel up north he bought a ticket and tried flying in like an ordinary traveler."

In her mind's eye Ingrid could still see the black slash of the police leopard streaking past her. "What do you think they'll do to him?"

Whispr shrugged. Among the many welcoming flads that was trying to cozy up to them was one for a vehicle rental company. Sticking a finger into the glowing sphere had instantly activated its functions. It trailed hopefully behind them as they continued on through the Arrivals area.

"Deport him if he's lucky. Slap him in detention if he's not. Feed him to cats if the cops are in the mood."

Her eyes widened. Where medicine and science were concerned Ingrid Seastrom was utterly up-to-date, but concerning Real Life she could be woefully ignorant.

"I'm kidding." A smile cut his angular visage and she favored him with a look of disgust.

Actually he didn't have a clue what the local cops did with illegal immigrants. With a lineage that included sjambok-wielding Afrikaans security, bomb-making ANC revolutionaries, fearless Zulu warriors, and modern police melds, it wouldn't have surprised him a bit to learn that the cost of securing borders that were under constant pressure from desperate would-be immigrants was occasionally offset by offering up pieces of said intruders in lieu of expensive leopard food. Did illegals from Mauritania taste different from, say, renegade Somalis? The thought would never have occurred to a Natural like Ingrid. To an ultra-slenderized Meld like Whispr it was perfectly—natural.

Hovering close to his left arm, the basketball-sized floating advertisement fended off competing flads with barely audible bursts of static electricity. As it urged them forward it declaimed with soft mechanical enthusiasm on the advantages of renting a roadster from the company it represented. Whispr ignored the sales pitch. They had engaged with the flad merely to help them locate the Arrivals Transportation desk. Whispr had no intention of renting a vehicle immediately upon entering the country. SICK had managed to track them down and send someone after the thread while they were in Florida. Though Whispr was pretty confident they had managed to subsequently elude the company's inimical attentions, he had not survived this long on the street by taking chances or moving too fast.

Once they reached the government-sponsored Transportation kiosk he dismissed the flad. It evinced no disappointment as it drifted off in search of other customers. Modern mobile advertisements preyed effectively on emotions but did not have any of their own.

Ingrid was already playing her hands over one of the several available holos. In response to her gestures all manner of public transportation lit up beneath her fingertips: taxis, buses, rail, aircraft, even maniped animals-for-hire. The latter were strictly for the tourist trade, an interested but realistic Whispr knew.

She eventually lowered her hands. "I've figured out how to get there, but how should we go? Where should we stay tonight?"

"Same routine as Florida," he told her. "Small hotel. Not too fancy, not too cheap. Same for the part of town. A suburb always draws less attention than the center of a city." He altered his voice to mimic that of an ancient Namerican actor whose work he had always enjoyed. "Ah'm a stranger here m'self."

As usual, she didn't get the joke.

With a nod she turned and put the request to the Transportation vorec. Connected to every other component of the greater Cape Town box it quickly provided half a dozen suggestions. One was quickly chosen, two rooms (Whispr let out a sigh but said nothing) reserved, and a deposit put down via her aliased credcard.

As they boarded the transport capsule at the airport's station they did not notice the two figures who stepped quietly away from the far wall and set off in their wake.

A small community of historic importance on the western shore of False Bay, Simon's Town was sufficiently developed to provide the facilities they needed while offering exactly the sort of quaint surroundings a pair of Namerican tourists would be expected to enjoy. Anyone looking for them in this part of Southern Africa would have a natural tendency to first seek them in central Cape Town. Simon's Town actually lay farther from the downtown area, with its famous harbor and grand tourist hotels, than did the international airport itself.

The main transport lines ran west from the airport to Downtown or eastward to Stellenbosch, the center of the wine and marijuana growing region. Every one of the automated cars departing the airport station was crowded with tired arriving passengers—except the one marked Muizenberg-Fish Hoek-Simon's Town.

Of the half-dozen other passengers taking the MFS service from the airport the one standing nearest to Ingrid boasted a full restaurant service meld. It took her a moment to realize that the impossibly short man was wearing nothing above the waist and that his bow tie, long-sleeved white shirt, pearlescent buttons, and neatly pressed pockets were nothing more than an artful spark tat. Such full body dimensional tats could be easily removed or customized should the owner change professions. They were particularly prevalent in hot, humid climates. A tat didn't cling, didn't show sweat stains, and never needed to be sent to the laundry.

Now that she saw that the little man had undergone skin stitching she found herself comparing the local work to its equivalent from Savannah. In addition to the uniform tat each of his hands featured two extra fingers apiece, the better to juggle trays, plates, glasses, and other dining paraphernalia.

Reflecting his country of origin his face was a neat checkerboard of black and white. It was the favored local melanistic meld. First at the airport and now on the transport she had seen alternating black and white stripes, spots, ovals, crescents, and in the case of one especially large woman, a direct vertical separation right down the middle of her face and exposed arms—half black and half white. Other Melds featured a smattering of brighter, less nationalistic skin colors. Turquoise seemed particularly in vogue this year, most notably among a group of loud, visiting Italians.

Seen firsthand it was clear that the old Rainbow Nation wasn't black or white. It was black *and* white.

Whispr could have fit his attenuated frame into any vehicle no matter how crowded, but he was glad of the space for his carryon pack. "Wonder why the cars on this transport line are so empty?" he mused out loud. An answer was soon forthcoming.

"Most folks are heading downtown or to the other main parts of the city. You're on a west bay express." The man boasting the restaurant service Meld and tat grinned at them. Every other one of his teeth, Ingrid noted with interest, had been stained a gleaming porcelain-black. "If this car was a local that stopped on the Wets it would be full by now also."

"'Wets'?" Ingrid inquired.

"The Cape Wets. Used to be called the Cape Flats, which were just what it sounds like, but since the worldwater came up—well, you'll see."

As the transport line curved smoothly to the southwest the higher country around the airport gradually descended until they were traveling atop a guide strip mounted on pylons. The million poor people who had made their ramshackle homes on the flatlands of the Cape Wets before the Greenland ice cap had melted had not moved when the sea level had risen. They could not move. They had no money, and no place to go if they had. So they stayed, and were joined by another couple of million of the Central African Diaspora who had migrated to the SAEC seeking work and a fresh start.

"It's like Greater Savannah," Ingrid insisted as she gazed out the transport car's window. But it was not.

"They say the Bangkok boatland has more people," the restaurant worker declared, "but there are more here than in any other stilted community, I think. Except of course for the Ganges Float."

Whispr's face contorted. "Never heard of it."

"It's where a country called Bangladesh used to be," Ingrid informed him.

Her companion grunted as he peered out the wide transparency of the transport car's wall. "Can't be any worse than this. I've seen a mess of buildings in my time, but this is just a mess."

"Careful what you say, visitor," the worker warned him. "People here are proud of their community, tumbledown as it may be."

The sleek air-conditioned car continued speeding on its way through a townscape unlike any Ingrid had ever seen. She had watched travelogue vits of South Africa, but those she could recall that featured Cape Town had made no mention of the Cape Wets. Passing through them, she could understand why. It was as if someone had engaged Escher's ghost to construct a vast urban landscape out of tin cans and toothpicks.

Like the transport track on which their comfortable climate-controlled vehicle rode, every one of the tens of thousands of individual structures they passed, whether domestic, commercial, or industrial, rose above the surrounding shallow waters on pylons or pillars or stilts that had been driven deep into the ground. Once a vast spread of flat dry land, the Cape Wets had been swallowed by the encroaching waters of False Bay. Now several million people lived just above the waterline in buildings that rose four, five, or more stories above the sea.

"I know what you are thinking," the restaurant worker guessed. "Those who live here thank God that the rising bay is one that is well protected from the elements and that the tide is sufficiently strong to flush it clean every day. Otherwise living here would be even more difficult than it is already."

"You don't live here?" Whispr asked him.

A foot shorter than the slender Namerican and hailing originally from central Gabon, the Baka immigrant drew himself up. "No, Meldbrother! I live in the town of Boulders, where I work. If you have time, come and see the penguins! Their beach has risen, but they still come to the same place regular as they have for hundreds of years."

"We don't have time to . . . ," Ingrid began.

Whispr cut her off quickly. "That sounds like a swell idea. We'll be touring around for a couple of weeks before we head up the coast to Durban and we sure wouldn't want to miss any of the local sights." He stared meaningfully at Ingrid. "Right, darlin'?"

"Oh, right," she quickly agreed, chastened at her forgetfulness. *Tourist,* she reminded herself. You are not here on a quest to solve scientific mysteries. You are a *tourist.* She held up her right hand and thrust out her forefinger. "I should have gotten that camera meld before we left."

"Don't worry about it," Whispr declared cheerfully. "I like you all Natural, just as you are."

The diminutive worker chuckled. "You like your women plain and simple, oo-ee? As Nature made them? Every man to his taste, I suppose. Myself, I like how science can improve on reality."

Ingrid bridled but said nothing. Over the decades national boundaries and much else had changed in Africa, but evidently not certain long-held cultural attitudes toward women.

The endless parade of makeshift structures flashing past the transport reflected the entrepreneurial skills of the locals and their ability to improvise construction despite a paucity of financing. Unable to expand horizontally because of the lack of available land, grown children built atop the homes of their parents, and parents atop those of their parents. Gazing in wonderment at the crooked, precariously leaning structures, it seemed to Ingrid that a brisk wind could bring down the entire district. But somehow, millions of impoverished citizens found ways to stabilize their clapboard and sheet metal and fiber dwellings, their half prefab businesses, and their salvaged shops.

The Wets might be poor and unstable, but it was not dull. Solar and wind and biomass powered the millions of lights that came to life as the sun began to descend over Table Mountain. Thousands of improvised walkways linked an equal number of buildings. Sometimes these informal paths floated on the water itself, elsewhere they hung like thick plastic vines connecting second- and third- and even fourth-floor levels. The transport raced past several ground-floor structures larger than most of the others. These blazed with cold fury, brazenly announcing the delights to be found within in a dozen languages or more: Xhosa, San, Afrikaans, Zulu, Baka, Himba, Shona, and Ndebele, every imaginable derivative of the Bantu languages, every worldwide variant of English, Hindi and Tamil and Bengali, French. . . .

"French?" Ingrid mused in surprise. The pygmy restaurateur explained.

"Some of the shebeen owners think it lends a touch of class to their joint."

"What's a shebeen?"

"Whorehouse." Whispr was less fascinated by the lights of the Wets than the glow that seemed to perpetually emanate from the doctor. He would much rather look at her than their surroundings. To someone like himself who hailed from a poor neighborhood one slum was much the same as another. Even one lying halfway around the world that was as well lit as the Cape Wets.

"Sometimes can be." Their helpful acquaintance sounded slightly miffed by the sinewy Namerican's explanation. "More often it is just a drinking place, like an informal club, where one can meet friends, play games, and . . ."

"Whore around." Whispr's attention reluctantly shifted from his view of the doctor to the dark bulk of the flat-topped mountain whose eastern flank the transport track was curving south to avoid.

Anxious to compensate for her companion's lack of tact, Ingrid tried indirection. "Do you work in a shebeen?"

Her attempt failed disastrously, as evidenced by the small man's reply.

"Madame, I am the sous chef at Chez Sebeli in Fish Hoek." Turning away from her, he moved toward the door. "And this is my stop. Yours is the one after the next. Do not worry about the fading light. Simon's Town is a tourist place. It is well patrolled and safe after dark. The beach is lovely in the moonlight, but stay out of the water."

Ingrid blinked. Not that she had a nocturnal swim in mind. Not after their long flight from Florida. But she was curious. "Why?"

"Government white pointers," the affable sous chef explained. "Or great whites as you call them. Fully maniped and on beach patrol. Looking for illegal immigrants, but they have been known to have trouble in the dark distinguishing honest residents from interlopers. Once bitten, it is impossible to retract a bite." With that he was out and gone through the softly hissing doors, an energetic small shape from Central Africa who had found his calling and made good in the SAEC.

"White sharks." Ingrid mulled over the intimidating image. "Somehow I don't think the government has much trouble with illegals trying to swim ashore here."

Whispr shrugged. The near vertical mass of Table Mountain had consumed the entire western horizon and the cold dark sheet of False Bay the other, leaving only a few lights directly ahead of them to mark the last of the shrinking peninsula that pointed ultimately toward Antarctica.

"How would they know how many tried and failed?" he told her. "Truly desperate people will try anything, no matter the risk."

She had to smile. "Even to searching out a doctor to remove police traktacs?"

"Even to enduring such a doctor's sarcasm," he snapped back irritably. He lusted after Seastrom, he desired her with every iota of his being, but he would have liked her a lot more if only she wasn't so damned smart.

Turning away from him she leaned close to the transparent wall of the transport car to catch the last twinkling lights of the outrageous physical and human morass that was the Cape Wets as it receded behind the transport. The night was incapable of consuming the millions. She had been wrong in her assumptions, and wrong early.

This place was nothing like Savannah.

Horizontal strips of light cutting the backside of Table Mountain revealed the locations of holiday apartments while off to the north and northeast the frozen nova of the Wets drowned out the light of the moon. But to the south the stars of the southern sky were becoming visible. Out in the salt-stung vastness of False Bay seals snugged down for the night, safe until morning on their barren rocky islands from the depredations of Natural great whites. Meanwhile a handful of the great predators who had been extensively maniped maintained their nocturnal patrol for illegal immigrants, unlicensed fishermen, and hard-bitten smugglers.

When the sea level had started to come up, old Simon's Town had simply been moved lock, stock, commuter transport line and historical buildings a little farther up the steep mountainside. Continuing to occupy the original town site, more recent additions had been constructed over the water. These were not the rickety, tumbledown structures that grew like stalagmites of sheet metal and fiber and resin in the Cape Wets. Well founded on sturdy supports; hotels, restaurants, gift shops, commercial buildings, and expensive residences reflected architectural influences that ranged from old Boer farmhouses to ultramodern windsail powerfices.

Standing on one of the walkways that connected their pleasantly modest hotel to the main street on the sloping mainland, Ingrid contemplated the moonlight on the bay. She was chilly. The season was the reverse of what she had left behind in Savannah. Tomorrow she would have to buy some warmer clothes. Turning away from the enchantments of the bay, which were as much olfactory as visual, she nodded to the northwest.

"This is charming, but we can't spend much time here. We need to get into the city proper so you can start making inquiries."

"Yeah, about that," he began, "just how exactly did you have in mind for us to proceed?"

She stared up at him. "You're the one with the street smarts. That's why you're here." When he didn't reply she sighed and continued. "SICK has two corporate headquarters: one in Joburg and one here. I was able to confirm that much while using the box on the plane. But I couldn't find anything that shows the locations of their research facilities."

He nodded thoughtfully. "Stands to reason. Big companies boast about the discoveries they make, but not *where* they're made."

"Then," she continued with becoming if naïve cheerfulness, "we'll have to infiltrate their headquarters to find the location of their principal research facility."

Turning to face her, his slim form nearly disappeared in the overhead lights that dimly illuminated the walkway. As always, he looked as if a strong wind could pick him up off the faux wood planks and blow him out to sea. His tone was somber.

"Listen to me, doc. I've lived most of my life on the streets. I can riffle and flan with the best of them. I can zift a pocket or purl a purse and disappear before the mark knows what's happened." Reaching into a pocket he withdrew the flattened, flexible, formfitting bottle from which he periodically sucked the fortified liquid that helped to keep his manip-thinned body properly fueled. As he pressed it to his nearly nonexistent lips he sensed that the curving container was almost empty. Tomorrow they would have to find a store that sold specialty foods for customized Melds like himself. Lowering the bottle he wiped his mouth with the back of an attenuated hand.

"But I'm not an industrial spy. I don't have the right physical tools to break into a box node, much less the headquarters of a company like SICK. And you"—he looked her up and down, admiring her in the rising moonlight—"you don't have the mental ones."

She stiffened. "I might surprise you."

"Yah. You've surprised me already, or we wouldn't be standing here at the ass-end of Africa having this conversation. I just don't want to be surprised when some security lod snaps your arms behind your back and securestrips your wrists before hauling you off to the company query cage for a private interrogation session with Mr. Volt and Mr. Watt." A sudden thought made him grin. "Of course, you could buy yourself something slink and low and distract the security while I slip inside."

She bridled. "You never give up, do you?"

He affected innocence. "What? You want to get inside SICK's offices, I'm just suggesting one possible avenue of approach."

"Let's take that car down a different street." She hesitated. "For now, anyway. I'll consider your suggestion only if we can't think of something better."

I can't think of anything better, he mused to himself as he envisioned her in the kind of seductive outfit he was proposing. Outwardly he gave no indication of where his imagination was straying. Leastwise, he hoped he wasn't.

"Okay. You're paying the bills."

"We'll go into the city," she reiterated firmly, "and you can start asking questions. You know how to ask. I know the address of SICK's administrative center: that's in the public box for anyone to see. What we need to find is the location of its main research facility: whether it's also here in Cape Town, or in Joburg, or somewhere else."

"Not the kind of information your average drift entrepreneur is likely to have readily at hand. But I suppose we might find somebody who knows somebody who knows somebody who knows how to get *at* that information." He didn't mince words. "Especially if you're willing to pay for it."

She sighed heavily. "That's becoming a familiar mantra of yours. How much is it likely to cost us? Me," she corrected herself.

He shrugged. "No telling. I don't know the local rates for that kind of inforeveal. Anyway, what price knowledge, right?"

Reaching out, she gave him a shove. "Easy for you to say. It's not your life savings we're spending here."

Turning away from her he headed up the walkway toward the town's single main street. His arm tingled where she had pushed him.

Then another hand was pushing him—far more forcefully. One of two very large black-and-white men slammed him up against the side wall of the two-story hotel while the other confronted a stunned Ingrid. Even in the fading light of early night Whispr thought he recognized them.

They had been on the transport car from the airport.

ABOUT THE AUTHOR

ALAN DEAN FOSTER has written in a variety of genres, including hard science fiction, fantasy, horror, detective, Western, historical, and contemporary fiction. He is the author of the *New York Times* bestseller *Star Wars: The Approaching Storm* and the popular Pip & Flinx novels, as well as novelizations of several films including *Transformers*, *Star Wars*, the first three *Alien* films, and *Alien Nation*. His novel *Cyber Way* won the Southwest Book Award for Fiction in 1990, the first science fiction work ever to do so. Foster and his wife, JoAnn Oxley, live in Prescott, Arizona, in a house built of brick that was salvaged from an early-twentieth-century miners' brothel. He is currently at work on several new novels and media projects.

www.alandeanfoster.com